THE HOLLYWOOD HIGH CHRONICLES

book 4

Ocean's Inferno

by **Melissa Velasco**

ISBN 978-1-960378-22-4   (paperback)
ISBN 978-1-960378-23-1   (eBook)

1st Edition

Models contracted through DMe Talent Agency:
Deidre Michelle (Agent) @dmetalentagency11

Front Cover Models: Maddie Dawn Cordero, Brody Pagan, Deidre Michelle, Neil Antonio, Julian Gopal

Back Cover Models: Maddie Dawn Cordero, Brody Pagan

Makeup and Hair: Xavier Visage
Costume Concept: Melissa Velasco
Cover Concept: Melissa Velasco
Photography: Tino Duvick @brokenchainphotography
Front Cover Design: Tino Duvick and Anna Hall
Editor: Kyle Fager
Proofreader: Doris Nehrbass

OCEAN'S INFERNO

My stepfather, Rich, wheels his minivan left into a driveway and comes to a stop at a security hut.

A security guard steps out with a clipboard just as Rich rolls down the window. "What brings you to the back lot today?" the guard asks cheerfully.

"Melanie Slate is scheduled to appear on the morning show," Rich answers, gesturing toward me in the passenger seat.

The guard looks past Rich and smiles my way. He glances at his list. "Melanie Slate, here you are. Go ahead and pull into the parking structure. You'll need these passes." He hands us two laminated cards on the end of lanyards. "Check in at sound stage fourteen."

Rich thanks him and pulls forward with a parting wave. He drives into the gloom of the parking garage, the overhead fluorescent lights creating shadows and bright spots as we pass.

I'm dreading this interview. It's happening because my school, Hollywood High for the Performing Arts, was held hostage by a militia—yes, for real—and my ragtag band of friends and I managed to form a resistance, fight them off, and create an escape for all of our classmates. Plus, well, I guess the whole siege kind of happened in the first place because of me. The militia was comprised of the rich friends of Daniel Stamp, who happened to be the father of my longtime tormenter, attempted rapist, and two-time attempted murderer, Joel Stamp. I use the past tense there because, fortunately, the scheming bastard of a vengeful father took a bullet to his head during the escape. Long story short, it's been an insane school year so far. The last thing I want to do is relive it on camera, and yet, here I am.

My injured shoulder is acting up, the arm sling causing me to ache and itch. I fuss with it nervously as Rich pulls into the first open spot and cuts the engine. Unexpectedly, my passenger door wrenches open. I gasp, raising my good fist, ready to take on the intruder.

Arch Terani grins at my side. "Hey there, firecracker."

I exhale with relief and playfully smack Arch on the shoulder. "You scared the crap out of me!"

Arch chuckles. "Sorry, Mel. You and Rich are the last to arrive. We've been waiting for you."

He takes my hand and helps me out of the van, where he gallantly presents me to my boyfriend, Trey Valdez. Trey's mirrored Oakleys mask his eyes as he wraps his arms around me.

"You all look fabulous!" I exclaim to the group.

Everyone's dressed up in posh outfits, and Trey's black, long-sleeved dress shirt and slacks look debonair.

I grin up at him. "You clean up pretty good, babe."

His jaw clenches tight. "I just want to get this over with."

Guilt flutters through me as I swallow hard. For the past month, Trey's been a sleepless, stewing basket case. His pensive dread brings my efforts at positivity to a screeching halt.

"Let's just try to get through this morning," Rich says soothingly. "You kids can do this."

Everyone in the group exchanges a variety of looks. Most are excited to be on TV. Trey and I don't share in the enthusiasm. If we had our say, this whole circus would just disappear quietly.

Trey puts his arm around my waist. "You and Valerie take point, okay?" he says to Adam Stone, our mutual friend and my ex-boyfriend. Adam and I have a soulmate connection that's vastly different from my connection with Trey. Losing Adam works out, though, because he's a button-pushing pain in my ass a lot of the time.

Adam nods. His fiancé, Valerie Merser, steps up beside him, and Rich, Trey, and I fall in line behind them.

"Seriously, guys," says Tanner Devick, our most flamboyant friend. "No one's getting on this production lot. Think about it. There's a security guard who checks everyone in. Trey's being silly."

Bear—the big, gentle energy worker striding at the back of the pack—belts his unmistakable laugh. "I think it's charming how you're still so optimistic after everything that's happened."

"As the new guy in the group," says Drake Santi, a star basketball player at Hollywood High, "I think it's bat-crap crazy that any of you are still capable of being optimistic. Our lives are ridiculous."

"I told Melanie that we should all move to Big Bear and form our own hippie commune," Rich says.

Bear's best friend, Darren Whipple, throws his arms in the air. "*Yes!* I'm so game!"

True to form, Marcus Vinsky is quick to chime in about food. "We could start a farm, and I'd bake all our cakes and cookies!"

"We could lie in the sun and enjoy the quiet," Valerie says.

"The guys would chop wood in the winter, and hunt for deer," Adam adds. "Back to our roots!"

"That's the spirit, kids!" Rich says.

Tanner alone appears disgusted. "*Absolutely not!* Not only do I refuse to be a recluse, but I have no interest in eating some strange, foraged mushrooms and wearing an earthy hemp shirt that Finley attempts to weave on a loom."

My best friend, Demitri Cantrell, laughs. "That took a quick turn. You do realize there are grocery stores and clothing shops in Big Bear, right?"

Tanner mutters something about how we've all lost our minds.

After passing through several long rows of huge, identical buildings, we arrive at studio fourteen, the number painted on the side of the building the only thing that differentiates it from all the other tan warehouses with dome roofs. A perky young intern awaits at the door. She checks our names and badges before escorting us inside. My eyes slowly adjust to the dimmer indoor light of a long backstage hallway.

"We're so glad you all could join us today," the intern says. "Your segment of the show starts in a few minutes. I'm going to leave you here in the greenroom to look over this list of questions the hosts plan to ask you." She hands Arch the list with a promise to return shortly.

We gather around the paper in Arch's hand and start reading.

Interview Questions: Hollywood High Heroes

1. Names

2. How did this situation begin?

3. Tell us about how the hostage takeover day unfolded.

4. How does it feel to be heroes?

"At least the answers to these questions will be easy," Arch says.

Marcus turns from the snack table. "You guys should get in on this! They've got brownies and muffins over here."

Nervous though I am, I smile and shake my head. It seems I'm not alone in being too nervous to eat. Marcus, on the other hand, has never turned down a snack opportunity in his life.

The production intern breezes back into the greenroom. "You all look dashing today. We appreciate that you arrived camera-ready. It's time." She turns on her heel and heads down the long hall outside the room at a fast clip.

We follow single file, with Arch taking the lead.

The intern stops next to a man with a headset on one ear. The man introduces himself as the stage manager, nods curtly, and quietly says, "When I give you the signal, you're going to walk across the set and get settled in the chairs provided. You need to move quickly. We have a two-minute commercial break coming up, and then we'll be live again."

A team of interns scurry around, efficiently clipping little microphones on our shirts and tucking the battery packs in our waistbands.

The stage manager puts a hand up, spends a moment listening to something in his headset, and then waves for us to proceed. When I round the corner, I'm awestruck by a morning show set I've seen a thousand times on TV. It looks different in person, smaller than I expected. The bright-blue cloud scene they use as a backdrop is painted on a wall, not at all unlike the sets that Hiram Friedman builds for our school plays.

Hiram inhales. "This is fantastic."

The stage manager grins at him and promises to show us how everything's built once our interview is over.

Hiram nods enthusiastically. "We'd love that," he says quickly.

We find our names on Post-it notes stuck to our assigned chairs. We all jockey about, arranging ourselves. All the guys wind up in directors' chairs in a row behind the girls. Separated from me by five chairs and one row, Trey glances at me and frowns. I send a pulse his way, trying to reassure him that the distance is fine. I've got Susan Cranz, Hiram's girlfriend, on one side and Kelsey Valdez, who's Arch's girlfriend and Trey's sister, on the other.

The "ready" light in the corner of the set flashes three times. One of the hosts, a bubbly woman who calls herself Kitty Kertle, turns to her cohost, Randy Fresh. "This is going to be super-duper," she gurgles girlishly.

My expression slides into deadpan judgment as I study our hosts. Randy Fresh is a conman type, a mid-forties, slick-as-snot ladies' man, complete with a tacky acrylic sapphire-blue sweater, perfect Superman hair, and plastic-surgery-addled eyes. When he hits us with his Ken-doll smile, I swear the rest of his face doesn't move. I tip my head and study him. *Bet you money he has plastic junk too,* I think.

Since we happen to have a soulmate connection that allows us to communicate telepathically, Trey overhears this, and I hear his resonant laugh in my head. Generally, I love that we can communicate this way, except that I still sometimes forget to block him off. That's led me into trouble more than a few times.

My judgy-wudgy gaze slides to Kitty, who's a regular source of strife in my home. Unfortunately, she's as physically impressive in person as she is on TV. On the daily, Kitty Kertle shares with the viewing audience her affinity for pink, skintight club dresses. She often attempts to professionalize these ensembles with shoulder-padded blazers that strain to cover her ample assets. Today's overworked blazer is black. She greets us enthusiastically. All the guys boil over with their "good mornings," while the girls sneer.

Internally, I wince as my stepfather beams from behind the camera line. He delights in this woman's newscast. Each morning, without fail, he says, "Good mooorning, Kitty," while tipping his coffee cup debonairly at the TV. My mother, in turn, fires off a ritual glare at both Kitty and Rich while she mutters about "the trollop." Rich then lectures about women supporting women, and how my mother should be proud of the twenty-something *amazing* phenom on the TV. My mother always gives him a blistering look, and comments that a tight dress and big jugs "do not talent make."

Only when Trey cracks up in my mind again do I realize I've been so lost in reliving the banter memory that I've apparently missed the transition to "live on air."

Trey fires off a winning grin my stepfather's way. Rich gives him a boisterous thumbs-up, and I fight not to roll my eyes.

I send to Trey, *"Knock off the bimbo worship."*

Trey sends back a mental snort but continues to grin like a nut while he surveys the pink-clad simpleton.

At least he's in a better mood, I think grumblingly.

The hosts' inane banter draws to a close, and Randy Fresh jovially says, "Today we have a special group of guests. We'd like to welcome the heroes of the Hollywood High hostage takeover!" Randy turns his attention to us as Kitty blinks emptily in our direction. The light on the top of one of the other recording cameras comes on, and Randy smolders out, "Please tell us your names."

I fight not to laugh at Kitty's empty-headed expression, my whole face spastically twitching as Trey guffaws in my head. I slide evil eyes his way. Trey's got an elbow on the arm of his chair, with his hand over his mouth. He's trying not to laugh, and it doesn't help my barely restrained hold over my sarcastic mirth.

We go down each row, dutifully announcing our names with a smile. My smile is fake, but it's the best I can do. In the monitor on the opposite edge of the stage, I notice that Trey's expression suddenly looks pensively strained.

Kitty asks the second question on the paper we were prepped with. "How did this situation begin?"

Arch fields this question, per our plan. Briefly, he explains the happenings before ending with an aside about how we pulled off some shenanigans, and it wasn't all so bad.

Kitty Kertle is clearly a bit taken with Arch, but who isn't? I can't hold it against the idiot. Arch could charm the bright-yellow sugar coating off an Easter Peep. "Arch," she says, "it sounds like you made the best of a tough situation with some hijinks while Principal Buttrum was in charge."

Arch grins at her. "If you can't beat them, join them, right?"

The hosts laugh, and Randy asks, "What was the most amusing mischief you kids pulled off before things got bad?"

Tanner pipes up, telling the host his humorous aside about our "Ants Go Marching One by One" marching plan, and the principal's reaction. Both hosts do their little TV-cackle, and we all chuckle.

"Way to keep him on his toes!" Randy switches gears. "Tell us about how the hostage takeover day unfolded."

Bear accepts the lead. "We knew something was coming because of Melanie's unique gift of intuition, but we didn't know exactly what we were in for." Trey looks at Bear like he's nuts for outing me that way. It does nothing to stop Bear as he lays out a little about the warning from the football team, and then adds far more than I would like about the nagging intuition I experienced.

When Kitty turns on me with brimming curiosity, I sigh deep inside. Bear just made me out to be some kind of mystical psychic, and it's all I can do not to grimace.

"How interesting!" Kitty's eyes light up as she leans forward. "Melanie, it really sounds exciting!"

My jaw drops. *Exciting! Almost dying is exciting?*

Trey frantically sends, *"Hold it together, Melanie."*

I ignore him, instead leaning forward in my chair. My friends inhale collectively, and I feel through my empathic gift as they radiate hope, along with a strong desire that I do everything I can to maintain my composure. Even under the best circumstances, I'm a loose cannon, so I guess they can't be blamed for their anxiety.

"Were you a cheerleader, Kitty?" I ask with feigned curiosity.

"I was," she bubbles over.

I smile, but it probably comes off as more of a leer. "I bet you were," I purr. I sit back in my chair and aggressively cross my legs in my black business skirt. "You'll be happy to know all the cheerleaders survived the *gunfire*." My eyes narrow.

Trey fails to stifle a quiet groan, and I watch the monitor as he rubs his face with his left hand. He had an affair with the lead cheerleader, Tiffany Savoy, who I detest.

Everyone else aims for neutral expressions, but there's visible tension.

Randy clears his throat and attempts to steer the conversation. "Not only are these remarkable kids heroes, some are royalty!"

"What the—"

"Down, girl," Susan murmurs.

"What does this have to do with anything?" I mutter back.

The light switches to a camera poised on a television screen hung on the wall. The homecoming picture of Presley Verelle, Marcus, and me flashes up on the screen. Our cheesy grins stare back at us.

The light shifts back to the camera aimed at us, and Randy Fresh crows, "Look how beautiful you three are in that picture!"

As we stare at the picture, I can feel my expression punching sarcastically.

Kitty catches me off guard. "Tell us more about this intuition of yours," she says in a gossipy way.

I decide to downplay it. "I would say it's just your standard gut feeling. Nothing that exciting."

My friends all smirk at me, and Deb Johnson rolls her eyes.

Randy looks disappointed, and to my relief, he switches gears. "How did you discover that trouble actually was afoot?"

Presley takes over the thread, explaining the beginning of the escape plan, and Mr. Jenson's involvement. The group takes turns enthusiastically laying out the whole tale, mercifully leaving me to keep quiet.

At the end of the story, Kitty Kertle turns to Trey and flirtatiously purrs out the final question. "How does it feel to be heroes?"

Trey clears his throat while I give him a snarly side-eye. "We did what had to be done. We're all relieved that so many made it out alive, but we must live with the knowledge that a handful didn't sur—"

Kitty interrupts with a cooed, "Oh, so sad." She shakes her head and hits Trey with big eyes.

I blister, and Kelsey puts a hand on my arm.

"The loss is a constant reminder of how precious life is," Trey says pointedly while he stares at Kitty. Apparently, our host's lack of tact has chapped his ass.

The news reporters give a thoughtful furrowing of their brows.

"Is there anything else you'd like to add?" Randy asks, apparently out of proper questions.

Trey looks deadpan into the camera. "We'd like to leave this all in the past now. We ask for privacy as we move on with our lives."

His statement is unexpectedly clipped, and the news reporters titter a bit, uncomfortably trying to rally.

"You heard it here, folks!" Randy charms out. "*The National Morning Show*'s exclusive interview with the Hollywood High Heroes! Thank you all for being here."

The camera lights click off, and everyone exhales.

CHAPTER 2

Randy Fresh beams at us. "Great job, kids!"

We all stand and stretch, relieved that the interview is over.

The stage manager comes around the corner. "How would you all like a tour of the station?"

"We would love that!" Hiram answers for the group. "Thank you so much."

The stage manager smiles and hustles us around the edge of the set as the newscasters get settled at their reporting desk before they're live on the air again.

The stage manager turns to us. "One of our associate producers has offered to escort you around. I think you'll like him. He's young and enthusiastic, much like your group."

He gestures toward a guy who appears to be in his mid-twenties. The guy is lounging against the wall a little way down the long hall, with his foot up, and he's reading a clipboard at his side. His long black hair is pulled back in a low ponytail, and he's wearing a black suit jacket and black slacks. I study the guy with my eyes narrowed. Something isn't right about the vibe slinking off him.

Hiram and Arch have already traversed the short distance and are enthusiastically talking with the producer. We all follow the man around while he points out the behind-the-scenes woo-hoo. I'd normally find it fascinating, but something about this guy has the hair standing up on the back of my neck. Maybe it's because he proves to be a showboating, braggadocious asshat. I fidget in my uncomfortable heels as we get to yet another set piece and he once again talks us through the intricacies of its floor supports. Apparently, he helped construct it. The theater techs in our crew are eating up this mundanity, but I'm having a hard time stifling a yawn.

"By the way, my name's Jet."

Of course it is. I roll my eyes at Trey, who smirks.

"What a tool," Trey whispers to me.

Jet takes us down a hall, where he introduces us to a few other executives. He's really laying on the suave-guy routine as he pals around with his older coworkers. I despise fake, and this guy has a never-ending supply. That's when I realize what really has me on edge about him: he can't seem to stop stealing glances at me. Our group is full of gorgeous girls, so it can't just be that he finds me attractive. He just won't stop *looking*. At the end of the tour, Jet takes us through the main door, and everyone fans out, thanking him for his time. I hide behind the guys, uninterested in dealing with Mr. Creepy.

"Where's the homecoming princess?" Jet asks. "Melanie, right?"

I sigh and step into view, hitting him with a neutral look.

A slow smile graces his angelic face, a touch of malice lurking just under the surface. "There she is. Hello, princess."

Everyone exchanges a glance, put on guard by the oddness of his words.

"Hello, Jet," I reply. "Thank you for the riveting tour."

"My father owns this network," he informs with a haughty air. He stares at me expectantly.

Unsure what he's waiting for, I finally say, "Nifty."

Jet flashes a brilliant smile. "Any chance I can treat you to dinner, princess?"

My face scrunches, and I tick my head from side to side. My friends snicker. They always delight in my quirks, and this one that happens whenever I'm flummoxed has always been one of their favorites.

Trey drapes an arm over my shoulders, giving Jet a look that says, "Back off my girl."

Jet barks laughter. "The offer stands," he says before turning and strutting toward the sound stage door. "It's been a pleasure." He tips his head my way and purrs, "I'll be seeing you" before closing the door behind him with a click.

Now that Jet's gone, I shudder from head to toe. "Oh, ick!"

The other girls scrunch their faces. "He's got that vibe," Presley says.

"What vibe?" her boyfriend, Marcus, asks.

"Kurt Moff vibe," Presley explains, and the girls all wince. Kurt Moff is an intolerable sleazoid at Hollywood High. We avoid him like the plague.

"Nothing like a pretty rich boy trying to be mysterious," Finley Farell says with a look of disgust.

Hiram shrugs. "He seemed all right to me. I loved the tour."

"He hit on my girlfriend," Trey reminds, miffed.

"Eh. He didn't know she was dating the Hollywood High savior," Bear teases.

All the guys razz Trey as we make our way back to the parking garage.

CHAPTER 3

I tip my head back and close my eyes, willing myself not to cry. I take a deep breath and hit my physical therapist turned torturer, Randall, with an exhausted glare.

Randall meets my gaze without wavering. "Ten more. Let's go."

"I can't." I shake my head and wipe sweat from my forehead.

A new voice rings out from the doorway, deep and serious. "What do you mean you can't? I never thought I'd see the day that Melanie Slate can't do something."

Bent over, with my hands on my knees, I smirk at Mr. Isley as he saunters toward me. "So, did you just show up to torture me with Randall here?" I ask him.

Mr. Isley's the head of the dance program at my school, which has been closed for the past month due to the rampant damage that resulted from the hostage takeover. The damage was caused in part by my group, a necessary evil as we masterminded and executed an escape plan for over fifteen hundred people. In anticipation of everyone's triumphant return to that hellhole, my physical therapist has been pushing me to my limit.

Mr. Isley puts his hands on his hips and stands up straighter, stretching to his full and mammoth height. My soul shrinks a little because I'm in for it. Mr. Isley's a force to be reckoned with. Everyone in the Magnet program loves him, but I know from experience that it's all fun and games until Isley's on a mission. He gets what he wants, and right now, I suspect he wants me to push through this excruciating session.

"I'm keeping you in the 'Vogue' piece for the dance show," Mr. Isley informs me. "I've taken you out of the other pieces, but you need to get through this physical therapy because I need you in the show."

I give him a speculative look. "I'm already in the theater production of *The Crucible*. Sorry to disappoint you, but I can't handle the dance show right now."

He ignores my point. "You need to get that shoulder back in working order, because you've got shoulders to roll while you jazz walk across the stage. I'll keep it to just walking."

I close my eyes, my entire body shaking from exhaustion. "I'm tapped out, Mr. Isley. There's nothing left."

Mr. Isley raises an eyebrow at me. "You took a rifle blast to the shoulder and had no idea. That's how tough you are. I'm not letting a few physical therapy reps beat you." He hits me with a stern glare. "Gut up! You can do this."

I glance at the door. Trey is leaning against the wall with his arms crossed over his chest, and he's smiling softly at me. Clearly, he's the one who informed Mr. Isley that I needed some motivation.

I narrow my eyes at him and snarl through our soulmate connection, *"You're gonna pay for this, Trey!"*

Trey smirks. *"I look forward to it."*

I tip my head back and laugh, a touch of my dark-water energy slinking through the room. I glance from Trey to Mr. Isley, and finally to Randall. "All right, let's get this over with."

Randall nods and gestures toward the dreaded elastic-band apparatus with a metal handle on the end. It looks innocent enough, but that giant rubber band is my nemesis these days. I pick up the handle, stretching my arm up to forty-five degrees.

"Here we go." Mr. Isley counts off my reps. "One . . . two . . . three . . . four . . ."

My arm shakes, and my shoulder feels like it's going to explode.

"Five . . . six . . . seven . . ."

My eyes fill with tears, and I whimper. I feel like I'm going to throw up from the excruciating pain.

"Don't you dare quit," Mr. Isley orders. "Your attackers don't get to win! Now push through."

I stop and squeeze my eyes closed, allowing the tears to spill down my cheeks. *Damn it! Isley's right. My attackers don't get to win.* I clamp my jaw tight and open my eyes with a growl, pulling willpower from somewhere deep. My arm moves again.

"Eight . . . That's it, Mel. You've got this. Nine . . . ten."

I let go of the handle, which snaps back and hits the metal stand with a whack. I double over, grab my shoulder, and wait for the burning to subside. This is harder than I expected, and it's testing every part of my resolve.

Mr. Isley puts his hand on my back. "That's the Melanie I know. Good work, kiddo."

I look up and grin at him. "All right. I admit it. You're right. I feel better knowing I didn't give up."

Mr. Isley nods. "Trey called and told me you're struggling. I'm going to be at as many of your physical therapy appointments as possible."

I smile. "Thank you, Mr. Isley. I appreciate you."

Trey pushes away from the wall and strides toward me. He wipes drying tears from my cheeks and pulls me in for a hug. I rest my forehead on his shoulder.

Trey pulls my tank top strap out of the way, showing Mr. Isley my shoulder. "The swelling's gone down substantially. It's looking a lot better. It's still a sick purple and green, but not like it was."

I nod. "It hurts terribly when I do these torture exercises, but it's been feeling a lot better the rest of the time the past few days." I glance at Randall. "I'm worried about the possible nerve damage we talked about. Sometimes it feels like a nerve goes haywire and sends shooting pain all the way across my back."

"Hang in there, Melanie," Randall encourages. "I don't think the damage is permanent. Think about it this way: a hole was blasted through skin, muscle, bone, and nerves. It all must knit itself back together. Every time you feel one of those nerve twinges, you need to be excited because that's one more thing that's closer to being repaired. I'm always more worried when a patient doesn't feel nerve pain. You want the nerves to be alive."

I rub my forehead. "I can work with that. If the pain means progress, that helps."

He nods and glances at Mr. Isley. "In all seriousness, I'd be thrilled for you to come to Melanie's sessions." Randall looks my way. "She's not exaggerating about how bad this hurts. I've had battle-hardened soldiers collapse in tears from these exercises. Melanie's the youngest gunshot victim I've worked with. She's also the only teenage girl I've done this with. I've been worrying I'm pushing her too hard."

Randall doesn't know that my energy-working friends have taken turns feeding energy into me that I've channeled into the injured area. Even though I have no idea what I'm doing, it seems to have sped up the healing process substantially.

Mr. Isley grins at him. "Don't let how young she is, or how little she is, fool you. Melanie's a beast, and she fights like a drunk sailor on shore leave."

Randall gives Mr. Isley a skeptical look. "You're serious?"

With a smirk, Mr. Isley rubs his forehead. "I'll come to her next PT appointment and hit you with a few Melanie stories."

"Deal," Randall says, grinning my way. "I'm curious now."

Mr. Isley turns to Trey and me. "Time to head to the school and look around."

"You're coming with?" I ask, surprised.

Mr. Isley smiles softly. "Principal Walker knows this is going to be hard, and he asked me to be there."

I smile. "I'm so glad Principal Walker's back."

Trey sinks into a chair, rubbing his face with both hands before glancing up at me. There's fear in his eyes, something I've only seen a few times. Literally, Trey created an entire plan to save over fifteen hundred people, and we only lost a few in the battle to escape. I know Trey's got some serious reservations about going back to the school. He's even mentioned that he'd rather get his GED than walk back through the front doors of that place.

I cross the short distance and wrap my arms around him, pulling his forehead against my chest. He takes a deep breath and exhales hard.

"Can you do this, Trey? I'll do whatever you want."

"What I want is to stay right here with my forehead in my happy place," Trey quips.

I laugh and turn to Mr. Isley. "Trey, and Trey's happy place, would love to join everyone at the school. Let's roll."

Mr. Isley looks down at Trey and puts a hand on his dejected shoulder. "I'm going to be there with all of you, Trey. And so will Mr. Jenson. I'm nervous too. How about you and I stick together? That'll make me feel better."

Trey looks up at Mr. Isley. "That might help."

CHAPTER 4

"**W**e toured the school before you kids got here," Mr. Jenson, the schools' maintenance man who helped us plan our daring escape during the hostage takeover, assures us. "I promise that you don't have to worry about enemies lurking."

Adam cracks his knuckles. "If that news came from anyone but you guys, I wouldn't believe it. Still, we're going to be wary either way."

"I trust nothing anymore," Trey says, "but I appreciate that you checked for us. I don't know if I'll ever walk into another building without looking out for danger."

Principal Walker is uncharacteristically blunt. "Principal Buttrum's only saving grace is that he helped spare Melanie's life. What he put you kids through was horrific. I'm sorry this all happened, but I promise you it's over. I'm back. You're all safe."

"Let's get through the catacombs and media room," Arch says. "We'll feel better after we face the ghosts we've been holding onto since the siege."

Principal Walker nods to Mr. Jenson, who crosses the room to the maintenance closet door, unlocks it, and moves the equipment out of the way to reveal another door. He unlocks the hidden door and pushes it open. Mr. Jenson flips on the light, and we crowd around, peering down a small staircase into the squat gray concrete catacombs that served as our secret route of passage during the hostage takeover.

Trey pushes to the front of our crowd. "Let's get this over with."

I step up next to Trey, ready for him to put his arm around me so we can head down into the catacombs together. He glances at me and descends the stairs by himself. Surprise zings through me. Trey and I do everything together, particularly when things get tough.

Bear puts his arm around my waist and gives me a gentle squeeze. "Give him a minute. If he doesn't come around, I'll talk to him."

I nod and wipe my sweaty hands on my leggings. Bear and I follow Trey down the stairs, where all our footprints from a month ago are still outlined in the dust along the walkway. We traversed these hidden halls so much during the escape planning that our mark was left on nearly every square inch. I shiver from the reminder, and the lingering panicked energy envelopes me. These halls still hold secrets full of anxiety and fear.

We pass the junction that leads off in the distance to the theater building, and all turn our heads in unison to look down the long hall to our right. There's a big, dried, brownish-red bloodstain on the floor and wall where I sat after the attack.

"I promise I'll get that cleaned up," Mr. Jenson says quickly. "We didn't get to the catacombs when we were doing repairs, so I didn't realize that was there."

Trey turns and looks at me. He's radiating grief, which makes the already claustrophobic space seem heavier.

He pushes through our group, heading back down the walkway.

When we come to the boiler room on our right, he's standing at the door that's still propped open by a doorstop. We crowd into the boiler room. During the siege, this was our break room, where we had cigarettes and a breather during the worst of the planning stress. The floor is littered with cigarette butts and water cups. My lipstick shines bright on the rim of Trey's discarded cup. It's sitting there on the floor next to one of the mismatched chairs. Trey walks across the room to his cup, picks it up, and looks at it with a far-off expression. A moment later, he turns and hits me with an intense stare. His pallor shifts to an ashen gray, his breathing gasping and ragged.

"You need to sit down," Ms. G says, clearly concerned for Trey. "You're going to hyperventilate."

Trey reaches behind himself, grips the armrest of the chair, and lowers himself into the seat. He drops the cup and puts his head in his hands. A moan escapes him, and a torrent of tears slide down his cheeks.

Ms. G sits in the chair next to Trey and puts her hand on his back, comforting him as he cries it out. She glances at us. "Why don't you kids all head to the media room across the way while I talk to Trey?"

Trey barks a panicked, "We don't separate!"

Mr. Isley kneels in front of him. "There's no danger."

My boyfriend hits Mr. Isley with a fierce expression. "There's always danger around here."

The adults' eyebrows furrow.

"I know you're trying to give Trey some privacy while he breaks down," Bear says, "but this group is past that kind of thing. When we thought Adam was dead, all the macho disappeared."

"I suppose that's likely true." Ms. G asks Trey, "Will you tell me what you're thinking so I can help you?"

Trey wipes tears from his cheeks. "If things had gone differently, I could be sitting here staring at Melanie's lipstick on my discarded cup, knowing that we'd just buried her."

Ms. G nods.

Trey glances at her. "If that had happened, I wouldn't have made it. Seeing that cup, and the blood in the hall, would've been the final straw."

"I understand, but it didn't go down that way," Ms. G says. "You can't go through this focused on the 'what ifs.' Melanie's alive. Torturing yourself over what didn't happen will get you nowhere."

Trey closes his eyes. "That's true, I suppose." He's forever pragmatic.

"Here's what I'm hearing," Ms. G says. "You've finally been faced with a situation you couldn't fully control. This is the same conversation I had with Adam after he was rescued from his kidnapping. His PTSD was built on fear about the idea that he couldn't handle the situation alone. You're both independent tough guys, and you finally couldn't fix something yourselves. So, Melanie almost died . . . You didn't realize she was shot and assumed the blood on her back was from the cut on her head. You weren't there when she coded on the ambulance gurney. She made it, Trey. Sure, she made it without you making sure she did, but she had her parents, me, Demitri, and the medical professionals who saved her life. Everyone worked as a team. You need to trust the rest of us. You aren't a one-guy army."

Trey takes a deep breath and nods once, hard and fast. He pulls himself together. "That makes sense. I'm ready to go into the media room." He stands up, slides through the crowd of our friends, and puts his arms around me. He exhales hard, and I wrap my good arm around his waist.

All of us follow as Trey leads the way across the catacomb hall to the media room door. Mr. Isley unlocks the door and pushes it open before reaching to flip on the light switch. The fluorescent lights buzz to life, flooding the room with their bright glow. We all blink and wince. Something about this windowless room makes the light uncomfortable.

We walk in and survey the scene. Piles of personal belongings from our backpacks are sprinkled on the floor like anthills. We had to dump out our backpacks to carry screw guns and metal plates that we used to secure doors throughout the school during stage one of our escape plan.

It's like time stood still in this room, locked tight and holding our secrets. The energy in here still crackles with bravery and fear. I shiver, and Trey rubs my goose-bumped arms.

"I can still feel the amped energy from a month ago," Bear murmurs.

"Me too," I offer.

We gather around the big conference table that served as our planning station during the siege. It's strewn with blueprints, leftover copies of the escape plan, and odds and ends.

Trey steeples his hands carefully on the table, as if not to disturb the past, and takes a deep breath. Slow and methodical, he turns the blueprints and rolls them up. Arch hands him a rubber band that Trey snaps into place around the thick roll. He turns and hands it to Mr. Jenson.

"I'll get this room cleaned up," Mr. Jenson assures us. "You kids just need to gather your stuff."

Trey shakes his head and turns to our group. "We need to put the past to rest."

Everyone works together, tossing the escape plan copies, turning off the still-humming copier, and throwing away trash.

We don't stop until the room is back in order. Next, we make our way to our individual piles. Ms. G hands out grocery sacks, and we fill them silently.

Once we're done, Trey surveys the room and then looks at each of us methodically before saying, "It's officially over."

We all nod and turn to the adults, who smile at us.

"You kids are the toughest students this school has ever seen." Principal Walker glances down at one of the escape plan pages in his hand. "I'm framing this and hanging it in my office as a reminder to never underestimate the students."

CHAPTER 5

The morning is bright and cheerful. I'm hoping it's a good omen for what's to come. Trey wheels into the student parking lot and pulls up next to Arch's car. Our friends are already gathered behind Bear's newly acquired Ford Bronco, enjoying a morning smoke.

Trey slides out of the driver's seat and walks around to open my door. I stand, and he puts his arm around my shoulders, careful not to press on my wound. He looks down at me, and my reflection stares back from his mirrored Oakley sunglasses. I've dressed for the occasion in a pair of swooshy black pants with a red crop top and red heels. I'm not feeling as confident as I look, but if you can't make it, fake it.

We walk silently to our group, everyone dressed to the nines in a menacing "don't mess with us" way.

"This is it," Arch says. "Moment of truth. You guys ready?"

Everyone nods and gathers up their backpacks from the discarded pile by the Bronco's bumper.

"Nice new ride!" Trey says to Bear.

Bear grins. "The insurance company gave me a heck of a settlement check for my burned-up car."

Yeah, that was a whole situation. Bear's car exploded by the theater one fateful night, part of a shockingly sinister plan carried out by the Drones, who thought the best course of action would be to kill as many of us as possible before we had a chance to testify against Joel, my attempted rapist and attempted murderer. Oh, and he and his friends were also Adam's kidnappers. Crazy place, Hollywood High. The teenagers in our little world will sometimes bypass the standard catty gossip and go straight to explosives.

"At least something good came of this mess," Hiram says.

"What do you all think it'll be like going back to school with everyone?" Finley asks.

"A disaster," Tanner jokes.

"Home sweet hell," Marcus says.

We all turn as a pack to walk across the street. Heads swivel as students get off the buses lined up along the curb. Some nod at us; others exhale with relief. They all look scared. Everyone seems to feel better knowing we're there, but none of them know how frightened we are. The student body collectively looks up to us. Not just because we're the student council, but more so because we've saved their asses, and their lives, more than once.

We turn the corner into the alley, and our footsteps echo and bounce off the walls. The students follow us, and everyone silently looks around. As we round the corner into Actors' Alley, the hangout spot for all the Magnet kids, we're unexpectedly accosted by media reporters rushing at us, yammering into microphones.

Trey grabs my elbow and instinctively pulls me behind him. All the girls end up in the middle as the guys circle us. Trey, Adam, and Arch take point, attempting to move our group through the crush of reporters, to no avail. Our hearts pound and panic rises. We're surrounded, and we've been in so much danger lately that everyone in our group amps up.

The reporters become more aggressive as they close in, jostling and jockeying for the best position. We're practically trampled. Trey's eyes are wild, the chaos pushing him over the edge. He wasn't ready for this. I glance at Adam, who's sharing Trey's panic, his fists raised. He's also still on edge after being so brutally kidnapped and nearly murdered by the Drones. Arch yells over his shoulder to the other guys to take Trey's and Adam's places up front. Deb and Valerie grab Trey and Adam and pull them behind our group. Darren, Bear, and Drake step to the front, and Bear takes over talking to the media. We don't want a brawl on camera.

I turn, searching for Trey and Adam, and spot them talking quietly with Marcus and Tanner. Tanner makes eye contact with me and nods slightly. He's got them covered. I turn back to find a microphone shoved in my face. I blink rapidly, trying to wrap my mind around the intrusion.

"What's your name?"

"Melanie Slate."

"Were you a part of planning the hostage escape here at Hollywood High?"

"Yes, ma'am."

"Inquiring minds want to know . . . What was it like in the trenches?"

"Terrifying."

"You're a brave girl, Melanie Slate." The reporter turns to Deb and asks if she was involved.

Deb snorts, tossing her curly black hair over her leather-jacket-clad shoulder. "I don't know you. Get to steppin'."

The reporter, more aggressive this time, demands, "Tell us what you know."

Deb's the wrong person to push. She's tough on a good day,

and today's proving to be bad. Her eyes narrow, and her mouth pulls back in a sneer.

From across the group, Drake, Deb's boyfriend, sees her shift and says to a reporter who's interviewing him, "Pardon me." He pushes his way past Hiram and Bear and puts an arm around Deb. Drake says to Deb's reporter, "If you'll excuse us." He steers his girlfriend in a circle and subtly snaps his fingers at Tanner. A gentle nudge moves Deb toward Tanner and Marcus, who have apparently become our safety zone for anyone who can't handle this chaos.

Another reporter slides through the melee and aggressively shoves a microphone in my face. I'm caught off guard again as the reporter asks, "How does it feel to be a hero?"

A booming voice comes into the fray. "Reporters have zero authorization to be on this property. Please leave."

Principal Walker to the rescue.

We exhale, and collectively try to push our way through the crowd. The pack of reporters is relentless as they continue blocking our exit. Trey's hand is quaking at my waist, and he's pale. Given his fragile state, this pandemonium isn't exactly working for him.

I turn to Arch and hiss, "We have to get Trey out of here!"

Mr. Isley, Mr. Jenson, and Ms. G push their way to us.

Principal Walker commandingly says, "All reporters, leave now or we're filing trespassing charges."

Mr. Jenson and Mr. Isley usher the reluctant reporters away.

As relative calm settles in, the principal turns to our group. "I'm so sorry, kids. We had no idea this was happening until Dante ran to find us."

"Where is security?" Adam barks.

A sheepish expression crosses Principal Walker's face. "Three of our security officers were killed by the militia during the hostage takeover. The remaining three quit. We haven't been able to replace them yet."

Trey's mouth drops open, and his wild eyes flash with accusation. "You told us we'd be safe coming back here!"

"I apologize," Principal Walker answers. "We called the police, and they'll be on campus the rest of the day to patrol and keep order. We'll redouble our efforts to hire security."

"I was excited about the new 'no-fence' concept until now," Tanner says.

"I agree," Principal Walker says. "We've clearly got a new set of problems."

CHAPTER 6

Presley glances my way. "What's up with the grin, Mel?"

"I'm just thinking about how good it is that things are dull and normal, finally."

She winces. "It certainly didn't start off that way."

"That's for sure, but everything leveled out after the reporters left." I scrunch my face. "I'm starting to think this entertainment business isn't for me. I despised the interview at the news station. I wasn't any more thrilled about the pandemonium this morning."

"We've got a long way to go before we hit that level of fame." Presley gestures flippantly. "I don't think this production we've been rehearsing is going to garner us any news recognition."

I laugh quietly. The show's quality is dubious at best. No one's heart has been in it, but in our defense, most of our rehearsals happened during the Principal Buttrum fiasco, so we've been a little behind.

Our quiet conversation is interrupted by Ms. Ferry. "Great job today, kids. *The Crucible* is coming along nicely. We've got a month before opening night, and I'm pleased with the progress. Anyone who's in the dance show, please grab your backpacks and head to the dance building for rehearsal with Mr. Isley."

Presley hugs me as I say, "Gotta bounce. See you at my house."

I head to the stairs on the side of the stage and make my way up the auditorium seating to where I've stashed my backpack.

Demitri catches up with me. "Javier and I are headed that way. We'll walk with you."

Javier Hernandez is another dancer—my first partner, in fact, until I wound up partnering with Demitri. A handful of us are cast in both shows, and to be blunt, I'm struggling with self-doubt.

I smile wistfully at Demitri, who laughs.

"Are you still having your usual imposter syndrome issues about being in the dance show?" he asks.

"It's only imposter syndrome if it's not actually true." I sigh. "We're about to see if my shoulder can handle this."

We make our way down the four-story staircase on the side of the theater building. My pinky finger catches an unfilled bullet hole on the bottom of the railing, and I wince. As hard as the repair crews tried, they clearly missed some of the damage from the hostage takeover.

The baseball field looms up on the right, and I scan the field in search of Trey. I find him standing statue still, staring toward the quad. His posture is rigid. He sends me a warning pulse through our connection.

"Trey's on guard," I inform Demitri and Javier. "Something's up."

We glance around the edge of the bungalow and spot a man leaning against the waist-high fence by the athletic field. Demitri glances at Trey, and they make eye contact. Demitri nods his way, and Trey nods back, silently communicating their mutual awareness.

I glance subtly at the stranger, whose long hair hangs over his eyes as he takes a drag off his cigarette, the cherry burning bright.

I inhale and quietly say to Demitri and Javier, "Is that that weird producer we met? Jet?"

"Who?" Javier asks as he surveys the guy.

"Producer from the morning show," Demitri murmurs to Javier. "He was polished and put together at the station. This version is a little slimier."

I raise an eyebrow. "My hair stood on end the whole time he gave us a tour. He asked me on a date." I scrunch my face. "The answer was no. Based on his whole grungy vibe, now the answer is hell no."

Demitri and Javier exchange a glance over my head.

"Just keep walking," Demitri says.

I take my new cell phone from my pocket and pretend to be on a call while Javier and Demitri loudly chat about what a hurry we're in.

Jet calls out, "Melanie," as we briskly rush past, pretending not to hear him.

—　—

The dance rehearsal is taking forever, and I'm flat worn out. My shoulder is killing me. It's clearly too soon for me to try to do so much. I should've dropped out of both shows.

Demitri and I aren't in the piece that's currently being drilled, and neither are Javier and his dance partner, Jayla Bethel. We all sit on the tumbling mat, waiting. I slump on the mat next to Demitri. He grabs his flannel and balls it up, putting it on his lap. Without saying anything, he reaches an arm my way and invites me to rest my head on the flannel. We've got at least a twenty-minute break. I curl up with my head on the makeshift pillow and wrap my good arm around his waist. I sigh and bury my face in his stomach. This would be odd with anyone else, but D and I curl up during breaks pretty often. I quickly fall into an unsettled half sleep.

After a while, Javier's voice drifts in. "You do realize you have a rattlesnake coiled up against you, right?"

Demitri chuckles. "Wrong. I have Melanie curled up against me."

"*How* can you handle her being like that with you?"

"She's one of my best friends, Javier," Demitri answers. "It doesn't bother me. She's only snuggly with a few people, and she trusts me."

Javier snorts. "The energy that rolls off her makes the hair on the back of my neck stand on end. Not to mention that every guy who touches her goes completely insane."

Demitri puts a hand on my sore shoulder, and the pain diminishes unexplainably. I sigh in my half-sleep state.

"Her energy doesn't bother me," Demitri answers. "I'm also not that guy, and you know it. I'm dating Victoria."

Ah, Victoria Garcia. She and I have had something of a rivalry when it comes to boys. She dated Trey just before me, and then had the nerve to try winning him back. I admit that she helped save me from Joel that one time, so I guess we've come to something of a truce. But the fact that she's now dating my best friend Demitri still puts me off in more ways than one.

Javier and Jayla both laugh.

"Victoria?" Javier exclaims quietly. "Really, Demitri? If you had the choice between Melanie and Victoria, you'd ditch Vic in a second."

"Since when is there a choice? Melanie's with Trey." Demitri pauses before adding, "She needs someone in her life who keeps her calm and takes the edge off. I'm happy to be that."

"You've got it bad," Javier accuses him.

"No," Demitri answers emphatically. "I don't."

"Sure, you don't. Answer honestly. Do you love her?"

"Of course, I love her." Demitri sounds exasperated. "She's one of my best friends."

"Are you *ever* going to come to terms with the fact that you've been in love with her for a while?"

"Nope." Demitri sighs. "This isn't a discussion. I'm in the friend zone and that's it."

"Your lap is the friend zone?"

Demitri laughs. "With Meley it is."

"This has disaster written all over it. Mark my words, that succubus is going to tear your willpower right straight out your ass."

They keep talking as if I'm not even there. I planned to catnap, not be comatose, but the conversation is intriguing, so I rudely continue pretending I'm asleep.

"Honestly, I hope they end up together," Jayla says. "Don't get me wrong. I like Trey, but things are so intense with him and Mel. It's like they're always boiling. She needs some calm in her life. I don't know Mel that well yet, but I really like her. She's only bubbly and happy around Demitri. Have you ever noticed how pensive she is around Trey and Adam?"

Demitri groans. "I worry about her more than I should. She has a side most people don't see. I know who she really is. And when she slides big, scared eyes at me, I want to rescue her."

"*See*?" Javier says. "He's got it bad."

"Good," Jayla says. "At least someone in her life cares about her soft side."

Mr. Isley's voice booms out, "'Vogue,' let's go." His voice gets closer. "Melanie. Up."

I groan and curl tighter around Demitri.

"I don't think she's up for this today," Demiri says.

"Of course, she isn't up for it," Mr. Isley retorts. "She's curled around the school's heartthrob."

"Don't you start," Demitri hisses. "I'm already getting it from Jav."

"Take five," Mr. Isley yells out to the cast. Then, he turns a glare at Demitri. "You're like a son to me, and we're going to talk later."

I roll over and stare angrily at our dance teacher.

Mr. Isley sits next to us and softly says, "Melanie, your life is a giant atom bomb, and I'm worried it's going to detonate all over Demitri."

"Can you *please* just let this be?" I ask.

"What would you do if Victoria stormed in here and threw blows over you curled up with her boyfriend?"

I crack up. "Knock her the hell out."

Mr. Isley gives me a look. "That solves your problem, but it does nothing to help Demitri. He loves her. Don't be selfish, Melanie. It's unbecoming."

I whimper and roll twice, my shoulder throbbing from the contact. I lie on the tumbling mat a few feet removed from Demitri. "Better?" I ask Mr. Isley, hitting him with big eyes.

Mr. Isley sighs. "How much of this is your shoulder hurting, and how much is it that you've got a thing for Demitri?"

My expression morphs into dejection. "I'm exhausted. Trey's been a basket case since the hostage takeover. He calls me every two hours *all* night long to check on me. My shoulder hurts, and it takes time for me to fall asleep. It's become a vicious cycle. Because of Demitri's calm vibe, I can zonk out right away. That's all this is about."

"It's not okay to put your friend in a compromising position to selfishly get what you need."

I curl up in a ball and huff while Mr. Isley chastises me. So tired and frustrated that I can't control my emotions, I tear up. "I wasn't trying to compromise my friend," I whisper. I blink back the tears and get a grasp on my inner turmoil.

"Everyone, stop," Demitri demands. "None of you understand her."

Javier snorts. "I don't think *you* understand her. Everything she touches explodes. I'm relieved Mr. Isley sees it too because maybe he can talk some sense into her."

My heart hurts. Javier tries to be civil with me, but he generally views me as a problem. It makes me sad that Mr. Isley does too. My friendship with Demitri is one of the few things that makes me happy, and I don't want to lose that.

Demitri turns a steely gaze on Javier. "That's the last harsh thing you're going to say about Meley." He turns to Mr. Isley. "You're worried the little atom bomb might detonate, right?"

Mr. Isley nods.

Demitri juts his chin my way. "Touch her back."

When Mr. Isley's hand lands on my back, his eyes snap wide. My energy is erratic and flaring. If Mr. Isley's at all intuitive, it won't be hard to feel what's happening.

The dance teacher looks worriedly at Demitri, who says, "She isn't trying to destroy my life. She's trying to stay sane."

Javier gives me a deadpan look. "Trey's eventually going to kill you for napping with her, D."

I roll my eyes. "No. He won't. I'm meaner than him, and we all know it."

Everyone but Demitri chuckles. He's watching me with worried eyes.

I groan as I stretch my shoulder. It burns again and causes a grimace. "I'm up." I get my knees under me and pull myself up to all fours, but my head hangs. "I apologize for compromising you with my evil snuggles," I say to Demitri. "I'm not trying to screw up your life."

"Melanie, none of that came from me. I never had an issue." Demitri stands and holds a hand out to help me up.

I shake my head and stand on my own.

"You're welcome," Mr. Isley says to Demitri.

My usually calm best friend snarls back, "Meley's the only female best friend I've ever had. I get to have fun when I'm around her. I don't appreciate you driving away the only girl at this school, other than Jayla, who doesn't paw at me."

Mr. Isley's and Javier's mouths drop open. Apparently, this is a revelation for them.

"It's true," Jayla says. "Watch." She motions to Demitri. "Take a lap."

We watch as gorgeous Demitri grabs a towel from his bag and crosses the dance studio. Every girl he passes reaches out and touches him. It's all friendly and flirtatious, but it's collectively a lot.

When Demitri comes back, Jayla says, "Now watch what happens." She nods at me, and I laugh quietly.

Demitri grins at me. "Come on, Fraggle." We walk through the middle of the crowded room, and no one touches him. They look at him, but he's left alone.

We circle back to Mr. Isley, and I put my hands out to the sides. "I'm the Bermuda Triangle. Feared, mysterious, and you sure as hell don't want to enter me because you might disappear."

Demitri belts out surprised laughter.

"It's true." I look to Mr. Isley. "I don't use or compromise Demitri. He's truly my friend, and we've discovered that we're less lonely and uncomfortable when we're around each other.

He's sick of being man-candy, and I'm sick of being a feared she-vamp. That's it."

"All right, Melanie," Mr. Isley says quietly. "Let's play 'what if.' What if you two can't keep a clamp over this oh-so-innocent friendship of yours?"

I rattle my head and say bluntly, "Then I'll climb Mount Perfect." I jut a thumb Demitri's way. "And I'll ring every freaking bell he's got, and a few he didn't know existed."

Everyone's mouth drops open. Demitri's amused.

"Yup, sure will," I say with my trademark sarcastic candor. "When we're finished, I'll make us milkshakes and we'll watch *The Price is Right* until I rev up again and hop on for another ride through Joyland."

Mr. Isley chuckles and shakes his head. "You, little miss, are quirky."

"I'm also sick of assumptions. You would've never asked anyone else what would happen if they dated their best friend. For some reason, everyone's convinced that I have zero control over myself *and* that I'm a selfish demon." I narrow my eyes at Mr. Isley and let a touch of my dark-water rage ripple from me. "You have *zero* clue how much self-control I have." I suck my rage ripple back in and roll my neck as it settles into me.

When I open my eyes again, they're laced with evil.

Everyone's mouth drops open—everyone's but Demitri's.

"Damn it! I better not lose my best friend over this." Demitri looks at Mr. Isley. "I'll be *pissed*!"

I leave them, crossing to places for the top of the grueling "Vogue" piece. Mr. Isley's promise that all I'd have to do is jazz walk turns out to be a lie straight from hell.

CHAPTER 7

Bear's laughter booms and echoes off the living room walls, his burger stopped halfway to his mouth as he doubles over at Tanner's typically hilarious antics. Tanner sashays across the room, cocking a hip and imitating Victoria's rant about missing "all the hostage escape fun."

Victoria sticks her tongue out at Tanner, and we all laugh. At least she's finally away from Trey. I welcome Tanner's actions. Trey and Victoria have spent the better part of this party talking quietly in a corner.

"It's on," my mother bellows from the den. We abandon our dinner, and the whole group of misfits races that way.

The news reporter says, "As previously reported on the noon and four o'clock broadcasts, tonight's breaking story . . . A group of young heroes saved Hollywood High from a makeshift militia. As we reported a month ago, Hollywood High was held hostage. The militia mastermind was Daniel Stamp, father of Joel Stamp, a senior at the school who was sentenced for the attempted murder of Melanie Slate."

Joel and Daniel's mug shots appear on the screen, followed by my homecoming princess picture, tiara and all.

I roll my eyes and tip my head back. "Fantastic. Of all the attention-seeking pictures they could have chosen."

Rich's eyebrows furrow. "I don't like you being the center of attention like that."

"As you're about to see," the newscaster continues, "the militia was no match for the student council."

My hands start to sweat. I've had anxiety most of my life. Trey instinctively grabs my hands, wiping them on his pants leg without taking his eyes off the screen.

"Do you always do that, Trey?" Mom asks.

Trey glances at Mom. "Do what?"

Mom grins. "Do you always wipe Melanie's sweaty hands on your pants?"

"Her hands get clammy when she's nervous," Trey answers absently as he looks back at the TV.

Mom and Rich exchange a "they're so cute" look.

The news report shifts to footage of the interviews from this morning. We watch the field reporter running our way, saying, "Let's see how students are handling the first day back at Hollywood High."

My parents' expressions morph with concern as the camera jostles and jolts, the reporters and camera operators shoving toward our group in the distance. We watch as Arch pushes Adam and Trey back. Both are in defensive stances. Trey is pale on the screen. The whole interview is chaotic as the reporters shift microphones rapidly from one of us to another.

It's weird watching how poorly those in our group hide their emotions. We come across as a bunch of ill-prepared, terrified hotheads.

The report ends, shifting to a story about rising gasoline prices, and everyone collectively exhales.

My mother gives us a mischievous look. "Wanna see a report that went a little better?" She pops a VHS tape into the VCR and fires a look my way. "I've never been prouder, for the record."

Mom hits the *play* button, and we experience the beginning of our interview with Kitty and her smoldering sidekick, Randy. Arch hits *pause* a few seconds in, saying, "Watch Melanie." He chuckles, and the video starts again.

I do exactly nothing to hide my shifting emotions. My expression changes rapidly from one Fraggle face to the next. Bafflement; disgust; a sarcastic head wobble; smirking, evil eyes. At one point, I scrunch my face so comically at Kitty that Marcus spews soda halfway across the room. My mom is roaring laughter at my cheerleader question. She finally hits the *stop* button on the remote because we can't hear the interview over all the cackling.

Rich gives me an aggrieved look. "I can't believe how rude you were to Kitty!"

Mom flashes a disgusted side-eye at her husband. "Kitty deserved it. Does that woman even *own* a bra?"

A ringing of the front doorbell interrupts.

"Saved by the bell!" Adam crows.

"There is a God," Rich mutters, clearly relieved to have evaded my mother's Kitty-irritation.

Three more dingdongs punctuate the air in rapid succession. We all look at each other quizzically.

We follow Rich to the front door. He opens it, glances out, and then turns back with a perplexed expression. "No one's here."

"What is *that* about?" Adam says.

Rich kneels and picks something up. He and Adam exchange a glance. Rich turns, revealing a gorgeous bouquet of huge, long-stemmed Ecuadorian roses peeking out of a gold box. He steps back into the living room and sets the box down on the coffee table. Adam closes the door.

We all lean in around the box, the heady scent of expensive roses wafting through the room.

Rich turns to Mom. "Carol, you got some secret admirer I don't know about?"

"I sure hope so," Mom quips. "Those flowers are gorgeous."

Trey hovers over the box and pushes the lid the rest of the way open with a flop. The flowers are perfectly arranged, with the kind of care that costs a small fortune. He reaches into the box and pulls out a card. After he opens the card and reads it, all the blood drains from his face, leaving him an odd shade of gray. His eyes shift to me.

"Yippee," Marcus spurts sarcastically. "We've got some *new* fun afoot."

Adam snags the note from Trey and reads it. He closes his eyes. "The flowers are for Melanie."

"New problem. Fantastic." Arch takes the note from Adam and reads it aloud. "Melanie, you're the one."

Trey's fists are balled up, and in a clipped tone, he chokes out, "I. CAN'T. TAKE. ANY. MORE!"

I look from one person to the next, my intuition nagging at me. I glance suspiciously down at the roses.

"You can guess who sent these," Demitri says.

"Jet," I announce.

Trey takes a grocery bag out of his backpack and hands it to Rich, who opens it and pulls out two massive industrial door bolts. Rich looks at Trey and smirks.

"You got new sliding bolts for our doors?"

Trey glares at Rich. "Will you humor me, given this new issue?"

Rich pulls Trey in for a hug. "Yes, we'll humor you. It means a lot that you go to such lengths to keep Melanie safe. I really don't think this Jet guy is that big of an issue, though. He asked Melanie out and delivered flowers." Rich shrugs. "Just a crush."

"Jet was at the school earlier," Demitri says worriedly.

"What did he say?" my mom asks.

"We didn't give him a chance to say anything other than call out Melanie's name," Demitri replies. "Seemed easier to walk fast and do the 'in a hurry' thing."

My stepdad disappears through the den and comes back with a screw gun. We all make small talk as Adam heads to the door with him, and they screw the thick steel sliding bolt into the doorjamb. Next, they go back through the kitchen, and we hear the screw gun as they attach the other bolt to the side door.

Arch steps to the front door and tests the new sliding bolt. He turns to us and smirks. "Short of the Incredible Hulk, no one's getting in through these doors."

Trey exhales and nods, his bloodshot eyes thick with relief.

"Now that we've turned this place into Fort Knox," Rich says, "you kids finish your dinner and try to have fun."

CHAPTER 8

I sigh and roll my neck from side to side to loosen the tight muscles. Third period is usually awesome, but the topic of the Industrial Revolution is lacking appeal. I'm bored, and it's an agonizingly hot day. There's no air conditioning in the two-story building, so I'm roasting to death. A bead of sweat drips down my forehead, landing in my eye. I wince, scrubbing at the sting.

"Melanie?" I open my eyes to find Ms. Tandy looking my way expectantly. She holds out a slip of paper and gestures to the TA who's standing by the door. "The office wants you. Looks like you're going home for the day."

I glance at Marcus, who's sitting to my right, and scrunch up my face in confusion. He stares at me blankly. Something must be really wrong at home. My mom knows that I have rehearsals for both shows after school. Trey was supposed to drive me home, and Mom promised to make his favorite meatloaf dinner. I narrow my eyes at Ms. Tandy, but there's no sense in arguing. My heart races a little as I ponder all the things that could be wrong. Is Rich sick? Did someone die?

I gather my textbook and papers and put them in my backpack, zipping it up as I stand. I make my way to the front of the room and take the slip of paper from the teacher. Sure enough, it's a "Request to Leave" slip.

"I'll take you to the office."

We leave the room, the door clicking closed behind us, and I turn to the left.

The TA shakes her head. "We're going to the main office."

That's bizarre.

All Magnet kids are usually excused from school through the Magnet office.

The main office is bustling with activity as we join the students in line. A gruff-looking woman motions us over. "Melanie Slate?" I nod, and she informs me, "Your brother is waiting for you outside. He's here to get you."

Alarm bells go off in my mind. I shake my head and lean in. "I don't have a brother."

The receptionist looks puzzled. "I must have misunderstood him. Either way, your ride is here." She shoos me away.

As I exit the office, I ponder about how the only people other than my parents who are likely to be assigned to take me home are the friends in my group. The long, wide hallway stretches out in front of me, empty of people. My head starts buzzing, and panic rises with each step I take toward the door.

Something is very wrong.

I pass the walls that once served as home to Principal Buttrum's metal cardholders, and from this angle, all the repaired holes are blisteringly apparent all the way down the long expanse.

My vision swims as my intuition flares. I gasp, unable to breathe, panic completely engulfing me. My feet feel heavier, like the floor is trying to hold on to me. I send a panicked pulse to Trey and Adam through our shared connection. I feel them both startle.

I stop and decide not to leave. I'm five steps from the main double doors when the right one opens. The sun is directly behind the person framed in the doorway in a halo of bright light and shadow. I can't see the person's face, but his stance is burned into my memory.

Jet. Run!

I start moving backward, and everything feels like it happens in slow motion as he rushes through the door, grabbing me by the arm and pulling. I start to scream, but Jet clamps a tight hand over my mouth.

He grabs me around the chest, yanking hard and spinning me around. My face cracks into the metal bar between the two doors, and I taste blood. I grab the bar and try to hold on, but he yanks again, clearing me through the door to the school's outside front steps.

I send a confused, chaotic image through the connection to Adam and Trey. I'm disoriented as I feel both guys running across campus. I fuzz the connection, knowing that I need to stay focused.

Jet drags me across the lawn toward a black luxury car that's parked illegally on the busy road. I'm ten yards from the car, and I fight like hell trying to get away. He throws me to the grass and grabs me by the back of the hair, dragging me across the lawn. I keep an iron grip on my backpack as I slide over the grass.

The street's crowded with people, but everyone ignores the tussle, continuing about their business. This is Hollywood, after all, and a public fight is nothing around these parts. Minding one's business is a survival skill in this town. Alone in my struggle, it occurs to me that this is what Adam and Trey must have felt like when they were finally in a situation they couldn't control. Looks like if I live through this, it'll come with a fresh case of PTSD.

Jet gets to the passenger door of his fancy car. The engine's still running. He yanks open the door, and I take the opportunity of his distraction, wrenching away from him now that he only has one arm around me. I scream, spinning out of his grasp, and take off running.

Jet yells, but I don't look behind me. I race to the building, yanking open the door, and run into Trey. He catches me, and I sob. Adam looks out the door and says, "He's gone."

I double over, panting.

Trey gathers me up and holds me tight. "This is insane," Trey says to Adam.

"Agreed," Adam replies. "Come on."

Trey wraps an arm around me, and we head into Ms. G's office. She takes one look at my mascara-streaked, bleeding face and waves us into her private office. She closes the door behind us and asks, "What happened?"

"I was pulled out of class and told I was going home, but it was the regular school office that called me out. Not the Magnet office. I knew it was weird because the lady said my brother had come to pick me up."

Ms. G narrows her eyes. "You don't have a brother."

"I'm aware. Anyhow, it was this guy named Jet. He works for the TV station that did our group interview. He grabbed me, smashed my head into the door pole, and tried to get me in his car."

"What!" Ms. G picks up her phone and dials security.

The newly hired security guards rush in, and I explain the whole mess again.

"Wait here," one of the guards says. "We're going to check things out."

"Jet Trippley?" the police officer asks again, dubiously.

"Yes, sir."

The officer raises an eyebrow. "Well, there's no way it was him. We called the station, and it was confirmed that he's been there all day."

My eyebrows rise, and I spiral into a panic. "I'm telling you that it *was* Jet Trippley. Black BMW. Long black hair. Alice Cooper concert T-shirt."

The officer shakes his head. "There's a lot of rockers around Hollywood that wear band tees. I don't doubt what happened to you, given that busted lip and your blood on the door latch pole, but it couldn't have been Jet Trippley."

Ms. G glares at the school security officer, who's also in the crowded office. "Someone must have seen *something!*"

He shakes his head. "I checked with every classroom on that side of the building. They all have their blinds closed to block out the sun. It's boiling today."

"Who said he was at the TV station?" Trey asks.

The police officer checks his notes. "Executive head honcho of some sort. Name's Dennis Rindon."

I look up at Trey, quietly imploring, "There's no way Jet's at work. It was him."

Adam sends to Trey and me, *"We're aware. We could see him through your eyes while he dragged you from the building."*

A furious heat rises to my face. It's so frustrating to know something for certain but the police refuse to believe it.

The officer sighs. "If there's any more trouble, give us a call." He hands his card to Principal Walker, and the officers take their leave.

Principal Walker appears incredibly unsure. "I called your parents. They should be here any minute. Let's get you to the nurse and put ice on that lip."

CHAPTER 9

"I'm Officer Blankenship. You're Melanie Slate?"

"Yes, sir."

"What's this about?" Rich asks.

Trey stands from the couch and crosses to me.

Officer Blankenship produces my sunglasses. "Are these yours?"

"They are. I was attacked at the school, and they went missing," I explain. "How do you have those?"

Officer Blankenship's eyebrows rise. "Who attacked you?"

"Jet Trippley. The police were called, but someone from his TV station lied and said he was there."

"Is that where you got that busted lip?" Officer Blankenship studies my face.

"Yes, sir."

"When were you last at the home of Jet Trippley?" he asks curtly.

"I've never been to Jet Trippley's home. Why?"

The officer's poker face returns, and I can't get a read on him. I can usually tap into the emotions of Normals with my empathic gift, but this guy is locked down tight. Clipped, he asks, "Where were you today?"

I look to Rich, who says, "She's been here all day."

"Alone?"

"Some of the day," Rich says. "We let her stay home because of the attack yesterday. Trey got here after school, but her mom was here with her most of the time. Why?"

"These glasses were found in Jet Trippley's home," Officer Blankenship informs. "There's a broken window, and evidence that his residence was robbed. He identified the glasses as yours and stated that you two used to date."

My mouth drops open. "That is *not* true."

Trey and Rich start to scramble to fill in the officer, but he cuts them off with a raised hand. "We'll let a judge sort this out. Melanie doesn't have a solid alibi because she was alone here part of the day." The officer looks down at me and says, "Please turn around."

I turn, disbelief washing through me as Officer Blankenship cuffs my right wrist.

Trey panics. "You can't do this! You don't understand!"

"Call Bruce," I implore Rich. Bruce is Marcus Vinsky's dad. He's one of the top lawyers in Los Angeles, and he's gotten us out of more than one mess.

Trey stares at me with terror in his eyes. "At least let her put on a shirt," he says to the officer. "You can't take her to jail in a sports bra."

The officer surveys me. "That's fair." He uncuffs my wrist.

Trey rushes down the hall to my room. He returns in moments with a plain black T-shirt that was sitting in a folded stack on my bed. He hands me the shirt, and I pull it over my head without saying a word.

"Wait," Rich says before I get my arm through the hole. He points out my shoulder to the officer. "Melanie was shot during the siege on Hollywood High. The wound still has to be cleaned out daily."

Officer Blankenship looks down at me with soft eyes. "That's where I recognize you from. You're the homecoming princess who was part of the escape. I saw you on the news." He glances at Trey, recognizing him suddenly. "And you were the mastermind."

Trey throws his hands out to either side. "The guy who filed assault charges is the son of the news station owner. He's obsessed with Melanie. We've been having issues with him stalking her since the initial broadcast."

I finish putting on the shirt.

Officer Blankenship's eyes widen. "All right, I'm listening."

Trey explains about the date request, Jet being at the school when I was headed to rehearsal, and the flowers. He then fills him in on Jet attempting to kidnap me, and an executive vouching for Jet's work attendance.

Officer Blankenship's eyes narrow. "What was the executive's name?"

"Dennis Rindon. Hang on just a moment." Trey rushes to his backpack and pulls a folded paper from the front pouch. He separates two sheets, stuffing one back in and hurrying to hand the officer the other one. "That's the officer who took Melanie's statement."

"He gave you a copy of his card?" the officer asks skeptically.

Trey shakes his head. "No, sir. He gave his card to the principal at school. I made two copies."

"Why?" The officer looks baffled.

"My father ran a security company," Trey explains. "I always think three steps ahead. I needed a copy for me and one for Melanie's parents."

Officer Blankenship gives a thoughtful nod. Finally, he asks Rich, "Do you have a lawyer?"

Rich nods. "Bruce Vinsky."

"This ought to get interesting. Mr. Vinsky is a force to be reck-oned with." The officer shakes his head, and his demeanor shifts from caged to cooperative. "Listen closely. JK Enterprises. Have Bruce look into it. Dennis Rindon is Jet Trippley's grandfather."

"What is JK Enterprises?" Rich asks.

"A law-skirting problem," Officer Blankenship replies. "*J* for Jet. *K* for Kitty."

Rich is confused. "Kitty's last name is Kertle."

Officer Blankenship gives him an aggrieved look. "Kitty Kertle. Really? Try Kim Trippley." He raises his eyebrows. "'Kitty' cer-tainly sounds more interesting."

"What do you think this is about?" Rich asks.

The officer takes a moment as if thinking about the best way to answer. "Now that I have background for your side of this, I don't think it's cut-and-dried. I need to take Melanie in, but you need to get information to your attorney. Everything I told you, Bruce could easily dig up. Whatever he finds, I'd prefer he kept my yapping about it quiet. The Trippleys are above the law. Bruce needs to work on airtight evidence. Melanie's facing breaking and entering, assault, and stalking charges."

Rich nods. "Thank you for the route. He'll look into it and keep your involvement under wraps."

Officer Blankenship looks down at me. "My hands are tied on this arrest. But after this is done, I promise to do what I can."

As I sigh into acceptance, he spins me around gently, clicking the cuffs into place around both wrists. Hands behind my back, I'm escorted down the front walkway to the police car. Every neighbor within shouting distance is watching the show.

I try to slow my racing heart. *I can't cry. If I lose it, Trey will go berserk.*

Officer Blankenship stops by the car as my mom pulls up

rapidly. "Ma'am, back up," he orders as she rushes our way, leaving her car running.

"Melanie is my daughter," Mom says as she continues her mad dash to me.

"Rich will explain everything to you," I say. "Just know that I didn't do what I'm being accused of."

"Which is?" Mom haughtily demands in her Texas accent, made thicker by her current state of upset.

"I'm being accused of breaking and entering at Jet Trippley's home, and stalking charges. According to him, we dated." I give my mom a snotty look.

Mom breaks into a cathartic chuckle. "Well, I can clear this up right now. The guy in question is scrawny, with stringy hair, and a creepy vibe. Melanie prefers dancers and athletes, ones that shower."

The officer considers this before looking Trey over, followed by me.

"I'll have Adam and Demitri meet with Bruce," Rich says before turning to the police officer. "I'll also call Melanie's school counselor, Ms. G. Can you be at that meeting?"

Officer Blankenship nods. "I just started my shift and can meet with you as soon as I'm done booking Melanie in. Would it be acceptable if we all meet at my regional field office off Olympic at ten? I know it's late."

Rich agrees, and Officer Blankenship says to my mom, "You can say goodbye."

Mom finally gives in to tears as she rushes to me and pulls me in for a soggy hug.

"It's going to be okay," I assure her.

Trey's next, and he looks beside himself with panic.

As he hugs me, I whisper, "You guys have to help figure this out."

He nods and backs away.

Rich comes up next. "Listen to me," he says, leaning down to whisper in my ear. "I know what I'm talking about. You keep your head down, try not to draw any attention in there, and do everything you can to fly under the radar. Got it?"

I nod, and Officer Blankenship helps me into the back seat of the police cruiser.

CHAPTER 10

Officer Blankenship removes my cuffs. "Stand in front of the blue wall, please," he instructs me.

The male booking officer, a rotund man with grandfatherly energy, glances at the ceiling. "I can't believe we have to do this."

"I don't want to book her either," Officer Blankenship says. "But we both know she could get lost in the system if we give her a juvenile processing pass." He looks me dead in the eyes and quietly asks, "Do you understand what I'm saying?"

"Yes, sir," I say with a nod. "I'd rather not get lost in here."

The male booking officer gestures for me to back up against the wall.

A female officer with kind eyes crosses the cramped space and hands me a paper with *Slate, M. 74792-1* handwritten on it. She gives me a sympathetic look and deflates before she glances back at my arresting officers. "You two can't be serious. You're going to put her in gen pop holding?"

"You got a better idea? Until she's put through the juvenile system, this is our authorized route."

The female officer thinks for a moment, rubbing her forehead. Finally, she says, "A solitary holding cell in Ward Three?"

"Again, I don't want her lost in the system," Blankenship responds.

The female officer sighs. "Good point."

I still my nerves and quietly ask, "How often do fifteen-year-olds get lost in this system of yours?"

The female officer gives me a dewy-eyed look. "More often than I'd like."

Boy howdy, you've really outdone yourself this time, Melanie. I gingerly take the paper from Officer Nice Lady and face the camera.

She takes my picture. "Perfectly manicured nails," she mutters. She glares at Officer Blankenship. "She doesn't belong here, and you know it."

In a whispered tone, she says something to Officer Blankenship that I can't make out. He nods, glancing my way, and crosses to me, clicking the uncomfortable handcuffs back onto my wrists, but in front this time. That's a little better, at least. We head through a door into a faded puce-green hallway that smells stale.

He leads me down the hall, steering me with my bad shoulder, but I'm so nervous that the pressure from his hand hardly registers. He stops in front of a crowded cell around the corner, and a sea of bored eyes shift my way. The women in the cell light on me and immediately perk up, catcalling and hooting.

Officer Blankenship turns a key in the cell door. "Pipe down!" he says loudly to the prisoners. "She's one of Mama Mabel's." He looks at me and flicks his eyes toward a woman who's holding court in the corner of the crowded cell.

He uncuffs me, and I step inside. The steel-bar door clangs behind me with an ominous *waaang.*

Officer Blankenship is careful to make eye contact with the

woman apparently called Mama Mabel, and they silently communicate something. Mabel nods the slightest bit in his direction. Officer Blankenship turns and makes his way back down the hallway, disappearing out of view.

I take a slightly shaky breath and face my new roommates. Mama Mabel stands and gestures wide, revealing her eclectic ensemble. She looks like a queen from an exotic land, and my eyes widen a touch.

"Cool off, ladies," Mama Mabel says as she hits me with an appraising stare. "Blankenship's calling in a favor. Pollyanna's under my protection."

The ladies simmer down, and all of them take their seats on the hard metal benches that line the cell walls. Brimming with curiosity, they look me over. I try not to shrink under their scrutiny.

Mama Mabel smiles at me. "Well, Pollyanna, here we are."

"Yes, ma'am."

Mama Mabel laughs, her shimmery low-cut blouse bouncing over her perfect cleavage. "It's Mama to you, not ma'am."

Flustered, and with my southern mother's upbringing unshakably rooted, I repeat, "Yes, ma'am."

Mama Mabel chuckles quietly. "We'll work on it."

Another of the ladies, a pretty brunette in a skintight, too-short, red leopard-print dress, asks, "You got a name?"

"Melanie."

"All right, Pollyanna," the leopard lady says.

The ladies all laugh, but it's friendly. Apparently having an "in" with Mama Mabel has shifted my odds. Relief trickles down my spine, but I know I still can't let my guard down.

Mama Mabel gestures toward the metal bench in the middle of the cell. "I assume you have questions."

I take the offer and sit in my assigned spot. In an effort to settle my nerves, I draw a deep breath. "I do. Why aren't we all in prison jumpers?"

Mama Mabel and the ladies cackle with amusement.

"You like orange, do you?" Mama Mabel asks.

Despite my racing heart, I grin a little. "Not particularly."

From her expression, it seems that Mama Mabel has taken pity on me as she sits down in her corner place of honor. "First time in the slammer?"

I nod, looking up at her with big eyes.

She smiles sweetly at me. "It's going to be okay. We've got you."

I glance around the cell, and indeed, all the gazes show sympathy. They're all at ease, and there isn't a hint of hostility. *Fascinating.*

"They aren't about to waste an orange jumpsuit on you just yet," Mama Mabel says. "Laundry services are expensive, and the budget's strained. This is where they put those of us who are likely to be sprung quickly."

I exhale, finally giving in to my mounting relief. Mama Mabel thinks I'm getting out of here soon, and she seems to know a few things about all this.

Her face lights with curiosity. "Well, Pollyanna, you must have a hell of a story. Pretty young thing like you landing in here." She spreads her hands out on her lap. "We've got nothing but time. Regale us with your tale."

I give a hesitant smile. "Would you prefer the long version, or the short version?"

Mama Mabel laughs. "It's late and nothing will happen before morning. Hit us with the long version. Something to do."

The ladies all settle in, getting as comfortable as one can be on a metal bench while leaning against a cinder block wall.

I clear my throat and start my story with the Joel mess. Something about the welcome reception of my new friends has brought out my humorous side, and I have them in stitches in no time.

Mama Mabel wipes laughter tears from her cheeks during a lull in my story. "How old are you, Pollyanna?"

"Fifteen. I turn sixteen in a few days."

Mama Mabel shakes her head. "Younger than I thought. All right, carry on. I'm enjoying this."

I take them through the whole Principal Buttrum fiasco and the escape plan.

Mama Mabel snaps her fingers. "*That's* how I know you! I knew you looked familiar."

With a quizzical gaze, I tip my head to the side.

"I run the streets of Hollywood with some of the gals in here," she explains. I must look confused because she adds, "We're high-class escorts in Hollywood. I'm their madam." When my mouth drops open, she grins and shakes her head. "You really are innocent, aren't you?"

I clear my throat. "It's nice to meet you all," I say politely.

"You aren't going to run screaming now that you know what we do for a living?" the leopard lady asks.

"First, there's nowhere to run." I gesture around the cell. "Second, prostitution's the oldest profession in the world. I don't judge."

Mama Mabel beams. "I like you."

The other ladies nod, and I make eye contact with each of them.

"You were a part of the planning?" Mama Mabel asks. "Of the hostage escape, I mean."

"Part of it, yes. My boyfriend, Trey, was the mastermind, though."

The ladies all catcall and make tittering noises at the mention of romance.

Mama Mabel leans in. "So, this Trey sounds like quite a guy."

I grin. "He is."

All the ladies giggle like teen girls. "She has stars in her eyes," one of them says.

Mama Mabel sighs. "Young love. Enjoy every moment."

I blush a little.

"Your tale hasn't disappointed," Mama Mabel says as she shifts in her uncomfortable seat. "But it doesn't explain why you're in here."

"All right, here it is." I hit them with the whole Jet saga, and they listen to every word, riveted.

CHAPTER 11

It's been the longest, strangest night of my life, but surprisingly, it wasn't all bad. Mama Mabel and my other cellmates have made me feel safe and oddly welcome.

Mama Mabel stretches her sore back and grins my way. "Well, Pollyanna, it's been a pleasure. You've made our evening a lot more fun than usual."

"Than usual?"

The ladies exchange knowing glances.

"Oh yeah," the leopard lady says. "We're in and out of the joint on occasion." With a funny cowboy drawl, she adds, "They frown on prostitution 'round these parts."

I laugh. "That makes sense, I suppose." I look down, studying my hands. "Thank you all. I never dreamed I'd land in here. When I walked through that cell door, I was terrified. I appreciate you taking me under your wing."

"Don't let tonight fool you, honey," Mama Mabel says. "You've got family in all of us, and we'll look out for you in here. But prison time won't be this pleasant. You need to keep your ass out of trouble. A tiny young thing like you is nothing but bait in here."

"Understood," I say earnestly. "If given the opportunity to get out of here, I don't plan to come back."

Mama Mabel tips her head toward the cell bars behind me. "I do believe your wish is being granted . . . Unless, of course, Archangel is here for a little dose of Mama Mabel." She shimmies her shoulders with a grin.

When I hear Arch laugh behind me, I whip my head around, surprised. "ARCH! You're here."

Arch winks at me. Bruce and an officer are standing by his side.

"You know I can't handle you, Mama Mabel," Arch says with a flirtatious smile.

Mama Mabel howls with laughter. "You can bet your ass I wish you'd try."

"How do you two know each other?" I ask, glancing between Arch and Mama Mabel.

"I told you, my Pollyanna. I run the Hollywood underground. Arch's an old friend."

I glance sideways at Arch, my eyebrows in my hairline. "You're a part of the Hollywood underground?"

Arch shrugs. "I've got friends in many interesting places."

The tall officer with a friendly face, whom I've yet to meet formally, chuckles. "I'm going to pretend I didn't hear any of that." He looks my way. "Melanie, we're releasing you. You either have incredible luck or Bruce here's a hell of a lawyer, because the booking outtake office isn't even open yet."

I nod at him appreciatively and look back at the ladies. "Thank you all. Is it weird if I say I'm going to miss you?"

Mama Mabel chuckles and stands to give me a hug. "No, my dear, it's not weird at all. We'll be seeing you around. Hollywood's a surprisingly small town. Now that you know us, you'll see us out and about. We tend to blend in, until we don't." She glances

Arch's way. "You need to talk to Big Joe, stat. Introduce him to Pollyanna and get the guys to keep an eye on her."

Arch nods. "Will do. That's a good idea."

The officer opens the cell door, and I step out with a final wave to my new friends.

Mama Mabel leaves me with parting words of wisdom. "Watch your back, Pollyanna, and don't take any shit."

"You too, Mama Mabel. See you around."

Arch wraps his arms around me, hugging me tight as he whispers, "Are you okay?"

I look up at him and nod. "Why didn't Rich come?"

"He's here. Just handling the paperwork."

We follow the officer and Bruce down the hall.

"Thank goodness for Mama Mabel," I say. "Officer Blankenship introduced us when he put me in the cell, and it saved my ass."

"Blankenship's a good guy," the officer says before looking to Arch. "This your girl?"

Arch shakes his head. "Just a good friend. Her boyfriend's outside waiting."

"How come you're in here instead of him?" the officer asks.

Arch smiles. "I run our crew, so I wanted to be the one who surveyed the situation on the inside."

We exit the door into the little booking room, where the officer has me sign a few papers.

Rich crosses quickly and gives me a huge hug. He looks tired, and older somehow, his face lined with worry. "Are you okay?"

I nod and wrinkle up my nose at him, excited by the opportunity to shock the usually unflappable Rich. "My new prostitute buddies got me through it."

Indeed, his face does register shock. "I can't wait to hear the details."

I laugh.

Rich signs the forms that the officer passes to him, then folds up his copy.

The officer hands me a copy of my mug shot. "Here you go, Pollyanna. Your souvenir."

I glance down at the picture and snort about this whole debacle. "Thanks," I say to him.

As we're turning to leave, Rich asks, "Pollyanna?"

Before I can answer, Arch pushes open the door to the outside, and I breathe in a gust of fresh early morning air. There, spread out before me in the parking lot, are all my friends holding up a copy of my mug shot.

I crack up and shake my head. "I hate you guys."

"See!" Marcus says. "I told you she'd think it was funny."

They all laugh and rush to me, hugging me one after another. Trey waits until last. He looks exhausted. When he wraps his arms around me, I finally relax, putting my head against his chest. He doesn't say anything, but he radiates relief.

"I present to you the newest member of the Hollywood underworld, Pollyanna," Arch says.

My friends all look confused.

"You even managed to get a cool prison nickname?" Tanner says.

I hold Trey's arms that are draped over my shoulders as I turn to face all of them. "Do I ever have a story to tell all of you. I spent the evening with a Hollywood madam named Mama Mabel, and all her prostitute employees."

Marcus whistles. "Leave it to Mel to have a great night in prison."

"I'm still working on the details," Bruce informs us, "but the charges have been dropped against you, Melanie."

"We'd like to file attempted assault and kidnapping charges against Jet," Rich says.

Bruce nods. "I'm looking into that through my connections at the DA's office, but you need to know that he has solid lawyers through his father and grandfather, and a mountain of cash to back it. The wealthy and powerful rarely play fair."

Rich scowls. "I think it's insane that he's gotten away with any of it."

"We can potentially convince the DA to file charges. They owe me a favor or two. But the Trippleys may wiggle out of it."

Rich glances at the guys. "I might unleash those hounds on him and settle this the old-fashioned way."

Arch cracks his knuckles. "Yes, please."

CHAPTER *12*

My new outfit is everything, and I grin at my reflection. This outfit is the perfect way to celebrate two major events that came together at once: first, the charges against me being dropped, and second, my sixteenth birthday. My denim hip-hugger jeans with a 1970s bell-bottom throwback flare turn out to be a lot cuter than I expected. My mom's generation knew what's up. The little skintight denim crop tank has a zipper up the front that matches the little ring pull zipper on the pants. My black platform heels are the latest rage, but I was warned by the salesgirl that one misstep is guaranteed to cause a sprained ankle. I'm chancing it because the shoes are fierce. My brunette hair is pulled back in a curled, bouncy ponytail. I'm ready for my special day.

There's a knock on my door, and my mom's cheerful voice rings out from the hall. "Hey, birthday girl, come out here!"

I grin and open the door.

Mom looks me up and down. "Gracious! That's certainly a flattering outfit."

"Too much?"

She shakes her head. "You know what? You're sixteen, and you should enjoy it. Work it while you can because you won't have that figure forever."

I raise a whimsical eyebrow. "You have *that* figure still," I quip, gesturing to my mom.

She chuckles as I follow her down the hall and find Rich in the living room. He's wearing a funny shimmery-red cone party hat and holding a giant present complete with a big red bow. He hands me the box. "Happy birthday!"

With a grin, I take the box from him, not wasting any time in ripping the paper off and opening the lid. Inside, there's another wrapped box that's a bit smaller. I laugh and pull the package out, ripping it open. Surprise, surprise, inside is yet another smaller wrapped box. I give my stepdad an amused look. "Really, Rich?"

He laughs and waves his hand my way.

I tear open the box, finding yet another. Finally, a tiny box emerges with an itty-bitty red bow on top. Inside, there's a little slip of paper that reads, *Go outside.*

I stare quizzically at the paper. "Well . . . all right."

Mom opens the front door for me, and there, at the end of the walkway, are all my friends standing shoulder to shoulder, grinning at me. They're all wearing red party hats. Trey's in front of them, smiling from ear to ear.

All my friends yell, "SURPRISE" at the same time, then rush out of the way, revealing a beautiful turquoise car with a giant red bow on top. Trey's still standing motionless in front of the car with a key dangling from his fingers.

My mouth falls open. "NO WAY!" I squeal.

Convinced this has to be a joke, I turn to my parents, but they smile and nod at me.

"Happy sweet sixteen, kiddo," Rich says.

I jump up and down and give Mom and Rich the biggest hugs ever. "It looks like a *jelly bean*!" I squawk.

My friends all laugh.

"Nickname achieved!" Tanner exclaims.

I run down the walkway, and Trey tosses me the keys.

"You ready to take this new toy for a spin?" he asks.

It's all I can do to contain myself.

Valerie steps up with Presley, Finley, Susan, and Kelsey in tow. She says to Trey, "Sorry, big guy, but the girls will be riding in the maiden voyage of Jelly Bean."

Trey laughs and steps aside. The girls all hop in.

"We can squeeze in one more," I say to Deb.

Deb throws her head back and laughs. "Not a shot. I'm taking my Harley and staying safely behind you."

I roll my eyes. "I'll have you know that I'm a fabulous driver."

Deb and the guys all laugh.

"Uh-huh," Trey says.

"Do we have a plan?"

Arch grins. "Follow me."

As I slide into my new car, I hear Bear loudly proclaim, "There goes the neighborhood."

CHAPTER 13

The girls are all chatting boisterously as we turn onto Sepulveda. I've spent the drive white knuckling the steering wheel. I thought I was a good driver until I suddenly was dealing with a car full of giggling teen distractions.

Valerie's in the passenger seat, and she says to the girls, "Would you bunch of cackling hyenas tone it down? Mel's a nervous wreck over here."

The girls all grimace and apologize. Arch turns right, and I follow him into the parking lot of the Malibu Castle minigolf course. I exhale, relieved to be where we're going. Arch parks, and I wheel carefully into the spot next to him. Our friends' cars and Harleys follow us. Everyone enthusiastically hops out.

I grin at Arch. "Was this your idea?"

"Actually, it was your mom's. She said you loved this place when you were little, and some lighthearted fun seemed like the perfect plan for your birthday." He gestures around our group of misfits. "With all of us here, Rich and Trey decided you were safe to leave the house."

The mention of my safety causes my shoulders to tense. Jet is still out there, the charges we tried filing against him failing to stick.

Tanner's snort snaps me out of it. "Lighthearted fun . . . *Right.*" He side-eyes the guys and says, "I'm about to whoop your asses at minigolf."

Adam's face splits with an evil grin. "Challenge accepted. You wanna put your money where your mouth is?"

The guys love a good competition. All of them take out their wallets. They pull out ten dollars each, placing bets on who'll win. Of course, they each bet on themselves.

We amble at a leisurely pace toward the Malibu Castle entrance.

Marcus grins. He jogs ahead, snagging Drake's baseball cap as he runs past. He hoots and hollers, teasing Drake as he ducks and dodges the basketball star's attempts to get his hat back.

Everyone laughs, and the guys all join in on the shenanigans, jockeying and joking as they rush ahead.

"I love every one of those morons," Finley says.

Valerie gives a wistful sigh. "Graduation's coming up. I'm going to miss this."

"Just because you graduate doesn't mean you can't hang out with us," Presley says.

Valerie looks down, her expression strained. "We all know how these things go. You'll all be busy with school and shows. Parties and gatherings will happen spontaneously. Adam and I won't be there for the planning. We'll drift apart. It's just how these things work."

Unfortunately, she's probably right. I glance at Valerie and then at Adam in the distance, realizing we're going to lose them soon. Suddenly, my heart hurts. Valerie's been like a big sister to me. She's a huge reason I learned how to stand up for myself. Valerie and Adam have changed my life.

All the girls look at each other, faces falling with sadness. "Valerie, I owe you for helping me become who I'm meant to be," I say. "I owe Adam too."

Valerie smiles softly at me. "I'm the one who owes *you*. You're the reason Adam gave up his player ways and became the guy I fell in love with."

I smile back at her.

We're interrupted by Adam's enthusiastic bellow. "Hey, girls! What's taking so long? We want to play minigolf!"

We glance his way.

"Let's enjoy today," Presley says. "We'll worry about the rest later."

We catch up and follow the guys up the winding walkway and across the drawbridge at the front of the castle entrance. I remember how enchanting this place was from when I was a little girl. We open the front door and are hit by an overwhelming cacophony of beeps and boops from a sea of video games. The whole place is lit up like a Vegas casino. Tag Team's "Whoomp" blasts over the game noise. Kids are everywhere, running and screaming. It's mass chaos.

Adam stops just inside the door. "I thought I wanted kids until now. This is insane." He looks at Valerie. "No kids, okay?"

She laughs. "No kids. Check."

We weave and wander through aisle after aisle of the noisy games. By the time we get to the back minigolf counter, I'm on sensory overload. A little boy screeches past us at top speed, nearly knocking Finley off her feet.

"Isn't this a charming idea?" Bear jokes.

I laugh. "I promise that it's far more pleasant outside on the course."

We pay for our golf session, each choosing a ball and a putter. We step out through the back door into a fantasyland. Rolling pathways adorned with different-colored festive lights meander and turn through a sea of themed obstacles. Windmills, frogs, jack-in-the-boxes, a haunted house, bubbling fountains, and waterfalls all dot the landscape.

The girls grin at each other.

"It's so pretty," Finley says.

The guys are equally impressed.

"If my dreams of becoming a film industry set designer fail," Hiram says in awe, "I'm going to build one of these places."

We wind down a walkway with beautiful flowers planted on either side and find the first hole. A giant frog is poised at the end. Its tongue drops down every so often, at random, to block the path into its mouth. We all get our golf balls through the hole in one try.

The guys' competition intensifies as we get to the tail end of our golf game. As good as the guys are at most things, they suck at minigolf. Trey and Drake are tied for the lead, and Drake just got a hole in one. The pressure's on.

At the final hole, a haunted house theme, Trey leans my way. "A good luck kiss from the lady?"

I bat my eyelashes at him. "Oh my! Good sir, how forward!"

Trey smirks. "I'll show you forward!" He backs me up against the wrought iron fence that surrounds the final hole and kisses me with a lot more conviction than I expect. He wraps an arm around my waist and picks me up effortlessly, putting his other arm under my tush to hold me. I wrap my arms around his neck, and we get lost in our own world.

Adam clears his throat. "Trey. *Earth to Trey!*"

"What?" Trey mutters.

"You want me to play for you?"

Trey ignores him.

"There's a hundred bucks on the line," Adam reminds.

Trey pulls away, setting me down. "Sorry, babe, but I've got to win this thing."

I sigh and close my eyes, attempting to come back to reality.

Adam laughs. "You all right there, Trey?"

Trey chuckles. "I think it might be Melanie who needs a second."

"Oh, hush," I growl.

He grins. "It's good for you. I've gotta hold your interest somehow." Trey turns and sets up his shot. He hits the ball, and it goes sideways on him.

"*Yes!*" Drake yells. "Winner, winner, chicken dinner!"

Everyone cracks up. Arch hands Drake the stack of ten-dollar bills. Drake waves the cash over his head. "Ice cream's on me."

CHAPTER 14

The guys have all opted to take advantage of the open-campus concept, ditching for a Monday-afternoon guys' lunch elsewhere. Marcus announced that it's justifiable because Mondays are long and intolerable. He would use the same excuse about all the other days of the week too, though. It's just as well because the girls need to hang posterboard advertisements for *The Crucible* and dance show ticket sales. We've been released from fifth period and plan to enjoy a leisurely lunch before we take our sweet time hanging the posters.

We're putting the finishing touches on the posters when Valerie groans and frantically barks, "Move, move, move." I jump up out of the way as she swings her legs out from under our picnic table and rushes to the trash can, losing her lunch.

Finley holds her hair. "How long have you felt bad, Val?"

"The past few days. Maybe I ate something questionable."

Deb snorts. "When's the last time you got your period?"

We look from Valerie to Deb.

Valerie shrugs. "My cycle's always been a mess. I can't gauge things that way. There's no way I'm pregnant. I've been on the pill for three years."

"I'm headed to the convenience store around the corner to get you a test just in case." Deb walks down Actors' Alley, quickly disappearing out of sight. A few moments later, we hear her Harley fire up in the student parking lot.

We all turn back to Valerie, who looks worried.

"You don't think it's possible, do you?" she asks.

Presley scrunches her face sarcastically. "Certainly, the virginal Adam and Valerie couldn't possibly get pregnant."

We all laugh hesitantly, knowing full well that Val and Adam have some steamy habits. Even if she's on the pill, crazier things have happened.

Valerie sits at our table and puts her head in her hands. "It's been at least six weeks . . ."

Susan and I exchange a glance over Valerie's head. Silence descends as we wait.

A few minutes later, we hear Deb wheeling back into Actors' Alley and shutting off her Harley in the middle of the walkway. The bell rings and the crowd clears out, leaving our group at the table with our posterboards and tape.

Deb grabs Valerie by the elbow, saying over her shoulder, "Get everything gathered up. We'll be back in a few minutes."

We watch as they disappear into the music building, heading to the ladies' room.

Finley sighs. "Let's all say a prayer that the test is negative."

"Let's get posters hung outside the cafeteria and the Actors' Alley bungalows while we wait," Presley suggests.

We spend ten minutes or so taping the posterboards up, and just as we finish, Deb comes out of the music building in a hurry and crosses the expanse of the quad. "We've got a problem," she says, short of breath.

Kelsey's eyes are huge. "You're kidding."

Deb shakes her head. "It's positive, and Valerie's panicking in the bathroom."

We abandon our posterboard stack on the table and run to the bathroom. Valerie is leaning on the sink farthest from the door, with her hair over her face. Her back gently racks with sobs. Finley pulls her in for a hug, and Valerie hands me the test she'd been clutching in her fist. Presley, Kelsey, and Susan gather around, and we stare down at the bright-pink lines. Yup, it's blazingly positive, all right.

"How do I tell Adam?" Valerie asks.

A knock at the bathroom door interrupts us, and Bear's voice rings out. "You girls in there?" Presley cracks open the door, and Bear says, "The guys just got back and found the posterboards and your backpacks on the table. We were worried something happened."

Presley grabs Bear's hand and pulls him into the bathroom. "We have a problem."

Bear furrows his eyebrows. "I'm not supposed to be in the girls' bathroom."

"This is an issue big enough to override social niceties." Deb turns to Valerie. "Do you want to tell him?"

Valerie practically throws herself into Bear's arms. He engulfs her, his mountainous form making her seem small as she cries against his chest. He glances at us, and I pick up the pregnancy test from the sink ledge, holding it out for Bear to see. Bear's eyes fall on the test, and his expression morphs through shock, panic, and finally settles into a happy grin.

We all exchange surprised glances as Bear takes Valerie by the arms and looks her in the eyes. He smiles softly at her. "Congratulations, Valerie."

Valerie blinks rapidly. "You're congratulating me?" she asks quizzically.

Bear nods. "Let's look at this logically. You and Adam are engaged, right?"

Valerie nods and sniffs, her breathing calming a touch.

"And you're getting married after graduation?"

Valerie nods again.

"Adam has a business that's already making enough to support you?"

"Yes."

"Obviously this is a surprise," Bear says, "but you two can handle it. Adam already has the down payment for a house, you've got your future locked in, and this is just another amazing part of the universe's grand plan."

Valerie smiles the slightest bit, and hope blossoms in her eyes. "You really think so?"

Bear belts his boisterous Bear laugh. "I really think so."

"How do I tell Adam?" Valerie asks.

A reassuring smile lights Bear's face. "Adam learned a lot after being held hostage. I promise that he'll surprise you." Bear sweeps his arm to the side. "No time like the present. The guys are all waiting at our picnic tables."

We make our way out of the bathroom, and Bear puts his arm around Valerie, leading us out the double doors of the music building into the bright sunshine. I survey the guys, discovering that Trey isn't there. Adam's sitting on the table. He jumps up when he sees Valerie crying next to Bear.

The guys gather around.

"What happened?" Tanner asks.

Valerie looks down and takes a shaky breath.

Bears takes pity on her. "Do you want to speak to Adam privately?"

Valerie shakes her head. "We're all family. I'm sorry, Adam."

She hands him the pregnancy test, and the guys all look at it, confused.

After a long pause, Adam gazes at Valerie. "You're pregnant?"

The guys all look shocked as she nods. Adam wraps his arms around her. My heart flutters. We stand in hopeful silence, just waiting for someone to say something.

Mr. Jenson's voice booms out from across Actors' Alley. "What's wrong, kids?"

We all turn to see Mr. Jenson and Ms. G walking swiftly toward us.

Adam smiles the biggest grin their way. "I'm going to be a dad."

Ms. G's mouth drops open. She reaches for the pregnancy test. "Valerie, are you okay?"

"Congratulations, Adam!" Mr. Jensen whoops at the same time.

Valerie looks up at Adam, baffled. "You were just saying the other day you don't want kids. You aren't mad?"

Adam cups her face with his hands. "Are you kidding?" He looks around the group, his face shining with elation. "We need to get on the wedding planning, stat! Valerie gets anything she wants. We're going to have a wedding for the record books!"

CHAPTER 15

"This is pointless."

Rich smirks. "Adam, it's not pointless. Don't you want to graduate?"

I look up from the history paper I'm proofreading for Finley, and my eyebrows furrow. We're all struggling with homework today.

As much as I hate this, it does feel kind of good to struggle with something so mundane. It helps take my mind off wondering what's happening with Jet. We haven't heard much of anything since Bruce said he would lobby the DA to charge Jet with attempted kidnapping. The sense Rich has gotten is that there won't be any legal action possible unless Jet does something new and chargeable.

Our waitress, Bambi, drops off my plate of hash browns and pancakes with a thunk before continuing down the line of tables, pulling plates from her big serving tray. She's harried, buzzing around like a hornet.

Adam nods his appreciation her way as Bambi sets his burger and fries by his elbow. He turns back to Rich. "No. I don't really care if I graduate at this point."

Rich gives him his infamous "disappointed dad" look, and I can't help but giggle. I've been on the receiving end of that look a million times. Adam glares over his shoulder at me, and I raise my eyebrows, pointedly looking back down at the paper I'm proofing. As much as Adam seemed excited when he first learned the news about Valerie's pregnancy, the reality of the situation seems to have set in. He's been in a hell of a bad mood for the past few days.

"I already have my business solidified," Adam grumbles. "I've got a building, an employee ready to start, and a list of clients who are driving me nuts waiting for their turn at a custom bike. I don't even need my high school diploma."

Trey leans into my shoulder and whispers, "Rich is about to reality check him."

I nod and glance up at the pair.

Rich leans back in the booth and crosses his arms over his chest. He hits Adam with an appraising look. "You're going to be a father. You need to set an example for your child, Adam. I have no doubt that you're capable of running a successful business without a high school diploma, but you're two months from graduating. You need the diploma. Life is long, and you never know what's coming. It's mandatory that you're scrupulous in your long-term outlook. I'm not letting you give up just because trigonometry's hard."

Adam's shoulders fall. "You're right. Let's get this done."

They hunker down, heads together, going over the dreaded trigonometry assignment again.

From across the table, Valerie leans toward me and quietly says, "It's big of Rich to come all the way down here to help Adam."

I chuckle softly. "He loves it. You know how those two are. When Rich painted the trim on our house, Adam showed up to help."

Valerie smiles. "I know it's odd, but they seem more like best friends than mentor and mentee."

I completely agree, but my response is interrupted when Bambi stomps up and curtly asks, "Is there anything else you guys need?"

I smile pleasantly at her. "No, ma'am. We appreciate you."

Bambi snorts, turns on her heel, and flounces off without a response.

Valerie snickers. "You'd think she'd be used to us by now, but she always seems pissed when we show up."

I grin and gesture across the long, narrow restaurant. "In her defense, our group's so big that we take up half the tables when we descend on this place."

"Eh. We tip well. She needs to get over it."

I love this seedy hole-in-the-wall. Even with all that has happened to us over the course of the school year, we've found time to meet at Snow White's Café once a week to do homework and eat dinner together. It's one of my favorite group activities, and I always look forward to it. If nothing else, this place has the best hash browns on the planet, and they serve breakfast all day. I love pancakes for dinner. Too bad Bambi doesn't share my enthusiasm.

Three booths down, Marcus throws his hands in the air and triumphantly whoops, "Finished! Thank God! I never thought I'd get through this assignment."

Next to him, Presley huffs. "Great! Let me copy your paper, show-off!"

Marcus hands over his paper, which she enthusiastically starts copying.

Rich glances Presley's way. "I'm gonna pretend I didn't see that," he says pointedly.

Demitri laughs. "You need to pretend you aren't seeing me answer my take-home test using CliffsNotes too."

"Integrity, kids!" Rich says with a roll of his eyes. "Be worthwhile people, please."

In unison, the whole group says, "Yes, Dad," and we all crack up.

Rich sighs and gets back to dragging Adam through the math.

We're interrupted by a familiar voice. "Bruce was right. Here you all are."

Surprised, we all turn and see Mama Mabel breeze in. She's wearing her usual layers of scarfs and various eclectic accoutrements. She has a huge guy with her. He's adorned in a badass worn leather motorcycle vest and riding pants. His no-nonsense expression lends him an intimidating vibe, but then he removes his dark sunglasses to reveal the sincerest brown eyes that survey us with care.

Arch stands to hug Mama Mabel. "Hi, Mama." He turns to the man. "What's up, Big Joe? I'm always glad to see you, but I suspect your presence means you two have bad news."

Mama Mabel and Big Joe pull up chairs in the middle of the restaurant, holding court in a spot where we all have a view. Everyone puts down their pencils and forks and prepares for whatever news is about to be revealed.

Once she has everyone's rapt attention, Mama Mabel begins. "I called Bruce to find out where you kids were likely to be. We've intercepted something you all need to see."

She takes a manila envelope out of her shoulder bag, pulls out a stack of pictures, and hands the stack to Arch, who walks them over to the end table. Arch looks at the pictures one at a time, handing each one to our friend Kenji Gwan as he finishes. Kenji does the same, and everyone passes the pictures from person to person down the line. When the first picture gets to me, I furrow my eyebrows in confusion. It's a dark, shadowy shot, taken from a distance. In the image, Trey and I are gazing at the view at Mulholland. I glance at Trey as I hand him the picture. The second one is of Presley and me laughing beside my new car in the student parking lot. The third picture is of our group walking down Highland Avenue. The fourth is me sitting at my desk. It was taken through the window of one of my classes that overlooks the front lawn of the school. Next is of me playing minigolf. The pictures keep coming, and the one similarity in all of them is me.

Trey looks up and asks Mama Mabel, "Who took these?"

"A local thug named Sharpie. And a friend of his who has transportation."

Arch snorts. "That crackhead's still alive?"

Mama Mabel glances my way pensively. "He might not be alive for long after you see this." She pauses hesitantly. "They get worse. Pollyanna and Trey, come over here for a second."

I break out in a cold sweat and scoot out of the round booth with Trey right behind me. We cross to Mama Mabel, who pulls another manila envelope out of her bag. She hands the envelope to Trey. It's full of a stack of eight-by-ten photos. He turns slightly to block my view.

His face goes ashen as he slowly fans through the stack. His mouth drops open, and he backs up two steps and sits down in an empty chair.

"Hand them over, Trey."

He doesn't argue, handing them to me with wide eyes. I look down at the first picture, and it's Trey and me in a rather com-promising moment, the shot clearly taken through his bedroom window at his house. The next picture is less provocative, from the night in Trey's car when we went parking at Mulholland.

Rich scoots from his booth and starts to head our way.

"Richard?" Big Joe says quizzically.

A look of surprise crosses Rich's face, and then awareness dawns on him. "Joseph?"

Big Joe pulls Rich into a hug. "It's been a long time, brother."

"Twenty years at least," Rich says with a grin as they pull back. He turns his attention to us. "Hand them over, Melanie."

My heart seizes. *I can't give Rich these pictures.*

Trey starts to protest, but Big Joe interrupts him. "How do you know these two kids, Richard?"

"Melanie's my stepdaughter."

Big Joe shakes his head. "Then you don't need to see the pictures." He looks Rich hard in the eyes. "Trust me."

The pictures are bad. They're all of Trey and me in our various amorous moments over the past few weeks. All taken through windows when we thought we had privacy. Some are worse than others, but all of them are reputation-compromising.

I look at Mama Mabel. "Our faces are visible in these pictures."

Mama Mabel nods. "I know, honey. I'm all over this. Don't you worry."

Big Joe comes to me and takes the photo stack out of my hand, careful to leave the images upside down as he slides them back into the manila envelope. He turns to face everyone. "Pollyanna is now under my protection," he announces.

I don't know what that means, but Rich seems to.

"You mean to tell me that you think Melanie needs the help of the *Hellhounds*?!"

Big Joe slides a challenging gaze Rich's way. "She's in deep, Richard, and she doesn't even know it."

Rich leans down on the table with his arms spread wide. His head hangs at a dejected angle, and when he looks up, he has fresh creases of worry all over his face. He glances at me, and for the first time in years, he seems at a loss.

Close to tears, and blushing bright red, I pulse to Adam, *"I need you to help with this. It's bad, Adam."*

Adam crosses the short distance, patting Rich on the back as he passes by. He stops in front of Big Joe and holds out his hand for the envelope.

Big Joe glances Trey's way.

Trey nods. "Adam's the only one who sees those."

Big Joe hands the envelope over.

Adam sits on top of an empty round booth, careful to put his back to the wall so no one else can see the pictures as he slides them out of the envelope. He starts shuffling through the images, and his jaw goes slack. He puts the photos back into the envelope, gets up from the booth, and hands the envelope back to Big Joe. When his gaze settles on me, my cheeks instantly burn fuchsia. He pulls me in for a tight hug and holds me while tears roll down my cheeks and settle on the front of his tank top.

He eases back and tips my chin up. "I'm gonna kill the person who commissioned those." He kisses my forehead hard, then turns to Big Joe. "They're mine to deal with."

Big Joe shakes his head. "Sorry, Adam, but we've got resources you don't. You have my word that this is going to get handled."

Adam moves over next to Rich, who asks, "How bad is it?"

"It's what you're thinking."

Rich closes his eyes.

Big Joe tips his head my way. "No innocent little thing like her is going to be compromised on my watch." He pauses before adding, "You know me, Richard. My word's good."

"Don't underestimate Melanie," Arch says. "She has the mark."

I'm confused by the statement, but Big Joe seems to get it. "You're kidding!"

Arch shakes his head and gestures for me to turn around. "Take off your jacket."

I slip off my leather jacket and hand it to Trey. Arch puts my hair over my good shoulder and pulls my black tank top strap out of the way, revealing my bullet wound. It's healed enough that it's no longer bandaged, but the newly formed scar tissue is still shiny red and angry-looking.

Big Joe and Mama Mabel whistle low.

"Guess I misjudged you with that Pollyanna nickname," Mama Mabel says.

"I could cover that for you," Big Joe offers. "I own Spiral Tattoo on Sunset. I'm the one who does all of Arch's ink." He grins. "Maybe a lotus flower?"

Without hesitation I say, "I want a firebird."

Rich's eyebrows shoot toward his hairline, and Trey looks at me like I've lost my mind.

Big Joe claps his hands once. "Done. It's on the house. Just make sure you bring Richard in to sign a consent form because you're underage."

Trey grins slyly at me. "Hot," he murmurs.

"Judging from what I just saw," Adam says, "it can't get much hotter."

I bare my teeth and snarl, "Shut up, Adam."

His hands raised in surrender, Adam amusedly says, "My lips are sealed, firecracker."

My hopeful gaze passes to Rich, but all he says is, "We'll talk about it."

"Are you ready to lure in Jet?" Big Joe asks as he looks down at me.

"Is that a good idea?" Rich asks.

Big Joe shrugs. "That sick fuck isn't going to stop. Would you rather he keeps taunting Melanie, or do you want to make a point?

The Hellhounds plan to teach him a lesson, but he has to come to us. If we go to him, he comes across as the victim. We're doing this our way, because law enforcement won't do anything until Jet really goes off the deep end."

Mabel adds, "When I spoke with Bruce about where to find the kids, he said the attempted kidnapping charges against Jet are officially dead. Now, we're dealing with Jet hiring crackheads to follow Melanie around. It's better to entice him in."

I close my eyes and take a deep breath before gazing up at Big Joe with steely eyes. "Let's do this."

"You've got more grit than meets the eye."

Bear snorts. "You have no idea."

Big Joe looks at Bear contemplatively. "She's really that tough?"

"She's a beast."

Respect is written all over Big Joe's expression as he looks down at me.

"You might as well all take a seat and finish your dinner while we hash out how all of this came to be," Mama Mabel says.

We take our seats, but I can't eat. My stomach's churning, and my heart's racing. The pictures are likely to destroy me.

Trey puts his arm around me and pulls my head down against his shoulder. He kisses the top of my head and murmurs, "It's going to be okay."

"I was at my office taking appointment calls when Sharpie came in more spastic and wilder than usual." Mama Mabel looks around at everyone's blank expressions. "A lot of you youngbloods must be new around here. Sharpie's a homeless local who's hirable for just about any odd job he can make some change on."

We all nod.

"Anyhow," she continues, "he presented me with the more suggestive photos, trying to sell them to me. Of course, I recognized the two stars of that show and immediately demanded to see the rest." She chuckles. "Sharpie charged me ten bucks and enthusiastically presented the pictures. I looked the stacks over and offered him another fifty-spot for all the information he had. He sung like a canary at that price." She clears her throat. "He said that some high-paying guy hired him to spy on Melanie. Sharpie was supposed to follow her everywhere and take photos for him. Sharpie reports to the guy every few days. It has to be Melanie's stalker."

Big Joe barks out a surprised laugh. "Damn, Pollyanna, you chose a hell of an enemy. I still can't believe the heir to the Trippley Broadcasting fortune is after you." He gives me a baffled look. "What's your tie to that weasel?"

I shrug. "None, really." I explain how we all met Jet at the station. "He has beyond creepy energy. I think he's an energy worker, given his vibe, but not the good kind of energy worker."

Big Joe's brow furrows. "Full disclosure, the Hellhounds I ride with are all Normals. Knowing this may have a metaphysical component is worrisome." He glances around at the group. "How many of you are energy workers?"

Trey, Demitri, Adam, Bear, Darren, and Rich raise hands. Mama Mabel does also, and I grin at her.

"Does Melanie have an enticing allure from that perspective?" Big Joe asks.

The guys who raised their hands all crack up.

"She's been stalked over it before," Adam informs.

"Not good," Big Joe says. "Jet's a creeper."

I side-eye him. "That tends to be my luck lately." I shiver as the memory of Joel wafts through my mind. I ask Mama Mabel, "He was trying to sell the pictures?"

She nods. "I gave him another hundred dollars, and a warning that I'm buying the exclusive rights to the pictures. He's supposed to bring me the negatives shortly, for another hundred bucks. Had to go pick them up from where he camps out—some fire escape behind one of the souvenir shops around the corner. I told him that if he showed anyone else, or I find out that he sold any copies of the pictures, I'll have him killed."

My eyebrows rise in surprise.

"No one messes with me and Big Joe," Mama Mabel says. "Sharpie knows I'm serious."

I'm a worried mess. "Do you think we can stop this before the pictures are plastered everywhere?"

Mama Mabel nods. "Buying Sharpie's easy. I was the first one he came to with the pictures because he knows I'm in the sex-trade industry. I don't deal in porn or smut magazines, but he took a shot in the dark. He'll bring me the negatives. The one issue we still have is whether Jet Trippley received his copies *before* Sharpie came to me."

"You mean you *don't know*?" Trey foghorns out.

Mabel winces. "I'm not sure, but I have to assume he has copies. He commissioned the pictures. Sharpie stammered and yammered around the topic when I asked."

Big Joe looks at Mama Mabel. "We have a name. It's not a name I want to deal with, but at least we have a direction." He looks Rich's way. "The guys will be here any minute. I'm going to figure this out with them."

Rich hits him with a hard gaze. "Do the Hellhounds still allow associate riders?"

Big Joe's expression registers surprise. "Hell, we'll allow you full membership if you're interested."

Rich grins, slow and malicious. "My wife would kill me, but since I used to ride with you guys as a friend, I can probably get away with that."

Big Joe's exuberant laugh bounces from the walls. "Didn't you sell your chopper years ago?"

"I've got a Harley I just finished last night," Adam says. "Black with orange pinstriping. It's cherry. The buyer backed out."

"How much?"

"Seven grand, out the door."

Rich nods. "I'll have cash for you in the morning. Melanie can drive me over to pick it up."

"Sold," Adam says, and he shakes hands with Rich.

I look back and forth between Big Joe, Adam, and Rich. "Wait a hot second," I say to Rich in exasperation. "Are you joining a motorcycle gang?"

Rich laughs. "No. I'm just a friend, but these are good guys."

"We prefer to be thought of as a philanthropic organization," Big Joe explains with a grin.

"Uh-huh."

"No, I'm serious," Big Joe says. "A lot of people have the wrong idea about us because we ride Harleys and look like tough guys, but we truly do more good than harm."

"That sounds an awful lot like how people describe us," Adam quips.

"When Mama Mabel filled me in on your lot," Big Joe says, "I was thinking the same thing. We run a toy drive rally ride every November that collects over five thousand toys a year. We go on child welfare checks with the youth and family officers when they're scared that there will be trouble. Several of our group work undercover for the police."

"So you're like Batman," Marcus suggests. "Good guys, but a little dark?"

Big Joe throws his head back, and his laughter booms. "Yeah. We're like a bunch of old, hairy Batmen."

"I can't wait to be there when you explain all of this to my mother," I say with a chuckle.

All my friends say in unison, "Me too!"

Rich does some fancy handshake thing with Big Joe. They bump shoulders, and all my friends stare at them slack-jawed.

Big Joe surveys the rest of us, and his gaze lights on me last. "Let's all meet on Sunday evening to make a plan. The Hellhounds normally work alone, but I like you kids."

"We can meet at my house," Rich suggests. "Carol will have dinner ready."

Marcus gleefully pumps his fist. "Yes!"

We all pay our dinner checks and gather our stuff to leave. As we're heading out the door, Mama Mabel exclaims in surprise, "Looky what the cat dragged in!" She points across the street at a wiry mess of a guy lurking near an alley.

"Sharpie?" I ask.

Mama Mabel nods. "You got what I asked for?" she yells across the street.

Sharpie holds up an envelope.

Rich takes out his wallet and hands Mama Mabel a stack of cash. "Here's money to pay you back for what you spent already, and to buy the negatives."

Mama Mabel takes the money and flashes the stack at Sharpie, who nods.

An idea comes to me. I take off my backpack and set it on the sidewalk. As I unzip my jacket, I say to the group, "If you don't want to be in a completely inappropriate picture, I suggest you move."

Never ones to miss out on a good time, they all fan out behind me and ready themselves in aggressive stances, to the amusement of Mama Mabel, Rich, and Big Joe.

"If my reputation's going up in flames, I might as well have some fun." I draw a breath and yell across the street, "*Yo, Sharpie!*"

He gives me a toothless grin.

"Still got that camera of yours?"

He unzips his backpack and holds up a camera. I grin at him and pull my white tank top up, revealing my six-pack and black bra. I cock a hip, sneer, and flash him a twin set of birds.

He takes the picture with a laugh.

"I've got fifty bucks for you if you deliver that to Jet," I yell.

Sharpie fires off an enthusiastic thumbs-up.

"Why do you think that's a good idea?" Rich admonishes.

I shrug as I tug my tank top back into place. "Big Joe says we have to lure Jet in." I tilt my head. "I just revealed some of the allure. I'm being cooperative." I grin evilly.

"You're being a brat," Rich mutters, but a mischievous grin is just under the surface. Rich is where I get my daring from.

"Oh yeah!" Big Joe says. "She's Reckless Richard's kid all right!" He throws back his head and howls like a wolf.

Rich joins in, howling at the top of his lungs. In response, howls echo a little way down the street. We follow Rich and Joe to a pack of Harley riders, all wearing black leather vests identical to Big Joe's. On the back of the vests, the word *Hellhounds* is embroidered in red.

Off to the side, I spot Sharpie conferring with Mama Mabel as the guys greet Rich exuberantly.

"You coming into the fold, Reckless?" one of them asks.

Rich juts his chin my way. "The wife would never let me join. But my kid's the target of all of this, so I'm going to ride with you guys as a friend."

Everyone in the motorcycle gang throws their heads back to howl again, sending shivers up my spine.

CHAPTER *16*

"**M**el and Demitri, front and center," Mr. Isley instructs. "Everyone else, take ten and clear out of the studio."

We're at the tail end of a grueling Saturday rehearsal for the dance show. Everyone else leaves as we step up.

Mr. Isley surveys us, and after a moment's consideration, he says, "We need one more piece for the dance show. Given the short time frame, I'm tossing the two of you in. You'll be performing 'Shhh.'"

I can't help but roll my eyes. I glance Trey's way. He's lounging against the wall, and he looks back at me with a blank expression. *Give it a second, and he'll be pissed. He's never seen 'Shhh.'* "No offense, Mr. Isley," I say in exasperation, "but every piece that Demitri and I do is naughty. 'Shhh' is a great one, but can the two of us *please* do something that doesn't create a week's worth of drama with Victoria? Just once?"

Mr. Isley looks surprised. "I give the two of you those pieces because you work well together."

I huff. "I'm aware, and I appreciate your faith in our ability to dry hump each other effectively in your dance studio."

Demitri cracks up. "Seriously, Mr. Isley, Melanie gets more action from me in these rehearsals than my girlfriend does at home."

Mr. Isley rolls his eyes. "We're an edgy department. We try to stay on top of trends, but I see your point." He looks at Trey, who's smirking, before turning back to us. "Do you have a better suggestion?"

Demitri and I side-eye each other. "Melanie and I have a song," he says.

"As in, the two of you have a 'two of you' song?"

We nod.

Trey clears his throat. "You, excuse me, *what*?" He doesn't look thrilled.

Demitri turns and hits him with an amused expression. He steps over to the stereo system and presses *play*. Tevin Campbell's "Shhh" starts, and Demitri raises his eyebrows Trey's way as the sultry song languishes from the speakers. He wanders the space, waving us back before singing the introduction of the song. Every time the girl's voice purrs, I say her lines in Demitri's direction with over-the-top sexy conviction. Demitri's singing voice is perfect, but he's so exaggerated that it's hilarious. We're known for goofing off in rehearsal, so we can get away with our little display. Mr. Isley and Trey look like they're trying not to laugh.

Demitri steps into a wide stance. "Allow me to demonstrate." He starts doing the sexy male-stripper-esq choreography. "Your girlfriend would be bent over here in this part of the song about her being the homework I'm doing." He strokes the empty air in front of him and pops his pelvis. "Her ample ass right here. Isn't that nice?"

He strokes again at the empty air, and I double over laughing.

He holds a hand to his ear comically, listening. "Oh yes, I remember!" He belts the next part of the song about doing it on the dining room table, then turns to Trey. "Meley's on the ground here, and I do . . ." He body rolls down and gyrates. He turns to Trey and smiles enthusiastically. "Yeah? That's good?" He hops up and hits *pause* after enough of the song has played to get the point across. "Would you rather *that* be our song, or can you chill long enough to hear the actual song we call 'our song?'"

Trey chuckles. "I'll hush because I don't want you to dance to *that*. That's for damn sure."

Mr. Isley shakes his head, amused. "This piece really *is* dirty!" We all laugh, and he offers, "All right, show me what you have."

"We choreographed this together, and we've got it down." Demitri gets a CD from his backpack and hands it to Mr. Isley. "Track seven."

We get into place, and "Wake Me Up Before You Go-Go" by Wham! bounces happily from the speakers.

"I can't even get mad about it," Trey admits. "This song is so them."

Mr. Isley laughs as we spin and bop, weave and twirl through the happy song. We're both grinning and making silly faces at each other. This dance is magic. It's happy and fun, with all the complicated lifts and turns that Mr. Isley likes.

At the end of the piece, I giggle as Demitri wraps me up in a hug. He sways me right and left, and then we turn inquiring eyes Mr. Isley's way.

Our teacher relents. "All right, you two. That was adorable. It's in. Nice work."

I squeal.

"I appreciate you, Mr. Isley," Demitri says. "We're always happy to do the pieces you select, but we like to try fun stuff too. There's only so many body rolls and leg wraps that two people can do before it becomes an issue."

Trey walks over and fist-bumps Demitri. "Thank you for that. I trust you two, but damn, it gets trying."

"'Vogue,' load up," Mr. Isley announces loudly enough to be heard by the waiting dancers in the hall.

I huff and give Demitri a good-natured side-eye while the rest of the cast comes back in.

Demitri scoffs and shakes his head. "Buckle up," he says to Trey. "I'm about to have to give your girl a rubdown again."

Trey sighs and says to me, "I have stuff I need to handle for the rest of the day. Are you going to be okay on your own?"

I nod, a little put off because Trey has been busy a lot lately.

"Can you drive her home after rehearsal?" he asks Demitri.

"I'd love that. Victoria's tied up again too. I was going to be bored."

I bounce happily because Demitri and I always have fun when we get to spend time together. "D, I have a test to study for. Think you can help me? You know how much I love math."

He high-fives me. "We've got this."

CHAPTER 17

Giggling boisterously, I boing into Demitri's living room. Mr. Cantrell looks up from his drafting table. The realization that I've disturbed him while he's working causes me to wince.

"I'm sorry to disturb you." I look Demitri's way, unsure.

Mr. Cantrell grins widely. "Little imp! I'm so glad to see you." He pushes off his chair and crosses the room to hug me.

I smile up at him.

He looks just like Demitri, especially with those sparkling steel-blue eyes. "What's up, kids?"

"Trey had stuff to do, and Victoria's got some kind of family thing." Demitri exhales. "A big thank-you to the universe for that. I need a vapid drama break. You good if Meley and I have some best-friend time? She needs help with a test."

Mr. Cantrell smiles. "Absolutely. Mel, would you like to stay for dinner?"

I look up at Demitri to see if it's okay with him. He nods.

"Yes, please," I chirp. I take out my phone and call home to update my parents on the plan.

———

I'm howling with laughter. Demitri wipes his wet cheeks. We're struggling to breathe around our chuckles.

Mr. Cantrell knocks on Demitri's open bedroom door and shines a grin on us. "Do you two ever do anything but laugh?"

Demitri shrugs. "Not really. It's a thing."

"How's the studying going?" Mr. Cantrell asks as he takes our finished dinner plates from where we left them at the end of the bed.

"Meh," I say. "As good as it can go. Math's not my strong suit."

Demitri rolls his eyes. "She does fine until parentheses and fractions get involved. She's getting there."

"Anyone up for *Trivial Pursuit*? The only time D and I get to play is when you're here, Melanie." Mr. Cantrell mutters, "If it isn't about the latest gossip, Victoria knows nothing."

I raise my eyebrows at Demitri. "You played *Trivial Pursuit* with *Victoria*?"

He chuckles. "We tried once, but it quickly became apparent that knowledge is important in that game, and she has none."

I point a finger at him. "I'm offended. That's *our* thing."

Mr. Cantrell appears amused.

"If it helps, I'll never play it with her again." Demitri cocks a hip and pretends to throw long hair over his shoulder haughtily in a perfect imitation of Victoria. "This is *boooring*. Let's go *shooopping*, Demitri."

Laughing, I shake my head. "I don't understand why you date her, D."

Demitri just rolls his eyes, and we head to the living room to set up the game.

———

I shift and mutter to myself, trying to remember where I am. My hand runs down someone's front. "One, two, three, four," I count sleepily. "One too many abs to be Trey." Without opening my eyes, I say, "Hello, Demitri. Am I about to take a walk of shame for something I don't even remember?"

Demitri chuckles, and then Mr. Cantrell joins him.

I groan. "Sorry, sir. My candid mouth strikes again."

"You're fine, Melanie," comes Mr. Cantrell's amused reply. "You fell asleep."

I rub my eyes and roll onto my back. My head is resting on Demitri's leg, and I look up at him. "I finally slept."

"Feel better?"

"Yes," I say with a shrug. "I hardly sleep anymore. I'm always waiting to be kidnapped by Jet."

Mr. Cantrell winces. "I called your parents and let them know you fell asleep on the couch while we were watching TV. They were relieved. Your mother asked if we could just let you sleep through the night here."

I slide a baffled gaze his way. "Seriously?"

"She filled me in on the sleeping issues you've been having lately," Mr. Cantrell says with concern in his tone. "I explained Demitri's calming ability, and she said she's going to call Trey and let him know that you're finally getting rest and you're turning off your phone for the night."

I look up at Demitri. "I really do need to sleep. I'm sorry, though."

Demitri shrugs. "I read a lot at night, anyhow. There's no reason I can't read with you asleep next to me."

I give his dad a sheepish look. "I apologize and thank you. I really have been struggling."

Mr. Cantrell nods and checks his watch. "It's one in the

morning. You two head to bed. Hopefully by morning, you'll feel better, Melanie."

My eyebrows rise, and I look Demitri's way. "Victoria and Trey are gonna be pissed."

Demitri shrugs. "Whatever."

It occurs to me then that this is a totally different sentiment than Demitri expressed back when he and Victoria first started dating and I needed a place to stay after being kicked out of my house. *Looks like there's trouble in Demitri's dating paradise.* I get up, and Demitri guides me into his room.

After a long moment staring at the wall, I ask, "Is this weird?"

Demitri sighs. "Is this the part where I'm honest, or am I supposed to give you a load of bullshit?"

"Be honest."

He takes off his watch and pulls off his shirt, a sight that causes my heart to skip. "No, it's not weird, which is really weird." Quickly, he changes into a tank top. Then, he tosses me a big T-shirt from his dresser drawer. "Go change out of that miserable leotard."

I step into Demitri's bathroom, a touch shell-shocked by how much I agree with what he just said. At a tap on the door, I crack it open, and Mr. Cantrell passes a wrapped toothbrush to me before closing the door again. I shake my head at the comfortable oddness of this situation as I pull the toothbrush out of the package and set it on the counter. I take off my sweatpants and leotard, then tug Demitri's T-shirt over my head. In the mirror, the shirt looks huge on me, more like a nightgown. I fold my clothes and open the bathroom door. Demitri comes in and brushes his teeth next to me. When we're finished, he hops up and sits on the counter. He grabs a brush from a drawer between his knees. He turns me around and pulls my hair out of the hair tie. He runs the brush through my hair lightly, and I close my eyes. I don't know why, but it always feels different when someone else brushes my hair.

I hear the brush thump on the counter. Demitri's hands land on my shoulders, and he rests his forehead on the back of my head. The room is suddenly heavy with the feeling that this is perfect.

My voice holds weight as I clear my throat and gravel out, "You okay?"

He inhales sharply but doesn't answer my question. "Time to sleep, Meley."

"What are you so conflicted about, D? I'm not sensing a sexual charge here. This feels heavier than a desire for a petty romp."

Demitri smiles softly at me. "It's not a desire for a petty romp. I'm not thinking about that." He shakes his head. "Some moments just feel right with you, and it screws with my head."

I turn and face him. "I get it."

"You need to sleep. I'm fine."

He slides off the counter and follows me into his room. He clicks on his nightstand light and leaves to grab his book from the living room. When he comes back in, he intentionally leaves the door open and turns out the overhead light. As I slide under the covers, he gets settled with his book and holds an arm out to me. I curl up with my head on his chest, and he sends a calm wave through his hand on my back. My eyes droop within moments.

Faintly, I hear Mr. Cantrell ask, "You okay, D?"

I slump into a deep sleep before he can respond.

I wake slowly and wiggle with contentment. That's when I realize I'm draped over someone. I hold still and assess the situation. My leg is slung around a hip, and I gather with a start that I'm curled around Demitri. I huff. Without opening my eyes, I ask, "You awake, best friend?"

"I'm awake. I'm reading."

"Lovely. Meanwhile, I'm draped over you like a needy hooker."

Demitri's isn't the only laughter I hear in reply—the other comes from the hall. I open my eyes and can't help pensively chuckling. "*Whyyy* do I always say this stuff without knowing you're there, Mr. Cantrell?"

"Because you're comfortable here."

I heft myself up to sitting and rattle my head. "I can't seem to wake up around you, D."

Demitri sets his book on his nightstand and smiles at me. "As long as you slept, that's all that matters."

I scoot out of bed, grab my hoodie, put it on, and flop the hood over my head.

"Coffee," Mr. Cantrell announces as he departs through the door. "Come on, Melanie."

He doesn't have to tell me twice. I trudge after him into the kitchen. Mr. Cantrell offers me a cup, which I gratefully accept before loading it up with cream and sugar. I take a sip and then wince from the pain in my back. I arch and pop my spine all the way up to the top.

"Back hurting today?"

"Mr. Isley's trying to kill me, I swear," I say. "My shoulder's on fire again, and my back is miserable. That overhead split lift about takes me to the limit every time." I shake my head. "Mr. Isley needs to give me some time, but he won't."

Demitri sighs. "He sees potential in you."

"Wrong." I give him a reproachful glare. "He sees a means to an end. I *can*, so apparently, I *must*." A glance down at myself stirs a groan. "Need pants."

As I trudge out of the kitchen, Mr. Cantrell says, "That shirt hangs to your knees. Your clothing is perfectly acceptable. Please just be."

"Spent the night latched onto best friend. Now I'm drinking coffee in his kitchen. Never been happier, and that's a problem. Conflicted and need paaants." I singsong the last word, sending the guys into a chuckle as I leave the room.

I return after donning sweatpants and help myself to more coffee.

"Breakfast will be ready in ten minutes," Mr. Cantrell says.

Demitri hefts himself up and sits on the counter. My phone rings from the pocket of my sweatpants. I take it out and put it on speaker.

"Hello."

"Hey, babe. You good?"

"I'm fine. Good morning, Trey. What's the plan today?"

Trey sighs. "I'm tied up until we meet the Hellhounds at your place tonight. You okay on your own?"

I rest my hands on the counter. "Trey, you've been busy every day this past week. What's going on?"

He pauses, and I turn and narrow my eyes at Demitri, who looks gorgeously pensive.

Finally, Trey says, "I'm just busy, Melanie. It's not anything to worry about."

"Whatever, Trey. Have a good day." I hang up.

"Victoria's still at her family thing all day too," Demitri informs me. "Wanna go to Tower Records and then have lunch?"

I give him a suspicious look. "Trey and Victoria always seem to be busy at the same time lately."

Demitri thinks about this and then shrugs. "Honestly, I don't care as long as she's not up my ass. It gives us a chance to hang out, which is what I generally want to do anyway."

I tip my head back and lean on the counter while Mr. Cantrell flips bacon. I decide to just say what's been on my mind. "At this point, I might as well be dating you, D. We go to movies together, we study together. Trey pawned me off on you yesterday. Can we please finally deal with the fact that this is insane?"

Mr. Cantrell looks at both of us. "I'm going to be honest. The difference between how things are when Vic is here versus when Melanie is here is telling."

"What's it like when Victoria's here?"

Mr. Cantrell takes a hesitant breath. "Demitri rarely talks. Victoria yaps constantly about how great she is. She follows him around while he finds anything to do other than deal with her. It's awkward."

I make a Fraggle face. "Sounds riveting."

Demitri doesn't laugh.

"What's it like when you and Trey are together?" Mr. Cantrell asks.

"He's pensive and brooding," I say with a shrug. "We talk, but it's generally off lately. Ever since I was shot, he's been strange. It got worse after the whole Jet mess fired up. He's been standoffish, elusive, and weird."

Mr. Cantrell sets down the tongs and turns the burners off. "Why are you dating him then?"

I hadn't expected the question, so I find myself blinking rapidly as I search for a way to respond. Finally, I manage to say, "Because we're soulmate bonded . . . I guess."

"Do you think Trey is cheating on Melanie with Victoria?" Mr. Cantrell asks Demitri.

Demitri sighs. "Victoria's given me no indication that anything like that's happening. She and Trey did date before he was with Melanie, though. And Trey had an affair with Tiffany earlier this school year, so I wouldn't put it past him. I'd like to think he learned his lesson and wouldn't do that again, but who knows?"

Mr. Cantrell's mouth is hanging open. "Trey cheated on you?"

The reminder of the Tiffany affair stings. My only reply is to nod.

With a disapproving shake of his head, Mr. Cantrell looks from me to Demitri. "It's ridiculous that you two are wasting your time. You're both gorgeous, smart, talented energy workers. You have all the same hobbies. You're literally perfect for each other."

The slightest sense of hope rises, but I clamp down on it.

Demitri doesn't look like he even wants to entertain the thought of us together. He takes a deep breath. "Dad, don't push. We do well as best friends. End of story."

His reaction makes me close my eyes. I've known for a while that I have a thing for Demitri, and I've had to work my ass off to avoid thinking about it. Mostly, I was able to keep the whole idea at bay because I'm not dumb enough to think I've actually got a shot with him.

The silence stretches.

I finally open my eyes, and Demitri's staring at me as his father finishes arranging our breakfast plates. After Mr. Cantrell hands a plate to Demitri, I politely decline the one he offers me. Suddenly, I'm not hungry.

"You need to eat, Meley," Demitri implores.

I shake my head. "I'm going to get showered, if that's okay."

Mr. Cantrell nods. "Grab a towel from the cabinet and take your time."

Just after I pass out of their sight, I overhear Mr. Cantrell say to Demitri, "I'm telling you now, that girl thinks she's invisible to you."

I pause, eavesdropping even though it's rude.

"No, she doesn't," Demitri snaps back.

"Demitri, I can feel what she's feeling. She thinks she's not good enough for you."

"What do you want me to do, Dad?" Demitri asks harshly. "I can't leave Victoria just because you think Melanie's perfect for me. Yes, Vic's annoying, but she has some good qualities too."

"After you two were both out cold," Mr. Cantrell says, "I checked on you. It was adorable. You were wrapped around each other, completely content."

"What's your point?"

"Would you have slept through the night with Vic as well as you did with Melanie?"

"Dad, please let this go. I'm not leaving the hottest girl at school for my best friend that's being stalked by a psycho. I mean . . . *baggage* much?"

"You need to get your head on straight," Mr. Cantrell says sternly. "Victoria might look like a brick shithouse, but she's a pain in the ass. You have a lot to learn about true beauty. Just because Melanie doesn't dress like a showgirl doesn't make her less attractive."

"I'm fully aware that Melanie is beautiful inside and out, Dad," Demitri snaps back. "That has nothing to do with this. I don't want to date Melanie given the drama quotient she experiences."

"Uh-huh. Your girlfriend looks like Jessica Rabbit, and now you can't think straight."

I shake my head to clear it, then go into the bathroom to get my shower. I turn on the water, strip down, and get in. My heart suddenly hurts as the hot water sluices down my back. I feel rejected. I already know that gorgeous Demitri is unlikely to be with anyone but Victoria. They look like a high fashion runway show everywhere they go. Humiliation burns in me as I ponder about how Trey's clearly avoiding me and my never-ending shitshow. Apparently, Demitri judges me for it too.

I open my connection with Trey and send, *"Can you please find time for me today? I'm feeling really out of sorts."*

Without even bothering to answer, he sends back irritation before fuzzing me out. I sigh and turn off the water. I dry off and get dressed in my clothes from yesterday. My makeup-free reflection stares back at me from the mirror as I run a brush through my wet hair. I sigh, realizing that today is the worst possible day for me to look like a blank slate in dirty clothes.

I grab my cell phone and dial Adam's number. He answers on the third ring.

"Can you do me a massive favor?" I ask.

"Sure. What's up?"

"Would you come get me?"

Adam's tone shifts. "Are you safe?"

"I am. I'm just out of sorts. I'm standing in Demitri's bathroom, in dirty clothes from yesterday, no makeup. I just want to go home."

"Did he hurt you?" Adam snarls.

I smile ironically. "No. He just makes me feel like a *no one* sometimes. It's not on him. This is my insecurity to deal with. All I want is a ride home with someone I can breathe around."

"You have a thing for Mr. Perfect, don't you?"

I snort. "Does it matter? I'm me. He's him. You know?"

"He's a fucking moron if he doesn't get that you're the best thing that could ever happen to him." Adam's clearly irritated.

"You think I can compete with Victoria?" I reply sarcastically.

Adam chuckles. "She ain't shit, especially compared to you."

"Just be a hero and save me, please."

"Done. I'll be there in five minutes."

I unlock the bathroom door and gather up my stuff. I fold the shirt Demitri lent me and leave it on the end of the bed. Next, I make the bed and arrange the pillows neatly. A peek in the bathroom confirms that I've left everything in its right place. I put my backpack on my shoulder and head for the living room.

When Demitri sees me with my shoes and backpack on, he frowns. "You ready for me to take you home?"

I shake my head. "I have a ride on the way. Thank you for letting me hang with you and helping me sleep." I smile at Mr. Cantrell. "Thank you for everything, sir."

The doorbell rings, and Mr. Cantrell, a curious expression on his face, crosses the room to answer it.

Adam greets him, then holds out a hand in my direction. "You ready to go, Mel?"

Demitri looks stunned. "You called *Adam* to come get you?"

With a nod, I step over to take Adam's hand.

Adam looks down at me and smiles genuinely. "I love you with no makeup. Reminds me of our beach days."

Clearly suspicious of our conversation, Demitri's watching us intently. "I'll drive you, Melanie," he insists. "I was planning to."

As I smile at him, I shield myself off hard to prevent my discontent from leaking into a room full of energy workers. "I'm good. You've done so much already. But thank you."

"*What* is happening?" Demitri asks.

Adam looks at Demitri and narrows his eyes. I can sense that he feels my closed-off vibe. "Come on, Mel. Let's roll." He puts his arm around me, and we make our way out to his Harley.

I put on my backpack, my wounded shoulder more numb than painful now that I'm fully awake and stretched out. Adam swings onto the Harley, and I expertly climb up behind him and wrap my arms around him.

Adam turns and puts a hand on my cheek. "You okay?"

I nod, but he isn't buying it. He says, loudly enough for Demitri and Mr. Cantrell to hear, "Tell me, Melanie. If you don't, I'm gonna ring Demitri's fucking bell until he tells me. Something's wrong."

I sigh and send, *"I just can't handle being here, wearing no makeup, doing the little-sister thing. He didn't do anything wrong. I'm in my head, and I'm a little screwed up right now. Please just drive."*

Adam narrows his eyes and smirks at me before looking Demitri's way. He juts his chin at him. "You thinking clearly, D?"

Demitri raises an eyebrow, clearly confused. "I think so."

Adam shakes his head slowly at him. "Don't be an idiot, D."

"What are you talking about?" Demitri's clueless.

"You're perfect just like this, Melanie," Adam says before kissing me on the forehead.

I rattle my head at him. "I don't need a pep talk for Demitri's benefit. Please drive, Adam."

He takes a fifth of tequila out of his leather jacket and swigs it back. Then, he pockets it away and fires up the engine.

Demitri rushes off the front porch. "There's no way you're drinking and driving with Melanie on that motorcycle." He throws his hands in the air. "It's ten in the morning, *Adam!*"

"It's five o'clock somewhere!" Adam crows. "Anyway, Mel and I've had a rough run of it the past few weeks. Go be uppity and let us live." With that, he backs out of the driveway.

Demitri gets to me and grabs my arm, forcing Adam to stop. "We obviously need to talk."

I chuckle sardonically. "I'm fine, D. Adam always riles you up on purpose. Don't fall for it."

"*We* aren't fine," Demitri retorts. "Adam being here makes that clear. What is happening?"

Adam rolls his eyes and shuts off the Harley so we don't have to yell over it.

"I'm legit good."

Mr. Cantrell comes down the walkway. "Melanie, I know exactly what's wrong. Let me help talk the two of you through this."

I shake my head at him. "I'm a lot of horrible things, but I'll be damned if *desperate* is one of them."

"It's what you want, isn't it?" Mr. Cantrell asks cryptically.

"What I want is to matter. The most frustrating thing about being Melanie Slate is that, unlike most of the other girls at Hollywood High, I'm not willing to be fake. Unfortunately, *everyone* buys the fake routine, so that makes me a *no one*. I can't and won't compete with it."

"I've got her," Adam assures with a harsh edge.

Demitri really studies me. "You heard what my dad and I said, didn't you?"

Adam hits Demitri with the full weight of his penetrating gaze. "It doesn't matter if she heard it or not. She can feel things, D. She's one of the strongest empaths I know. Just let her be. Do your own thing."

"Please come back inside," Demitri says to me with a slightly desperate lilt. "We need to talk. I'm going to be a nervous wreck all day until we discuss this."

"You slept here?" Adam asks me.

I nod. "Demitri's calm vibe helps my insomnia."

Adam raises his eyebrows. "You slept all night in his *bed*?"

I nod again. "It wasn't a thing."

"How'd that go?" Adam asks Demitri.

"Never slept better." Demitri looks away. "I had all these bizarre dreams that were actually really pleasant. I woke up with my energy reserves completely full."

Adam nods knowingly. "Sleeping with an energy worker is a whole different ball game. Buckle up, though, because it's messed with her head. Melanie feeling insecure is rarely good for anyone." He grins. "Except me, of course. So I guess I should thank you, D. The only time I get to be alone with her is when you and Trey screw up."

"If you're so in love with her, why'd you propose to Valerie?" Demitri asks.

Adam's eyes narrow, and from the energy he's projecting, I wonder if he's about to explode. Instead, he pointedly asks, "Ever been handed something so perfect for you that you're suspicious it's a trick?"

Mr. Cantrell gives Demitri a knowing side-eye. He and his son squabbled about this exact same point earlier.

Demitri closes his eyes and inhales slowly.

"Yup," Adam says, smirking at him. "Looks like you do. It was the same way for me with Mel."

When I rest my chin on Adam's shoulder, he side-eyes me.

"You got Val out of the deal," I say with a soft smile. "And you love her. It all worked out."

Adam shakes his head. "No, it didn't. You got broken in the deal, remember? So did I. Val isn't faring much better."

I shrug. "Broken and busted is what we do, babe."

"Melanie thinks Trey and Victoria are screwing around," Demitri says.

Adam rolls his eyes. "I swear to God, I hate him." He smiles at me. "If they are, you're better off. He's mean, selfish, and dismissive of you. It hurts my heart." He looks from Demitri to me. "Why isn't Trey picking you up right now?"

I look down, sad. "I asked him to make time for me today. He got irritated and blocked me."

Adam rubs his face hard. "I'll always show up when Trey and Demitri leave you flat on your face." He tips his head Demitri's way. "Thanks for being a shallow jackass, bud. I'm about to take every detour I can think of and spend as long as I can with her arms wrapped around me." He fires the Harley up with a deep rumble.

"Damn it, Melanie!" Demitri demands over the racket. "Don't leave with him."

With a contemplative gaze at me, a slow smile builds on Adam's face. "I'm not taking you home. I'm taking you where everyone loves you and they're always asking when you'll show up again. They open at eleven."

I smile. "I don't have a swimsuit on me, Adam."

He shrugs. "There are shops all along PCH. The only rule is, I get to pick out the one I buy you."

I tip my head back, belting surprised laughter. "Fine. I'll spend the day practically naked at the Beach Bar with you. My one rule is that it's not a date."

Adam smiles. "It's not a date, but you're dancing with *me* this time. All those damn Surfrider Beach vultures always try to steal you."

"Deal."

Adam laughs heartily at Demitri's expression as he guns the engine, and we take off down the road. I hold on to Adam's waist and close my eyes.

CHAPTER 18

As I make my way through the crowd, I'm stopped right and left by everyone I pass. I've missed this place. The Beach Bar is full of energy workers who are searching for inner peace. The guys do flirt, but it's got a harmless feel to it. I've always felt at home in this crowd.

When I get to Adam, he hands me a hard cider. We clink bottles and take our first sips just as "Feeling Irie" by Gregory Isaacs comes on. Adam grins and pulls me in. I'm wearing his chosen bikini. The gold shimmery material doesn't hide much, but it covers enough that I'm unlikely to get arrested, at least. Among this crowd, my teeny bikini is acceptable, and I revel in the freedom of letting go and being comfortable.

Pressed seductively against me, Adam sways me front and back. He's an incredible dancer. I opt to enjoy the flirtatious moment instead of feeling bad about it. I won't let this go to a place that winds up causing guilt and conflict, but a little flirting with my soulmate is allowed on occasion. That's when it occurs to me that we still haven't had a chance to discuss the pregnancy news one on one.

"How are you holding up, Adam? About the whole becoming a father thing, I mean."

He smirks as he looks over my shoulder and evades the question. "Look who decided to haul his ass down here," he calls out.

I glance over my shoulder to find Demitri and his dad striding our way. I sigh and brace myself for the confrontation, but I don't get a chance to even greet them before I hear behind me, "Holy crap! If it isn't ba-*by* girl!"

I know the voice without having to look. I giggle bawdily and then announce with a hint of flirtation, "Rocco Rutelle."

He crinkles his nose and grins down at me as I turn to face him. He's six foot four, and I'm tiny in comparison. Rocco is something of a big dog among the surf crowd—boisterous and charming, and with a whole lot of swagger. He's harmless, though. Well . . . he's harmless with me. I wouldn't ever want to find myself on the receiving end of his fist-fighting tendencies.

Rocco says with an edge of amusement, "We miss your bitty ass around here. Goddamn, baby girl. You're looking good!"

Demitri clearly doesn't enjoy hearing someone else use one of his nicknames for me, but Rocco's been calling me that longer than Demitri has.

"You too, Rocco."

He picks me up and hugs me. "I forget how teeny she is," he says over my shoulder to Adam. He sets me down and asks, "Will you do the thing? Just one more time?"

I laugh. "You ask that every time I see you. I always say yes." I place my hands on his chest and put my head on him with my eyes closed. A moment later, I've topped off his energy reserves.

He groans softly. "That's intoxicating."

I open my eyes and smile up at him.

Rocco hands me his lit joint and says to Adam, "This girl. I've never felt anything like that."

Adam smiles, but his energy is laced with remorse and nostalgia. "I know."

Rocco gestures for me to pass the joint around our group. "How are things with Val?"

After a dismissive shrug, Adam takes a hit from the joint before passing it to Mr. Cantrell. Adam doesn't enthusiastically share his baby news, and it worries me. I don't think he's handling it well.

Rocco's gaze shifts back to me. "Good to see you, Wildcat." He rubs his nose on mine before sliding through the crowd to the other side of the porch.

Adam puts his arm around me and hands me my cider. "You and your surfer boys." He chuckles.

The silence hangs for a moment as Adam and I stare at Demitri and his dad.

"What's up, Peter Pan?" Adam says, jutting his chin D's way.

Demitri looks me up and down, seeming to disapprove of my swimsuit. He takes off his shirt and hands it to me. "Please put this on."

I take the shirt and scrunch up my face. "Tempting. It smells like your cologne, and if I wear it, you'll be shirtless, so hooray. On the other hand, I'm among old friends, this is what all the girls here wear, and I'm safe, so *eh*." I tuck the shirt into his waistband, leaving it hanging. "There. Now you fit in." I polish off my hard cider just as the waitress walks by and exchanges a fresh one for my empty.

Delroy Wilson's "Dancing Mood" bounces cheerfully from the speakers, and Adam spins me around before pulling me in and dancing with me to the reggae song. I slide my knee up Adam's side, and he holds my leg suggestively as I backbend.

An old friend of ours named Pepe sidles up. No one has ever told me Pepe's last name, but I do know he's a rascal. Always laughing and cutting up. He does nothing but surf. I have no clue how he affords rent. He's usually disheveled, and I've never seen him in anything but board shorts. I don't think the guy even owns a shirt. "Think I can steal Wildcat for a dance?" he asks Adam.

Adam shakes his head. "She promised me her dance card spots this roll around. Sorry, Pepe. You never give her back."

Pepe laughs. "Can you blame me?"

As he walks away, Adam chuckles.

"Grant me a convo, Meley?" Demitri requests.

"There goes my happy buzz," I say with a sigh.

Adam rolls his eyes. "Why can't we ever just have fun? It's always something." He drops my hand and leans on the railing with Mr. Cantrell.

They strike up a chat while Demitri hauls me to the other side of the patio. Along the way, I'm stopped by several people who want to say hi.

We make it to a spot that seems to please Demitri, who turns to me. "You're apparently popular around here."

I shrug. "I like this place. They don't card me, and it's chill."

Demitri stares out at the ocean, his vibe tense. He doesn't say anything for a long stretch.

"We're standing in a beach bar," I say finally. "There's reggae music playing, and you need to lighten up. If your dad's cool with it, grab a beer. Catch some sun now that your shirt's off."

Demitri exhales loudly. "Melanie, we both know we do better when we don't get things confused between us."

I shrug. "Okay. It's not confused. Now what?"

"It is confused because you confuse it. Why can't we just do the best-friend thing?"

I scrunch up my forehead and give him a slightly arrogant gaze. "I'm fine. I left, totally in best-friend mode. *You* followed me, were uncomfortable with my bikini, and now you're bringing up all this serious stuff while . . ." I listen for a second to figure out the new song that just started. "While Peter Tosh is playing."

"We're confusing, and you know it."

I rattle my head, baffled. "Then discuss what confuses you."

A local named Luis walks up and interrupts us. "Wanna dance instead of looking miserable?" he asks me as he gives Demitri a judgmental once-over.

"*No*," Demitri snaps back. "She doesn't." He turns me and puts my back against the railing. Then, he steps in front of me, effectively blocking anyone from coming up to talk to me.

I gesture in the direction of my retreating acquaintance, Luis. I don't know him well, and didn't want to dance with him, but that's not the point. "What's your deal? You're acting like a jealous boyfriend."

Demitri rubs his face. "I just don't like all these guys hovering. It's weird."

I scoff. "Coming from *you*, that's rich! You're constantly accosted by flirtatious girls. I never give a shit about that, do I?"

Demitri looks uncomfortable. "I'm just not used to it. People are always so standoffish around you."

I shrug. "Here, they're not. Maybe that's why I like it so much."

"You never wear stuff this revealing."

"Last time I checked, you don't mind revealing outfits. You're dating a girl who wears practically nothing on the daily."

Demitri nods. "It works for her."

Did I just hear him right? "I work my ass off in the studio and gym," I snap, "yet you treat me like your dumpy sidekick. It's offensive."

"I don't think you're dumpy," Demitri snarls. "Don't put unfounded accusations on me. The problem is that you're *better* than dressing like this." He looks around pensively. "The last thing we need is for Jet to see you wearing *that!*"

As our voices rise, Adam and Mr. Cantrell cross to us.

Adam gives Demitri a menacing glare. "One of the reasons I brought Melanie here is that these Beach Bar guys will kill Jet if he shows up and harasses her. I can keep her safe here." He gives Demitri a pointed look. "That's not the issue you have with the bikini, though. You give Melanie a morality check again, and I'll have you launched on your ass."

"What's the problem?" Rocco hollers to Adam.

Every guy on the patio turns and stares at us, all silently asking if I need help.

I wave my hand casually. "We're fine, guys. Sorry to disturb you."

Everyone goes back to their chatter, but I can sense that they're keeping one eye on me in case I change my mind.

"You're playing with fire, riling these guys up," I warn Adam. "Everyone needs to chill." I turn to Demitri. "Keep it down and let's deal with this. I'm sick of dancing around the issue. You don't get to have it both ways, Demitri. You can't be my happy-go-lucky best friend, but then also hit me with boyfriend judgment and jealousy. I've got Trey for that."

Mr. Cantrell puts his hands up as a peace gesture. "I think the problem is there's more between you two than gets discussed."

Adam hands me my drink, and I take a swig.

"Discuss it, then," I snap at Demitri.

"I can't," Demitri snaps back. "It'll be overstepping where Victoria's concerned. The conversation I need to have would hurt her feelings."

I look around the bar and yell comically, "Victoria? Has anyone seen Victoria? Ohhh, Victooooria."

No one answers, although I earn a few amused looks from the other patrons.

I turn back to Demitri and make a Fraggle face at him. "No Victoria. I guarantee she wouldn't make it five minutes in this place. This crowd hates fake flotation devices."

"Obviously she's not here," Demitri says with a dead tone. "It's the principle of the thing that bothers me."

I nod with over-the-top sarcasm. "Lovely. You go worry about your principles while I enjoy my day."

When I start to walk away, Demitri grabs my arm, stopping me.

I glare up at him. "Say it."

He just stares back.

"Your issue is that there's blazing attraction between us," I say. "Yes, I'm with Trey, but let me tell you, a fairy tale it's not. You"—I point to him—"are dating a waste of air, but God forbid you ditch her. I mean, how could you dump someone who *looks* like she's worthy of your Greek god ass? I'll tell you this, she's not even close to worthy of you, Demitri. She's rude and self-centered. You've finally discovered your flaw, and it bugs the shit out of you. Turns out you're shallow." I nod enthusiastically at his shocked expression. "So, Mr. Perfect, you're going to go on your merry way and worship Victoria. I'm going to drink another cider and dance with Adam." I turn to Adam and joke, "Unless you'd rather call Victoria and haul her vapid ass down here to see what all the fuss is about."

Adam smolders down at me as he swigs from his beer. "I would rather die." He gives Demitri a snide look. "D, you're just bugged because you think you've got everything you want in Victoria, but you don't. *Melanie's* everything you want. She comes with problematic baggage you don't want to suffer through, though, which I guess I can respect."

Demitri's jaw is tense.

Adam grins down at me. "You need a new backup plan, because you and Trey are going to implode. That motherfucker parks his car in other garages, and you know it."

I shake my head. "Coming from you, Adam? Really?"

He shrugs. "I'm not faithful. That's no secret."

Silently, I wonder if any of that will change with a baby on the way. I think about asking him, but then decide against it because it'll kill what's left of the mood.

My gaze catches Rocco's from across the patio. He's tanned and gorgeous, with the top of his wet suit draped around his waist.

"Maybe Rocco's my next conquest."

Adam chokes on his beer, then quickly collects himself. "A capital plan, my dear. You could move right into the filthy beachfront shack Rocco shares with six other surf bums." He gives me a sarcastic look. "He sells weed."

I bite my lip and take on a vampy expression. "I don't want to marry him, silly. I just thought I'd play with him for a while."

"I'll call in an order for penicillin so you're all prepped and ready."

Demitri glares down at me, and Mr. Cantrell sighs.

I grin and hold a hand Rocco's way.

Rocco cuts his chat off mid conversation and strides through the crowd to me. "Wanna dance, baby girl?"

I nod happily, and he picks me up and scoots through the gap between Demitri and Adam.

"Excuse me, pardon me, Prince Charming," Rocco says to Demitri.

Demitri glowers as Rocco sets me down and starts dancing with me. Adam chuckles, then swigs from his bottle.

"That seriously doesn't bother you?" Demitri asks Adam, loudly enough for me to hear.

Adam and Rocco exchange an amused look. Rocco spins me around.

"Isn't he cute?" Rocco says of Demitri.

"The guy she's dating is too busy for her," Adam says with a roll of his eyes.

Rocco dips me flirtatiously. "So here you are, back to your roots with her, huh, Adam?"

"Nope." Adam tips his beer bottle. "Just friends. I won't lower Melanie to being my sidepiece. She's better than that."

"Does that make her your sugar baby then?" Rocco says, looking to Mr. Cantrell.

"Seriously, Roc?" I say, offended. "You know damn well that I would never be with someone for money!"

Mr. Cantrell looks both shocked and amused. "I'm trying to hook her up with my son, who's dating a waste of air. Unfortunately, my son isn't cooperating."

Rocco turns me around and drapes his arms over my shoulders while he surveys Demitri. "Nope. He won't work. You need someone real, and that guy"—he points at Demitri—"isn't going to ring your reality bells."

I cover a laugh with a fake cough and look away.

"Hey!" Demitri snaps. "Wait just a damn minute!"

Rocco looks mischievously at him. "You're used to being the most perfect God in every crowd, I suspect." He stops, and his expression morphs curiously before he says to no one in particular, "I wonder . . ." He turns and bellows, "Yo, Riptide. Come here."

A stunning—I'm talking *holy-crap* gorgeous—guy wades through the crowd to us. I swear I've never seen anyone more captivating. My heart nearly hammers out of my chest, and my head spins. I reach up and steady myself with a hand on Rocco's arm.

He grins.

As Riptide approaches, Demitri gapes at my reaction.

Riptide's perfect surfer body is deeply tanned. My brain liquifies as I survey his curly hair, still wet with ocean water. As he gets to us, he looks down at me with deep-brown eyes I get lost in. He glances at Rocco as he touches my arm and smiles, but it's not naughty. Instead, it holds an edge of wonder. "Hel-*lo*. Who, and what, is this? Oh *my* God."

I blush, suddenly shy.

Riptide melts a little. "Ohhh! You're adorable." He pulls me in, hugging me.

I giggle happily.

"This is Melanie, but she's known as Wildcat around here. She's currently unhappily taken. She used to date Adam and is apparently stuck in an unreciprocated mesmerization with that guy." He waves his hand flippantly at Demitri. "He's new around here, and no one gives a fuck."

Riptide chuckles at Rocco's dismissiveness as he looks Demitri's way and tips his head right, then left, unimpressed. Demitri seems shocked.

Adam snorts. "Good times, huh, Peter Pan? You're hot shit, but Riptide's hotter shit." Clearly elated, he looks at me and says, "Melanie appears to like the other Greek god more."

I giggle, still wrapped around the Greek god in question.

Riptide studies me with his captivating gaze. I smile the slightest bit.

He smiles back flirtatiously, reaches down, and laces his fingers with mine. Eyes closed, he examines my energy, a sweet expression on his face. He opens his eyes and says to Rocco, "She's amazing."

Shaking his head slowly while he studies me, Riptide breathes out, "Damn. I'd sell my soul to the devil for a soulmate connection with you. I have an ability that allows me to study the heart of relationships. I've looked over you and pretty boy. You're perfect just the way you are, and to hell with anyone who can't see that." He gently puts his hand around the back of my neck and sends a wave of this calm, capable, soul-bending energy into me.

I gasp and close my eyes. My back bows. Riptide holds me while I lie limp in his hand. I come back to my senses and look up at him.

He guides me upright as he says with a tone that holds great weight, "You, my wildcat, don't settle."

I smile and rattle my head, trying to clear it.

"I teach surf lessons," he says, lightening the mood. "Any interest?"

"Actually, yes." I nod appreciatively.

A baffled Demitri barks out, "I've been trying to talk you into letting me teach you to surf for months! It's always no."

"Any excuse to see *him* again," I say, still gazing up at Riptide.

"I'd have you ripping and curling in a day," Riptide says, as he flirtatiously winks at me. "Hit me up." At his request, the waitress gives him her order pad and a pen so he can jot down his number for me. "I found an excuse to give her my number," he says to Mr. Cantrell and Demitri. "Smooth, right?"

I laugh lightly at his candor and read the paper he hands me. "Pierre?"

He grins. "You deserve my actual name."

"Thank you, Pierre."

He nods, and I watch, starry-eyed, as he melts into the crowd.

"Holy crap," I say to Rocco. "I can die happy now."

Rocco laughs, squeezes my arm, and winks at me before walking away.

"We need to talk," Demitri insists. "Will you come back to my house with me?"

"Not in the mood," I say with a shrug. "I want to eat and stare at Riptide."

"Yo, Rocco!" Adam yells. "Melanie wants to gaze at Riptide while she eats."

Adam and I laugh as Riptide wheels around comically. "Food's on me," Riptide calls.

Turning to Mr. Cantrell and Demitri, Adam says, "Nice to see you. Have a good one."

He puts his arm around my shoulders, and Rocco and Riptide wave us over to a four-person booth they've just commandeered. Demitri follows like a lost puppy. Adam slides in next to Rocco, leaving me with the spot next to Riptide. I sit, and Riptide looks over the menu I'm holding, intentionally pressing against my shoulder. We banter about the crappy choice I was apparently about to make.

"Melanie, it's fish-and-chips. End of story. They're insane here."

"Eh."

"Trust me," Riptide says flirtatiously.

"All right. Fish-and-chips, it is."

"What the . . . ," Demitri says, throwing his hands up. "Am I hallucinating? She's never turned down a chance to hang out with me."

"Maybe you need to switch gears," Mr. Cantrell says, shaking his head at his son.

Riptide smirks at Demitri. "Your problem is solved, pretty boy. Melanie's out of your league anyway." His arm glides around my shoulders, and my eyes widen. No one has *ever* told Demitri he's not good enough.

Rendered speechless, Demitri looks from his dad to me. He

gestures wordlessly from me to Riptide, and I giggle and wiggle my shoulders.

"Happy girl," I chirp.

Demitri gives me a hurt look. "Meley, you can't be serious."

"Meley, huh?" Riptide grins. "I like that. I'm going to steal it."

Adam cracks up, slapping the table. As he looks up at Demitri, he gasps out, "Watching you reduced to 'ain't shit' is fucking hilarious."

"You're still the bestest best friend," I assure Demitri cheerfully. "All that confliction you were bitching about is *over*. You're in the friend zone, just like you wanted." I purr at Riptide, "You're not in the friend zone. Sorry."

He crinkles his nose charmingly at me. "I don't want to be in your friend zone."

I bounce like a happy Fraggle. "Problem solved."

Demitri snarls, clearly not happy.

Riptide hits him with sparkling eyes. "You're welcome. I got your problem off your jock, and I've decided she's welcome to adore me instead." After a moment, he asks me, "Does that wound hurt?"

I nod sheepishly. "Gunshot," I inform him before he can ask.

Riptide winces. "I don't even want to know." He rotates me and puts a hand lightly over the wound. I feel an odd energy waft, and then my head drops as all the tension leaves my body. Something is shifting in my shoulder, and then, all at once, it stops hurting.

"I've been at energy work a long time," he informs. "I've developed a healing ability."

He switches to rubbing out knots in my sore back. He grips my good shoulder gently and holds a moment while he sends calming energy into a knot, forcing it to release.

"Ohhh," I groan. "You're magic."

His energy swirls through me as he shifts to another knot.

I slump over the table. "Best back rub ever."

Demitri glares at Riptide, then narrows his eyes at me as I look at him from my flopped-over position. My eyes roll into the back of my head as Riptide hits the perfect spot.

When I can coherently think again, I side-eye Adam. "I hate modern-society rules about age. I'd drag his ass out of here and have him moaning a three-thousand-year-old deity's name in five minutes flat if I didn't think it would get him arrested."

Rocco breathes out, "Holy turn-on, Batman."

Riptide freezes. "Adam, how old is she?"

"Sixteen, but she's on at least her two hundredth lifetime." Adam shrugs, blasé.

Riptide's voice is suddenly gravelly with heat as he says to Adam, "Please tell me it wouldn't be worth it."

Adam grins at me. "Unleash the beast, Mel."

I drop my shields, and my dark-water seduction thrums from me in blisteringly sensual waves. Riptide has me revved.

His head droops, and he whispers, "Holy shit."

As I turn my face a touch, I find him staring at me. "My seductive dark-water side is a lot," I murmur.

When I sit up, Riptide slides a hand along my jaw and puts his forehead on mine, squeezing his eyes closed. His hand is trembling as he gasps out, "I'm only eighteen. Think statutory laws still apply?"

"Yes, moron," Demitri says.

I toss my shields back up and cut off the dark-water energy flow. Riptide throws his head back and exhales hard.

After a moment, he comes back to his senses. "That's what you specialize in?"

"That's the fun one." I crinkle my nose and give him a cute, big-eyed look.

Riptide grins and holds my gaze.

"I'll deal with your back, Melanie," Demitri offers. "You don't need this guy all over you."

I rattle my head and look Demitri's way, having forgotten he was there.

Riptide squeezes my shoulders seductively just to irritate Demitri.

"I really do need him all over me." My whole body goose-bumps.

"I hate you for introducing me to her, Rocco," Riptide says. "I swear I'm in love, and I've known her ten minutes. This girl is pearl worthy."

Rocco fist-bumps him. "Damn right she is. You're welcome."

Demitri rubs his face before snapping at his dad, "Let's go."

Mr. Cantrell and Demitri leave to the sounds of Rocco's, Adam's, and Riptide's laughter.

After Demitri's out of earshot, I inform Riptide, "You just destroyed him. For the record, he's a nice guy."

"I know he is," Riptide says with a nod, "but he's been put on a pedestal for too long. I saw his feelings about his girlfriend when I searched his intent. He needed a reality check. You're a catch, and he's an idiot for dismissing you."

I roll my eyes. "I'm over it. Whatever."

"You aren't over it, Melanie," Riptide says, shaking his head. "You're quite thoroughly in love with three guys: your boyfriend, Adam, and Demitri."

I sigh in frustration.

"Sorry. I shouldn't have said that in front of Adam."

"He knows," I groan. "He and I don't have secrets."

"All true," Adam says. "Thank you for helping her, Rip."

"My pleasure," Riptide says, smiling down at me.

"So, eighteen huh?" I say curiously.

"In this lifetime." Pierre smiles, his eyes sparkling.

Younger than I thought. I smile and blush at the potential this raises. "Thank you for being nice to me."

Riptide looks baffled. "You don't have to thank me for that. You aren't a charity case, Meley."

We all sit in silence thinking about this for a moment.

Finally, I break the lull. "We need to head out after we eat," I say to Adam. "We're meeting the Hellhounds so we can deal with the picture mess."

"What picture mess?" Rocco asks.

My cheeks instantly burn with embarrassment, and I duck my head.

"Whoa," Riptide says. "What's happening?"

Adam leans in and quietly explains the situation.

"We're going with you," Riptide says. "We might be useful."

Rocco nods.

Blazingly embarrassed, I tell Adam, "I don't want these guys to see the pictures."

Riptide tips up my chin to look in my eyes. "Then we don't see them. This isn't about that. This is about us making sure you're safe."

"Now Mr. Perfect is taking Trey's job," I say to Adam. I look up at Riptide. "Keeping me 'safe' is my boyfriend's big contribution."

The grin on Riptide's face is a touch sadistic. "Ah, now I'm definitely in. Meeting the boyfriend sounds like a *great* plan."

I crack up.

CHAPTER 19

I walk through the door with Adam, Rocco, Pepe, Luis, and Riptide. Most of my friends are already here.

Trey crosses to me. "You good?" he asks as he pulls me into a hug.

I nod.

He looks the surfers over, doing nothing to hide his suspicion. "Sorry I wasn't available today."

"These guys kept me busy," I say with a shrug. "I was fine."

"I bet they did." Trey looks at Adam and mutters, "What the hell?"

Adam gives him a blasé look in response. "She's allowed to have friends, Trey."

"Not these friends," Trey snaps back.

The argument is interrupted as Rich comes into the room and starts greeting everyone.

"No way!" Riptide exclaims. "*Richard?*"

As Rich surveys Riptide, his mouth drops open. "Pierre!"

Riptide strides across the room, and the two guys hug like long-lost friends.

"What are you doing here, kid?" Rich asks.

"I was hanging with Melanie and Adam," Riptide says with a grin. "They informed us that there's a problem, and we tagged along." He glances my way before asking Rich, "Is she your daughter?"

"She is, indeed. Stepdaughter, technically—not that there's a distinction. That girl is me through and through."

Riptide gives me a soft look. "Rich is my favorite person on the planet. You just somehow became even more perfect."

With narrowed eyes, Rich looks at him and murmurs curiously, "Actually . . ." before he grins at me. After a brief contemplation, he says, "Thanks for dragging them here."

Charmed by their reunion, I ask, "How do you two know each other?"

Riptide pats Rich's shoulder. "Rich and my dad were old surf buddies. They taught me to surf when I was little. He's my godfather, but I never see him now that he doesn't have time to surf."

"I'm the one who gave him his nickname." Rich turns to Pierre. "Congrats on winning the Haleiwa Challenger, by the way."

Jaws drop all around the room.

"You won Haleiwa?" Trey asks.

Riptide nods humbly. "I caught the right waves. The universe aligned on that one." He grins at Rich and then at me. "I got my endorsement deals, and I'm full-time pro. Still teach surf lessons though because I love it. Melanie's gonna give it a shot."

"There's no one better to teach you than this guy," Rich says, beaming as he pats Riptide's arm.

The doorbell rings, and Rich crosses the room to open it. Hellhound bikers pour in, joining the Hollywood High teens and surfers in the crowded living room.

The last of the Hellhounds arrive. "You must be Firebird," one of them says to me. "They call me Stubbs."

I grin at him. "Nice to meet you, Stubbs."

When he gives me a thumbs-up, I notice he's missing half his thumb. He grins at me, and I laugh and nod.

"You earned a great nickname from Big Joe on day one," Stubbs says.

Marcus pipes up. "Melanie's got a lot of nicknames. Mama Mabel calls her Pollyanna from her stint in jail."

The Hellhounds all look at me in surprise.

"*You* were in jail?" Stubbs asks.

I nod.

"For what?"

I grin sheepishly. "Assault charges."

Stubbs cracks up and says to Big Joe, "We're gonna need to have a teeny-tiny Hellhound vest made for this chick."

Rich laughs. "Not a shot in hell."

My mom comes through the hall door and gives Rich a disapproving headshake. She turns to Big Joe. "You've certainly caused quite the fuss since you popped back up."

Big Joe grins. "I was worried you might say that. It's nice to meet you, Carol."

Despite her irritation, Mom smiles at him affectionately.

"Before you ask, I want to clarify a few things for everyone." We all gather around, and Big Joe continues, "The Hellhounds aren't just some trouble-making motorcycle gang. That's a misnomer, although we rarely dispute it because having a reputation like that tends to keep people out of our hair. But we truly do more good than bad."

Mom looks at him with genuine curiosity. "You're doing good so far. Keep going."

Big Joe grins. "We have two factions. Your husband, Reckless, was always part of the good guys, but he's never been an official member. His professional career would've frowned on it. He drew our Christmas card for us every year; he ran a food drive four times a year; he rallied all of us to help build a homeless shelter with a volunteer organization."

"He made all of us join a bowling league," says a big guy with *Buzz* embroidered on his vest. "It was awful."

We all crack up.

"Hey!" a grinning Rich says. "That wasn't so bad. They had free beer."

"Sounds like the good guys actually really *do* a lot of positive things for the community," Mom says.

Big Joe nods.

"So, what about the bad guys?" Arch asks.

"We don't do bad things just for the sake of it," Big Joe answers. He clears his throat. "Think of our bad guys more as vigilantes. Some of what we're likely to have to do to help Firebird would be considered *bad* things by most of society, but it's necessary for her well-being. Do you see the distinction?"

We all nod.

"When shit hits the fan, we send in Stealth and Mercury," Big Joe says with a gesture to two guys who give an awkward wave. It's obvious that these two prefer not to be in the spotlight.

"Mercury?" Finley asks.

Clearly charmed by our sweet Finley, Mercury grins sheepishly. "When I get involved, the temperature rises."

"And Stealth is like a stealth bomber," Big Joe adds. "You won't see or hear him until it's too late."

Mom glances around the room. "You sound like the grown-up version of my scrappy pack of alley cats here. I love all these kids for exactly those qualities. One more question though . . . How did Rich get the nickname Reckless?"

Stubbs cackles. "When he was younger, he'd do anything on a dare. Snort wasabi, eat fire ants. The list is long."

"I thought it was because he was a thug," Mom says with a laugh.

Big Joe side-eyes Rich mischievously and says in a sweet, convincing voice, "No, ma'am. Uh-uh. Old Reckless has never been a thug a day in his life."

All the Hellhounds make innocent faces, but one by one, they start to crack around the edges, and finally they're all doubled over laughing.

Mom joins them with a chuckle. "Well, Big Joe, either way, I appreciate you clarifying all of that for me. I feel better about this now, and to be honest, the Harley Rich bought from Adam *is* gorgeous."

Adam gestures his appreciation at Mom, and she crosses the room to give him a hug.

Glancing around the packed room, Rich says, "It's a little crowded in here. There's a round courtyard out back that's big enough to fit everyone."

"I've got every lawn chair I could borrow from our neighbors," Mom adds. "Make yourselves at home. I'll have lunch ready in an hour."

Valerie takes pity on her. "Should the girls stay inside and help you?"

Mom smiles endearingly at her. "I don't mind the help, but all the fighters in the group need to be at the meeting. Any chance some of you *aren't* scrappy?"

Jayla raises her hand. "I'd be happy to help you. I'm not big on the war room stuff."

"Me too," Susan says.

"I'm not big on the battle stuff, and I'm a heck of a cook," Drake says as he takes the damp dish towel out of Mom's hands and whips it onto his shoulder. "My mom owns a catering business."

"Well, you three come with me then. I'd love the company."

Mom's chosen helpers follow her to the kitchen. She's got her hands full today with so many to feed.

"Riptide, why don't you and the surfers get a fire going in the firepit out back?" Rich suggests. "I need the Hollywood guys to help me unload lawn chairs from my truck."

After the boyfriends disappear, the girlfriends saunter up to the surfers and grin.

"We need to spend more time at the beach, gals," Presley says.

"Yeah, we do," Finley chirps.

Adam laughs and puts his arm around Valerie as we head out back. The surfers make quick work of getting a fire going while Hiram sets up a boom box, hitting *play* before he leaves to help haul chairs.

Bobby Brown's "My Prerogative" blasts from the speakers. The surfers turn to my friends. Riptide asks me to dance, and I flirtatiously agree.

"I want that one," Presley barks out, pointing to Luis.

Luis grins. "That'll work. Come on, gorgeous."

Finley happily accepts Pepe's dance offer, and Deb slides into Rocco's arms with little argument.

The Hellhounds are all drinking beer and watching the sexy dance display, as our boyfriends round the corner with armloads of chairs.

Trey sets his down with a thud and boils out, "What the *hell*?"

The Hellhounds crack up, clearly enjoying this turn of events.

Victoria fluffs her ample rack and sways her hips dramatically as she struts to Riptide, who's dancing with me. "I don't have anyone to dance with," she purrs. "Mind if I cut in?"

Riptide surveys her, and his expression morphs into pity. He holds me tighter and can't seem to help it when he busts up laughing.

I look from Riptide to Victoria, and then at Demitri, who rolls his eyes.

"Are you laughing at *me*?" Victoria asks. If looks could kill, Riptide would incinerate.

He ignores Victoria and says to Demitri, "Seriously?"

"We need to set up chairs, Vic," Demitri says as he crosses to Victoria and pulls her to him.

Victoria pouts. "I want to dance, though."

"He doesn't want to dance with you," Demitri informs her awkwardly. "He wants to dance with Melanie."

"Will you dance with me?" Victoria asks flirtatiously.

"No," Demitri says in a deadpan tone.

Riptide chuckles and says to Rocco, "That empty shell thought I was going to pick *her* over Melanie? She's lost her mind!"

"She has no mind," Rocco quips back loudly.

I shrug. "Everyone always picks her over me."

"Your boyfriend picked you," Riptide reminds me.

"He dated her before me." I give him a pointed stare.

Riptide looks Trey's way, and his eyes narrow. He glances from Trey to Victoria and then back at me.

"Ease off, Hang Ten," Trey snaps. He takes my hand and pulls me away from Riptide.

— —

After a little more dancing and a lot of arranging, everyone gets settled, and Big Joe clears his throat. "We've got several things to tackle tonight." He looks around at his guys, who are lounging about, perfectly comfortable in their motorcycle tough-guy gear and sipping from beer cans. "Melanie's under our protection. We owe Mama Mabel for getting us out of the Trixie incident."

I don't know what the Trixie incident is, but I'm suddenly curious.

Big Joe continues, "She's also Reckless's stepdaughter, and that makes her family."

The guys all nod.

"I'm getting ready to date her," Riptide pipes up to his friends, "so that makes her your family too."

The surfers crack up, and Rocco high-fives Riptide.

"Like hell, you are," Trey growls.

Rich's eyes morph huge as he says to Riptide, "You're opening up a can of fistfight." But then he nods his approval almost imperceptibly at Riptide.

I tweak my shoulder and glance at Riptide flirtatiously. He looks down, clearly pleased with Rich's approval and my interest.

Mama Mabel takes over. "The first thing we need to do is get back the photos Jet Trippley has."

A biker with the name *Grip* embroidered on the front of his vest asks, "How imperative is it that we get the photos?"

Big Joe levels Grip with a weighty look. "They're reputation ruining."

Grip and the Hellhounds glance my way, and I shrink a bit under the anticipated scrutiny, but none of them have judgment in their eyes.

"She's a kid," Grip says. "The police would throw Sharpie and Jet in jail in a heartbeat on child pornography charges."

Big Joe nods. "True, but she's also been in the media at length lately, and we can't go to the police. It'll be all over the news if we do.

We need to get her out of this as subtly and quietly as possible."

"What were you in the media for?" Grip asks me.

"The Hollywood High escape. My homecoming princess picture was flashed on every station. Then my mug shot was on the news after Jet pressed assault charges against me. His dad owns Trippley Broadcasting. They can ruin me."

"We'll get the pictures back, I promise," Rich says as he rubs his forehead.

I give him a desperate look.

He sighs. "We have to get the pictures back just so she doesn't look so sad anymore."

The guys all look at me with conviction, and Stubbs assures me, "We've got your back, Firebird."

Mama Mabel reminds everyone, "Let's not forget that Trey's in these pictures too. We're doing this for both of them."

Adam snorts. "He'd be the prize stud of Hollywood if those pictures got out."

Trey gives Adam an exasperated look and turns red, but the Hellhounds all jokingly give him a standing ovation. Everyone cracks up, and even Rich can't help but laugh.

"How are you handling all of this, Reckless?" Stubbs asks Rich.

"Melanie's a good kid. She's only had two boyfriends, Adam and Trey." Rich gestures to the two guys.

The Hellhounds glance at both before settling their attention back on Rich.

"I guess I don't really find it awkward so much as I'm trying to help the kids out of a bad situation. They didn't ask for a voyeuristic stalker, and I don't think any of this is their fault. No one deserves to have some crackhead photograph what they do behind closed doors."

Big Joe grins impishly. "I'm glad to hear you're being so

reasonable. If you decided you were mad at them, I was going to dust off your old stories in their defense."

"Don't you dare."

With a wink at Trey and me, Big Joe promises, "Later."

We both laugh.

Mama Mabel asks, "What's the plan for getting back the pictures?"

Dante waves his hand. "I actually might be able to help with that." All eyes turn to him, and he explains, "Just so happens that my band is playing on Jet's dad's 'Teens of Tinseltown' segment of the morning show tomorrow."

Mama Mabel snaps her fingers. "Ain't it grand when the universe aligns?"

"That's damn convenient. What does this gig entail?" Big Joe asks.

"There's five of us in the band. We're cleared to have three extra roadies with us to help set up."

Big Joe grins and glances at his guys. "I think Hog and me should go in with the band. Hog, you'll help the kids. You've got band experience, and you know how to set everything up." He glances around the group of kids. "We need one of you who hasn't been a part of all the media coverage. Most of you are too recognizable."

Victoria raises her hand. "I'm the only one in the group who wasn't there during the big escape. I haven't been a part of any of the interviews or media coverage."

Mama Mabel and Big Joe exchange a look, and Mama Mabel says, "These are the prettiest pack of teens I've ever seen." She glances back at Victoria. "Gorgeous gal, any chance you're good at manipulating and distracting guys?"

All of us crack up, and Trey says to Mama Mabel, "It's your lucky damn day!"

Victoria smiles, slow and vicious. "It would be my pleasure."

"Jet gave us a tour of the studio when we went in for our live interview," Adam explains. "He was a braggadocious, arrogant shit that day, but it's about to work to our benefit. He made a huge production of pointing out his office as we walked by."

"Adam, I need you to draw out a clear map."

Adam nods Big Joe's way. Valerie takes a notebook and pencil from her backpack and hands them to Adam, who gets to work with Hiram on blueprinting the studio layout.

"This should work as long as Jet doesn't act on the pictures today," Big Joe continues. "I don't think he will. He's likely enjoying this. We'll have Hog help the band while he keeps a lookout. Victoria will be generally gorgeous and distracting, which will clear the way for me to sneak into Jet's office and find the pictures."

Victoria preens.

"What if the pictures are at his house instead?" Trey asks.

"Hell, that's a whole lot easier. If the pictures aren't in his office, then we just run an old-fashioned break-in while he's not home." Big Joe glances my way. "It's your job to be very visibly apparent at school tomorrow morning."

Mama Mabel asks, "Trey, do you think you and Melanie could manufacture a huge breakup that gets everyone talking? We're going to need word to get back to Jet that Melanie's single and her friendships have splintered. It'll help lure him in."

Trey looks my way. "We can try."

CHAPTER 20

I pull into my usual parking spot and take a deep breath before shutting off my car. Trey's Camaro is parked across the parking lot next to Kendra Poth's car.

I hate this plan! I sigh. *Might as well get this over with.* I grab my backpack and open the door. My skintight, bright-red tank dress is blazing in the early morning sun. I slip on a pair of obnoxious, sequin-outlined sunglasses that I borrowed from Tanner, and stride to my friends across the parking lot.

Arch grins at me and whistles. I'm not happy and can't share his enthusiasm. He puts his arm around me as I reach the group.

"You look like a million bucks," he says. "This outfit should do the trick. Everyone will notice."

"The perfect *I-still-got-it* breakup outfit."

"Just remember that none of this is real." Arch gives me a pointed look. "We're actors. You can do this."

I glare up at him. "Trey's not an actor."

Adam grins at me. "Today he is. I spent the better part of yesterday coaching him in my garage while I tuned up Big Joe's Harley."

I pulse to Adam, *"Fill me in."*

He shakes his head.

"I hate this."

"Mama Mabel's plan is airtight," Bear says. "A madam knows how to manipulate men better than anyone."

I glance down at my hand, and it feels naked without my promise ring that I had to leave in my jewelry box at home because of this blasted plan. I reach up and touch the hematite necklace that Trey gave me as a secret replacement until this whole charade is over. "It feels weird not having the whole group together," I say grumpily.

Bear nods. "I've already watched the others head into the school. They should be in place."

Our plan is for the dancers to separate and take Trey's side in our imaginary breakup scheme. The others of our group are siding with me in this fiasco.

"Kelsey's got to do her sisterly duty and side with Trey for our plan to work. You and I can stick together." Arch sweeps his arm toward the school. "Lead the way, Firebird."

"Here goes nothing," I mutter as I walk toward the school, hips swaying, heels clacking aggressively on the pavement.

Heads turn, and people start whispering.

Looks like I've got their attention. This just might work.

Our small group turns the corner into the alley, and I spot the rest of our friends surrounding Trey in the distance. They're in the quad, right where they're supposed to be. Trey turns to face me, half the length of the school between us. The plan is for as many students as possible to see this little act. We want the word to spread like wildfire.

I try to pulse down our connection to Trey, but he's shielded off so tight that I can't get through. *I don't like that one bit.*

After crossing half the distance between us, I take an aggressive wide-legged stance, my right leg pouring out of the slit that runs up to my thigh. Judging from the look on most of the students' faces, I have their attention. Heads whip from me to Trey. That's when Kendra steps up next to him. She presses herself seductively against him, her stunning black dress hugging every curve. He turns his head in slow motion to look down at her and then kisses her passionately.

This wasn't part of the plan!

Panic explodes through me, and I feel my heart swell nearly to bursting. I gasp, unable to breathe as my lungs seize. I look at the ground, willing myself not to cry. Suddenly, my trusty dark-water side roars up from my depths. I look back up just in time to see Trey end the passionate kiss. Kendra turns to flash an arrogant smirk my way.

"What the *hell*!" I move like lightning, aggressively eating up the distance between me and Trey.

A huge crowd has gathered, and they're all staring at us with their mouths hanging open. I pass Mr. Jenson, Ms. G, Mr. Bentley, and Mr. Isley, who are clustered in a tight clump with their eyes practically bulging out of their heads.

"You've *got* to be kidding!" I growl as I reach Trey.

Our plan was to make it clear that we'd broken up, but there was nothing discussed about Trey hooking up with Kendra right here in front of everyone. I'm not acting anymore. This charade's been replaced with an actual breakup.

Trey smirks at me arrogantly. "I told you yesterday that we're done."

My mouth drops open, and I slide my borrowed sunglasses off so I can stare Trey in the eyes. He counters by slipping his Oakleys on. I snap my mouth closed with an audible pop and slide furious eyes to Kendra. Never one to shrink from confrontation, the gorgeous dancer meets my gaze head on.

One clipped word slices from me. "SLUT!"

Kendra throws back her head and belts laughter.

"I got tired of your whole goody-goody act," Trey says to me.

Shocked, I rattle my head. *Since when am I a goody-goody?*

Kendra wraps her arms around Trey and practically melts against him. She kisses him on the neck, and Trey shivers a little.

He only shivers when I DO THAT! I'm internally spiraling. *He isn't acting anymore. I've actually lost him!* I reach up, my hand shaking noticeably, and grasp my necklace, yanking it hard. It snaps, coming free from my neck. I toss the necklace at Trey's feet before turning on Kendra and lunging.

Arch grabs me. I strain against him, screaming obscenely.

Adam rushes between the two groups and yells at Trey, "Get the hell out of here. *Now!*"

Trey squares up and faces off with Adam. Every spectator gasps in unison. A fight between Adam and Trey would be one for the record books, and everyone knows it.

Arch whispers quietly in my ear, "You need to stop fighting me. I have to get between them. This wasn't part of the plan."

I relax, and he lets go just as Trey and Adam throw blows. I take the opportunity to backhand Kendra. She moves just in time, only my fingertips catching her cheek.

The teachers rush into the fray. Mr. Isley grabs Adam, wrenching him back, while Mr. Jenson wrestles Trey to the ground.

Ms. G steps between Kendra and me and hollers, "*Enough!* To my office! *Now!*"

CHAPTER *21*

Mr. Isley brings up the rear, closing the door to the Magnet office.

I whip around, ready to take Trey to the floor, when Ms. G laughs bawdily. "The Oscar goes to Trey!"

Trey and Adam grin at each other and high-five. Everyone else looks confused. Then, as one, they exhale with relief.

"You were in on this?" Mr. Isley asks Ms. G.

"Yup," Ms. G says with a grin. "Adam called me last night."

Mr. Isley holds out his still-shaking hands. "I'm glad someone knew what was happening. I nearly had a heart attack when those two guys faced off. Of all the students, they're the last two we need fighting."

"I'm out," Kendra says, rubbing her red cheek. "You guys can run this little scheme on your own." She turns to me. "I barely got out of the way in time. I can't imagine how bad it would've hurt if you'd caught me with your whole hand." She glances at everyone, adding, "Melanie strikes like a rattlesnake. No wonder everyone's terrified of her."

"This isn't over between us," I snarl at Kendra. "Your time is coming." My brain is sputtering, trying to comprehend this mess.

I glare at Trey. "WHAT THE FU—"

Arch clamps his hand over my mouth before I can finish the sentence. "Someone needs to fill the rest of us in," he says, "because that little production wasn't part of our plan."

"This is my fault," Adam says. "Melanie was unsure how she could pull off her part of the breakup charade." He gestures to Trey. "No one knows her better than the two of us. We decided that the best way to get a convincing performance out of Melanie was to take her off guard."

I glare at the two guys, and my gaze finally settles on Trey.

He shrinks a little. "I'm sorry, babe."

I grind my teeth and take a deep breath, before snarling, "As if your little disappearing act lately wasn't enough . . . You had to kiss her, huh? Aren't you quite the method actor!" I'm so mad I can barely think.

"I'm sorry, Melanie," Kendra interjects. "Adam chose me because I'm one of the few girls in the group who doesn't have a boyfriend. It seemed easier than adding a second breakup to the gossip."

I slide a furious gaze her way.

She throws her hands in the air, exclaiming to Adam, "I told you she was going to be mad at me! I don't need this nightmare."

"Don't blame Kendra," Adam says to me. "It really was all part of the act."

Gently, Mr. Jenson says, "Someone fill us in. There's obviously a whole lot happening that at least a few of us were in the dark about."

Arch nods. "Is there ever."

The adrenaline subsides, and my eyes fill with tears. "The kiss I can forgive," I inform Trey. "But when she kissed your neck, you shivered. That's only for me."

Trey looks stunned. "I didn't even know I did that."

Tears fall hot down my cheeks, and I whisper down our connection, *"I'm done."*

Trey's mouth falls open, and he nearly doubles over, panicked. He breathes, "Melanie!"

I shake my head and say to Kendra, "He's yours."

Kendra's eyes are the size of hubcaps, and she blinks rapidly at me.

Everyone's frozen in place.

"Melanie, it was all an act," Adam desperately assures me.

I shake my head and close my eyes.

"Melanie, look at me." I open my eyes, and Adam's right in front of me. He tips up my chin. "I *promise* it was all an act."

"The shiver wasn't an act, Adam. I know Trey—body, mind, and soul. I know what I saw."

Arch raises a hand to get everyone's attention. "How about the rest of us go into the conference room while they work this out?"

Everyone moves to the door that leads to the conference room, grateful to get out of the middle of this very private discussion.

"Don't bother leaving on my account. I'll see myself out." I turn on my heel and open the office door, stepping quickly into the hallway in a daze.

Presley rushes to follow me.

CHAPTER 22

"**D**id you find them?" Arch asks.

Dante quietly answers, "No. The pictures weren't in Jet's office. Big Joe's switching to plan B. How did the breakup situation go?"

"It was a disaster. They broke up for real."

Dante squawks, "*Why*? What happened?"

"Trey shivered."

Dante snorts. "He shivered?" he asks skeptically.

Arch pauses, and I feel his gaze on my back. "She's been asleep all through lunch."

I'm not asleep. My head's on my arms that are resting on the picnic table. I've cried myself to exhaustion and been a mess all day. I let them believe I'm asleep though because I want to hear this.

"Adam and Trey had a side plan that involved Trey and Kendra kissing in the quad," Arch explains. "They thought Melanie would be more convincing if she was taken off guard. That part went fine until Kendra curled around him like glaze on a donut and kissed his neck. He shivered the slightest bit, and Melanie caught it. She backhanded Kendra."

Dante whistles low. "In Trey's defense, I dated Kendra for a while. She can be shiver inducing. She has an energy about her."

Arch chuffs. "Apparently Trey's shivers are only for Mel. She broke up with him in the Magnet office after Ms. G hauled us all in."

"How many are suspended?" Dante asks. "That's going to screw up our whole plan."

"None of us. Ms. G was in on all of it. Apparently, Adam called and filled her in last night. We explained everything to Mr. Isley, Mr. Bentley, and Mr. Jenson too."

"Is everyone at school talking?"

"Oh yeah."

"Then we're still on track. Jet will get word through Sharpie. That weasel hears everything. The rest of it will work itself out. Let me try talking to her."

"You think you can fix this?"

"I'm going to try," Dante says. "Where's Trey?"

"He left with Kelsey right after the breakup this morning. He's not doing so good."

I hear footsteps, and the picnic bench shifts slightly as Dante sits next to me. He rubs my back and says softly, "Melanie, wake up."

I whisper, "I'm not asleep." I look at Dante.

He turns sideways on the bench and scoots closer to me. "Then I don't need to fill you in on my conversation with Arch?"

I shake my head and lean my shoulder against Dante's chest, with my head buried back in my arms on the table.

Dante puts his hand on my back. "You and I both know that you can't break up with Trey for real."

He waits for me to say something, but I feel empty, and no words come.

He sighs. "If you two weren't so obviously meant for each other, I'd let this go, but you are, and I can't."

A fresh round of tears wells up as I look at him. "Something has to be just for me. He was with Victoria before me, and she took all the shiny new out of most of the physical stuff. He's never even around anymore, anyway."

Dante laughs. He raises an eyebrow. "If I'm really open with you, will you forgive an overshare?"

I nod.

He thinks for a moment before saying, "You know I'm in a band?"

I nod again.

"Musicians get a lot of tail. I mean a *lot*. Women throw themselves at us after shows. Not to toot my own horn, but we're really good, and the band's actually going somewhere."

I sit up at rapt attention. Dante and I are friends, but he's never told me anything like this before.

He smiles softly. "As a guy who's been around blocks that are a lot more exciting than Victoria and Tiffany, I can tell you there's a big difference between going through the motions of a one-night stand, and actually being in love with a partner." He takes a breath. "I'm not going to blow smoke up your ass . . . Kendra's a damn good time. She has a dangerous energy that rivals yours. I wouldn't be surprised if she did have an unexpected effect on Trey . . ."

I start to shut down.

Dante holds up a hand. "Let me finish before you lose your marbles. I was about to say that she can't have the effect on him that you do because he's not connected to her. His heart's with you. Period. If you two don't get back together, you're going to be the one great love that haunts him for the rest of his life." He shrugs. "Regarding his being busy all the time, maybe he just needs a breather."

I look down. "I'm not okay with Adam and Trey adding the whole Kendra aspect to the plan. Why her of all people?"

Dante smiles at me endearingly. "You wouldn't have been okay with any girl they chose. You need to stop being pissed at Kendra. She's a decent girl. You have my word that she isn't the home-wrecking type. Kendra's a good time, but she's also a loyal friend."

"You promise?" I quietly ask.

He nods. "I promise. I haven't talked to her yet, but I guarantee she feels like crap about the whole situation."

I sigh. "Now I feel bad."

"Don't," he says, shaking his head slightly. "She'll understand. From my mouth to God's ears, you have my word that Kendra's a stand-up girl. I'll talk to her."

"Fine. But I need some time where Trey's concerned."

Dante puts his hands on my cheeks and looks in my eyes. "I understand where you're at, but I need you to consider Trey's feelings. I guarantee he's dying inside right now. Trey's got a really soft heart for you. You tend to need time, and the time you take hurts him . . . badly."

"What about the time *he* spends away from *me*? Does it matter that his dismissive aloofness hurts me?"

Dante waffles his head right and left. "I'll see what I can find out about that. You're likely worried about nothing. Trey's just a solitary type."

CHAPTER **23**

Fantastic.

Trey's leaning against his car that's parked sideways behind mine. Big Joe, Stubbs, Rich, and Mack are all gathered around Rich's newly acquired Harley, chatting a few yards away from him. I can't help but smile a little through my heartbreak fog. Rich is so proud of that silly motorcycle. He's like a kid again.

I narrow my eyes and study the bikers. Mack is new to me. He's different. Where Stubbs and Big Joe have laughter lines permanently creased around their eyes, Mack has frown lines. He seems more like a thug than the others.

My friends catch up with me as I cross the street, and we're still maintaining distance from the other half of our group that are pretending to be on Trey's side.

Arch sees Trey and cuts across the parking lot to him. "What are you doing here?" Arch quietly hisses, "We can't have every kid on the buses see our whole group together or it'll blow our cover."

Trey takes his sunglasses off, revealing his red, puffy eyes. Rich looks his way and immediately walks over, putting his arm around Trey.

Arch throws his hands in the air. "We must keep a clear division for this to work," he says in exasperation. "You snuggling with Melanie's stepdad is a bad look."

"I don't care about the plan anymore," Trey says loudly, shaking his head. "I'll just deal with Jet myself. All I care about is getting Melanie back."

Rich's head snaps to Arch. "I'm sorry! What?"

Arch sighs and glances my way as I lean against the driver's-side door of Jelly Bean. I'm tired, and I don't have any fight left in me. The stress of every ordeal we've faced this school year has finally caught up with me.

Realizing that neither Trey nor I plan to speak, Arch says, "They broke up for real. It's a long story that you probably don't want to hear, but it involves another girl and a shiver."

Rich squeezes Trey's shoulder, and Trey's face falls. Rich looks shocked as he wraps his arms around the distraught boy. "Fix this," Rich mouths to me.

Before I can say anything, Kendra crosses the street and walks up to me. She holds up her hands in surrender. "Before you light my ass up, let me speak."

I nod and glance at Trey. He and Rich are watching Kendra. Trey looks both hopeful and worried.

She waits as all the buses loudly rumble away from the curb, leaving us without the student audience. "Dante talked to me."

Dante winks at me.

"I'm not after Trey," Kendra continues. "One hundred percent honesty. I've literally never thought of him that way. I met Trey and you at the same time, and the two of you are connected in my mind. Frankly, I wouldn't date him even if he stayed single." I look at her quizzically, and she explains, "You're so inside his head that any girl he's ever with again is going to compete with you every moment. And anyway, I respect you, Melanie."

I exhale, letting go of a breath I didn't realize I was holding.

"Ask me anything you need to," Kendra adds. "I want this squashed right here, right now. I don't want bad feelings to drag out. A warning, though . . . I'm going to answer honestly, so make sure you want the answer."

Everyone gathers around, dropping any pretense of our planned group separation now that we don't have an audience. Big Joe, Mack, and Stubbs join the circle, looking surprisingly interested.

I bark out a laugh. "You three are going to think this melodramatic teen crap is ridiculous."

"We're ass-kicking bikers, but we're also people," Big Joe says with a soft smile. "We'll help where we can." He surprises me yet again as he adds, "I didn't realize how much trouble this charade would cause in your actual relationship. We'll think of something else. You two just need to fix this."

I turn back to Kendra and cross my arms over my chest. "It looked like there was a spark."

Kendra nods without hesitating. "There was."

I glare at Trey, and he looks at Kendra like she's lost her mind.

Kendra says to Trey, "I'm not going to lie to her."

Clearly frustrated, Trey rubs his eyes hard. "I'm begging you to."

Kendra shakes her head. "She's got that crazy superhuman intuition. And the temper of a gorilla on PCP."

Trey gives her another pleading look.

Kendra sighs and shifts her attention back to me. "Here's the deal. Trey's hot." She makes a sardonic face. "I'm hot too. Hot people have sparks. I'd be dead inside if I felt nothing. Frankly, I see the draw you two had at first now that I've kissed him."

I look back at Trey, and he's clearly fed up. He turns his back to us, putting his hands on the roof of his car with his head hung.

He huffs, making his shoulders rise and fall hard.

Kendra continues. "There was a spark, but not a fire. I'm not after him. He obviously isn't after me. At some point, you must get past this idea that a brief spark with someone else is enough to destroy your life. Don't give me that much power, and don't give up so easy on Trey. He doesn't deserve that. He's a good guy."

My eyebrows rise as I contemplate what she said. "Actually, oddly enough, that helps."

Kendra smiles. "All right, here it is. I'm going to show you all my cards, which I don't do often, so enjoy the moment." She looks at Dante. "I haven't told him, but Dante's my guy. If I'm going to torch the lives of the people I care about, it's going to be for him."

Clearly surprised, Dante gives Kendra a flirtatious look.

"I'm sorry we hurt your feelings," Kendra says, hugging me. She jokingly grins at me and adds, "And I'm sorry we're all hot, and there were sparks."

"I'm sorry I hit you."

"Remind me not to ever get in a fistfight with you," she says with a grin, "but you can back me anytime."

I tip my head Dante's way. "I think Dante might be waiting for you."

She nods. "I've been waiting for him about as long as I plan to." She scrunches up her nose coyly at me.

"Go get him."

Kendra strides Dante's way and stops in front of him. He brushes her hair from her face before he whispers something to her that we can't hear.

Her eyes soften, and she quietly says, "Really?"

"Really."

She nods, and he kisses her.

We all grin at each other, and Tanner's eyes sparkle mischievously as he over-the-top belts out a lyric from "Reunited" by Peaches and Herb.

Adam, Bear, Arch, Hiram, and Marcus join in the song.

The Hellhounds sway from side to side and loudly belt out, "Hey, hey!"

Dante cracks up mid kiss. "I hate you jackasses!"

We all double over laughing. Everyone turns expectant eyes on Trey and me.

Trey pushes away from his car and crosses the distance to me. He cracks his stiff neck. "We're not doing this. I respect your feelings, but sometimes they get in the way of reality." When I glare up at him through my lashes, he falters for a moment.

His shoulders start to sag, but Adam rescues him. "I screwed up, Melanie. I know how you get, and I didn't think things through." He side-eyes Kendra. "I apologize to everyone involved." Now he looks pointedly at Trey. "You need to make more time for Melanie or you're going to lose her."

Trey nods.

I glance at Adam and then look back at Trey. Finally, I say, "No more sparks with hot chicks."

He smiles hopefully. "Kendra was the last hurrah."

I roll my eyes and can't help but laugh. "I'm not ever kissing your neck again, for the record."

Trey relaxes and chuckles, wrapping me up in his arms and hugging me tight. "We'll see about that."

"Thank God that's over," Adam says, sounding relieved. "Can we *please* get back to the problem of Melanie and Trey's sexy child porn now?"

Rich scoffs. "You kids have weird issues."

Everyone laughs, the tension breaking.

CHAPTER 24

Tanner and Big Joe are talking with their heads together as we walk down Highland. They look like they're scheming, but I'm so worn out from this day from hell that I can't muster up the energy to care.

We amble left onto Hollywood Boulevard, cross the street, and turn down a back alley, where we pass a lamppost sporting a red light and walk up to a burgundy door under a frilly awning. When we pass through into a beautiful Victorian parlor, we all freeze, mesmerized by this cozy world full of burgundy velvet and goose down throw pillows. It's the last thing I expect, but I should have known better because the whole room feels and looks like the embodiment of Mama Mabel's soul. Everything is mysterious yet soft. The room smells like roses and sugar, with an underlying hint of spicy exotic incense.

Mama Mabel greets us boisterously, and the ladies lounging about on chairs and love seats turn our way. I recognize several from my stint in jail, and they all greet me with an enthusiastic, "Pollyanna!" Laughing, I cross the room to hug my new friends.

Mama Mabel says to her ladies, "Please be ready to meet and greet customers at seven. Until then, you're free to do as you like."

The ladies gather their things and wander away for some downtime.

"All of you, welcome to Mama Mabel's," the proud madam says with a wide sweep of her arm. "Please make yourselves comfortable."

Trey chooses a cozy love seat and glances hesitantly at me, raising his eyebrows. I sit down and curl up next to him with my legs draped over his knee. He closes his eyes and takes a deep breath before wrapping his arms around me and pulling me close. I settle in with my head on his chest, and he rests his cheek on the top of my head. This is how we sit to watch TV in my den, and something about the familiarity seems to make him feel better. His heart rate slows under my hand.

When we all get settled, Mama Mabel says, "I heard through the grapevine that there was trouble in paradise today." She looks at Trey and me with raised eyebrows. "I trust that all's well now?"

Trey says, "I hope so," at the same time I say, "I think so."

Mama Mabel laughs boisterously. "Sounds to me like you both know so, but you're cautiously unsure of what the other is thinking."

We nod, and Trey says, "That's fair."

We've had our soulmate connection shut down tight all day.

Mama guides us with her words. "Then the air is clear, and you both know where you stand. Put the fight to rest in your hearts right here and right now."

I gaze at Trey, who looks down at me. I reach up, put my hand against the side of his neck where Kendra kissed him, and lightly rub the spot a few times with my thumb. Eyes closed, he shivers, which makes me smile. He opens his eyes and brushes his fingertips featherlight from my forehead down to my chin. It's my favorite thing he does, something I've always described as the most oddly settling thing I've ever experienced. We both take a deep breath and turn our attention back to Mama Mabel.

"That was magic," she says. "Do you always communicate that way? No words, all energy?"

We glance at each other, and Trey grins at me before explaining, "Our energy connection usually works a little better than our verbal skills."

Marcus snorts and says sarcastically, "Hothead and Smart Mouth over there tend to pop off when they talk too much to each other."

"Oh yeaaah!" Trey retorts. "Because your communication skills and Presley's are the prize gem of Hollywood."

Everyone chuckles.

Mama Mabel softly says, "All joking aside, a big part of what I do here is counsel people through human interactions. You two really are remarkable." She turns her attention to Big Joe and nods his way.

He clears his throat. "The picture recon was a bust. They aren't in Jet's office. I think I should take Stealth and head to Jet's house to do a quick search."

"You know where he lives?" Mama Mabel asks.

Big Joe smirks. "I put Intel on it as soon as we knew the pictures had to be somewhere else. He's our tech and information specialist. Now I know Jet's address, what his car looks like, where he banks, where his grandfather lives in Iowa, and even the name of his second cousin twice removed."

Mama Mabel grins at him. "Tell Intel I said hi."

"Oh, I'm sure he'll be by sooner rather than later."

My cell phone rings, and I answer.

"Wildcat, where are you?" Rocco barks through the line, all hyped-up.

"I'm in Hollywood. What's up?"

"Is Adam with you?"

I glance at Adam, who stands and gestures for me to join him in the parking lot. Trey and Demitri follow, with Big Joe in tow.

Outside, I put the call on speakerphone. "I have you on speaker. Adam, Demitri, Big Joe, and Trey are here."

"Did you get back the pictures?"

I huff. "No. They weren't in his office."

"Jet Trippley has a black Beamer, right?" Rocco asks.

"He does."

Riptide's sultry voice rings out from the background of Rocco's end of the line. "Long black hair. Looks like a goth serial killer?"

"That's the guy."

"Then I know him," Riptide says. "He's at Moonshadows. He just pulled up. Adam, are you available?"

"Yup. What's the plan?"

"Get your ass down here and bring my girl. I'm handling this picture situation."

"Let's get something straight," Trey snarls. "She's my girl. She's Demitri's Meley. She's Adam's brunt-of-his-jokes. She's not *your* anything."

Riptide chuckles. "Well, Trey, perhaps you should get your shit together. One of my many metaphysical abilities is reading relationships. You're one iceberg from sinking, there, Ocean Liner."

Trey sharply inhales as Adam cuts off the nonsense. "We're on the way. Meet you there." I hang up and Adam informs, "Parking's tight at Moonshadows. We shouldn't take more than two cars."

Trey nods. "I'll drive. Adam and Big Joe, come with me. I need to hear what Intel found out about this guy."

"That works." Demitri murmurs to me, "We need to talk."

I pout, disgruntled.

After filling everyone in inside Mama Mabel's, Trey, Adam, and Big Joe jump into Trey's car and take off.

I climb into Demitri's passenger seat. He starts the Jeep, and we follow Trey, quickly catching up. When Demitri turns to me, he looks really vulnerable.

"What's wrong, D?"

"You know what's wrong, Meley."

I smile affectionately at him. "You're my favorite. You know that, right?"

He huffs. "I *thought* I was the favorite, but then *Riptide* came along." He says his name like it tastes bad.

"You will forever be the first 'perfection' I ever laid eyes on," I say, wobbling my head comically. "But *damn*, is Riptide gorgeous. Seriously, if I was ever going to leave Trey, it would have to be worth it, and Riptide is *definitely* worth it."

Demitri side-eyes me like a grumpy toddler. I can't help but laugh.

"I don't want you with Riptide," he says. "Melanie, I secretly liked being the one that made you tongue-tied."

I giggle. "You still make me tongue-tied, but it's awkward knowing that I felt like I did when you weren't in that same zone. I really hate being the lost-puppy best friend. It's better now."

"I know, but now I'm not happy," Demitri says with a glower. "I wanted the friend zone, but I didn't want someone who's perfect to slide into my spot in the process."

"You don't get to have it both ways. So, Riptide's perfect and interested. The only one who needs to worry about that is Trey."

Demitri rolls his eyes and glances my way. "I want to clarify some things. I don't view you as my dumpy little sister."

I shrug. "It doesn't bother me anymore, but I appreciate that." I clear my throat. "I apologize for staying at your house. I needed to sleep, but I still shouldn't have. It confused me."

"Seeing you through Riptide's eyes was enlightening," he says as he wobbles his head.

I shrug and smile at him. "I'll never be what impresses you. I'm just not that polished. And anyway, it was nice being admired by Riptide."

As we pull onto Pacific Coast Highway, Demitri rubs his forehead, then turns on his CD player. I roll down my window, letting the ocean breeze waft through as the Doors' "Five to One" thumps through the speakers. I put my feet on the dashboard, close my eyes with a smile, and enjoy the sun on my face. Luckily, Demitri doesn't push the conversation for a while.

Just after Jim Morrison finishes belting in that gravelly way of his, Demitri finally breaks the silence. "I'm not proud of being shallow where Victoria is concerned, and I'm sorry for it."

"I just want you to be happy, D. I'm glad you're getting what you need."

As the car slows down, I open my eyes just as we turn left into a packed parking lot. Demitri parks as close to Trey as he can, and we all get out of our cars as Rocco and Riptide come down the front steps.

Rocco informs, "Jet's on the back balcony, eating and being an arrogant sleaze to the waitress. He should be thoroughly occupied."

Riptide steps up to me and smiles. "Good to see you, Meley. Let's see if I can fix this."

I give him big, scared eyes, and his expression softens.

"I promise that if I don't find the pictures, I'll beat the shit out of him until he hands them over."

I melt a little.

"What the fuck is happening with this guy?" Trey asks yet again.

Riptide ignores him and struts over to a black BMW. The valet attendant comes over and performs a bro handshake thing with him.

"Dickhead owner of dickhead car has something of my girl's," Riptide says. "I'm going in."

His friend shrugs. "Dickhead comes here constantly and never tips. Steal whatever you want."

Riptide pops the trunk and gestures for us to look through it while he gets into the car. I open the trunk and discover that it's nice and neat. *This should be easy.* I look between two folded blankets but find no pictures. Then, I open a big duffel bag and gasp.

Trey closes the back seat door and comes around to me, shaking his head. Apparently, the pictures aren't in there.

I point at the duffel bag, and he follows my gaze. "Oh my God," he breathes out.

"This guy is dangerous," Adam says.

Big Joe nods. "Yup."

Riptide hollers out, "Boom."

We glance around the trunk lid and see him standing outside the car, peeking in an envelope. When he looks at me, a question on his face, I nod my permission.

He slides the pictures out and fans through them quickly, then puts them back in the envelope. He holds it up with a sneer. "They're all of Melanie."

I exhale, relieved.

Trey gestures him over, and we point to the duffel bag. Adam pulls a little Pentax camera out of his back pocket and snaps several pictures. I zip the duffel bag closed, careful to leave things how I found them, and close the trunk.

Riptide hands Trey the picture envelope. "Jet has a murder bag in his car. Rope, duct tape, knives, zip ties, and a jar of some kind of mystery liquid. He's after Melanie. It's time I deal with this."

Trey glares at him. "I'll deal with it, but thank you."

Riptide hefts himself up on the BMW and stretches out on the top.

Adam laughs. "Gotta love surfers. Any opportunity to catch some sun."

Trey grumbles and strides to his car with the picture envelope in hand.

Riptide holds a hand my way, and I scoot to him and lean on the car door. "I've got you on this, Melanie."

I smile at him and murmur, "I really am taken, you know."

Riptide nods. "I know. I'm legit your friend. I'm also scarier than I seem. I know Jet. We don't get along."

Jet chooses that moment to strut out of the restaurant. He sees Riptide on his roof and snarls, "Get the fuck off my car, Rip."

Riptide sits up and blisters back, "I'm the king of this beach, and I'll lounge anywhere I want."

Focusing on me and radiating obsession, Jet breathes, "Melanie," and it sounds dirty.

"Let's be clear, Jet. If you ever *look* at her again, I'll end you." Riptide hops down and wraps his arms around me.

"You don't have the balls to end me."

Riptide lets go of me and reaches out lightning fast, grabbing Jet by the front of his shirt. He whips him around and slams him into the car. He pulls him back and slams him a second time, knocking the air out of him. "You think I'm scared of you, rich boy? Oh so scary goth poser? Really?" He sneers and lets loose a blasting wave of menacing fury that makes my arms goose-bump. "You know where I live. Feel free to show up anytime. I'll fucking end you in my living room while I make popcorn and watch a movie with Melanie." He points at me, then turns back to Jet. "You aren't dealing with a bunch of high school kids anymore. Now you're dealing with my crew. If you hurt Melanie, we'll slaughter you and dump your body in the fucking ocean. My boat's always gassed up. Got it?"

Jet looks legitimately terrified as he nods slightly. When Riptide lets go of him, Jet rushes around the car and gets in, starting the engine and hauling ass out of the parking lot.

I quietly say, "Thank you." Tears fill my eyes, and when Riptide holds an arm out my way, I curl up against him.

Rocco sets his hands on my shoulders, and over my head, Riptide says to him, "I swear to God, I'm going to kill that creepy pervert. I flat can't stand that she's crying."

"Can I please have my girlfriend now?" Trey growls.

Riptide says, "Nope," and holds me tighter.

I grab two handfuls of his tank top and shiver in his arms, scared.

"I have to get back to my chopper and close up my tattoo shop with my staff," Big Joe informs us. "I'll come back this way after. And I'll bring Rich."

Adam nods. "I need to go, too, but I can come back after I handle something with Valerie."

Demitri quietly assures Trey, "I'll stay with her and make sure she's okay."

Trey sighs and asks Riptide, "Do you swear you have her covered?"

Riptide nods. "Give me the pictures, and I'll destroy them."

Trey grabs the pictures from his front seat and hands them over. "Where are you headed? We'll be back."

"Surfrider Beach."

Trey turns to me and holds out an arm. Riptide lets me go,

and Trey wraps me up in his arms. "You know I love you. Right, Melanie?"

When I don't respond, he tips up my chin. Finally, I say, "Trey, something's not right."

He glances to the side and shakes his head. "I'm just burned out," he says before kissing me on the forehead. "It's one damn thing after another. There are only so many stalkers, gunshots, rape attempts, and death scares that one guy can take with his girl."

I nod and look down. "I get it. I hate my life. I just want to disappear."

Trey tips my chin up again and looks in my eyes. "Don't say that. We'll get it figured out. I love you." He kisses me, and I melt a little.

When he pulls away, I huff. He rounds the car, climbs in, starts the engine with a roar, and pulls out of the parking lot with Adam and Big Joe in tow.

Riptide smiles at Demitri and me. "I've got a van full of boards, and I put a new swimsuit and wet suit in the back this morning for Melanie." He gives me a charming look. "It's surfing time."

I shake my head. "I'd love to swim, but I'm not about to try surfing in front of Demitri."

"Why?"

Suddenly insecure, I glance Demitri's way. "Because he's perfect at everything, and I'll just embarrass myself."

Riptide surveys Demitri and waves his hand dismissively. "He actually looks like a surfer," he admits to Rocco.

Demitri smiles. "Been at it since I was five."

"All right, pretty boy," Riptide says. "Let's see what you've got. Will you tolerate a lesson?"

Demitri rattles his head. "Why would I need a lesson?"

Riptide and Rocco side-eye each other, amused.

"People fly here from all over the world for brush-up lessons from Rip before they hit the international competitions," Rocco explains.

Demitri grins. "All right, I'm game. Let's have some fun." He holds out his hand. "I want the envelope, though. It stays with me until it's destroyed."

Riptide hands it over. "Our friends already have a bonfire going on the beach. We'll burn them in a few minutes."

He gestures to his van, and we cross to it. He pops the back door and hands me a black bikini. I look up at him and grin.

Demitri leans in to inspect the goods inside the van. "No way!" He looks to Riptide. "Rusty boards?"

Rip nods. "They sponsor me. We'll size you out, and one's yours." He grins at me. "I've also got a bitty board for you, little miss. It's meant to be a youth board, but you're adorable, and it reminded me of you." He raises his eyebrows. "It's blaaack. With a skull and crossbones that's wearing a red booow."

I laugh. "It sounds really cute."

"It *is* really cute. Hop in and change."

After he closes the door behind me, I change into the snug black bikini, tapping on the door when I'm finished.

Riptide opens it, letting me out. "Perfect," he says, biting his lip as he surveys me. "We're headed down the way to Surfrider Beach."

Demitri holds a hand to me, and I take it. "We'll follow you."

Rocco surveys us. "You two are rather striking together."

Demitri looks down at me. "No one lifts or partners her but me. I don't even bother working out anymore because we dance in the studio two to three hours a day. Everything that's choreographed for us is complicated, and we train through counterbalance movement together on our off time."

Riptide asks, "She's that good in the studio?"

Demitri nods. "She's the beast of the dance department. And that's saying something. Mr. Isley trains top talent."

"I should talk to Chelsea," Riptide murmurs cryptically.

Demitri puts an arm over my shoulders and escorts me to his Jeep. We follow the guys up Pacific Coast Highway.

We see a bonfire on an expansive beach. The lifeguard on duty is talking with a group of guys that I recognize from the Beach Bar. They turn as we approach, and Luis yells out, "Yesss! Wildcat's here!" He runs to me and picks me up, spinning us around.

I squeal happily and greet all the guys. Rocco, Demitri, and Riptide put down the boards they're carrying, and I hold up the envelope.

"We've got some stuff to burn, boys," Riptide explains.

The guys all cheer. Apparently, bonfire burning is a thing with this crew.

"You need to make sure they're all here, Meley," Demitri tells me.

I sigh. "The negatives and copies we had were destroyed by Mabel. These should be all that's left." I cross the beach to a private spot and fidget nervously as I open the envelope.

Riptide and Demitri come to me.

"Do you want one of us here while you do this?" Rip asks.

I look up at them with big eyes.

Riptide says to Demitri, "The big-eye thing . . ."

Demitri nods. "I know. It slaughters me. Slaughters Trey and Adam too."

"You can add me to that list," Riptide says with a sigh.

For a moment, I survey both guys. "I don't want to browse

through my nightmare alone, but neither of you are on my list of partners where this is concerned."

Demitri steps up behind me and wraps his arms around me. "Look through, Meley. Best friend's on duty."

I pull them out and start shuffling through. The photos near the top are more innocent. I hand those to Riptide. "So far, they all seem to be here." I look down at the rest with Demitri. These are the bad ones. I fan through them, quick enough not to linger, but slow enough to make sure none are missing.

Demitri's eyebrows rise. "Jet's sick. These are worse than I expected."

I turn them over and start to hand them to Riptide, but Demitri shakes his head and takes them from me. I look down at the pictures that are left, and my mouth drops open.

"Holy shit," Demitri says. "Rip, look at this."

We stare down at four pictures that are of someone other than me. It doesn't take long to pick up that the girl is dead. Her lifeless eyes stare blankly at us. Each picture is taken from a new and gruesome angle, as if the photographer was attempting not to miss a single lurid detail. She's wearing nothing, and she was clearly badly beaten before she died.

Riptide's mouth drops open. "I know her." He corrects himself. "I guess it's more accurate to say that I knew her." He yells, "Hey, boys, come here."

The surfers run up to us and crowd around. Riptide takes the dead-girl photos from me, and I grab Demitri's hand that's holding my naughty pictures. He wraps his arm around me and presses the pictures, facedown, against my stomach.

"Is that Tenisha?" Riptide asks.

Pepe is clearly sad. "Holy crap, guys. It is. We're going to have to find a way to tell her brother." He looks at me and explains,

"She's a Malibu local who went missing a few months ago."

I hand the guys the empty envelope. "We should get these to the Hellhounds, and then make sure the police are contacted."

Rocco holds his hand out to Demitri. "Give me your keys. I'll put these in your Jeep, and we'll burn the rest now." He slides the corpse shots into the envelope.

Demitri hands over his keys, and I look up at him. "So Jet's killing girls?"

Radiating fear, Demitri squeezes his eyes closed and pulls me in. He explains to our friends, "Jet tried to kidnap Melanie from school. It was a close call."

Rocco jogs back, and the guys rally around me. They guide me to the bonfire, where Riptide hands me the innocent stack of photos. He announces, "We do this our way, guys."

Luis takes some pictures from the stack. "With the burning of these photographs, may Jet Trippley be caught."

Rocco takes several. "With the burning of these photographs, may Jet Trippley be punished."

Pepe takes a handful. "With the burning of these photographs, may Jet Trippley's victims find peace."

They toss them into the bonfire, and we watch them burn. The smoke smells acrid.

Demitri takes the naughty pictures he's holding and divides them into three stacks that he holds facedown. He hands a stack to Riptide.

"With the burning of these photographs," Riptide says, "may Jet Trippley realize his fate."

"With the burning of these photographs, may Jet Trippley heal," Demitri says thoughtfully.

"No matter what, you always want the best for people," I say to Demitri as I smile softly. Then my expression morphs sadistic, and

I allow my evil dark-water side to boil to the surface. My eyes glaze demonic as I snarl, "Unfortunately, I can't say the same." I turn and stare at the bonfire. "With the burning of these photographs, may Jet Trippley burn in hell."

We toss the lurid photographs into the fire. I send a massive energy wave into the flames, and the bonfire flares eight feet into the sky, incinerating my embarrassment along with the pictures. My friends watch in amazement as I fuel the inferno with my energy. When I drop the bonfire back down, their mouths fall open.

Rocco breathes, "Wicked."

"Leave your boyfriend, Melanie," Riptide says in awe. "I'm serious."

I smirk up at him, radiating evil in thrumming waves.

Demitri puts his hands on my back and sends a wave of calm through me.

My head falls, and my eyes close. I exhale.

"Cool off, baby girl." When my energy hums normal, Demitri takes my hand and guides me to the ocean. We wade out waist-deep, and he turns to face me. "I'm sorry the pictures happened. They're gone, and I'll never tell anyone what I saw."

"Thank you."

He nods and raises an eyebrow. "You don't get to leave Trey for Riptide. That's a no-go."

"Look who's jealous," I say with a laugh.

He nods. "I am, indeed."

I shake my head subtly at him. "Don't get confused now. Remember that you're you and I'm me. That's always been the problem."

Demitri scoffs.

I shrug a shoulder, feeling shy but clear on where I stand. "I need to be good enough, D."

Demitri starts to argue, but when Riptide calls to him, he sighs, wades over to Riptide, and takes the board he's offered. I watch as the two guys move past me and paddle out into the water. Riptide straddles his board and motions me over. I swim to him, and he pulls me onto his board. I lean back against his chest, and we watch Demitri catch a mammoth wave.

My eyebrows rise as I witness my best friend do all the surfing stuff I've seen in movies but know nothing about.

Demitri paddles to a stop next to us and surveys how I'm lounging casually with Riptide's arm slung across my chest.

"You're actually good," Riptide says, impressed. "Now I'm going to make you better."

By the time Demitri and Riptide are finally done surfing, I'm stretched out on a beach towel, enjoying the heat from the bonfire. The sun is low in the sky, and it's getting cold.

I look up at the guys and laugh. "Holy crap, you two are gorgeous. It's like staring at a Versace ad."

Both guys grin, and Demitri holds his hand out. I take it, and he hefts me up.

"You need to tandem ride with Demitri," Riptide says. "He needs the balance challenge, and you need to get a feel for the board."

I nod, baffled. "I have no clue what that means, but sure."

Riptide asks, "Do you want me to take her out first, so she's got an idea?"

"No," Demitri responds sternly. "I'm doing this with her."

Riptide narrows his eyes, surveying us. He quietly says to Demitri, "You're getting there. I like the energy shift."

Demitri smiles. "For the record, it was never that she wasn't good enough for me."

"I hear that." Riptide's lips twitch, and then he laughs so hard that he tears up.

We watch him curiously.

Finally, he sighs happily, having enjoyed his chuckles. "I'm sorry, Demitri, but Victoria is hilarious. We all laughed our asses off when we left Melanie's house. All she does is pose, pout, preen, and bitch." He scrunches up his face. "She's really not that pretty. There's nothing worse than getting a girl home, unwrapping the package, and realizing the eyelashes are fake, the bra is padded, and she's wearing two pounds of makeup."

Demitri studies him and seems to think hard. "She's become less and less attractive in my mind lately, to be honest."

Riptide seems to consider this. "You, sir, are flawless. I'm also flawless. It's a tough position to be in."

"It's really lonely," Demitri says.

"Indeed," Riptide agrees. "That's why we must have our people. The ones who give us shit, let us be normal, appreciate our internal flaws, and love us for who we really are." He sweeps his hand to the surfers, who are listening. "Hence, these guys."

"Screw you, Riptide," Pepe hollers. "You ain't shit."

"Don't you forget it." He grins at Demitri, and I crack up.

Demitri nods. "My people are Melanie, Javier, and Adam. Adam likely doesn't know that, though."

"Then why are you giving the most intimate parts of yourself to Victoria?" Riptide asks. "She's repulsive."

Demitri shakes his head. "I don't have an answer except that I have some serious evaluation to do."

Riptide sweeps an arm my way. "If I were to guess, Melanie leaves you vulnerable because she knows too much about who you really are. You can't pull the suave, aloof card with her. You don't want to give up that wall you live behind with your girlfriends, and Melanie's already seen who you really are."

Demitri's eyes snap wide.

"Melanie's one of your people," Riptide says with a knowing nod. "Your girlfriends aren't your people because you don't show them who you really are."

As Demitri studies me, I try to be as unthreatening as possible. Softly, I inform him, "If it helps, I love who you really are, and don't particularly have much use for your 'perfect guy' façade."

Demitri briefly looks shell-shocked before he pulls it together.

Riptide takes a sharp breath and then drops a bomb. "Demitri's learning, and that means I hit the gas. Melanie, I have no interest in wooing you with a bunch of charming bullshit. I won't ever play games with you. I have no fear of you getting to know my darkest secrets."

I stare up at him, mesmerized by his unexpectedly candid outpouring. "Your upfront, honest way makes my soul pound."

Smiling endearingly, he says, "I love that about you. You pull no punches. You say exactly what you're thinking, and I never have to wonder if you're telling it to me straight."

I laugh sardonically. "I'm not good at the coy, girly games. I'm blunt. It's a blessing and a curse."

Riptide sweeps my hair from my cheek and wraps his hand around my jaw. "That's exactly what I want."

Looking strained and uncomfortable with this exchange, Demitri says, "I'm sorry that I'm just realizing a lot, Melanie."

I glance Demitri's way. "Love, I need to really level with you. My life is a wreck. It's not polished. When I'm not trying to escape the grim reaper, I'm destroyed. I don't have time to pamper and preen. I don't have that luxury, but even if I did, I wouldn't. There's beauty in the ugly of my life, but you'll never see it. All you try to do is yank me from my reality. Sometimes it's welcome, but I am what I am. My life is ugly, and you're beautiful." I look up at Riptide with big eyes. "You're beautiful also." Realizing that I'm way out of my league, yet again, I shake my head.

As I start to walk away, Riptide stops me with a hand on my arm. "I'm vicious, Melanie. No one messes with me. Evil really doesn't scare me."

"Will you please back off?" Demitri implores him.

Riptide shakes his head. "No. The second I laid eyes on her—hell, I was still halfway across that patio—my heart hammered out of my chest. I touched her arm, and my knees nearly buckled. I know what I want. The only person who has a shot of shutting me down is Rich, because I respect the hell out of that man. He helped raise me. I lost my dad two years ago, and Rich was next to me at the paddle-out memorial."

Demitri inhales and swallows uncomfortably.

I smile at him and singsong, "Friend *zooone*."

Demitri's glare turns into a sad smile as I bounce like a Fraggle.

My gaze slides flirtatiously to Riptide.

"All right, surfing," he says with a grin. "Tandem. Give it a shot."

Demitri snags his board, and we walk out into the water. He instructs, "Lie down." I do, and he hops on, lying over me. "This is why you aren't tandem surfing with Riptide."

I laugh. "Instead, I get to be all hot and bothered by you? How nice."

"Precisely. Now paddle out."

We do and get out to the right spot. We let a couple of waves pass as Demitri instructs me. "When I tell you, paddle hard, then get your feet under you. It's called a pop-up. Grab my arm like we're going to counterbalance. Engage your abs and legs. It's just like dance, only deadly, with sharks and drowning."

He laughs at my grimace. A wave comes our way, and he positions us how he wants us.

We paddle, and he barks, "Now!"

We hop up to our feet, and I grab his arm and figure out how to lean and move with him. He twists us hard, making me squeal happily. We're so in sync from working together in the studio all the time that it's perfect. Our surf friends scream their approval. I high-five Demitri, and we both bail off into the water at the end of the ride.

Demitri hugs me hard and rattles his head. "Are you *kidding*? I've never seen anyone pull off a tandem ride the first time. I'm so freaking proud of you."

I giggle. "Thank you for taking me."

We get back to shore, and Riptide runs to me, picks me up, and swings me around. He's so excited that he's practically vibrating. "Yes! You have to take a tandem trip with me."

I laugh and nod. "One more tandem trip and then I want to try going out on my own."

Riptide throws his head back, laughing. "I knew you'd love this." Rocco hands him his board, and Riptide says, "Let's go, girly."

We wade out and load up on his board. He settles on my back, and we paddle out.

"Hold your breath," he instructs me, and we dive under a wave. As we emerge, he shakes water from his face. "That's called a duck dive." He turns us around, and we sit up. "We're at the break line now. You ready?"

I nod nervously.

We paddle, and he says, "Now."

I pop up and find my balance. When he snakes an arm around my waist, I can't even wrap my mind around surfing with Riptide.

We curl and twist before hitting the barrel. I grin as I look up through the arching wave. It's like being surrounded by magic. As we come out of the barrel, he throws his hands in the air and howls. I laugh and let myself fall backward into the water.

Riptide sits on his board. I lean against it, and he smiles down at me. "Nice work, Meley. That was awesome."

"Thank you for taking me out. This is fun."

He nods, and we head back to the shore.

Pepe high-fives me. "You've got what it takes. Now go do it on your own." He hands me an adorable little board, and I grin girlishly.

"You like it?" Riptide asks.

I nod. "Thank you." The black board is the perfect size for me, and the girly skull and crossbones make me shrug my shoulders happily. Riptide melts a little while he observes my reaction to the gift.

All the guys wade into the ocean, and we paddle out together.

Riptide gets situated next to me. "You're taking the same wave I do. Let these guys go first and watch what they do. You won't have a partner there to steady the board."

I watch as the other guys head off on one wave after the other.

A fresh wave comes our way, and Riptide says, "Here we go. Your only goal is to make it to the end. I'm staying behind you."

I nod, and we paddle out before I pop up. I find my balance and work through the twisting. I curl to the top of the wave and twist back down, hit the barrel, and make it out the other side. Wondering if I did it right, I look at the guys. Their mouths are hanging open.

"You did it, baby girl!" Rocco yells. "Holy crap!"

Riptide pulls up beside me. "Some people just have it."

Demitri laughs. "It helps that she's physically strong enough to handle it."

"I guarantee she surfed in a past life," Riptide says, grinning. "People don't just do it like that."

As darkness falls, we all sit in a happy circle on our boards, laughing and joking. I revel in the exchange.

Suddenly Riptide's expression changes, and he growls. He's staring at the shore.

I follow his gaze to spot someone on the sand watching us. I realize it's Jet, and my heart thumps in my chest. I open my soulmate connection with Trey and pound on the blockage between us.

Finally, he drops his wall and asks, *"What's wrong?"*

"Jet. Get to Surfrider Beach."

"On our way. We've been trying to call you. We're on PCH."

"Who's we?"

"Adam, Rich, Big Joe, and me."

My mental conversation is cut short as we hear a boom and something whizzes past my ear.

"Jet's got a gun!" Rocco squawks.

Disbelief swirls through me as we bail off our boards. Riptide grabs my hand. He pulls me, and we swim out and around, dragging our boards behind us by their ankle tethers. The tide tries to carry me too far out, but Demitri gets on my other side, helping me behind a massive rock outcropping. We all grab on. It's jagged and cuts my hand.

Pepe asks, "What do we do now?"

Riptide shakes his head. "This is insane."

"Trey, Jet just shot at me. You guys need to stay away. We're trapped."

Trey snarls in my mind. *"Big Joe is packing. We're almost there."*

I relay the message to the guys, but we all know we're in big trouble. We hear something above us and look up. Jet's perfectly outlined in the moonlight on the top of the cliffside.

"Go, guys. Now." I unlatch my board tether and heft myself

up on the top of the outcropping. I'm scratched all over from the jagged rocks.

Jet smiles in the full moonlight, radiating seductive malice as I reach the top and stand.

Irritation overtakes my fear. "What is it with you broken-ass boys hunting me? This isn't new or alluring, Jet."

"It's different with you and me," Jet hollers across the distance between us. "I want to kill you so I can keep you and enjoy my time."

My mouth drops open.

He's clearly enjoying my shock. "I can't wait for you to rot." He makes his way down the boulders, headed my direction.

The thought of what he's implying is so gross that I can't even summon the fear I should feel.

"Oh my God," Riptide says from somewhere below.

Demitri hefts himself up next to me and grabs my hand just as Jet raises his gun.

I have to end this. With no clue what I'm doing or how I'm doing it, I gather an energy load. It quakes in my chest, threatening to burst. Unable to figure out how to release the blast, I race toward Jet and hit him with an evil right hook. He screams and falls, and his shot goes wild, harmless. I look over the edge as my friends trot up behind me. There's no sign of Jet on the rocks or in the water. He's nowhere to be found. I wheel around when I hear people approaching. Trey runs around the corner on the beach with Adam, Big Joe, and Rich close on his heels.

They look up at me.

"He's gone," I announce.

Gingerly, I make my way down, and Trey helps me off the last big boulder. Clearly worried sick, he hugs me tight.

Riptide frantically tells Rich, "We found and burned the

pictures. There were several of a dead body that are in an envelope in Demitri's Jeep. Jet has a murder bag in his car, complete with everything he needs to do some really *sick* shit. Apparently, necrophilia is his kink. He announced that he wants to kill Melanie so he can get off on her while she rots." He takes a breath and calms his frantic energy. "I leave for Hawaii in two days, but my agent can rebook me for the morning. I hire two bodyguards on my trips, and they're damn good. Why don't I take Melanie with me to give you guys time to get this sorted out?"

My eyes snap wide, and then I blink spastically, shocked by the offer.

Trey explodes. "WHAT? You can't be serious. It's obvious you're not trying to protect anyone. You're just after my girl."

Rich holds up a hand. "Riptide, you do realize Melanie's sixteen, right?"

Riptide snorts. "I'm eighteen. Is two years really that stunning in the world of energy workers? We've all lived how many thousands of years in past lives?"

Adam chuckles. "Last time I checked, Rich, you're a lot older than Carol."

Rich gives Adam an exasperated look.

Trey beats him to saying, "Really, Adam? Whose side are you on?"

Adam grins. "Melanie's. I think getting the hell out of town is the best thing she can do. She has a creepy necro after her. Do you want her to spend a few days regrouping in paradise, or do you want her to rot?"

Trey grimaces. "Why does it have to boil down to Riptide-paradise or Jet-murder? Can't we settle for her just staying home and being scared but safe?"

Rich levels Riptide with a harsh stare. "Sixteen, Rip."

Riptide's face bunches. "Yeah . . . That whole *she's-younger-than-you* reasoning would work on anyone but me. I think you need to give Melanie a little credit. She can handle sitting on an airplane, staying in a hotel, and eating food in a resort restaurant."

"Pierre, can I fill her in?" Rich asks when he notices my confusion.

Riptide nods.

"All right, here it is," Rich says. "Riptide is a rare man. His dad died two years ago, leaving his beach store and condo to him. I helped him get through the legalities. His dad knew he wasn't going to make it, and so, to smooth the way, Pierre was emancipated while his dad was still with us. He's been living on his own and running a business since he was sixteen—hence why he thinks jet-setting teenagers is a normal thing." Rich huffs. "Meanwhile, his surfing career took off, and he's lived more life in a few years than most people do in a lifetime."

I'm stunned as I stare at Riptide. "I'm so sorry about your father."

He smiles sadly. "My mom died when I was little. Dad's with her. It left me alone, but it worked out."

"You dropped out of school, which I need to whoop your ass for," Rich scolds him.

Riptide chuckles. "The purpose of school is to gain job skills. I have those." He gives my stepdad a puppy dog look. "My bills are paid, and I have a winning career."

Rich rolls his eyes. "Yeah, yeah. You're the luckiest turd I've ever met . . . minus the whole orphaned teenager part." He deflates again. "I need to be around more. I apologize, Pierre."

"I've got Rocco to guide me," Riptide says with a shrug.

We all give Rocco an unsure look, and he flashes a bright grin, complete with a boisterous thumbs-up.

"Oh Lord," Rich groans out.

"She's not going," Trey says venomously. He snaps a fierce glare Rich's way. "Wasn't it you who said I couldn't propose to Melanie until she was eighteen?"

"Wait, *what*?" I yammer out. I look from Trey to Rich.

Rich rolls his neck around dramatically. "Yes. That was different. Being engaged is different from hopping a plane to Hawaii to get away from a murderous stalker."

To my surprise, Adam and Demitri crack up. Rocco spurts laughter. Riptide grimaces. I scrunch my face up.

"How exactly is being adorably engaged at sixteen different from hopping a plane to paradise with Wonder Nuts over here?" Adam asks as he juts a thumb Riptide's way.

Rich tosses his hands. "I have no clue." He rubs his face hard. "I can't believe I'm about to ask this. Melanie, what are your thoughts?"

I swallow hard, unsure. "Umm. I'm so overwhelmed. It's been nothing but issues and danger. I don't sleep. My stomach is always in knots. I'm a nervous wreck all the time. The thought of a break . . ." I look at Rich with pleading eyes. "At the same time . . ." I look to Riptide and bashfully say, "Hawaii is far away, and . . ."

Riptide smiles softly at me. "I get it, Melanie. I know you just met me. With that said, you're being hunted. Jet has a damn murder bag in his car. We need to get you away from danger and let the police deal with him."

I do nothing to hide my insecurity. I glance to Trey. "It's really sweet that you asked Rich's permission."

Trey's eyes narrow. "His double standards piss me off." He turns his glare at everyone. "I'm getting ready to just do what I want, seeing as how that's apparently acceptable now. Being a gentleman has gotten me nowhere."

Rich holds up a hand in defeat. "This all went in a direction I didn't anticipate. You did the right thing asking, Trey. At the time, I gave you the best answer a dad could. I didn't say no. I said to wait."

Pissed, Trey holds out a hand in Riptide's direction. "Yet, *he* doesn't have to wait?"

"Trey," Rich says patiently, "he isn't asking Melanie to marry him. He's asking her to leave for a few days, purely for her own safety. While unorthodox, I trust Riptide. Honest to God, there's no one more on the up and up. Riptide, if you take her, you have to promise me you'll keep her safe."

"Done," Riptide says.

"We can work to track down and deal with Jet while you're gone," Big Joe offers. "If nothing else, it'll give us time to get the police involved."

I nod. "I need to leave and clear my head." I slide an unsure gaze Riptide's way. "I have a bad history with psycho stalkers and attempted rape. If I do this, I need to know your intentions are good." My chin quivers. I'm suddenly terrified.

Riptide's expression crumbles. "You have my word that I'm not trying to lure you away to hurt you."

"He's a bastard, but not a dirty one," Rocco assures us.

We all look at him like he's nuts.

"That's so helpful. Thank you!" I manage to get out around my baffled chuckle.

"Don't talk, Roc," Riptide says, but he's laughing too.

"What?" Rocco says flippantly. "It's true. Riptide's a good guy."

"Trey, please help sort out this Jet situation while I'm gone," I say to encourage him.

Trey grits his teeth, pissed. Finally, he relents.

Rich thinks for a moment. "I'm okay with letting you go, but I need to figure out how to tell your mom."

"Just let her know that I'll take care of Melanie," Riptide says calmly. "I promise."

"Okay then, Rip," Rich says. "Have your agent book the ticket. I'll pull cash for Melanie to take and can wire her ticket fee to your agent."

Riptide shrugs. "My sponsor always grants funds for two tickets, so it's no problem." He grabs his cell phone from his bag and dials a number. In less than a minute, he's made arrangements with someone named Chelsea to add a plane ticket for me and to switch him to a two-bedroom villa.

"We'll see you at the airport at six-thirty," Rich says once we have all the details.

As I say goodbye to my friends, Adam, Demitri, and Trey set to squawking.

"She isn't left alone for a moment, Rip!" Adam insists.

"She's allergic to sulfa drugs and corn," Demitri adds.

I look at him like he's nuts.

Adam piles on again. "She's also allergic to lidocaine and apricots."

"She has night terrors," Trey informs. "She wakes up screaming."

I rattle my head and say over the boy-angst, "I'm not this fragile! Stop."

Riptide holds up his hands, and the guys hush. "She'll be fine. As long as she's not allergic to the ocean and sunshine, all is well."

Trey and Demitri say at the same time, "She's allergic to both. She can't go!" They glare at each other while Rich laughs.

"She'll be fine," Rich says, raising his eyebrows at Trey and Demitri. "What she's allergic to is Jet. Melanie, let's get you home. You need to pack, and I need to talk to your mother."

CHAPTER 25

As we pull up to the airport, the sun is just rising, and we get out of the car in the calm light of dawn. Driving Riptide's van, Rocco pulls up behind us at the curb. Trey, to my surprise, pulls up behind him, followed by Demitri, who has Adam in his passenger seat.

The guys get out of their cars, and Riptide chuckles. "Good morning, boys. I see that Melanie's going to get a five-alarm send-off."

Rocco and Riptide pull two long black padded cases out of the van and lean them against the side. "Melanie," Rocco instructs, "your board is in the smaller case. Keep an eye on it. Things rarely get stolen at these events, but boards sometimes go missing."

I nervously nod. "I will, but I don't plan to surf while we're there."

Riptide looks at me like I'm crazy. "You think I'd let you go to Hawaii and not surf? You'll be an expert by the end of this trip." He turns to Rich and my mom. "The competition starts day after tomorrow. It's all televised, if anyone wants to watch."

"Melanie may end up on national television?" Trey asks with a tone of suspicion.

Riptide shrugs. "It's possible, but I wouldn't worry about it. Even if she winds up on TV, these competitions are *covered* with beach bunnies. Everyone blends in."

As we're talking, I spot a woman in a professional-looking suit as she's exiting the airport and striding toward us. She greets Riptide.

"Good morning, Chelsea," Riptide says with a smile.

She hands him our plane tickets, then turns and smiles at me. "Well, aren't you lovely?" She holds out her hand, and I shake it.

"Good morning. I'm Melanie Slate. It's nice to meet you."

Chelsea nods. "You, as well. I'm Chelsea Alice. Pierre tells me you're a dancer."

"I am."

Chelsea surveys me appraisingly. "Can you pull off triple turns?"

I smile, confused. "I can."

"Show me, please."

I look at Rich, suddenly feeling awkward. After he takes my carry-on backpack from me, I prep and hit a quad. *It's a little early for this nonsense. I need coffee.*

Chelsea smiles. "Tumbling?"

I nod again. "Within reason. I'm no Olympian, though."

"We need illusions, pike tosses, and hitch kicks also."

I shrug. "Child's play. What is this about?"

Chelsea smiles. "I don't just represent surfers. As it happens, I'm the agent for a dancer whose partner broke her leg in a rock-climbing accident. We need a replacement, and I've been charged with the task. Riptide filled me in on you, and I'm hoping you're up to it because the performance is happening in conjunction with the competition." She looks to Riptide and says with concern, "Think she can hold her weight in lifts?"

"I think this will actually work," Riptide says before adding cryptically, "I talked to him."

Demitri steps to me. "Overhead split lift," he says as he grips my waist.

I prep and hop. Demitri tosses me up and grabs my legs. I point my feet and hold in a full split over Demitri's head. I plunge over, hands landing on Demitri's stomach, and flip back to my feet.

Chelsea nods, impressed. "You're right, Riptide. This might just work."

I smile at her warmly. "I can do everything you mentioned, and I learn fast. How many pieces are in the show?"

"Two. There's an easy piece. But the tough one is set to 'Wipe Out,' and it's no joke."

I grin. "I'd love to give it a shot."

Riptide jumps in with a hurried, "Hang on, hang on. This one actually has parents she needs to get permission from." He introduces Chelsea to Mom and Rich.

Chelsea winces a little. "My apologies. It's nice to meet you. Would you be open to Melanie getting a résumé credit?"

Mom and Rich glance at each other. They both smile and Mom nods. "This solves my problem," she says. "If Melanie's going for a gig, then I don't have to tell people my daughter is shacking up in Hawaii with a hottie."

Riptide blushes a little and covers a laugh with a cough. My guys look irritated.

Rocco belts laughter. "Damn, Richard!" he caws. "That wife of yours is both beautiful and blunt."

"As long as she's happy, I'm happy," Rich says. He smiles at Chelsea. "We give permission."

"Done. You solved my problem too. It pays twenty-five hundred dollars, plus your room, ticket, and food. Your trip is now covered." She looks at Riptide. "You're welcome."

Riptide laughs. "I wasn't worried about it, but that works."

"Is the dance show televised also?" Mom asks.

Chelsea nods. "It opens the competition every day. It's fun. You should watch." She checks the time on her pager that's clipped on her slacks. "You two need to go."

Trey grabs my hand. "I need to talk to you." As I step to the side with him, he looks at me with confliction. "Melanie, we're having issues."

"Indeed, we are. We can't discuss them now, though."

"Do you plan for this to be a romantic trip?"

I shake my head. "No. I planned to hide and decompress, but now I'm apparently working too."

"I don't want you to go," Trey says.

"I'm sorry, but I'm going," I quietly reply. "I need a break, Trey."

His jaw tightens. He's clearly angry. "I have to admit I've had some serious reservations about our relationship, even before you decided to shack up with Riptide."

"I'm not shacking up," I retort angrily.

Trey snorts. "So sorry that I don't want my girlfriend in Hawaii with another guy."

I sigh. As usual, I can't catch a break. "I get it, Trey. Can you please view this for what it is?"

"I *am*," Trey snaps back.

My heart squeezes tight.

Trey takes my hand and slides the promise ring off my finger. I watch, full of conflicting emotions.

"I'll be honest," he says, "I don't know if I'm ready for this level of commitment. I want to be a teenager and have a good time. Apparently, you do too." He side-eyes Riptide.

"I'm being hunted, *again*," I remind him, exasperated. "Why can't you see that I need a break from terror and drama?"

"I'm done," Trey says with finality.

To my surprise, I'm not feeling any regret. I fuzz Trey out to avoid him realizing how unhappy I've been. It takes me a second to catch my breath. I expected heartbreak, so this warm sense of relief takes me off guard. "If that's what you want," I say, "that works."

"I'll deal with the Jet situation however I can," Trey assures me. "I'll help get whatever information they need. Marcus's dad is going to do his lawyer thing too."

"Melanie," Riptide cuts in, "we've gotta bail."

Without hesitation, I grab my backpack from Rich. He and Mom are looking from me to Trey, but there's no time to discuss it.

I hug Rocco, and he says, "Have the best time ever, Mel."

I grin up at him.

Demitri steps up next and hugs me tight. "I despise that you'll be dancing with another partner. Don't let the guy do anything stupid." He sets his hands on my cheeks. "Don't get trapped in a room alone with your new dance partner. Do you understand me?"

I scrunch my face, baffled. "Weirdo. I'll be fine, D."

"Eyes open," Adam says, next in line to give me a hug. "Watch for trouble. Know your escape routes."

"I will. I promise."

"Be safe, please," Mom implores.

"She'll be fine, Carol," Rich admonishes.

I give him and Mom a hug. I grab the handle of my suitcase, and then the handle of the surfboard case that Riptide turns over to me.

After Riptide gets his stuff situated, he tips his head toward the door. "Paradise awaits. Let's roll."

CHAPTER 26

Although I know it's a waste of energy, I can't shake the notion that Jet is still watching me somehow. I shift in my seat and turn the page of my book. Subtly, I glance around again, but there's not much to see among the other first-class passengers. I'm too short to see over the seat, and besides, I know Jet isn't here because I spent the whole boarding process obsessively watching every person lining up to get on the flight. *You're worried about nothing. Relax and try to enjoy this.*

Riptide pulls off his headphones and asks, "You okay?"

My eyebrows rise. "I'm sitting in a first-class airplane seat, on my way to Hawaii when I should be suffering through second period at school. I think I'm good."

He laughs. "You're also a little nervous."

I shrug. "That too."

He takes my book and sets it on the tray table in front of him. "Jet didn't follow us, Melanie."

"You were searching for him too?"

Riptide smiles like I've just said something completely adorable.

"I promised to take care of you. So, yes, Melanie, I've been on the lookout for your necrophiliac stalker."

I laugh bashfully. "Thank you. I apologize for the drama."

Riptide shifts in his fancy airplane seat and puts an arm on the cushioned armrest. "All right. Now let's get to the other thing that has you bunched up. Here it is. I'm old-world." He gives me a pointed look. "You, Demitri, and Adam are the oldest souls I've met, but I'm older than all of you. I have no intention of dating you on this trip. I plan to court you, and that's a very different situation."

I look at him quizzically, while leaning my elbow on the ample armrest.

"Courting is formal dating," he says with a smile. "No rushing. No pressure." He looks at my hand. "With that said, I need to understand why your ring is suddenly missing."

"Trey took it back. He said he wasn't ready."

Riptide nods. "He's not ready. Trey's still in casual dating mode. There's nothing wrong with that. Your situation has a lot of layers that I'm still trying to get a handle on. You and Adam clearly have a soulmate bond, but Adam needs a breather. His fiancé is nice, and I kind of get them, but not really."

I smile softly. "Adam and I are intense, and I'm relieved he's with someone else. He's a full-time job, and it gets old."

Riptide chuckles. "You and Demitri are a different animal. There's no soulmate bond there, but there's deep respect. I like him." He tips his head right and left. "Demitri's trying to figure out some final pieces to himself. On one hand, he really does see the best in people. On the other hand, he's attractive and enjoys the attention more than he lets on. He'd have to move past his ego to be what you need, because the last thing you need is a runway model. To be honest, once you get to know me better, you'll realize that I'm like the mega-Demitri."

"I like Demitri, but he's just a friend." I scrunch up my mouth. "I don't like chasing guys."

Riptide laces a hand with mine and plays with my fingers pensively. "How do you feel about the breakup with Trey?"

"On one hand, I'm relieved. I'm so sick of his brooding moods and disappearing act. On the other hand, I'm upset and worried he'll quit helping keep me safe. Even before Jet started stalking me, the need for a bodyguard or two has been kind of a thing in my life." I sigh and shake my head.

"Fair enough," Riptide says. "You're now single, and if I can be forward, I'd like the chance to give some innocent dating a shot. I understand if it's too soon, though."

I tilt my head to the side. "My age really doesn't bother you?"

Riptide appears amused. "If I was still in high school, I'd be getting ready to graduate," he says. "I'm the same age as Adam, and you dated him."

"Oh. Right." I relax a little. "Umm . . . I'm interested," I shyly admit.

Riptide smiles softly at me. "You really are charming, Melanie. Relax and don't stress about the dating stuff. I'll make this easy. I want this trip to be a fun break for you. Dance in the production. Drink mai tais. Enjoy the sun."

I really study him, and my heart rate picks up. Even though I've only known him a short time, it's already clear to me that he's the single most beautiful person I've ever met. After a long moment, I ask, "Why are you doing this? You could have anyone you want."

He smiles. "Sometimes you have to explore. I don't do that often. I'm very career driven. I'm also selfish with my time. I'm on my last lifetime before I become a spirit guide. Time is different for souls like me. It's all fun and games when you've got future lifetimes piled up. When you're on the last one, every day counts in a new way."

"That's the last answer I expected."

He chuckles. "I know. I don't tell people that, but you deserve the answer." Putting a hand on my cheek, he says, "I've decided to test the waters with you, and I'm grateful that Trey is done, and Demitri missed his opportunity. You're young as far as physical body age goes, but soul is a different matter. I'm going to send you something."

He puts his forehead on mine, and I close my eyes. A memory pops up in my mind, and I watch it, confused. I'm in the mind of a guy who's walking on a beach. A pretty, tanned woman is watching him. He thinks, *I love her. I don't know how I got so lucky.* He gets to her and brushes her wavy black hair from her forehead. She looks up at him, and shock zings through me as I realize she has my brown eyes. In her expression, I can see what makes me who I am. She smiles, and her eyes twinkle.

I open my eyes as the memory ends. "That's remarkable," I say in wonder. "How did you do that?"

"I can share memories, and I recall a lot of my past lives. I searched for you in my past life memories. We've known each other, although that's the only lifetime I can recall with you."

"We dated?"

He nods. "We did, although it was an affair, which I'm not thrilled about. I don't believe in them."

I get lost in thought.

Riptide quietly says, "Tell me what you're thinking."

I sigh. "Trey and Adam are deeply ingrained in me. Adam and I have a solid understanding this roll around. I'm comfortable there. Trey, on the other hand, is a constant battle. We fight over jealousy. We fight over commitment. We fight because he's so closed off and

I'm so nervous. Nothing is easy with him, and it gets old."

"You're too young to be at the 'gets-old' phase of a relationship."

I huff. "If I'm being honest, I just want to enjoy my life."

We're interrupted as the stewardess stops a cart next to Riptide, sets plates down in front of each of us, and pulls the metal covers off. A mouth-watering chicken dish is revealed, complete with vegetables, rice, and an orchid garnish. She sets fruity-looking drinks on our tray tables before asking, "Mr. Strader and Ms. Slate, is there anything else I can bring you?"

"No, ma'am," Riptide says. "Thank you."

As the stewardess pushes her cart to the row behind us, I unwrap my silverware from the cloth napkin and say, "Strader, huh? I probably should have found that out before I agreed to this trip."

Riptide chuckles. "Quit looking for things to worry about. We've got three more hours before we land. I have deep-tissue massage appointments on our villa patio scheduled for an hour after we check in. Then, we're meeting up with the other surfers and their wives and girlfriends for dinner. There's nothing but good today."

"Massages?"

"Indeed. Later, we'll soak in our private hot tub before bed."

I smile softly at him. "You keep getting better and better."

He sips his cocktail. "My life is a dream, if you can handle the travel and media pressure."

"I guess we'll find out. I'm enjoying this first-class travel pressure so far, if it helps."

He chuckles. "You're built for this. You just don't know it yet."

My heart skips when I remember that this is no longer just a vacation to get away from a stalker. "When am I supposed to rehearse for this performance?"

"Morning after next at eight. The competition opens at three. You'll be occupied from eight to noon."

I wobble my head. "Four hours, huh? I've worked with less time, but it was with Demitri, and we know how to partner together. This is going to be tight."

"You'll be fine. You're worrying again instead of eating your chicken."

I take a bite and wiggle happily. The chicken has a tangy sweet sauce, and it's so good.

Riptide smiles. "You like it?"

"A warning: If you like waifs who don't eat, I'm not your girl. My goal in life is to die full and laughing."

He chuckles. "You'll enjoy this trip then. I eat constantly during these events. I burn off calories like crazy."

The conversation shifts to him telling me all the ins and outs of how these competitions work. It's fascinating.

—

The plane taxis to a stop, and the departure hustle and bustle begins. I hastily put my backpack on my shoulder, getting ready for the deboarding nightmare to ensue.

"Chill, Meley. We exit a different door. There's no rushing and jostling in first class."

I grin. "Yes, to that. I'm not a fan of crowds or fast-paced pressure."

Riptide looks at me pensively. "Then I need to warn you about what's coming. There's going to be a lot of media. They're really pushy, and I'm intentionally very caged. I don't like my personal business out there. I'd prefer that you don't answer their questions."

I panic a bit. "What questions?"

"They'll be curious about who you are and how we met. Just stay behind me and be politely aloof."

"You didn't warn me about this."

Riptide smiles. "The good outweighs the bad on these trips. Once we're in our villa, we're safe from the vultures. I've hired security, and they won't let reporters through. In public is a different story. Everything you say and do is fair game for them. You're here as a dancer in the show. Less is more."

I huff.

"I guarantee our mainland friends will see news reports. Plan your behavior according to what you want them to see." I nod, and he sweeps his hand to the aisle. "Let the games begin."

CHAPTER 27

The villa door closes, and I exhale, relieved. "That was crazy."

Riptide sets our surfboards along the wall and blows out a frustrated breath. "It's worse than usual. I won this competition, along with two others, last year. The media attention seems to be ramping up accordingly."

As I look around, I'm blown away. This villa has a luxury-hut feel, if that's a thing. Big woven fans spin delicately, creating a breeze from the expansive ceiling. We're standing in an airy living room. Riptide takes my suitcase and wheels it into a hall. He flips on switches as we go. We find two identical bedrooms, and he puts my suitcase in one and his in the other.

"Thank you."

He kisses my forehead. "You're welcome."

When Riptide leaves to answer the villa doorbell, I slip off the gorgeous purple orchid lei that I was gifted as I stepped off the plane and sit on the edge of the bed trying to regroup. I think about what just happened.

We descended the stairs from the plane, and that's when chaos ensued. Two huge guys met us at the stairs, and we were escorted through throngs of reporters. I kept my sunglasses on, stayed between the huge bodyguards, and just kept moving. Riptide handled it well, answering questions when he chose to, and charmingly wiggling out of the ones he didn't like. We dealt with that same chaos through the whole airport, and in front of the resort. The competition is hosted on the resort's private beach, and from the crowds, it seems that surfing is a far more attention-worthy event than I realized.

Riptide comes in and surveys me. He's wearing a puffy white robe and has another in his hand. He crosses to me and lays the robe on the end of the bed. He kneels and puts his hands on my cheeks. "You okay?"

"Can you be Pierre to me?"

Apparently taken off guard by the question, he still seems charmed. "Of course, I can. Love, what's wrong?"

"This is a little scary. I didn't realize I was taking a trip with the star quarterback of the Super Bowl."

Pierre chuckles. "I didn't warn you because I wanted you to get to know me before you found out my professional status."

"For the record, I like you for you."

Pierre sits next to me on the bed and puts an arm around me. "Why do you want me to be Pierre to you?"

"Riptide just became way out of my league."

He shakes his head. "No, he didn't. With that said, I get that Riptide's more of an image. Pierre is who I really am, and I keep him really private. So, yes, you can be a part of my private side. I'm honored that you want to be a part of that side. Girls usually chase Riptide. They're rarely interested in quiet Pierre, who reads and likes crossword puzzles."

I giggle. "I like reading and crossword puzzles a lot."

He gestures to the robe. "Put on the robe and meet me on

the patio. The spa team is setting up. You're getting a lemon hair treatment and a facial while we're at it."

"Thank you," I say as I smile up at him.

As he leaves, I head to the bathroom, rinse off quickly, and put on the robe. I survey my now-makeup-free face in the bathroom mirror, but the girl who looks back at me is different from the one in Demitri's mirror. I've spent so much time in the sun that I've gotten surprisingly tan. My cheeks charmingly flush, and I like what I see. I opt to just enjoy being me, free from the pressures of gussying up. After running a brush through my damp hair, I leave the private bathroom.

When I get to the patio, a lady meets me at the door, all business in a crisp white spa uniform. She hustles me to a massage table next to Pierre, who's facedown on a matching blue cushy table with a white towel draped over his tush.

An assistant efficiently moves our way. She turns my back to Pierre, unties my fluffy robe, yanks it off, and unhooks my bra, causing me to squeak.

"You're fine, Melanie," Pierre says with a chuckle. "Relax."

Unsure, I look over my shoulder at him. The masseuse plunks me down on my back, and I find myself largely exposed before a towel is draped over my midsection. I look Pierre's way and mutter, "I guess we got the awkward nudity phase out of the way."

He rolls his eyes good-naturedly. "If it helps, I wasn't worried about it."

Hands land in my hair, and the smell of lemon fills my senses. I sigh happily as another set of hands land on my constantly sore quads. I drift happily, half-asleep in a fog as my legs are rubbed.

My masseuse asks, "Too hard?"

I shake my head.

"You're full of knots," she informs me. "I need to really dig in."

When I nod, she performs her threatened digging in, and I sit up like a jack-in-the-box that's cranked one turn past *boing*. "Yowzers!" I squawk.

Pierre cracks up.

"Okay," the masseuse says, laughing. "I'll take it one notch down."

As I lie back, the assistant who was smearing goo on my face puts the towel back over my chest, and I drift again.

When the masseuse gets to my feet, I sigh happily. I look to Pierre, who smiles softly, reaches a hand across to me, and laces his fingers with mine. We both close our eyes. There's an unspoken studying of each other's energy as we enjoy the moment. Somehow, there's no pressure. Pierre brings out the calmest side of me, and I enjoy basking in peace.

The masseuse's voice rings out, "Both of you flip over."

I turn over, lying on my stomach. Pierre flips onto his back.

"Hold hands again," the masseuse orders. "It's cute."

I reach my hand out, and Pierre laces his fingers with mine. The masseuse digs what I think might be an elbow into my back, and I groan as she hits a horrible spot. It sends lightning through my entire back, causing me to tense.

"Oh boy," she says, stopping. "Not good. Call in reinforcements. This girl is a mess."

I giggle and look up at her. "Thank you so much."

"You really are," she says with a laugh. "Is that a bullet wound on your shoulder?"

I nod and huff.

She tells her assistant, "Have them bring scar cream."

The assistant scurries off while my torturer finds new spots to mash and roll through her hands. A few minutes later, I hear many footsteps, and there are suddenly hands all over me. Just as one painful moment ends, a different one begins.

I realize with a start that I've got a death grip on Pierre's hand. "Sorry, love," I groan out through numerous pressings.

He chuckles. "Go easy on her. She's never had one of these."

"No can do."

My eyes snap wide at the sound of an electric buzzing. Pierre's watching me, and I ask, "What the heck is that sound? Did you order a service I need to be warned about? I don't do battery-operated hardware without a warning."

He cracks up. "Lucky for you, this one plugs into an outlet." His eyes widen, and he warns, "Incoming."

Something heavy lands on my back. It vibrates me nearly out of my skin, the sensation causing me to laugh. My chuckles sound funny. Pierre laughs with me and rubs my hand with his thumb. I grin at him.

Mercifully, the hardware is removed, and more hands land on my back. I'm rubbed and squished within an inch of my life, but it becomes quite pleasant after a while. I find myself drifting off again.

"Riptide, hop up a second," someone says.

There's a shifting, and I hear him settle. Hot stones are placed on my back one at a time. I groan happily.

Someone pats my shoulder. "You two relax."

Soft hypnotic music comes on, accompanied by the sound of a water fountain that's been switched on. The patio door opens and closes, and it's suddenly calm.

Pierre's arm glides along my back and settles between two of the hot stones. When I open my eyes, he's smiling at me with his cheek resting on his table. Our tables have been pushed together, and it's pleasantly intimate. He rubs his thumb back and forth on my back but doesn't say anything. Happy in the moment, I close my eyes again. The stones on my back cool down, and I feel them lifted off one at a time before Pierre runs his hand up and down my back. I open my eyes and shift, then take the heavy stones off Pierre's back. He watches me, and it occurs to me too late that I'm not dressed, but there's no sense in worrying about it now. As I settle on the table, he pulls the sheet over me and curls up against my back. He inhales and exhales with me.

"Want to take a nap?" he asks. "We've got three hours before dinner."

I nod and sit up, stretching before scooting off the table.

He picks up our robes. "You want this?"

I shrug lethargically and head through the French doors into the living room.

He catches up with me and takes my hand, guiding me into his room. He turns out the light, and I slip under the covers. When he lies down, I curl up around him with my head on his chest. Choosing not to worry about how little I really *know* Pierre, I fall asleep the second his hand settles on my back.

CHAPTER 28

I wake slowly. It takes me a moment to get my bearings, but nothing about it is unpleasant. I'm curled around Pierre, who's still asleep, and I opt to lie still and enjoy the moment.

Pierre wakes a few minutes later and rubs his eyes. He stretches his back before wrapping his arm around me again and putting his other hand on my leg that I move up by his waist. We lie there in silence, and I give him a minute to wrap his mind around the current situation.

After a long while, he says, "I'm done searching, Melanie. You're what I want."

My heart doesn't do the rapid beating thing. Instead, it beats softly, completely in harmony with the moment. I nuzzle his chest with my cheek. "We're okay, right?"

"We're perfect. Everything about this is right."

I smile and close my eyes.

"We have an hour and a half before we need to leave," he says, rubbing my back. "Want to get in the hot tub for twenty minutes before we get ready?"

I nod and sit up. "I feel permanently sleepy."

He smiles. "Good. You're relaxing. Come on, love." He guides me through the living room and out the French doors, where I survey the back patio, noting the ten-foot privacy fence.

"Security is patrolling. No one's around. You're safe." Pierre slides into the hot tub and looks up at me in the moonlight.

I sink into the little hot tub and lounge back with my head on the deck. The water bubbles and boils away any concerns I've ever had. After a long moment, I look his way. He's watching me with a sweet expression.

"Thank you for bringing me. I'm completely content for the first time in my life."

Pierre stretches. "Good. That's exactly what I was hoping for." He holds an arm out to me, and I cross the brief distance to him.

As he pulls me into his lap, I giggle quietly. "What happened to courting?"

He chuckles. "I just want to kiss you."

I give him a jokingly suspicious look. "We'll see how that goes. We're in Hawaii, naked in a hot tub."

He shakes his head while he smiles. "Nope. Nothing to worry about."

I shrug cheerfully. "I didn't say it because I was worried about it."

My arms drape around his neck, and he leans in, kissing me. I melt as this calm energy climbs up my spine like warm oil. Everything about it is seductive and unthreatening. I moan the slightest bit against his lips, and my dark-water seduction slinks up Pierre's spine. He gasps and puts his forehead on my shoulder.

"You okay?" I ask.

He nods but doesn't say anything. As I rest my cheek on his wet hair, he holds me in the warm water. Everything about the moment is perfect. Finally, he loosens his arms that are around me, and I lie back in the water with my legs still wrapped around his waist. I pop my back all the way up with a spine flex before I just drift. Pierre's hand lands by my neck, and then runs softly down the center of my chest. He puts his hands around my waist and lets me be, completely content.

I open my eyes and look up at the moon. "Is it time to get ready for dinner?" I murmur.

"Unfortunately."

I sit up and wrap my arms around Pierre's neck again, lean in, and kiss him. It starts off innocent and calm, but things quickly heat up. I wait for him to end the kiss, but he doesn't, and so I settle into the moment. Finally, I pull away and scoot to the other side of the little hot tub before things rev up more than Pierre's promise of a simple courting would allow.

"Do you want to order room service instead?"

I shake my head. "No. I want us to get ready and go to dinner with your friends. This is *your* trip, and I don't want you to miss the stuff you're looking forward to just because I'm here."

He smiles. "I wouldn't be missing anything. I see these guys at every competition."

I stand and step out of the hot tub. "We need to get showered."

CHAPTER 29

I leave the bedroom and head down the hall, where Pierre is engaged in a serious chat with our bodyguards.

"This guy is trouble. He's tried to kidnap her, and he shot at us when we were surfing. I don't think he knows we're here, but I want you to keep an eye out just in case."

I watch as Pierre hands them a picture that I assume is of Jet. While they study the picture, Pierre looks my way. His eyes widen slightly as he takes me in.

He pulls me to him, wrapping his arm around my waist. "Nothing happens to Melanie on this trip," he says to his two bodyguards, both of them reassuringly massive. "I want her to feel safe."

The bodyguards nod. "No worries," the bald one says. "Thank you for filling us in."

"Are you ready, Meley?" Pierre asks.

I nod and thank everyone. As we leave the villa, the two bodyguards take the front and back position, and Pierre squeezes my waist. My freshly curled hair bounces around my shoulders. I can't help but smile to myself. Something about how Pierre treats me makes me feel really pretty. I'm wearing a flowy dark-red dress that drapes alluringly in the front, has an open back, and a slit up to my hip. I feel good in it. Pierre surprised me with the dress. Apparently, the concierge at the resort is damn good at his job.

I look up at Pierre. "Thank you for the dress. I love it."

He winks at me, but before he can answer, we get to the beachfront resort restaurant, where media are ready at the entrance with a fresh barrage of questions. I slip past with one bodyguard, who guides me to a rowdy table full of people. They're all sun-kissed, everyone dressed in tank tops, breezy skirts, and pants. There's an easy, carefree air about them that's vastly different from the Hollywood fuss and muss I've gotten so used to.

"Ms. Slate, Riptide will be along shortly," the bald bodyguard informs. I watch him cross to the two-person table near us and take a seat.

I have no clue what to say or do. I don't know any of these people.

My problem is quickly alleviated as a gorgeous blond lady in a tropical print sarong squeals, "Fresh meat! What's your name?" She bounces up to me and puts a tequila shot in my hand.

I take it and laugh. "Melanie. It's nice to meet you all."

The guys set in whooping and hollering, and shots are distributed along the packed, long table. When Pierre arrives, he's greeted boisterously.

Everyone demands details about me, but Pierre shakes his head. "Sorry, guys. Tone it down. I don't want Melanie caught up in a bunch of media drama." He takes a shot glass, and a guy at the end of the table slurs out a profane cheer.

I lick the salt off my hand that the blond lady liberally sprinkled, take my shot, and bite a lime. Everyone plunks down, and conversation flows easily. We order dinner and get through another round of shots before our food is delivered. It seems this restaurant couldn't care less about carding us. Pierre and I prove to be the youngest of this group, but given the lighthearted behavior of several, we come across as mature. Pierre holds my hand the whole time, and I discover that I love his habit of toying absently with my fingers. Even though it's completely innocent, it's oddly personal. The girls prove to be an easy bunch, and this crowd feels like the Beach Bar regulars back home. The tequila shots likely help, because I find myself laughing and talking with everyone like we're old friends.

As dinner winds down, one of the guys says, "Damn, Rip. I think you finally found your seashell." By now, I know him as Ruckus, and he's a man who has clearly earned his surfer name. He's tall, body-builder huge—a rarity among surfers—and has a mouth on him that easily rivals Adam's.

I melt a little. "That's a new one."

Ruckus smiles. "Surfers are a lot like otters. We mate for life. Some of us tend to be hoes."

The other guys all toss napkins at him.

"But that's not how it works for most of us," he concludes.

"I've definitely found my seashell," Pierre says, looking sheepish. "But we're new, so go easy on her. I don't want her scared away." He gestures to a girl across the table. "Caroline, Melanie is dancing in the opening show. Take care of her, would you?"

Caroline, a gorgeous redhead with a tall, lean dancer's body, smiles enthusiastically. "Nice! I'll help you get it down." She pushes her chair back and waves me over to the empty spot behind our table.

My eyes snap wide. "I'm several tequila shots in. This might be a bad plan."

A tanned man sitting next to her stands and says, "I'm Caroline's partner in the show, and her husband. I know all your lifts, so I can help her teach them to you." He looks to Riptide. "Who's partnering her?"

Riptide grins. "Beastie Boy."

"Ooohhh," Caroline coos. "They're going to be *adorable!*"

I look around and see that the restaurant has emptied, save for our massive group.

Caroline's husband takes my hand. Guiding me around the table, he asks, "What are you wearing under that?"

"Little shorts."

"Perfect. Up you go." He grips my ribs and dead presses me into a side split lift.

I stretch and point my feet as I hit the top of the lift.

He spins me twice and informs, "Basket toss down," before launching me into the air and catching me. "You're partnered with a guy named Zane, but we call him Beastie Boy. He's going to love you. He's used to a partner twice your size."

The surfers all watch as Caroline drags me to the open dance floor and we work through the choreography. When we finish, Caroline says, "You've got this." She turns to the bartender and hollers, "Kai, do you have the Eliminators' 'Dawn Patrol' back there?"

"Of course," Kai yells back. "I've got all the crap tourists like."

I ask, "What do the locals listen to?"

"Led Zeppelin."

I throw my head back, belting surprised laughter. "Yesss! I love that."

"Here you go, girls," Kai says. "Music's hot."

As "Dawn Patrol" bounces through the speakers, Caroline and I start the choreography. The piece is flirty and fun. It's a lot of hip wiggles and playful arms, and I quickly have it down.

"Nice, Melanie," Caroline compliments. "That's it."

We get to a fresh wiggly section, and Caroline and I body roll and gyrate through it. She asks, "Belly dancing or Hawaiian dance training?"

"Belly dancing. I know zero about Hawaiian dance technique."

Kai yells from the bar, "I assure you no one cares what it is as long as you keep doing what you're doing."

I laugh and glance at the table of friends. Pierre's mouth is comically open, and he does nothing to hide the seduction in his eyes. His friends all tease him, and he shakes his head. "I don't give a damn about anything but her right now."

"Sorry, babe," I say with a giggle. "Guess you've never really seen me dance."

The song ends, and Caroline says, "Now for 'Wipe Out.' It's fast, and incredibly complicated. Your first tumbling pass, I can't do. Three front flips into a leap in second. You'll split-star eight times and then get pulled up by Beastie. Same thing from the other side of the stage. That'll get you through the first minute of the song."

I wince. "Gymnastics isn't my strong suit. Let's see what happens." I take off my bracelet and set it on the table, then tie the bottom of my skirt up and walk to the end of the big dance floor. I mark through the series with my hands before taking a grounding breath and focusing on the diagonal other end of the floor. I open my dark-water energy reserves and boost up before launching into the three requested front flips. I spring into a leap in second and land in my center split on the floor. Finally, I whip through the split stars and stand.

Caroline's mouth is hanging open. "Okaaay. I don't know how you just did that. So, I forgot that you illusion twice after the front flips, slide into the splits, and then do the split stars."

I rattle my head. "Oh. That's easier."

Ruckus blinks rapidly and asks in disbelief, "Did you just leap seven feet in the air, out of a front flip, and land in the splits?"

I laugh. "I did."

Ruckus pats Riptide on the shoulder. "Congratulations, my dude. I recommend you marry her tonight and have matching tattoos by morning."

Riptide rubs his forehead with his thumb. "I know you said you were a dancer, but I didn't think you were a *dancer* dancer."

I hit him with a quirky shoulder shrug and pop my foot behind me. "There's a distinction?"

The guys all laugh, and Kai yells from the bar, "Hell yes, there's a distinction."

Caroline says, "Try it again with the illusions."

While the surfers gape at me, I go through the flips, leaps, illusions, and split stars successfully.

Caroline is grinning as I stand. "You'll be fine, Melanie. The choreographer's going to eat you up. You should see some of what we've been stuck with over the years."

I exhale, relieved. "Excellent news."

Kai waves me over and hands me a shot. "Ankle warmer. Take that down, and it'll be the best night of your life."

"It's already the best night of my life," I say with a grin.

Kai smiles and leans on the bar. He appears to be a Hawaiian local. He has a charming smile, but there's a sense of boredom to his demeanor. My empathic gift picks up that he's not happy in his bartender job. "Rip is the best guy I know," he quietly informs. "He's never brought a date to any of these dinners. He's a complete ghost rider where dating is concerned. I guarantee you're special."

I smile and look down at the bar. "I really like him."

Kai grins. "I think you really love him."

I roll my eyes a touch. "I always fall fast, and it's a mistake."

"Maybe that's because you really live," Kai says as he wipes the bar down with a damp towel. "There's nothing wrong with giving in and letting go."

"How do you know these things?"

Kai hits me with a deep expression. "There's no better therapist than a bartender. We see and hear it all. I know people, Melanie. I know love and lust. I know anger and irrationality. It all lands here." He points subtly Pierre's way. "That guy loves you. Doesn't matter if he met you five minutes ago or five thousand years ago. It is what it is. True love works that way. It's supposed to be easy, especially when it's new. Bask in it. You're in paradise. Do all of it and enjoy your life."

I take the shot and toss it back. It's smooth going down, and I close my eyes. Suddenly my whole body is pleasantly warmed through. I smile at Kai. "Thank you."

He nods and winks at me, then switches out CDs. Sultry music wafts from the speakers as a warm ocean breeze drifts by. I turn and untie my skirt, letting it drop back into place, before leaning my back against the bar. I watch Pierre push his chair back and cross the distance to me. He's perfection in his breezy white linen shirt.

He gets to me and slides his hands around my neck and through my hair. "You're captivating," he says quietly.

I smile up at him. "My splits do tend to be well received."

He laughs. "Your splits aren't what captivated me."

I smile softly at him while he backs up, pulling me with him to the dance floor. Everyone partners up, and we dance the night away with the lapping ocean in the distance.

CHAPTER 30

My head is whamming like a jackhammer as the smell of fresh coffee forces me awake. I groan and put a pillow over my face.

Pierre chuckles and rubs my back lightly. "Tequila is the devil in the morning, but we had fun."

"Please kill me. But *damn*, it was a good party." I sit up and take the cup of coffee he offers, croaking out, "What time is it?"

"Six."

I groan.

Pierre laughs. "Morning soak before you have to leave for your costume fitting?"

"Definitely."

We make our way to the patio, where Pierre lays two towels and our robes on the lounge chairs by the hot tub. "I have breakfast ordered. It should be here in thirty minutes."

I slide into the hot tub and set my coffee cup by the side. As I soak, my headache starts to burn off.

Pierre takes one of my feet and rubs it.

"This is so perfect," I groan out.

"Does that mean you'll come with me to the next one? It's back here in two months."

"I'd love to. But are you sure you want that?"

He nods. "I want to officially date you."

My heart flutters. "That's really sweet. How does your courting work in that situation?"

He smiles and switches to rubbing my other foot. "We've already moved faster than my courting should have allowed. With you, it seems to be more corrupt than I intended."

I laugh. "You kissed me. I think your virtue is safe so far."

"True, I suppose," Pierre says with a smirk. "The guys all love you. Even Kai is enamored, and he hates everyone."

I laugh bawdily. "He's quite the counselor. We had an interesting chat last night."

"Do tell."

"It was about my habit of falling fast. He enlightened me to the fact that it can be attributed to really living life to the fullest instead of my assumption that it stems from immaturity."

Pierre smiles. "I fell in love with you the second I laid eyes on you."

"Same, love. You walked up, and my brain melted."

Pierre's expression slides vulnerable. "Really?"

I laugh. "You're seriously surprised?"

Pierre chuckles. "What else did Kai say?"

"That we need to do whatever feels right and enjoy love in paradise."

"Kai's a smart man." Pierre tugs my foot, pulling me through the warm water to him. I wrap my legs around his waist as he settles me in his lap. He isn't hesitant when he kisses me this time. We get lost in the heat of the moment before he picks me up and carries me, dripping wet, through the living room. He pulls away, only to crack the door and inform the bodyguards that our breakfast delivery needs to be left by the door. He closes the door and carries me into the room we've apparently decided to share instead of staying in separate spaces. After closing the bedroom door, he sets me down on the bed, and I scoot back, sliding my legs under the covers. He flips off the light and crawls over me.

"This is part of courting, kind sir?" I quip.

He laughs seductively. "To hell with courting."

I gasp in the dark.

His brand of warm energy oozes up my spine, and when I unleash my dark-water seductive side, he growls out, "I want to marry you."

I giggle. "A warning that my dark-water side has a tantric element that makes it impossible for my lover to keep his deepest thoughts a secret."

"I have no need to keep secrets from you."

All further conversation is cut off as Pierre's courting rules are obliterated for the next forty-five minutes.

I race out of the bathroom and grab my backpack that's on the dresser. I throw my room key in and run into the living room. From the breakfast tray, I grab two pineapple chunks and pop them in my mouth. I slip on my flip-flops and twist my wet hair into a bun. Pierre rounds the corner and hands me a breakfast sandwich wrapped in a napkin. I take the to-go coffee cup he offers, and he hauls me to the door.

He opens it and informs the bodyguard, "She has to be in Ballroom B for a fitting in seven minutes."

The other bodyguard wheels around in a golf cart and grins at

Riptide. "I've got her covered. Good to see you so happy, Rip."

Pierre grins at him. "She doesn't leave your sight! Take care of her. It shouldn't take long, and I want her back the second she's done."

The bodyguard agrees, and I start to rush to the golf cart, but Pierre snags my arm and pulls me back. He kisses me, and I giggle.

We get distracted, and the bodyguards both clear their throats.

Riptide laughs and insists, "Go, go."

I run to the golf cart and hop in.

Pierre is reading on the couch when I return. When he looks my way, I ask, "What's the plan?" He just stares at me, and I giggle. "You okay?"

He rattles his head. "Repeat the question. I heard none of that."

I blush. "That would be a first."

He looks at me quizzically.

"No one's ever been so enamored with me that they lost track of their hearing abilities."

Pierre looks shocked. "I really don't get that, Melanie. I've never been more captivated by someone."

I shrug happily. "I can say the same about you, although you're used to it, I suppose."

"We have the whole day to do whatever we want," Pierre says, taking my hand and pulling me into his lap. "What would you like to do?"

I shrug one shoulder. "I'll give you my list if that's okay?" When he nods, I inform him, "I want another surf lesson from this *gorgeous* guy I know."

Riptide rubs his nose on mine and smiles. "Okay, what else?"

I bite my lip. "I want to get back in the hot tub and have my way with you."

He nods.

"And I want to have dinner with your friends again." At his askant expression, I chirp, "That's all."

He looks at me curiously. "That's your list? You're in Hawaii, and you want dinner, surf, and sex?"

I nod.

"How about we knock out the sex and surfing before lunch, skip dinner with my friends, and I take you to do something that will blow your mind?"

I squeal and kiss him.

He laughs and stands up, taking me out to the patio.

— —

My mouth drops open as I look out the window of the helicopter. I turn to Pierre. "No way!"

He snuggles up against my back, leaning over to enjoy the view with me. We're flying over a volcano, and we spot lava boiling and bubbling inside the opening.

"I've never seen anything like that," I say, glued to the window.

Pierre kisses my shoulder and lets me enjoy the moment. We start to fly away, and I crane my neck to look for as long as I've got a view.

"Alex, please circle," Pierre says into the headset. "Melanie's enjoying this a lot more than I expected."

"No problem, Mr. Strader."

We circle again, and I can't get enough of the view. I gasp out, "I've never seen a more beautiful color than that lava. It's so vibrant."

Pierre seems beyond pleased that I'm enjoying his special idea so much.

The pilot asks, "Another go-round?"

"She's good now," Pierre says with a chuckle. "Head to the next surprise."

"There's more?"

He nods.

We enjoy the flight for a time before we lower to the ground and the noisy helicopter quits whirring. Pierre thanks the pilot, and we get out and walk down a pathway surrounded by tropical flowers.

I close my eyes and inhale. "The flowers smell amazing."

"What are your favorite flowers?" Pierre asks.

"Pansies, tiger lilies, stargazer lilies, honeysuckle, a rare rose called a Claude Monet, and morning glories."

"Interesting list."

I grin. "Honeysuckle grew outside my grandmother's front door and smelled like happiness to me. Claude Monet roses remind me of Renaissance Italy. It's one of the few lifetimes I clearly remember. I love morning glories because they're hidden, and you must catch them at the right time to realize their beauty. Pansies and tiger lilies are the cutest flowers in *Alice in Wonderland*. Stargazer lilies smell like nothing else in this world."

He stops and looks at me, then wraps his hands around my face.

I giggle. "What?"

"I love how you think." He leans in, kissing me softly. He ends the kiss and puts his forehead against mine.

"You love me because I'm quirky about flowers?"

"Melanie, it's not quirky. You have sweet reasons for why you like those."

I shrug. "I'm a little odd. I'm glad you're open to it."

"I love everything about you."

"I love you too, Pierre. I've never been happier."

He puts his arm around me, I snuggle against his side, and we continue our trek. We round a corner to discover that the view is unreal from up here. There's a gazebo up ahead and a waitstaff. He guides me to the gazebo, where a tall, slender waiter with easy eyes says, "Mr. and Mrs. Strader, welcome."

I side-eye Pierre, and he shrugs. "Test it out and see if you like it," he says.

I laugh. "That's not the answer I expected."

"My apologies," the waiter says with a smile. He asks Pierre, "What is your date's last name?"

"Stick with Strader. It sounds good on her."

I laugh and shake my head. "You know what? I've decided I'm going to enjoy it instead of worrying."

He pulls out my chair for me. "Perfect."

"That was the most unreal lunch I've ever had."

Pierre laughs. "I love that you enjoy food so much."

I shrug happily. "It's one of the great joys in life. Between lifetimes, I greatly miss ice cream, sex, and hot water."

Pierre looks at me wistfully. "At the end of this lifetime, I'm going to miss food, the ocean, and you."

My heart suddenly seizes up, and I'm unexpectedly panicked at the reminder that this lifetime is the last one for him.

"I'm sorry I said that, Meley," he says, closing his eyes tight. "I don't want you to worry about any of that right now."

"I need you to know that my soulmates are freaking busted. I'm not ready to lose you after one lifetime. I can't keep doing this with them."

Pierre gives me a quirky half smile. "All I can do is ask if you'll give me the rest of this lifetime."

I smile. "If you insist."

The waiter hands him a bill folder, and he opens it. After looking the check over, he takes the pen and writes something, then hands everything back to the waiter. "Please bill my account."

"Done and done."

"Thank you."

Pierre takes my hand, and we make our way down a hillside path, descending more steps than I've ever seen in one place. Our bodyguards follow at a respectful distance. A sleek yacht is waiting, and my mouth drops open as I look at Pierre. He guides me on, and I breathe out, "This is unreal." Suddenly, I'm worried. "Pierre, Rich gave me money for the trip, and yeah I'm getting paid to dance, but I don't think it covers this."

Pierre puts a finger over my lips. "It's handled, Melanie. Quit fretting."

As the yacht leaves the dock, we lean on the railing. A stewardess brings us champagne glasses, and we enjoy the view as we circle the island. Pierre proves to be hilarious, telling me stories from his time growing up with my stepfather. We settle on a couch, looking out over the ocean, and laugh and chat for an hour.

When we pull up to a little dock off the shoreline, Pierre instructs, "Dress *off*. It's time to swim."

I pull off my breezy floral sundress, revealing the bikini Pierre gifted me. We step off the yacht and are greeted by a man who appears to be an old friend of Pierre's. He's short and built like a tanned cinder block. With an enthusiastic smile, the man turns to me. "Pretty girl! Look at that." He pats Pierre on the arm.

I blush a touch, and Pierre hugs me. "Melanie, this is Akamu."

Akamu guides me to a ladder, and I get in the ocean.

Pierre gets in with me. "We're on a sandbar. Can you touch the bottom?"

I shake my head.

"Come here, Meley."

He pulls me to him, and I wrap my legs around his side like a toddler. I'm so happy that I don't bother feeling weird about it.

Akamu blows a high-pitched whistle, and I get scared as fins start zooming toward us. "No, no, no. What is happening?"

"They won't hurt you," Pierre assures me. "You're safe."

Watching the fins circle us, I hold on to Pierre like the world is ending, while he laughs at me. Suddenly, a nose pops up out of the water, and a dolphin imitates Pierre's laughter.

I turn into a two-year-old as I clap my hands and giggle.

Akamu cracks up. "She's adorable."

I giggle up at him and ask, "Can I touch it?"

He nods. "Her name is Cruiser. She's friendly."

I hesitantly reach out, and Cruiser nudges my hand with her nose playfully.

"Ohhhhh. She's really cute. Pierre, look!"

He nods. "I know. Touch her side. They feel really odd."

I put my hand delicately on her side and chirp, "She's rubbery."

Another dolphin swims up and looks at me.

I giggle and exclaim, "Hello!"

"She talks to them like they're people," Akamu says with a laugh. "I love her."

Pierre seems enchanted by me as I ask Akamu, "How do you communicate with them? I want to understand them."

Akamu gets in the water, and the dolphins circle him while others join in. When he makes a clicking sound, the dolphins all nod their heads. He pulls a bucket full of fish from the dock and hands it to me. "Give them each one. They like food."

I take one of the fish and wince. "Slimy." One of the dolphins makes a noise at me, and I give it to her. Other dolphins take up the chatter, and I hand out more fish. When Cruiser decides she wants another one and tries to take the bucket from me, I admonish her. "Oh no, you don't! You're a piggy." I take back the bucket while Pierre and his friend chuckle. I give Cruiser another fish, and she swings around and bumps me with her side.

"She likes you," Akamu says. "Grab her fin."

"I don't want to hurt her."

"You won't."

When I grab her fin, she takes off swimming at lightning speed. I squeal and hold on tighter. The other dolphins follow, and I laugh happily while they play around me. A big dolphin bumps my hand, and I grab his fin. He pulls me in a wide circle around the huge, netted-off area that they apparently live in, then drops me back with Pierre and looks at me.

"What's his name?"

"Bolt."

"I love your home, Bolt," I say, smiling at him. "Thank you for the tour."

He squeaks at me, and Pierre rubs my back lightly with his thumb under the water while I wrap my legs around him again, tired from swimming for so long.

Akamu blows a whistle, and the dolphins all take off in a wide circle. They arch through the air, and I gasp. Bolt leaps last, really close to us, before turning on his side mid arch and blasting us with a tidal wave of water as he splashes down.

As I sputter and laugh, Bolt comes to me and looks into my eyes.

"Very funny, sir."

Seeming pleased with himself, Bolt nods his head.

Pierre takes me to the ladder, and I get out of the water. The dolphins all line up and look at us.

I kneel. "It was nice to meet you all."

At the flick of Akamu's hand, the dolphins swim away together. "You truly understand them," he says to me.

I nod happily. "Thank you. That was magic."

"I love her," Akamu says as he pats Pierre on the arm. "No one ever talks to the dolphins like they're people. They're really smart, and they like it." He squeezes my hand. "Thank you for coming out today. It's been a pleasure."

After thanking him, Pierre guides me back to the yacht, and we climb aboard.

"I can't believe we just did that!" I exclaim.

"You surprised me yet again. You're adorable with animals."

A sheepish feeling bubbles through me. "I think I connect with them because they're helpless. I like delicate creatures."

"So do I," Pierre says as he stares at me with a hint of nostalgic longing. "Are you ready to head back to our room now?"

I give him a heated look and bite my lip. "Yes, please." I grip the side of his neck and kiss him, doing nothing to hide my blazing interest.

He gravels out, "We'll be there in twenty minutes."

We walk through the door, and as Pierre locks it, I wrap my arms around his neck. He looks down at me with heat in his expression. "Think we can go to the bedroom this time?"

I nod and take his hand, guiding him through the foyer. When I flip on the light, my mouth drops open. Every piece of furniture holds a vase of Claude Monet roses and stargazer lilies. "Oh!" I rush to the first vase and deeply inhale the scent of the captivating burgundy-and-white lily.

"How do we have a villa full of my favorite flowers?"

He laughs. "Note written on the lunch bill."

I giggle. "People jump through hoops for you."

"I don't take advantage of it often, but I'm flexing my status a little to pull off some magic for you."

I guide Pierre over. "Have you ever smelled one?"

He shakes his head and leans down, smelling the gorgeous flower. "They really are incredible."

I look up at him. "This is unbelievable. Thank you!" I guide him to the couch. "Sit down with me for a second before we disappear into the dark and can't make coherent thoughts."

He sits, looking at me curiously.

"Pierre, I need you to understand that I'm not a gold digger. I love today so much, but I didn't expect any of what you set up. I promise that I'm just as happy with grilled cheese sandwiches and a movie at home. You don't have to do all of this."

Pierre leans in and quietly says, "I'm fully aware that you didn't expect any of this. I'm also aware that you're not a gold digger. Your reactions today are part of why it's fun to do these things for you." He tips up my chin. "You deserve it, Melanie."

I take his hand and guide him to our room. "We don't have to be anywhere else?"

"Nope."

"Good."

CHAPTER 31

I'm panting, covered in sweat.

"Great job today, Melanie," the choreographer says. "We'd love to have you join the circuit."

My eyebrows rise, and Beastie Boy smiles down at me. "You're the easiest partner ever. You hardly weigh anything, and you hold your weight. I'd love for you to join us."

I nod my appreciation, though it's clear I need to seem aloof and keep a little distance from Beastie Boy, whose real name is Zane. *Damn*, is he stunning. He's massive, muscular, and he has kind eyes and the most gorgeous jawline I swear I've ever seen. He also happens to be the most solid partner I've ever worked with.

"I need to check on a few loose ends," I tell them. "Can I get back to you on that tomorrow?"

"I'll talk to Chelsea about you," Beastie Boy says. "She'd be crazy not to sign you to the agency."

"Thank you. That's really sweet."

"You need a passport right away," the choreographer instructs. "We come here again in two months, but New Zealand is after that."

My eyes snap wide. "Seriously?"

She grins. "Then Australia. Riptide's on the circuit. It's a good gig." She turns and announces, "Break's over. Places, please. This run is being filmed. Big smiles. You're happy, carefree beach angels."

I survey the dancers in their bouncy little blue skirts, bikini tops, and board shorts. We load up in our spots, and the music starts as Pierre walks through the ballroom door. He watches us blast through the "Wipe Out" routine.

Beastie Boy is a breeze to work with. There's not a waver, he never loses his grip, and he's always dead-on with the timing. The camera circles us as we smile and flirt happily, in character.

When the piece ends, the director of photography announces, "Time to head out to the beach. I need an opening credit shot, and some material for promos."

We all gather our stuff, and I move to Pierre as dancers greet him while they pass by, headed out the door. "You okay if I go do this promo stuff?" I ask him.

He nods. "I already got a feel for the water and took my practice runs. I've got lunch ordered, but we have an hour until it's delivered to the villa."

Zane joins us, and Pierre fist pounds him. "How are you holding up, Beastie?"

"Exhausted. I managed to sleep some on the plane." Zane smiles down at me while he informs Pierre, "This one's a breeze, though."

"You two are acquainted?" I ask.

"Zane is like my big brother," Pierre says. "We've been friends a long time."

"I'm headed out," Zane says. "Good to see you, Rip."

Pierre puts an arm around my shoulders, and we start to walk out.

The director of photography scurries up and says, "Ditch that stuff, Melanie. I'm going to film the two of you walking out to the beach. Shirt off, Rip."

I look up at Pierre and murmur, "You ready for the couple-status cat to be out of the bag?"

He nods and pulls off his shirt, stunning in a pair of black board shorts. I put his shirt in my backpack, and the bald bodyguard takes it from us.

As the cameramen leave, the director of photography holds up his hand for us to wait. "Melanie, I need you to take the sunglasses off and slowly look over your outside shoulder as you walk past the first camera. Sexy and carefree, please. Riptide, you already know the drill. Is your board out there?"

He nods.

"Perfect. Head to the beach, do the sexy smolder thing, then grab your board and hit the water. We'll knock the promos stuff out all at once."

"Can she tandem with me?" Pierre asks.

The director of photography grins. "Definitely."

"Melanie," Pierre says, "when I get my board, you strip that skirt off and come out with me."

When the director of photography gives the signal, Pierre drapes an arm around my shoulders, and we walk out the door and head to the beach exit. We find cameras set up all along the beachfront walkway. As I pass the first one, I take off my sunglasses and slow-pan a look over my shoulder with girly eyes. Then, I turn back to look at the beach and keep walking, hips swaying. Pierre grabs his board while I drop the skirt, revealing my dark-blue bikini bottom. He takes my hand, with his board under his other arm, and we run into the surf together. I lie on the board, and he lies on top of me. We paddle out and duck dive under a passing wave.

When we're by the break line, we both sit up and wait for the next wave. "We've only done this a few times," I remind him.

"We're going to be fine. Here we go."

A monster wave comes our way, and we pop up. Pierre wraps an arm around me and braces his leg against mine. We get our tension right, and he wrenches us to the side. We fly up over the crest and slide back down, before ripping up and back down a few times. As we hit the barrel and come out the other side, I flash devil horns, and Pierre throws a fist in the air. The already-gathering spectators roar their approval. We both look at the shore and smile, and he playfully grabs me and falls backward into the warm ocean water. I sputter and come up laughing while he kisses me.

As we get back to the shore, a photography assistant hands me a towel, and I dry off while a makeup person slicks back my wet hair. I wiggle the skirt back on and join the line of dancers all posing with the ocean in the background. When we finish, Pierre grabs my hand, pulling me through the backstage area to the waiting golf cart. We hop in, and our bodyguards drive us to our villa.

We rush through the door, and I jump in the shower, then get my hair and makeup ready for the show. When I'm finished, lunch is waiting. Pierre sits across from me at the outside table, and we soak up the sun while we eat.

"The choreographer asked me to join the circuit."

Pierre's mouth drops open. "Please tell me you said yes."

"I need to know how you feel about me homing in on your career this way. I'm temped to say no, Pierre."

He shakes his head before grabbing my hand. "This is exactly what I want. I have zero doubts. We'll tour the circuit together, and it'll be perfect," he says with a grin. "I'm so proud of you for being offered the long-term gig."

I take my cell phone from the table. "Let's see if I *can* say yes." I dial my parents' home number. "Hey, Pops," I say when Rich answers.

"What's up, Mel! We're watching a dance commercial you're in. This is wild!"

Surprised that the crew managed to turn the edited commercial around so quickly, I laugh. "We haven't seen the commercials yet, but they spent all morning filming rehearsals. So . . . the choreographer wants to hire me to join the circuit. It means international travel, but Pierre's on the whole circuit and we have bodyguards."

"It sounds like a hell of an opportunity," Rich says hesitantly. "What do you think?"

"I want to do it."

He sighs. "What about school?"

I wobble my head right and left. "I want to be a professional dancer, and it's a good long-term gig. The school makes absence exceptions for working teens in the industry. I'd be nuts to turn this down."

"Is Rip there?"

"He is. You're on speaker."

Pierre says, "What's up, Rich?"

"Hey, bud. How did she do?"

"She's amazing. She fits right in with the dancers and the surfers. Her dance partner works well with her. It's all exactly right."

"What about the two of you?"

Pierre chuckles. "Unfortunately for you, that's exactly right also."

"I figured it would be," Rich says with a laugh. "You two are well matched. Hang on."

We hear the murmur of conversation, and then I hear my friends all exclaim in the background.

"Everyone's there, huh?"

"Yes. We're all going to watch together. Your mother and I approve, as long as Rip's on the circuit. Take the gig."

I squeal, then Mom's distant voice hums through. "Richard, Melanie and Riptide are on TV! You're missing it."

"Hit record," Rich instructs. "We're recording the whole thing."

"Thanks! Talk to you later, Pops."

I hang up, and we rush to the living room. Pierre clicks on the TV, and we watch our slow-motion, music-enhanced exit from the building. It looks like a fantasy. We really are gorgeous together. I look like a beach beauty, and he's sheer perfection. I smile up at him.

"Damn," he says. "I'm suddenly jealous of me. You're beautiful in slow motion."

I swoon a little.

The whole promo's been perfectly edited, even with the short time frame. This event has incredible talent behind the scenes. We come through the barrel and grin at the spectators, both of us clearly elated. I study my face on the screen. All my usual pensiveness is nowhere to be found, replaced by happiness.

Pierre wraps his arms around me as the commercial ends. "We're going to travel the world together, girl."

I gaze up at him in disbelief.

CHAPTER 32

I'm nervously staring off into space in the wings. We dance, live on international TV, in less than five minutes, and I'm suddenly questioning my ability.

Beastie Boy steps up next to me and says, "This is easy. The crowd loves it. It's the happiest, most appreciative audience you'll ever dance for."

"Good to know, because I'm taking the gig," I say with a nod.

He high-fives me and waves over the choreographer.

The choreographer gives me a questioning look.

I nod. "I'm in."

"Yes! I'm thrilled. I'll get your contract ready. We do the same two routines to open each day of competition. The hardest part about this tour is the airplane travel."

My response is cut off as the stage manager calls us to places. Beastie Boy stands next to me, and we sweep onto the stage as the first song starts. We smile and flirt, bop and sway through the piece, and it's effortless. I'm hardly winded as the song draws to a close, which is a good thing because "Wipe Out" starts quickly on its heels. I get through the tumbling passes, and the whole piece goes well. At the end, I race Beastie Boy's way, and he presses me into my final overhead lift.

We quickly bow and scoot off the stage, to the cheering of the crowd. The announcer's voice rings out, and the competition starts. I'm waved over to the wives and girlfriends of the surfers, who are assembled on a private viewing platform. Caroline and her husband follow me. The girls apparently saved me a chair, and I sit shoulder to shoulder with them, watching the guys' surf event.

I lean over and quietly ask Caroline, "Should I expect jealousy and issues with the other ladies now that these guys are in competition instead of enjoying dinner?"

"Nope," she murmurs back. "Everyone gets along."

A lady named Jocelyn informs, "These are heat qualifiers. They determine who gets to compete."

Baffled, I ask, "People come here and don't get to compete?"

She nods. "The gremmies are encouraged by the pros, though. There are only good vibes at this thing."

"Gremmie?"

"It's what the new guys are called. The pros help them along. Today's easy for us. Jim and Riptide already earned spots because they placed first and second last year. They'll surf their asses off in qualifiers, but it's more for fun today. Tomorrow's when things get wild. You'll see."

"Riptide," the announcer blisters out.

The audience goes wild, and we watch as Pierre spots his chosen wave. He gets through qualifiers with a perfect set, and everyone screams.

I smile and say to the girls, "This is a good time."

"You have no idea," Jocelyn replies. "All our guys own surf shops. The lifestyle is amazing. Money comes easy. The food is great. The travel is unbelievable. We get to do it all with our best friends."

The girls grin at me, and we watch our guys gather their boards as the sun sets at the end of the qualifiers.

We carefully descend the steps, and Riptide makes his way across the sand to me. He picks me up and spins me around while I laugh.

"You did great, Pierre."

"So did you," he says, smiling at me. "I got to watch the show from the surfers' box." He rubs his nose on mine.

That's when I notice a bank of media personnel snapping pictures of us. "We're being filmed," I murmur.

He sighs. "That happens a lot." He sets me down and heads to the media box for an interview.

I melt into the background and slide behind one of our bodyguards, who asks, "You doing all right, Ms. Slate?"

"Yes, sir. Just trying to avoid the coverage."

He nods and says over his shoulder, "That's exactly right. You're handling this well."

My chest tightens a little, and I narrow my eyes as I survey my intuition.

Beastie Boy stops next to me. "You okay?"

Before I can answer, a blistering alarm sounds, and the announcer yells through the speaker system, "Bomb threat! Everyone, clear out."

Panic ensues, and people start running for their lives.

My bodyguard grabs me and covers, looking around frantically.

"It's him," I yell over the noise and chaos.

"Jet?"

I nod again. "Intuition pulse." I rattle my head, scared and frustrated. "Just trust me. I'm an energy worker."

Beastie Boy puts an arm around me. "We have to get her out of here," he insists to my bodyguard.

My bodyguard yells, "Kalino, where's Rip?"

"I don't know. Get Melanie out of here."

My bodyguard tries to pull me, but I frantically shake my head. "I'm not leaving without him!"

"Yes, you are."

He picks me up and slings me over his massive shoulder. He takes off running past the crowd and around the far side of the bleachers, where we hit a chaotic wall of people. Beastie Boy helps get us through the crowd.

"Put me down," I yell.

He sets me down, wraps his arm around me, and pushes me with the crowd. Here and there as we pass, Zane pauses to help pull a fallen person back to their feet. Some people aren't so lucky, and wind up trampled. Everything is insane.

"Where do we go?" I ask frantically.

We come to a dead stop, but he bulldozes his way to the side and climbs through the back of a set of bleachers. When we get to the other side, Beastie Boy lifts me over the guardrail, and we take off running through a parking lot. After the police wave us through, my bodyguard's walkie-talkie screeches, and he plugs in the earpiece that detached during our mad dash. He listens and weaves me through the crowd. Media reporters try to stop us. I'm close to tears, but Beastie Boy distracts the reporters as my bodyguard barrels past, blocking and shielding me through the crush. We round the far side of the resort, and he rushes me into a private patio at the backside of the restaurant. As the patio gate clangs shut behind us, I turn to find the surfers and wives huddled up.

Kai rushes through a door and sets down a tray of ankle warmers. "Thank God, Melanie," he says. "Where's Riptide? He's the only one still not here."

I shake my head frantically as panic bubbles up.

Beastie Boy rushes through the gate. "It's crazy out there."

"Where's Rip?" I ask him.

"Didn't see him."

I close my eyes and search the booming energy of the crowd that's scattered all over the resort. When I locate the deep pulse that's distinctly Pierre, I gasp out, "He's in the center of the resort. He's headed this way."

My bodyguard radios, "Do you have him?" He listens and then nods at me. "I've got radio back. He's safe."

A few moments later, the gate opens, and Pierre is shuttled through. The other bodyguard, Kalino, pulls the gate closed, and I exhale. Pierre puts his surfboard with the others.

"You scared the crap out of me!"

Pierre crosses the patio and hugs me. "We had to go around the backside. Anyone know what happened?"

Ruckus snorts. "No, but what I do know is Melanie found you by closing her eyes."

I laugh quietly. "I can sometimes locate energy if I know it well and it's strong enough."

"You're remarkable," Pierre says, resting his cheek on the top of my head.

Everyone smiles softly at us.

"Do me a favor and don't disappear in the opposite direction again," I say as I wrap my arms around him.

Pierre looks to my bodyguard with intense gratitude in his eyes. "Thank you, Kaipo."

— —

I'm lounging against Pierre, on the tile patio, and we're all wasted. Food isn't an option because the kitchen can't reopen until we get the all clear. Kai finally just hauled a bunch of booze on a cart to the private patio, and we helped ourselves. We're two hours into drinking, and now Kai's so hammered he can't walk, so it's unlikely that the bar will open tonight.

I crack up as the guys get to the tail end of a story about a pack of ambitious cougars who decided that Riptide was going to be their conquest during last year's circuit.

Riptide wipes laughter tears from his cheeks. "They were ridiculous. I've never had to hide and sneak like that in my life."

Kai's walkie-talkie buzzes, and we hear, "All clear. The bomb squad has completed their work. The resort lockdown is lifted."

I look over my shoulder at Pierre. "Now what? I don't even know if I can stand."

He laughs. "I don't either."

"You guys up for dragging the little grill to the beach?" Kai asks. "We can grill hot dogs and make a bonfire."

Everyone enthusiastically agrees.

"Jet was behind the bomb scare," I say to Pierre.

His brow furrows as he looks to Beastie Boy. "This guy's dangerous." He fills Beastie Boy in on the murder bag and the pictures of a dead girl.

Beastie Boy gives me a worried look as he and Pierre quietly confer.

"Think it's safe?" I ask.

Pierre glances around at everyone. "There's enough of us that I think so. If we're out of the villa, I'd rather be with the group, though." He smiles. "I want to show you how to night ride."

"We can ride at night?"

"Yup. Full-moon rides are magic."

I smile and attempt to get up. It doesn't go well. "Oh no," I mutter. I roll twice and use the momentum to stand. Once I'm on my feet, the world tips sideways, and I groan out, "So much upside-down, right side up."

Beastie Boy chuckles as he helps steady me.

When Ruckus falls over, it takes three guys to heft him back to his feet. Riptide manages to stand, but he requires the help of the fence. We all stare at each other and laugh.

I shake my head at Pierre. "I don't think I can find the beach, but if I do, I don't think I can get back to the villa." I swallow hard. "Jet's no joke, Pierre. We need to lock down."

Pierre nods. "You're probably right."

"We've filled in the circuit security," our bodyguard Kaipo informs. "They're actively searching for him. Reinforcements have been brought in. It's safe to go back to the suite."

Pierre grabs his board, and we head through the gate. He wraps his arm around me, and we wind and weave through the resort walkways with our bodyguards keeping a polite distance.

"I'm so sorry my crazy stalker caused this issue," I say quietly. "I didn't know life could be this amazing, and then reality came crashing in."

"I'm not going to let you get derailed. Jet is no match for security here." He takes a deep breath and admits, "All that was missing from my life was love, and I want to enjoy it."

"Your ease in the face of danger is bizarre," I say while glancing around pensively.

Pierre laughs a little. "If you only knew how many crazy stalkers I've had in the past year." He shrugs casually. "This is why we have security. Fame, obsession, insanity . . . I'm not new to it. What I *am* new to is love."

I snap a curious gaze his way.

Pierre smiles. "I was never willing to settle. I've had exactly one girlfriend, and that was for all of two weeks. Girls always have the wrong intentions with me. Because I can see the heart of relationships, I could always see their motives. I was waiting for someone who loved me for me."

I'm suddenly stone-cold sober as I pull him into a gazebo off the path. "Wait, what?"

He nods. "The only people who know that are Beastie Boy and Rocco. I was baffled that Rocco called me over to you, but he said he knew that you and I were meant to be. I told you I knew you were the one the moment I laid eyes on you. Your intentions are completely in the right place."

"Flings though, yes?"

He shakes his head.

"One-night stands?"

He shakes his head again. "I waited for my seashell."

My mouth drops open. "So . . . I was . . ."

He nods.

I put my hands over my face. "If I had known that I would have handled things differently. I certainly wouldn't have rushed us through forty-five minutes before my fitting."

Pierre laughs. "Everything is perfect. I wouldn't have changed anything."

I scrunch up my face awkwardly. "I'm sorry. I assumed. It never occurred to me to have this conversation. Seems like every guy I know who's over sixteen is a busy hoe."

Pierre wraps his arms around me. "I don't discuss it, and I specifically chose not to bring it up. I didn't want you to second-guess yourself." He gives me a look. "I've had a lot of lifetimes, Meley. The whole first-time thing loses its shock at this phase of reincarnation."

I laugh a little. "That's true, I suppose. You sure you're okay?"

"Positive. You're exactly who I want."

I lace my hands with his. "Think we can go back to the room, and you can have a new first time?"

He tips his head curiously. "We're well past the first time, Meley."

As I lead the way, I pull the key out of my backpack and then unlock the door for us to slide through. Riptide says goodnight to the bodyguards. After locking the door and bolting it tight, I lead him to the patio and turn on the waterfall fountain and overhead twinkle lights. I pull my Discman and little speaker from my backpack and set them on the table. As Pierre watches me curiously, I shuffle through my CD choices in my soft travel case and pop one in. With UB40's "The Way You Do the Things You Do" wafting from the little speaker, I walk to him and hold out my hand. He takes it, and we dance.

"You're worried for no reason, Meley," Pierre insists. "I'm fine."

I wince a little. "Will you tolerate some bad social decorum if I overshare?" Pierre nods, and I hesitantly say, "So, I was in your position with Adam. I didn't tell him my virginal secret. He felt bad about it, but . . ." I wince.

"Spill it, Meley," Pierre says as he stops dancing.

I sigh. "He was just using me. He proposed to Valerie right after. It wasn't exactly the whole magical fairy-tale virginity loss." I stare up into Pierre's eyes. "I'm not an Adam, and I need to right this with you."

Pierre scoffs. "I'm going to kill him. He's a known man-whore, so I'm not surprised, but he doesn't get a pass with you." His face scrunches. "What a jackass."

I crack up. "Surprise, surprise. Adam Stone is a selfish douche-kabob."

We start dancing again, and I revel in it. Finally having a chance to not dwell on a deadly nightmare with post-traumatic melt-downs is the most freeing experience. I despise all the worrying and brooding. Choosing to trust that the circuit security is what Kaipo assured, I let myself enjoy the moment.

Pierre turns me out before guiding me back in. I wrap my arms around his neck, and he leans down, kissing me. He picks me up, and I wrap my legs around his waist. He leans against the wall and hooks his other arm under my tush. I giggle.

"What?"

My eyes sparkle. "You make me feel really little."

He chuckles. "I think all your guys love that you're tiny. It seems to be a point of agreement."

"I don't have other guys, Pierre. You have zero competition."

He seems to melt a little, but then his expression morphs sad. "We have to go back to reality in a few days. Trey and Demitri will have watched the competition footage. There are conversations looming."

I shrug. "That's too bad, so sad, for Trey. Demitri's my best friend and always will be, but I'm not good enough for him roman-tically. I'm covered in things like gunshot wounds, and he finds flaws revolting."

"Flaws tell your story, Melanie." He contemplates this and finally sighs. "You deserve to know something about Demitri."

"Ugh. Let me guess. He really can't stand me?"

Pierre chuckles. "Quite the opposite. He adores you, and it bugs him. You're right that he loves perfection, and he's aware that your life path doesn't allow it. By the time you die in this lifetime, you'll likely be riddled with scars from everything you deal with." He smiles softly at me. "Demitri sees flawless women as up to his standards, but what he's yet to realize is that, for a woman to be flawless, she must be one of two very annoying things."

I grin. "Do tell."

"She's either so privileged that she'll drown him in debt and expectation, or she's so pampered that she'll smother him with neediness. Either is revolting. To be covered in scars means you lived, grew, conquered, and handled your shit."

I nod. "I take it that you plan to discuss this with him?"

Lost in thought, Pierre smiles and looks off at nothing. "Demitri's a good guy, and I won't allow him to get trapped by a black hole like Victoria. He needs to understand his errors so he can grow." He smirks at me. "His growth can wait until after you're thoroughly mine, though."

"He must strike you as competition," I tease.

"He would be my only competition."

I purr seductively, "I promise that you're the only one for me."

He puts me down and smacks my tush. "Inside, now please."

I guide him back inside with a giggle and lock the patio door behind me. We head to our bedroom, where I inform him, "We have nowhere to be for the rest of the night. So . . ." I unplug the clock on the nightstand. "That doesn't get plugged back in until we go to sleep." I close the door and pull the curtains shut.

He unties my bikini top and drops my skirt. My bikini bottoms tie at the sides. He unties them and picks me up, carrying me to the bed and carefully setting me down. I scoot back and lie with my shoulders propped on the down pillows. Pierre scoots next to me, and I pull the covers up.

I roll on my side and trace his abs absently. I giggle.

"What?"

"I can't help it. You're so cut, and I love it. You make my brain melt. My thoughts literally stutter when I'm around you."

"I'm blushing," Pierre says. "It's too dark to see it, but you should know."

We laugh.

I run my hand up his chest slowly and open my dark-water ability just enough for it to be teasing. He gasps and I lean in, kissing him lightly. I smile against his lips and whisper, "Your job is to lie here." Smiling through the dark, I hand him the drink he brought from the bar. "Now, you sip that while I make something crystal clear. You don't get to touch me. You lie there, and that's not up for argument. You, my love, are the best surfer on the planet. You're literally the hottest guy I've ever seen. I want you to be an egotistical dickhead for the next two hours because I want to do unspeakable things to the guy all the girls in the spectator stands are fantasizing about right now."

Pierre chuckles seductively. "You know I'm not that guy."

"That makes it even better." I kiss him.

He whispers, "Come here."

I shake my head flirtatiously. "What do you say?"

"Please?"

"Nope."

He growls, "Now."

"That's better."

CHAPTER 33

We wake to a call. I grapple blindly in the dark for the phone receiver and finally find it. "Hello?" I sound sleepy and hung over.

"Hey, Mel. Where's Rip?"

"Asleep. What's up?"

"Tell him to wake the hell up. We've got somewhere to be."

I groan. "There was just a bomb threat. Really? We're not going anywhere."

"Up. Now."

"Ruckus, I assure you we need showers."

Pierre laughs and takes the phone. "We really need showers. What do you want, bro?"

I can hear Ruckus laughing. I roll over and snuggle on Pierre's chest. He wraps his arm around me, pulls me in tighter, and runs his nails lightly up my back.

I whisper, "Hanging up nooow."

Pierre groans and stretches. "Please tell me you're kidding."

Alarmed, I sit up.

"Damn it. I can't miss that, but I'm incredibly happy lying here with Meley."

I raise my eyebrows as he hands me the phone.

I hang it up as Pierre informs, "Storm's coming in."

"And?"

"Recommended evacuation of the area."

I groan. "We have to pack up?"

He chuckles. "No. We need to grab our boards and head to the beach. Waves are massive."

I look at the clock on my nightstand. "It's four in the morning."

"Yup. Welcome to Dawn Patrol, baby girl." He hefts himself up. "I brought your wet suit. You'll need it. It'll be cold. Screw showers. That's what the ocean is for."

With a wince, I inform him, "I'm a shower girl."

"Yeah, well, I'm a covered-in-sex, roll-out-of-bed-and-surf guy, apparently."

I laugh, heft myself up, and start rotating my sore neck. "All right. I'm up." My mood shifts pensively. "What about Jet and the bomb threat?"

Pierre shrugs. "The whole group will be there. If that scrawny freak shows up, we can take him out."

Pierre pulls our wet suits from the closet and hands mine to me.

I throw on my bikini but have trouble tying it. "My fingers are protesting this plan."

He chuckles and ties the back of my bikini top for me. I put on the bottoms before tugging on the skintight wet suit and following Pierre to the living room, where he unzips my surfboard case and hands it to me.

"Now for the real lesson. Let's see what you can do when the energy gets wild out there. You can harness and use it. Someone with your energy-working ability should be impressive once you get the hang of it. It's intense."

My grin is laced dangerous, and my dark-water side slides up behind my eyes. Pierre smirks to match and grabs his board. We step out of our villa into the rain. Pierre searches right and left before informing, "Coast is clear."

"Where are our security guards?" I ask, unsure about this plan.

"Asleep in their villa next to ours. They have to sleep some-time." He raises an eyebrow my way. "So does Jet. Let's roll"

When I start to back up, he says, "Nope. Come on. Trust me."

"Warm bed. Warm hot tub. Warm boyfriend. Ugh." I wince at the rain.

He grins at me. "We'll get in the hot tub and back in bed in a few hours. The competition starts at one, and there's plenty of time. Also, *aw* . . . I like being your boyfriend. Think you're up for a tattoo with me?"

I nod. "I would love that."

He grins. "I want a seashell."

"Perfect. You pick it, and we stick it."

He puts an arm around my shoulders, and we lug our boards through the rain and down the winding pathways to the beach. When we get to the wet sand, the beach is covered up with our surf crowd. They all greet us, seeming thrilled with the weather. Meanwhile, I feel like a wet pure-bred puppy left out in the cold.

I grimace as Ruckus runs our way and asks, "What's the matter, Melanie?"

Everyone gathers around as I explain. "Ever been wrapped around a Greek god and been interrupted?"

Ruckus appears amused. "Can't say I have."

"Well, I have, and it's irritating."

Everyone laughs, and Caroline informs, "Trust us. Naked Riptide doesn't compare to that ocean right now."

I huff. "I don't know . . . He's something."

Pierre warns that I'm on edge about Jet. Most of the guys

showboat in reply, clearly quite convinced they can take him. Pierre laughs, but I'm unsure. I study my intuition and find that there doesn't seem to be any Jet danger looming.

I sigh. "All right. Let's do this."

"Wait," Beastie Boy barks. He points to the turbulent ocean. "Do you really think Melanie can handle that?"

Pierre looks out at the ocean before grinning. "My girl is a metaphysical beast. She'll harness it."

Zane blinks rapidly. "You energy workers are always convinced you're superheroes. You're not. That ocean is a mean mother right now, Rip. I think this is a mistake."

"She'll be fine," Riptide insists.

"I'll take Melanie out while she gets a handle on it," Zane offers.

"Beastie, back off," Pierre says irritably.

"I'm not making a play for your girl," Zane barks back. "I'm twice your size, and I have a better chance of helping her if it goes bad."

"Enough," Pierre says forcibly. "Don't put doubt in her. Give Melanie a shot." The two guys stare at each other for a long stretch. Finally, Zane shakes his head and relents.

We all head down to the water and paddle out. I struggle to stay on my board. The water churns and crashes, and I'm tempted to turn back. We get to what I assume is the break line, but everything out here is chaos.

"I don't think I can do this," I yell over the pounding waves and storm.

"It's just surfing, Melanie," Pierre assures me. I look around hesitantly, and he grimaces. "You're really good on this board. I know you're new to this, but the only way to get better is to do it. If you back out, I think the daredevil in you will regret it."

I slide a cagey gaze Pierre's way. "When your life regularly boils down to impending doom, you don't intentionally put yourself in danger."

"It's just a storm. Sometimes we have to face our fears. That said, I have a safety measure." He pulls a glowing strap from his wet suit that he unzips a little. "Whatever you do," he yells over the crashing thunder, "don't take this off." He puts the glowing wristband tightly on my wrist. "If you go under, that will help me find you."

I attach my ankle strap, so I don't lose my board, and wait at the break line. Every wave that comes my way scares the crap out of me. The ocean boils, and I'm overcome with fear. I have a lot of post-traumatic issues from past-life deaths, and apparently, I can add stormy seas to the list.

Pierre takes off on a wave. I was supposed to go with him, but I flat couldn't do it. I'm frozen on my board. I decide to paddle back to shore, but then a massive wave comes my way and crashes over me, rolling me over. I scream and swallow ocean water. I flail and can't figure out which way is up as I'm swirled violently and dragged by an undertow. I try to swim, but my hand hits sand, and I suddenly realize I went the wrong way. I push hard off the bottom and feel like I swim forever. My head finally breaks the surface and I gasp, but another wave crashes over me, and I inhale lungs full of water. They burn, and I panic again as I flail deep in the water. My vision goes spotty.

I can't find the surface!

I kick hard, but it doesn't help. I fight for what feels like forever. My lungs seize, and I'm jerked back and forth in a way that I've never felt before in this lifetime, though I'm positive I've experienced it in the past.

I'm drowning. It's not actually as bad as I always feared.

My world goes black.

— —

"Damn it, Melanie! Come on!"

Something pushes on my chest repeatedly, and then I sputter. Someone turns me over.

"Barf it up, baby," Pierre says.

"Thank God!" someone else exclaims. "Holy shit, we almost lost her!"

I hack out a lungful of salt water. It hurts, and I try to gasp. I curl around the pain of my burning lungs.

Someone rolls me back over, and Pierre's looking down at me. He's clearly been crying. He shakes his head as we're hit with pelting rain. His expression crumples, and he puts his head on my chest, exhaling hard. "That scared the shit out of me."

"You brought her back. It's okay, Rip." Ruckus asks me, "Do you know where you are?"

I nod. "Hawaii."

Ruckus smiles. "What's your name?"

"Melanie."

"She's fine," he announces. "Everyone, calm down."

I look around, and all our friends are there. It's obvious from their expressions that things got bad.

Pierre pulls me into his lap. He presses his cheek against my head, which is resting on his chest. "I took off and thought you were right behind me. Next thing I know, we're all headed to shore, and you were gone. Thank God for that fluorescent band on your wrist. Your ankle tether came loose. We found your board a long way from your body. You didn't have a heartbeat when I hauled you in."

I flop my head back. "Thank you for rescuing me, and sorry to worry you guys."

Another coughing fit starts. I gag and choke. Zane hauls me up from Pierre's lap. He drapes me over his forearm and squeezes my stomach. It hurts terribly.

I throw up a massive round of salt water. I wince and sheepishly say, "I'm sorry."

Zane helps me stand. "That was the goal. It needed to come up."

I nod a little.

"You okay?" Zane asks.

"I think so." Managing to stand on my own, I discover that I feel all right. I grab my board from the sand next to me and start walking.

"What do you think you're doing?" Pierre hollers.

I grin over my shoulder. "Fuck that ocean. I'm going back in and making it my bitch."

Everyone throws fists in the air and yells, "YEEESSS!"

Pierre grabs his board and jogs to me. "You're definitely my girl."

We all paddle out together and stop. I have Pierre on one side and Zane on the other. Zane's watching me with a caged expression. A massive wave comes our way.

I grin wickedly. "Here we go boys." I pop up and take off, dropping every shield I have and replacing my energy with the ocean's raging pulse. This time, I work with the ocean and surf my ass off.

Riptide pulls up next to me as I flop down and straddle my board. I shake my drenched hair from my eyes and yell over the storm, "Again!"

He grins at me in the soft light of dawn, and we paddle back out. We bring in the sunrise with a few more runs and then wade back to shore.

Ruckus high-fives me as the rain calms to a sprinkle. "Welcome to the dark side, Mel. You died, came back, and kicked ass!"

I beam from ear to ear, and my gaze meets Pierre's. "Naked pancake time, now please."

Everyone laughs, and we haul our boards up the beach to the pathway leading to the villas. I thank everyone again for helping me.

Pierre's arm drapes over my shoulders, and we say goodbye to our friends as they disappear to their villa turnoffs. Pierre unlocks our door, and we get our boards situated on the tile entryway. I strip off my wet suit and hang it on one of the drying hooks, then untie my swimsuit and head to the patio.

After calling in a room service order, Pierre comes out to the patio just as I sink into the hot tub. He climbs in after me and pulls me into his lap. "I've never been that scared."

I look up at him. "I'm okay."

He closes his eyes tight.

My hand slides onto his cheek. "Will you show me? Like you did with the past-life memory?"

He nods and puts his forehead on mine. I close my eyes as the memory plays in my mind. I see through Pierre's eyes as he gets to the safety of waist-deep water. He scans the group, lit by the moon.

Panic zings through him. "Where's Melanie?"

Everyone looks around, and chaos abounds. They paddle into the crashing waves and fan out.

Pierre yells, "Look for a pink emergency wristband!" As they all search frantically but come up empty, Pierre desperately paddles farther out. His mind is racing with every possible thought. *Oh my God, if I lose her now, I won't make it.* He's completely overcome with raging turmoil.

Suddenly, he spots a faint glow and unhooks his ankle band. Someone grabs his board as Pierre dives in and swims hard. He sees me deep in the water. I study myself in the memory. I'm creepily pale. My hair floats around me as I look like I'm hanging, suspended in time. My eyes are open, with a dead emptiness.

Pierre's heart nearly explodes as he realizes I'm already gone. He grabs me and kicks hard. His head breaks the surface, and he gasps to fill his burning lungs. Rolling to his side, he presses me to his chest and propels us in the direction of the shore. Several people grab onto him and help him contend with my dead weight.

When we reach the shallows, he stands and picks me up before running to the sand and laying me down. He laces his fingers together and pumps my chest hard, starting CPR. My mouth spurts water. He keeps at it, but I don't come to.

Pierre thinks, *Nooo! This can't happen. She can't do this.* He screams, "Come on, Melanie!"

Everyone's kneeling around me, and he keeps up the chest compressions for what feels like forever.

"She's gone, Riptide," Ruckus says tearfully. He tries to pull him away, but Pierre won't stop.

"There's no way this is happening," Pierre growls.

Zane grabs Pierre's arms. "Stop, Rip." Zane flips me over, holding me up around the waist with his arm.

"Can you do it?" Pierre begs.

Zane thumps the middle of my back hard, and water spurts from my mouth again. "Come on, girl," he snarls. He leans my limp back against his chest and grips my stomach with his clasped hands. He pumps hard, and water pours again. "Try now," Zane instructs as he lays me on my back in the sand.

Pierre starts chest compressions again, and water doesn't spurt this time. Finally, he says beggingly, "Damn it, Melanie! Come on!"

That's when I take a gurgling inhale, and Pierre drops his head back and exhales hard. His arms burn from the effort to save me.

He rolls me over. "Barf it up, baby."

There's a ton of chatter, but I don't remember hearing anything but his voice.

The memory ends, and I open my eyes. "Are you okay?"

He shakes his head. "No. Beastie was right. I shouldn't have taken you out there."

"I appreciate that you had faith in my ability. It's okay, Pierre." I change topics. "You're really sweet," I say with a smile, "and you actually do love me." I study him. "Your memory-sharing ability is crazy. In the memory, I can even hear your thoughts and feel your emotions."

He smiles softly. "I'm glad my feelings didn't bother you. Indeed, I do love you. Wait here. I need to handle something." He hefts himself out of the hot tub and heads back inside.

A few minutes later, there's a knock at the door.

Pierre comes back out and announces, "Your pancakes are here."

I dry off and head in. We sit at the table and start eating as we watch promo commercials and news coverage of yesterday's qualifiers, culminating with the bomb threat. Riptide and I seem to be the hot new gossip, and we're featured in a lot of what's shown. I smile as a commercial for the competition comes on. At the end of the commercial, the on-screen Pierre runs to the on-screen me and swings her around. We watch as he rubs his nose on mine with the ocean at sunset in the background. It looks like a dream vacation scene.

He doesn't say much, but he keeps looking at me with fear in his eyes.

I clear my throat. "After yesterday's bomb threat, I'm worried about the competition today."

Pierre shakes his head. "Nah. Management will be extra cautious. We're fine."

We finish breakfast, and he instructs, "Get showered and dressed. I laid out two new dresses for you."

"*More* new dresses?"

He nods.

In the bedroom, I find a gorgeous black dress exactly like the red one that I wore to dinner. The other dress is a pretty blue one unlike anything I'd normally wear, but I instantly love it.

I get in the shower, and after a few minutes, he slides in with me and closes the glass door behind him. We make quick work of cleaning up. I hand him a towel, and we dry off.

When I cross to the vanity and reach for my makeup kit, Pierre shakes his head. "Brush your hair and get dressed. No makeup. I want you just like this."

With a soft smile, I start brushing my hair. "I love that so much. I've never been as comfortable as I am with you."

He smiles. "I hate makeup. The whole beauty industry's a racket designed to make women feel like shit about themselves so makeup companies can make millions. I'll be damned if someone plays my girl that way. The universe made you perfect."

I slip on the blue dress before turning and burying my head in his chest. The gesture comes off as more frantic than I intended.

He puts a hand gently on the back of my head. "You okay, Meley?"

I nod. "Thank you for letting me be me. I despise feeling like I'm not good enough."

He wraps me up and holds me lightly. "I promise you'll always be good enough." He tips up my chin and looks in my eyes. "I love you."

I melt. "I love you too."

He's wearing a pair of white linen pants with a long-sleeved white linen shirt featuring blue embroidery.

"This is the outfit," I say, wiggling my shoulders. "Yup. I want you to wear this *always*."

He smiles and laces his hand with mine.

As we leave the villa, I ask, "Where are we going?"

"For a walk on the beach."

Our bodyguards join us at a respectful distance. Knowing they're watching for trouble, I decide this is an okay plan.

I squeal happily as we get to the sand and enjoy the mostly vacant expanse. It's still early, and people haven't quite gotten started for the day.

As we reach a private spot, our bodyguards turn their backs, scanning for trouble.

Pierre faces me. "I'm not a formal guy. I've been through too many lifetimes to give a damn about societal rules and bullshit. With that said, I want you to be mine." He pulls a white leather-covered little box from his pocket and opens it.

My mouth drops open. Inside is a stunning delicate gold band. On top are two pearls, one silver and rainbowy and the other white with a pink shimmer.

"I love you, and I'm asking for the rest of this lifetime with you."

I delicately touch the pearls. They're soft and somehow feel alive.

"You need to understand something," he says. "What I'm asking holds weight. They're Hawaiian wedding pearls. It's a thing, kind of like a Celtic claddagh wedding band. Not all traditions require all the ceremonies and nonsense. Surfers tend to keep it simple. If I put this on you, every surfer on the planet will view you as married to me."

I look up at him and nod, unable to speak because I'm choked up.

His eyes light up as he smiles and slides the ring out, closing the box and putting it back in his pocket. He slips the ring on my finger, and it fits perfectly. He leans down and kisses me softly. Everything about the moment, including the clapping thunder in the storm-cloud-filled distance is perfect.

"It's beautiful," I breathe out as I gaze at the ring. I look up at him. "Thank you. How did this happen?"

"I went shopping for it while you were in rehearsal. If everything went how I thought it would on this trip, I vowed not to leave here without seeing what you'd say."

Suddenly overwhelmed, I wobble my head. "I'm sixteen and already promised myself to another guy once."

He shakes his head. "You aren't sixteen. Don't get caught up in the number from this lifetime. You're ancient and allowed to do as you please, at least in your own heart." He cups my jaw with his hands. "I wanted desperately to marry you in our one other lifetime together, but you were married to Trey. The second I saw him take that ring off your finger at the airport, I vowed to put my own in its place."

I study him. "There's a big difference between a cute high school promise ring and this." I hold up my ring-bearing hand. "You've known me for a week. This trip is a fantasy, and yeah, we have the tour ahead of us. But eventually, I'll need to go back to reality, where I have two soulmates and have to sit through six class periods a day. Oh, plus, I'm currently being stalked by a murderer."

Pierre shrugs. "I'll flatten Jet for coming near my wife, and you'll be done with school sooner rather than later. None of that bothers me. You'll move in with me. I plan to talk to Rich."

"Rich is going to shit kittens, Pierre! He said no when Trey asked permission to get *engaged* to me," I remind him. "You're talking about us already being surfer married and moving in together."

Pierre squints. "Trey's a douche, and I'm awesome. Therein lies the distinction." He smiles with vibrant sarcasm as I crack up.

"I agree about the douchey distinction, but my parents still might not hop on this bandwagon." My face scrunches. "I don't even know where you live."

He laughs. "I guess I should show you when we get home. I have a surf shop on the beach, the business I inherited when my dad passed. I live in the condo above." He gives me a come-hither look. "You'll love it."

"Yes, to all of it. This is exactly what I want." I give him a pointed look. "I'm letting *you* be the one to con Rich into this, though. I'm staying out of that battle."

Pierre laughs.

By the time we enter the restaurant, the rest of our party has already gathered around the same table we occupied for dinner a few nights ago. They enthusiastically greet us, and all the ladies hug me.

"Is she your Brenda?" Ruckus exclaims.

Pierre chuckles. "That didn't take long."

"Brenda?" I ask.

"It means wife," Pierre explains. "Or love of your life."

I rattle my head. "You guys have all this slang. I have a lot to learn."

The girls grab my hand and inspect the pearl ring. Several tear up and hug me again. They squeal and hug Pierre.

Zane's staring at Pierre with his mouth open. "Seriously? That was quick."

"She nearly died, and I couldn't wait," Pierre says with a shrug. "It is what it is. I'm in love with her."

Despite his clear misgivings, Zane congratulates us. I'm unsure if his issue is that he really doesn't like me, or that things are moving so fast.

As we take a seat, everyone simmers down. I lace my hand with Pierre's, and he absently toys with my ring. I smile softly.

A mimosa is plunked down in front of me. I thank the waitress.

Zane sits on my other side and quietly asks, "You okay?"

"I am. Thank you again for saving me." I smile brightly. "Also, thank you for partnering with me. You helped drag me through the fastest rehearsal ever."

He chuckles. "You learn quick. I give you credit. I'm glad you're coming on board."

"Do you have an issue with me?" I say bluntly.

"No," he says in surprise. "I'm just shocked. Pierre doesn't date. Apparently, little bro knows what he wants when he meets it, though."

"Seems like you two are really close."

"Our group's been at it a long time. Welcome to the inner circle, Melanie."

"Thank you," I reply, relieved that he seems okay with me.

Pierre checks his watch. "We have to be at the competition in two hours."

Everyone starts excitedly chattering and speculating about how each surfer is likely to rank. The general consensus is that Riptide's got first place in the bag, but he proves humble about it.

"Any new trouble with Jet?" Zane asks, putting a damper on the mood.

Pierre rubs his face. "You're usually the jokester of the group. Why are you suddenly such a downer?"

Zane sets down his coffee cup and leans forward to hit Pierre with a penetrating stare. "I guess I have questions that you should be bogged down with, Pierre."

Pierre sighs. "Hit me with them."

Clearly frustrated, Zane shakes his head. "Every once in a while, you remind me how young you are. All right, let's get down to the nut cutting." He calls over our bodyguards. "After the threat yesterday, was a bomb *actually* found?"

"No," Kalino replies. "Just a threat."

"Was it called in? Did they trace the number? Where was the call tracked to?"

"Called in. Number was untraceable."

"It was Jet," I say. "Intuition knowledge. I have no way to prove it, though."

Zane studies me. "How accurate is that intuition of yours?"

I shrug. "When it gives me info, it's right. This time, I got clear information that it was Jet who made the call. It doesn't always work that way, though. I trust it when it's clear, but when it's vague, it's *really* vague."

"So, we have no idea if this psycho is here on the island, or if he called in the threat from California?"

Zane is met with blank stares from everyone but me.

This appears to aggravate him. "Don't you think that's an important bit of intel? Someone needs to check plane records! The police need to be tracking this guy. I mean, have the police even made *any* move to arrest him over the murder kit you found and the dead body pictures?"

I shrug timidly. Zane's intensity makes me nervous. "I have no update on that," I admit.

"Why?" Zane demands. I cower a little, and he softens his vibe. "I'm not trying to scare you, but you've been here several days.

You haven't called for an update?"

"I should have. I got so caught up in having a break from the bad stuff that I guess I lost track of reality."

Zane gives Pierre a harsh look. "I get that you're all bubbly over her, but if you're as serious about Melanie as that ring indicates," he motions toward my ring hand, "then you need to take care of business. The Jet situation doesn't just *poof* because you're having such a good time surfing and rolling around with that tiny dance fantasy."

Clearly annoyed, Pierre laces his hands on the top of his head and closes his eyes. He doesn't say anything for a long stretch. Finally, he opens his eyes and levels Zane with a steely look. "I appreciate your concern. I know you mean well, but I've hired security, we have a safe villa, I filled all of you in on the threat and what to look for, and we're being careful. Yes, there are risks, but I refuse to lock Melanie away. Never mind what's going on between us. She's dancing in her first paid gig, in Hawaii, on national television. I won't ruin that for her. She's fully aware of the danger she faces. Talking like this is only making things worse."

Zane studies me again with soft eyes. "I'm sorry to put a pall on the fun. Congratulations on your first big gig. I didn't realize any of that."

I shrug a little, and happiness lights in my eyes. "You've made the dance show really incredible. Thank you for that. I'll never forget this."

Charmed, Zane quirks his mouth. "You're welcome. That was nice of you to say. I'm sorry I was harsh."

"It's okay. I get that you're just concerned."

Ruckus laughs a little and raises his eyebrow my way. "The fact that your first pro gig is with Beastie Boy is a little baffling. Your luck with stalkers sucks, but your professional luck is astronomical."

I look to Zane curiously, and he shakes his head at Ruckus. "Leave it at that, please," he says.

"Why?" Ruckus asks. "Tell her."

Zane makes a sound like a scoff and a laugh at the same time. "She's having fun. She's comfortably confident. Let this be." He gets up and says goodbye before leaving.

My expression slumps as blazing insecurity bubbles up. "He doesn't seem to like me much," I say quietly.

Ruckus is suddenly serious. "That's not true. When Beastie Boy doesn't like someone, he ignores them. I think the problem is that he respects you, he's incredibly concerned, and you're now his family because he views Pierre as his best friend and little brother."

"What about that whole cryptic exchange?" I ask timidly.

Ruckus winces. "Sorry, but Zane's about to be pissed. I'm going to fill her in."

"You *should* tell her, Ruck," Caroline encourages.

"Do you watch movies, Melanie?" Ruckus asks encouragingly.

I shake my head. "I read a lot. I watch a little TV, but it's not really my thing. Why?"

"You have no idea who Zane is, do you?" Ruckus appears a touch amused.

"Well, he's known as Beastie Boy. He's really patient and taught me two lifts I've never done. Does that count?"

Ruckus chuckles. "Zane's a big deal. He obviously has a dance background, but that's not his main career. The only time he still dances is on this circuit, and he only does that to spend time with all of us. He left a movie set to come do this show."

"He's an actor?"

Pierre's forehead scrunches. "Do you really not know who he is?"

I shrug. "No clue. He's an amazing dancer, though."

"I vote that we get the concierge to rustle us up some movies for a viewing party tonight after the competition," Ruckus says.

"Bad plan," Pierre says. "It'll piss off Beastie. He asked us not to fill her in. I think he's taken with the way Melanie treats him like a normal guy."

"Is he not normal?" I ask, amused.

Pierre laughs quietly. "Zane is a very normal, down-to-earth person. The problem is that other people rarely treat him that way. You talk to him like he's an everyday guy, like he's part of the cast. I sense that he likes it and doesn't want things to get weird."

I wobble my head about. "Well, nothing that's been revealed so far really fazes me. I'm hoping to work with him again in the future, and I don't want to make him mad. I'm not generally someone who gets starstruck anyhow. I vote we leave it at that. Don't rent movies. If he's enjoying being a normal guy, there's no reason that can't continue."

"No curiosity?" Ruckus asks.

I laugh. "You're trouble, Ruckus. No curiosity about his movies. I just want to enjoy this trip. He's fun. You're all fun. Dancing in the show is fun. Let's not worry about anything. My guess is that Jet saw the competition footage of me and Pierre and figured out we're together. He's petty and had to make it known that on top of being a necrophiliac stalker, he's also a jealous, immature mess. So he called in a threat from California."

I stand and toss my napkin. "Now, you all have a competition to get to. I apologize that my crazy life interfered with what matters. Let's get to it."

Pierre stands, taking my hand. Everyone says goodbye and heads to their villas to get ready.

CHAPTER 34

As the other girls and I sit in the bleachers, I'm wearing my opening show costume, and the media have taken more pictures of me than I prefer. The one downfall to being with Riptide is that I've been pulled into the chaos of his celebrity. I do my best to ignore the scrutiny.

The ocean is boiling with angry black clouds in the background. Pierre tried to talk some sense into the judges about postponing, but they deemed this a newsworthy wave day. Several of the best competitors wipe out brutally, and I'm nervous for Pierre's upcoming run. My intuition is nagging at me, but I shove it aside while simultaneously praying it's nothing. There's no distinct information, just an undercurrent of mild panic. The last thing I want to do is be deemed a crazy overbearing wife a few hours after he put a ring on my finger.

Riptide's name is announced, and he pops up and takes on a terrifyingly huge wave. He's having a jaw-dropping run. I'm just about to relax into a smile when I hear it: a white-hot flash ripples from somewhere underneath him. An instant later, there's a massive boom, and a ball of fire rises from out of the water and blasts through his board. I slowly stand, watching in horror as Pierre flies ten feet up and then smacks hard into the water. What's left of his board is pulled in two different directions, the fire extinguishing in the waves. A disbelieving hush falls over the crowd. Tears fill my eyes. I'm frozen in place.

Stunned and confused about what just happened, everyone watches the ocean, but Pierre doesn't surface. Now panic starts to rise, and every surfer hits the water, paddling out in a line.

It's as if the crowd suddenly wakes up all at once. Screams punctuate the air, and people crush toward the exits, screaming about a bomb.

I have to find him!

My legs feel like gelatin as I run down the stairs. Zane's racing my way. He gets to me, and I grab his arm, trying to steady myself. I close my eyes, searching for Pierre's energy. I find him in the ocean and run for the water. Ruckus sees me make a racing beeline and waves me over. I skid flat on his board, and he lies on me. We paddle hard, our friends following, and I dive off and swim under the surface. Pierre is deep in the water, his energy leading me straight to him. I grab him just as Ruckus gets to us, and we kick hard together, hauling Pierre up, breaking the surface with a gasp.

Emergency paramedics pull up on a jet ski, and Pierre is strapped to a backboard and raced to the shore. Everyone gathers around and picks up the board while I wrap my hands around Pierre's head. He's covered in burns and missing one leg from the thigh down. My mind jars violently between relief that he's breathing and shock at the sight of the bleeding stump where his leg used to be. I look up at Zane, who's gaping in disbelief at his best friend. Unable to breathe, I allow my dark-water side to rise from deep inside me. Suddenly able to think, I focus down and in, finding Pierre locked within his mind.

When we get to an ambulance, paramedics try to pull me away from Pierre. I turn and frantically explain to the surfers, "I've located him in his mind. I have to be there to try to bring him back."

"You must let her go with him," Ruckus yells to the paramedics over the sounds of chaos. "She's his Brenda. She's also a *Hese*." At my quizzical look, he explains, "Witch."

This seems to be all the explanation the paramedics need, because I'm herded into the ambulance, and we take off with sirens screaming. A paramedic puts a neck brace on Pierre and starts assessing his vitals while the other tourniquets his leg. They attach a breathing bag on his face, while I clamp my hands on his forehead. I close my eyes and drop into meditation.

I open my eyes in my mind and draw Pierre in.

He looks down at me, dread in the apparition of his eyes. *"Melanie, this is bad."*

"You can survive the leg amputation!"

Pierre shakes his head. *"It's not about my leg. My neck's broken, and my brain's swelling."*

I frantically shake my head in my mind. *"No! We're not doing this. You're not leaving. The doctors will figure this out."*

In our minds, Pierre wraps his arms around me and holds me. Though he doesn't say anything, his silence speaks volumes.

"Please don't go," I beg him.

"I need you to listen to me, because I don't have much time." In the realm of our minds, he pulls back and holds my cheeks in his hands. *"My time with you has been brief, but it has completed me. This is my last lifetime, and it's been truly fulfilled because I got to love you. I want you to live your life, and I never want you to doubt that you are the love of my life."*

Tears stream down my cheeks in reality and in my mind. I rattle my head, frantically protesting what he's saying.

He whispers, *"Baby, I know. I'm destroyed too. I really thought I was going to get to live an entire lifetime with you."* He turns his head and seems to listen to something before looking down at me. *"I'm being called. I have to go."* He leans down and kisses me before suddenly fading away.

My eyes snap wide just as the heart rate monitor in the ambulance hits a dead, never-ending trill. As my entire body collapses around my seizing lungs, I cry myself sick while the paramedics frantically work to save him. We pull up to the hospital, where a swarm of reporters is gathered to record my heartbreak as I get out of the ambulance. A van pulls up, and all the surf guys in Pierre's group rush out. One look at my hysteria is all they need to know. While reporters yap and carry on around me, I collapse to my knees.

Ruckus pushes through the crush and hauls me to my feet. He picks me up and cradles me as the paramedics run through the doors with Pierre on a gurney. When we're stopped at the waiting room door, Ruckus, Zane, and the guys crowd tightly around me.

"He's already gone," I whisper. "I dropped into meditation, and he said goodbye to me."

Ruckus turns, and the guys all surround him as he carries me out the doors to the van, where they lay me on the floor in the back of the carpeted but otherwise empty vehicle they use to haul their boards. I curl up in a ball and die inside as the guys all sit around me with tears rolling down their cheeks.

While we wait for news, our bodyguards let us know that authorities are searching for Jet, but he's nowhere to be found.

"My guess is that he hired out the hit," Zane says, seething with quiet anger.

I look at Zane with huge eyes. "What do we do?" I manage to get out around a strangled sob.

"We wait, honey," Zane says. His eyes are haunted. He looks to Ruckus and quietly says, "She looks really young when she's destroyed."

Ruckus's chin shakes, but he holds it together. "She's sixteen, Zane."

"Holy crap." Zane says with sincerity, "I have a little sister your age. Can you trust me to help you?"

I nod spastically.

Ruckus says, "Come here, Melanie. I've got you."

"Back off, Ruck," Zane says. He gathers me into his lap, leaning his back against the metal wall of the panel van. He holds me like a toddler for a long stretch. When his phone rings, Rocco collects it from Zane's dance bag.

The moment Zane answers, a woman starts screeching from the other end of the line. Zane swallows hard. "Ms. Alice," he says with a quiet but firm tone, "I need you to calm down. I'm holding Melanie. We're hiding in the back of a van in the hospital parking lot because there are media vultures all over the hospital. I'll call you when I have an update." Zane pauses and listens. "No."

I hear Chelsea lose it but can't make out what she's saying.

"I know," Zane says. "I need you to take a deep breath. There's stuff that must happen. If I give you a list, can you help me?" He must get an affirmative because he immediately starts in with the instructions. "I need you to call Pierre's lawyer. I don't know who he has down as his power of attorney in case of an emergency. Someone's going to need to make choices, I fear." He listens again and says, "Yes, he pearled Melanie, but we can't put this on her. There's no legal paperwork, and she's underage. Even though all of us respect where they're at with things, she still wouldn't be considered his wife legally." He pauses to listen, nodding. "You need to call Rocco also. I think we have a lot to handle, but I'm waiting for official word." There's another pause. Zane closes his eyes. "As well as you can expect. I'll make sure she's covered." He listens again before saying, "You need to get her mom or stepdad here. The police are involved, so we need someone who has legal authority over her. I'll stay with her until you have an update." With that, he ends the call.

"This is bad, isn't it?" I ask.

Zane nods calmly and pulls me in tighter. "We'll get help here for you. For now, it's enough that you're safe. Kalino and Kaipo are outside. We'll figure out what to do."

After what feels like forever, there's a knock on the van door.

Ruckus opens it, and a doctor slides inside and closes the door to block out the media vultures. "Is this his girlfriend?"

"No," Ruckus answers, gesturing to my hand that bears Pierre's ring.

The doctor seems to understand what it means. I sit up from my spot on the van floor and look at him.

Before the doctor can say anything, Zane says, "Full disclosure, Pierre has no living blood relatives. He and Melanie aren't legally married either, and she's not old enough to make life-or-death decisions."

The doctor looks at him all starry-eyed but doesn't say anything.

"I spoke with Jessica Suriah, Pierre's lawyer, about an hour ago," Zane continues. "Apparently, I'm down on his medical 'Do Not Resuscitate' paperwork, along with his other friend, Rocco, who isn't here."

The doctor finally snaps out of it. "Zane Drell. It's so nice to meet you."

"Likewise."

From his expression, the doctor apparently recognizes Zane from his movies. "Okay," he says. "Then we need to make some decisions." He levels Zane with a heavily weighted look. "In your opinion, would Riptide want Melanie involved in the decision-making?"

Zane blinks rapidly. "Some of it, yes. The harder stuff, I don't know. I'll be the one to make final decisions, *but* I'll consult Melanie. This keeps you out of hot water at least. If the answer comes from me, you're in the clear legally."

The doctor takes an even breath. "That works for me." He quietly informs, "Riptide has a broken neck and a fractured skull. His right leg is missing from the thigh down, as you likely know. His other foot has irreparable damage from the explosion. It was definitely a bomb that harmed him. We have him on life support, and his heart is currently beating. Scans show that he has suffered a tremendous brain bleed."

It's all I can do to hold myself together. I'm numb with shock but feel like I'm going to lose my mind.

Zane rubs his face hard.

"Zane and Melanie," the doctor says before pausing for a calm inhale. "I'm afraid Pierre is brain-dead. We need to take him off life support before his body heals enough that he can breathe on his own. If we don't, he'll spend the rest of his life as an empty shell. I know you don't want that, and I'm positive a man like Pierre wouldn't want that."

"What happens now?" I'm terrified of the answer.

The doctor gives me a look that breaks my heart all over again. He switches his broken gaze to Zane. "As his DNR assignee, you need to decide if you want to keep him alive, or end life support."

Zane tips up my chin to stare in my eyes. I know he's destroyed, but he does a remarkable job of holding it together. "Do you understand everything the doctor has said?"

"His body is destroyed," I say, my voice quivering. "He's brain-dead. Even if he heals enough to breathe on his own, he won't be anything but an empty, breathing body."

With his brow furrowed gravely, Zane nods. "I'll make the final choice, but I want to give you an opportunity to have a say in this."

I fight to breathe around tight lungs.

"Do you have asthma?" the doctor asks as I start wheezing.

I nod, and Ruckus quickly hands me his inhaler. I take a puff and squeeze my eyes closed. I put my quaking hands over my face. "There's no chance?" I barely manage to get out.

"There's nothing I can do," the doctor says.

I nod jarringly.

"Zane," Ruckus says, his eyes on me, "I don't think this pressure is good for her."

Zane holds up his hand. "I agree, but Pierre felt strongly that Melanie could handle things. I want to give her the respect of an opinion."

"I can do this," I manage to get out. After a long moment of brain-rattling thought, I choke out, "Zane, I think you need to end the life support." The moment I get the directive out, tears roll down my cheeks, and I can't breathe around the pain in my chest.

The doctor takes my hand while I lose every square inch of my shit. After I calm enough to breathe again, he says, "I know that's a hard decision, but it's my medical recommendation." He looks to Zane. "Now, I need your official answer."

"I'd like to end life support." Zane is rock solid in his declaration. He puts an arm around me and assures, "I made the decision, Melanie. You didn't. It's not on you."

The doctor asks, "Would you all like to come in and say good-bye to him?"

Everyone nods as they silently cry.

I try to dry my tears as the van door is opened, but it does no good because the stream is too steady. I opt for crying as calmly as I can. I get out of the van, and Ruckus puts an arm around me. Zane walks in front of me, blocking some of the cameramen's views. Pierre's bodyguards flank us and keep the media back.

We walk through the doors and are guided into a hospital room on the first floor of the small two-story hospital. A nurse closes the door behind us, and we all completely fall apart as we look down at Pierre. His wet suit has been cut down the arms and chest and peeled back. He looks alive, save for all the machines and the breathing tube he's hooked up to. There's a blanket over his legs, blocking the view of the damage.

"Melanie," Zane says. "I want you to double-check that there's no chance he's in there and his brain is somehow functioning without us knowing."

The doctor looks at Zane curiously.

"Melanie's an energy worker," Zane explains. "The reason they were even able to locate Pierre in the ocean was because she can find his energy. I want to know that there's zero chance he's in there before we do this."

"Interesting," the doctor replies, somehow accepting this insanity.

Nodding as I step forward, I gently wrap my hands around Pierre's head and watch as our friends all join hands and close their eyes, bowing their heads in prayer. I close my eyes and drop into meditation, searching for the energy that makes Pierre, Pierre. It doesn't take long to discover that his body has no soul hum, and he's truly gone.

"I love you," I hear Pierre say in my mind. *"Pull the plug, Meley. I'm gone from my body. I'll watch over you."*

As he disappears, my knees give out. I feel Zane hold me up as I take a deep breath and an almost howling cry rises from my throat.

Hands land on my shoulders, and everyone starts sobbing. They take turns saying goodbye to Pierre.

As the last one to go, all I can say is, "I love you."

I turn and bury my head in Zane's chest. While he holds me tight, I hear a button pushed. The creepy, rhythmic inhale and exhale of the breathing machine halts, and we all watch as Pierre's body stops breathing.

The doctor waits a few minutes before putting a stethoscope to Pierre's chest, after which he quietly announces to a nurse, "Time of death, five thirty-two p.m."

Zane and the surfers guide me out of the hospital room, down the hall, and through the invasive media throng. We climb in the van, and I sit between Zane and Ruckus the whole drive back to the resort.

We're met in the parking lot by the wives, who all have tear-stained faces. After getting the "all clear" from the bodyguards, I step out of the van. Caroline hands me my backpack. Everyone surrounds me to provide cover from the throng of reporters jostling around us and filming the moment. When we get to my villa, I unlock the door, and the heady smell of flowers hits us as we enter. It's exactly how Pierre and I left it. I shake my head as a fresh wave of tears rolls down my face.

Caroline hugs me.

Kalino brings my surfboard in and zips it into its case. "Melanie," he says quietly, "we're supposed to take you to the airport."

I nod, and Kalino steps out to guard the door.

Ruckus looks into my eyes. "No one knows Riptide better

than us and his surf buddies back home. We've never seen him that happy. I promise you, he died complete."

Anguished, I draw a shuddering breath.

Caroline wraps her arms around me. "I'm so sorry, Melanie. Damn it, but we need to get you packed and take you home."

I nod. "I'll take his suitcase and get it back to his best friend, Rocco."

Everyone makes quick work of packing me up, and Caroline brings me the black dress Pierre got me. I head into the kitchen and change out of my dance costume into the dress.

There's a tap on the doorjamb, and I quietly say, "Come in."

Zane steps to me. "I'm going to handle things here and deal with the media. I'm hoping to distract them so they don't follow you to the airport."

Though I don't really know him well, Zane seems to be taking me seriously. My instinct is to joke about it. "Are you *that* distracting?"

Zane makes a humorless scoffing sound. "Yes," he answers simply.

"Umm . . . I want to thank you." I look up at him with big eyes. "I'm sorry you had to help me through Pierre's death. You have far more right to fall apart than I do."

Zane's expression collapses. He tears up before quickly pulling it together. "It's okay, Melanie. I'll process everything once we know you're handled. Can I hug you?"

I nod slightly.

He wraps me up and assures me, "I put my number in your backpack. I'm a call away."

"Thank you."

Zane lets me go and guides me back to the living room. We watch while everyone does a final sweep. When they're confident that they got everything, I'm shuttled out of the villa and whisked into the van with Ruckus. My suitcase and Pierre's are loaded into the van, and someone slides my surfboard in last. Ruckus and I sit together in the back on the way to the airport.

We park at a private airstrip, and as I get out of the van, there's a little plane waiting. I look to Ruckus. "Wasn't someone sending for my mom or Rich?"

Ruckus shakes his head. "There wasn't time to get him here. Your stepdad booked you on a private flight."

"My family can't afford a private flight!" I insist, panicking.

"Don't sweat these details, Melanie," Ruckus assures. "Your stepdad will be waiting for you when you land."

"I'm flying home alone?" I say in a panic.

Ruckus's forehead creases. "You are. But it's going to be okay, sweetheart."

My eyes are huge.

"We're almost done with a security sweep of the plane," Kalino informs gently. "It's safe."

Ruckus takes a paper and pen from his pocket and hands them to me so I can write down my phone number. "I'll call as soon as we have transport information for Riptide's body," he says.

"Wait, what?" I gasp out.

"It's okay. I shouldn't have said that. Just focus on getting home. I'll get information to you through Rocco."

"Thank you, Ruckus," I say, having no idea what else to express. I thank the bodyguards too, and they head off to finish their search, leaving Ruckus and me in an awkward silence.

Finally, the sweep is over, and all is clear. Ruckus leads me up the steps of the plane, where I pass through the open hatch alone. The door is shut as I take a seat. My hands shake as I pull my cell phone from my backpack. I dial Rich, but he doesn't answer.

The slip of paper with Zane's number peeks out of the front pocket. I pull it and dial the number. When he answers, I kind of squeak out, "I'm flying home alone. What do I do?"

"Damn it!" Zane says. "Ruckus didn't tell me that. I'll rush that way and join you."

The engine whirs, and my voice shakes as I say, "There's no time. We're taking off. What do I do?"

"Buckle up, Melanie. Private flights are easy. Just sit there and look out the window. You're going to be okay." He sounds exhausted.

"I'm sorry I called you," I whimper. "I feel stupid. I guess I know how to sit on a plane."

"I know you can sit there. The problem is that you're scared to face this reality without someone to process it with. It's okay that you feel that way."

"I have to go. Thank you for helping me."

"Call me when you land, please," Zane softly requests.

"Okay," I whisper.

"Deep breath, baby girl."

I manage to inhale.

"Good. Now exhale."

I do, and he says goodbye hesitantly.

The plane catches altitude, and we soar away as I stash my phone. Through the window, I spot the stretch of the beach that had been designated for the competition. It's still so brightly lit. My heart hurts. Tears fill my eyes, and I draw my knees to my chest.

CHAPTER 35

It's late when my plane lands. I descend the steps onto a tarmac, where Rich, Mabel, Mr. Cantrell, Rocco, and my guys are waiting.

Rich runs to me. The second he hugs me, I dissolve into tears again, and we both sob. Rich looks down at my ring and squeezes his eyes closed while he shakes his head, devastated. "Damn it. I'm so sorry, Melanie." He pulls himself together with considerable effort and quietly explains, "I know what that ring means. For Pierre, of all people, to give you that ring means you were his everything." He hugs me again and waits until I cry myself out.

I tearfully ask, "Are you mad because I'm too young for this ring?"

Rich shakes his head. "I've known what you are for much longer than you have. Part of parenting you is understanding that you can't live your life like a teenage first-timer. You're an old soul, and Riptide was perfect for you. I would have approved this."

Rocco crosses the brief distance and pulls me in. He looks like death warmed over. "I'm sorry you rode here alone. None of us were thinking clearly. We got our asses handed to us by Zane after he talked to you. I just let him know that you landed safely."

"I just had to sit there," I say lifelessly.

"It's the principle of the thing," Rich says. "I'm sorry. We should have had someone ride with you."

"I'm okay," I say with no inflection.

When Rich tips his head subtly, Rocco looks at my hand and murmurs, "Oh, fuck."

The others gather around, and all subtly survey my ring.

Adam wraps his arms around me and lays his cheek on the top of my head while I silently sob. "I'm so sorry, Melanie."

"You want to explain that?" Trey glares at Rich.

"We'll talk, Trey," Rich assures him.

"*That's* fine, but when *I* asked for her hand, it wasn't okay?" Trey clips back.

"I didn't know about this," Rich says placatingly. "I promise, we'll discuss it."

Adam lets go of me just as my luggage and surfboard are pulled from the cargo hatch.

The suitcases are wheeled my way. I gesture to Rocco and say to the steward, "The black suitcase goes to him." I look up at Rocco. "It's Pierre's."

He shakes his head. "It's yours."

Demitri holds an arm out my way, and I lean into him. "We'll get you put back together, Melanie," he says, carefully holding me. "I don't want you to worry about anything."

Gently, Mr. Cantrell guides me a few steps away from the group. He waits until Rich gets back from quietly talking to Trey before saying, "Jet's gone missing, and the police don't know where he is. Your family has been put in hiding. That's why Rich sent a private plane. Mama Mabel was the one whose name went on the flight booking because we didn't want anyone connected to you to have their names on public itinerary logs. For safety, your parents are staying with some friends."

I frown. "I don't want . . ." I look hesitantly at Rich.

"What do you want to do, Melanie?" Rich encourages me to speak.

I look up at Demitri. His expression melts.

"Umm . . . I think I need to head to Pierre's and figure stuff out."

"Wait. Slow down, Melanie," Demitri says. "Jet's on the loose."

I squeeze my eyes closed. "Fuck Jet. I don't give a damn if he finds me." *I hope he does and this ends. I don't want to live like this.*

Mama Mabel steps forward and wraps me in her arms. "I'm going to personally counsel you through this loss, Melanie. It's going to be okay." She turns to my stepfather, "My place has security. I'd be happy to host anyone who needs somewhere to go."

Rich clears his throat. "Melanie, what would you like to do?"

My chin shakes as I look up at Demitri. "Would you stay there with me?" I ask softly.

Demitri looks to his dad. "I think you and I both should stay at Mabel's. Melanie's going to need help."

"I'll gladly stay there if it helps," Mr. Cantrell says.

Mabel hugs me. "Does this work for you?"

I nod against her chest and thank her.

"Do you want me to load your suitcases in Demitri's Jeep?" Rich asks. "Maybe it'll be easier if you go through them with Demitri by your side."

I look to Demitri, who agrees. "Strap her surfboard to the top rack," he says.

"No," I say, shaking my head. "I'll never surf again. I want to know that my last time was with Pierre." I chuckle, but there's no humor in it. It's pure irony. "I died at five o'clock this morning."

Everyone looks at me with extreme concern in their eyes.

"What do you mean?" Rich asks.

"We were out surfing during a storm. A wave took me down, and I drowned. Pierre and my dance partner brought me back. Pierre and I thought that was the end of what we needed to worry about . . . Like, we survived the big trial." A shuddering breath escapes my lips. "He was dead several hours later."

Rich, Adam, Trey, and Demitri all reach for me at the same time, clearly shell-shocked by the news that they almost lost me too. I choose to hug Rich because it seems easier than dealing with the three guys. He pulls me in tight.

"I need to get home to Valerie," Adam says. "She hasn't been feeling well." He says goodbye to me and takes my suitcase and Pierre's to Demitri's Jeep.

"Are you sure you've got this?" Trey asks Demitri.

"She chose me to help her," Demitri says with a nod. "I'll get her through it."

Trey side-eyes me. "Why don't I stay with you?"

"That's sweet of you," I say, "but I think it's better if Demitri does. This is a lot, and you and I have yet to discuss anything about our breakup. I can't handle that right now."

Trey runs a hand down my arm. "I'm a call away, Melanie," he says, clearly unsure.

"Thank you," I murmur.

Trey takes his leave before things can get any more awkward.

Rich promises that he'll be anywhere he needs to be. Before he leaves, he assures me that he'll call the moment he knows more.

"Follow me," Mama Mabel says. "We'll get you settled in."

Demitri guides me to his Jeep, and we follow Mabel's car out of the parking lot. Mr. Cantrell pulls up the rear of our caravan.

CHAPTER 36

I step into the parlor and look around.

Mama Mabel smiles softly. "Melanie, do you remember Mack?"

I study the Hellhound biker, who looks at me stoically. "I do," I reply. "Hello."

"Hello, Melanie," Mack says. "I'm going to arm our security system. Gates will slide down over all the windows and doors. You're safe here."

"Thank you."

"I'll show you to your room," Mabel offers.

I follow her down a hall, where she unlocks what turns out to be a guest room. Inside, I'm greeted by mostly light-blue, delicate décor.

"Will this work?" Mama Mabel asks.

"Yes, thank you." I look up at her with huge eyes.

"I'm going to get Demitri and Mr. Cantrell settled. I promise I'll be right back."

Demitri clears his throat. "This is going to sound odd, but Melanie has stayed with me before. I'd rather she wasn't alone tonight."

Mama Mabel's eyebrows rise. She slides an unsure look Mr. Cantrell's way. "Dad opinion?" she asks.

"I'm fine with it," Mr. Cantrell says.

"Melanie?"

"Yes, please," I whisper.

Demitri steps in and wraps his arms around me. I press my cheek against his chest.

"I've got her," he assures. "Give me some time to talk with her."

"Okay." Mabel thinks hard for a moment. "Spend some time talking with Demitri, but I'm here when you need me."

I'm barely holding it together. "Thank you," I manage to say.

Mama Mabel switches to talking with Mr. Cantrell as she leads him down the hall. Demitri closes the door, and the moment it clicks shut, I fall apart completely. A torrent of tears gush, and my knees go weak. I sink to the wood floor, clutching my stomach. A keening sound blisters from me, and soon, it becomes an animalistic howl.

Demitri gathers me up and holds me tight. His jaw is clenched as I look up at him, so distraught that I can't inhale. My midsection starts to spasm, making my whole body seize. Demitri looks to the door, and I see Mabel and Mr. Cantrell through my peripheral vision.

"Wastebasket," Demitri orders.

A wastebasket appears just as I start to throw up. Demitri gets my hair gathered back. He holds it in one hand while he keeps me steady with an arm around my chest. I vomit again, so violently that he has to brace himself to keep me upright.

I sag, shaking, as tears continue to fall. I stare blankly into the trash can, but don't recognize or smell the revolting mess. Mabel's hands remove the can. The floor comes into view as the wastebasket disappears. The lines and knots in the wood look unusually pronounced.

"Here, honey," I hear Mabel say.

"Thank you," Demitri replies. A wet washcloth swipes over my mouth. "Melanie . . ."

I hear Demitri faintly but feel no inclination to answer. It's like I'm somewhere else.

"Meley . . ."

Nothing. I have no clue how to reply. I'm Meley, but I'm empty.

When I turn over, I find myself staring up at Demitri. He shifts, supporting me with an arm around my back. I'm bent at a weird angle, but I don't care. I can't feel my body. My mind hums, staticky. I blink blankly and study Demitri.

"You have the prettiest eyes," I think, and the thought is audible in the room.

Demitri's eyes widen in fear, but he manages to say, "Thank you, Meley." He slides his stunned gaze to Mabel and his dad.

"Is that new?" Mabel asks, having apparently heard the thought as well.

Demitri nods, careful to keep his movements subtle and calm.

"Pierre loved me," I think. *"I was real to someone."* Again, the thought projects audibly through the room.

"Good, Meley," Demitri says softly. "You need to be real."

"I'm not real to you."

"You're real to me," Demitri assures, clearly aiming for neutral even though he's creeped out about this whole incorporeal communication thing.

I shake my head slowly. *"You hide from pain. Shallow is real to you. This isn't for you."*

Demitri grabs my cheek. "Wrong. I'm here. I need you to inhale with me, Meley."

When I do as he suggests, my eyes widen in my emotionally detached state. Something's coming, but it doesn't register. Spastic jolting starts in my chest and shoulders before my head drops back and everything shakes distantly. I hear exclamations and panic, but it does nothing for me. I lie, content in the shaking, unconcerned. Feeling my body's chaos in a detached way is a deep emotional relief.

After an indecipherable amount of time, voices slowly come into focus. The more the voices sharpen, the louder they sound, and the harder I quake.

Fingers land on my forehead, sending a tingling sensation into me. "Shhh, Melanie. It's okay."

At once, the spasms cease. I'm left still and unexpectedly settled. Draped over Demitri's arm and lap, I inhale deeply and give in to the sensation.

"I've got her mind rolled," Mr. Cantrell says. "What do we need to do?"

"I've got her," I hear Demitri say, but it's as if he's in another room, or dimension, or something. I'm lifted but don't care. I feel a weight shift and flop chest-to-chest with Demitri, unable to control my body in Mr. Cantrell's energetically induced catatonic state.

"Tired," I think. *"You smell like home."* The disembodied words drift through the space.

Demitri lays me down on the bed. "I know, Meley."

Vaguely, I feel my shoes being removed.

"I'll get her changed," I hear Mabel offer.

"I've got her," Demitri assures distantly. "She can stay in the dress. She needs to sleep. Dad, don't release her until I tell you to."

"What's your plan?" Mr. Cantrell's voice wafts through.

"Don't judge me for it. I apologize in advance, and I'll apologize to her tomorrow. I can get her to sleep."

I feel a shift before I'm flopped over, my head landing on

Demitri's bare chest. His arms wrap around me, and I shiver violently.

"Breathe in, baby girl," wafts through.

I inhale deeply, and the scent of Demitri blazes through my confused senses. With a primal groan, I exhale.

"Like I said, I apologize, but Melanie and I have that effect on each other," Demitri says. "She's wouldn't normally react so obviously. Guess she's not exactly in her right mind."

"What is it?" Mabel asks.

"Some kind of connection. We don't discuss it, but it rolls my mind with hers when I let it. Apparently, I'm not alo—"

I slip into a sleep so deep that I'm unaware of anything but the dark.

CHAPTER 37

I look at Riptide's driver's license, my thumb covering his picture while I read the address.

Demitri pulls into an alley driveway and parks. "Wait here," he says as he shuts off the engine.

I survey the blueish-gray two-story building through the windshield. Just as Pierre described, there's a shop below and wood stairs on the side to what I assume is the living space above. The shop lights are off, but the condo lights are bright as the sun sets.

I feel oddly detached still. I've said little since I woke up three hours ago. I'm still in the black dress, uninterested in any changing or human activity.

My door opens, and I slowly look that way. Demitri's staring at me, and I startle.

His brow creases. "It's me, Meley. You're okay."

"Where's Jet?" I ask with no intonation.

"That's an excellent question. We need to get inside." Demitri sighs. He fought me on this plan when I heard from Rocco, insisting that we bring people with us who can bodyguard. I refused Mack's help, and Demitri finally relented.

He helps me out of the Jeep, and I watch as he closes the door after grabbing my backpack from the floorboard for me. He puts an arm firmly around my waist, guiding me to the stairs. We climb them, but I'm on autopilot. Demitri knocks on the door that opens. Rocco is on the other side and looks exhausted. His eyes are puffy from crying. He smiles a sad, silent greeting and gestures us in. We step into a living room, where I'm greeted by heavy energy. Pepe and Luis are slumped on the couch, balling their eyes out. A woman sits in a chair in the corner.

Demitri must have called my stepfather, because Rich steps through the door.

Before I get a chance to greet him, the woman gets up from her chair and approaches me. She's tall and slender with harsh, angular facial features. Her eyes are kind as she asks, "Are you Melanie?"

"Yes, ma'am."

"I'm Jessica Suriah, Pierre's lawyer and financial adviser. He called me after he gave you the ring." She reaches out her hand, and I put my hand in hers. "It's beautiful."

"Thank you."

"Anyhow," she says, clearing her throat and blinking back tears, "three days ago, he called and had me put you down as his beneficiary on everything. You're on his bank accounts, his business, his house, his life insurance. I rushed it all through. Pierre wasn't patient with things like this, and it's a good thing in this case because it means we aren't faced with a bunch of legal red tape."

"You've got to be kidding!" Rich says.

"And you are?" Jessica says.

"I'm Melanie's stepfather. Rich Fairtrade."

Jessica shakes his hand. "Excellent. You're down as Melanie's executor until she's twenty-one, per Pierre's instruction. Pierre was dead serious about Melanie. I had all the paperwork already drawn up and on my desk, waiting for the go-ahead. He called me the night before they left for Hawaii and laid the whole situation out. I thought he'd lost his mind, but his intuition was never wrong. He signed everything before he left." She hands me two stacks of papers. "Those are his bank statements from his personal and business accounts."

Rich stands next to me, surveying the paperwork. On the top are Pierre's name and mine, with his address. I blink rapidly as I scan through it all.

Jessica gestures toward the papers. "You're now a multimillionaire, Melanie."

It's such a stunning statement that it doesn't process as real.

"What is happening?" I look to Demitri with blank eyes.

Demitri clears his throat. "Melanie's dealing with some shock. She slept for a long stretch, but it didn't help. She's very emotionally detached right now." He puts his hands on my cheeks. "Melanie, Pierre put his assets in your name."

I blink in response.

Worry mars Demitri's stunning face. "He considered you his spouse. You own his stuff," he clarifies.

I rattle my head and absently hand the paperwork to Rich. "Stuff," I murmur, before slowly walking around the living room. I look to Demitri and hold a hand his way.

Demitri crosses to me while everyone glances at each other, unsure. Their tears have stopped as my odd behavior distracts them.

"Are you two together?" Rocco asks, sounding pissed.

I stare at Rocco with no understanding.

"No. I seem to be who she's depending on," Demitri answers vaguely. He takes my hand, and I guide him around the room, picking up pictures as I go.

I smile at a picture of Pierre when he was a kid, along with

Rich and another man I don't know. They're all wearing wet suits and holding their surfboards, with the ocean in the background. I hold the picture out to Rich, and he chokes up for a second before pulling it together.

I keep slowly making my way around. I point at a picture of Pierre and his surfing friends. "Pierre," I say matter-of-factly to Demitri.

"It's a nice picture, Meley," Demitri says softly. "He looks happy in all of them."

I nod.

I pick up a picture of a man who is unmistakably Pierre's dad, and he has his arm around a pretty woman who has Pierre's eyes. She's holding a baby, and they're wearing swimsuits at the beach. I carefully set the picture down and turn to face everyone who's watching me.

My line of sight shoots past them as I spy a stereo system. I cross to it and hit the *power* button on the five-disc CD player.

A song comes on midway through.

Rocco smiles softly. "Riptide must have left the CD in the player. He was listening to it the night before you left for the competition. I came up after work to join him for a beer. He said the song reminded him of you."

I hit the *back* button and start the track over. Richard Marx's "Keep Coming Back" wafts from the speakers. As I listen, hands land gently on my shoulders, and Rocco turns me around. I put my forehead on his chest.

"He loved you from the first day he saw you," he says quietly.

I step back and look at Demitri with huge eyes. A lot of emotions that scare me are bubbling deep in my gut. I reach out a hand and Demitri steps to me.

"Dance?" I ask.

"Of course," Demitri says, though he sounds unsure. My distant state clearly has him in a cautious emotional place.

The song hits a swell, and though my mind can't quite keep up, my dance training clicks in and guides me. Demitri dances with me like only he can. He lifts his hand and spins me through four pirouette finger turns before getting a hand on my lower back and lifting me over his head. I drape over his hand, my head meeting my calf, and he turns us twice before lowering me to his shoulder. He wraps a hand around my waist and lunges. I somersault up and over his shoulder, landing draped on his angled back. I slide down, and he turns and takes my hand. He launches me off the floor and holds me against him while he turns across the room. When he dips me low, I giggle, surprising myself.

Demitri smiles vibrantly, saying, "Hi."

"Hi," I reply.

"Looks like you're a little more aware," he says as he guides me to standing and pulls me into a formal waltz position.

More mentally connected, I tighten my form, and Demitri breezes me through a quick-paced waltz across the room.

"Wow," Jessica breathes out. "They're lovely." She says to Rocco, "I see why Rip loved her and wanted Demitri at arm's length. He and Pierre are so much alike."

Rocco nods. "He even *surfs* like Rip did."

The song ends, and "Hazard" comes on. My eyes widen as I look to the stereo. The beginning of the song is hauntingly ominous. Dread swells in me, and I moan quietly.

Demitri hits the *stop* button. "Let's nix 'Hazard.'" With concern in his gaze, he looks to Jessica. "Do you think you could discuss the legal details with Rich for now and check in with Melanie later?"

Jessica wobbles her head. "I suppose that's okay. Melanie has paperwork she needs to sign, but we can handle it later."

"Explain," I say, sliding a confused gaze up to Demitri.

"Settling an estate seems like a lot at the moment," Demitri calmly informs the room. "I need her to stay stable. Given some new metaphysical stuff that's popped up, *unstable* seems like it would be problematic."

"Melanie?"

I look to Jessica.

"I need you to sign for the business and personal accounts," she explains.

"But I'm sixteen," whispers from me.

"Of course. Rich will sign also."

I look to Rocco and tip my head ponderously. "You surf?"

He nods. "I do." He's watching me like I'm some kind of unpredictable exotic creature.

"Me, too, but not like you do." I blink rapidly before looking up at Demitri. "I want to be a dancer with you and Beastie Boy."

"Who?" Demitri asks.

"Zane. Surf competition." My eyes widen fearfully.

Demitri rushes to inject calm by saying, "Got it. Dance with me and Zane."

"Where is he?" I ask.

"Honey, Zane had to go back to a movie set," Rocco says in a placating tone. "He isn't here. Do you want me to call him?"

"That's weird. Here is where we are," I say matter-of-factly.

"Okay. Apparently, Zane's a part of 'we,'" Rocco says, sounding unsure. He grabs the cordless phone from the coffee table and dials a number. He puts the call on speakerphone.

Zane answers.

"Hey, Beastie," Rocco says. "We're at Rip's. Melanie, Rich, and Demitri are here meeting with Jessica."

"Fill me in."

"Melanie's been hit with a lot. Pierre left everything to her, but she seems to be a bit . . . flummoxed. She mentioned you and wanted to know if you were around."

"Melanie?" Zane calls out.

"Hi."

"Hi," Zane says softly. "What has you confused?"

"I don't want to sell swimsuits," I inform emphatically.

Zane spurts laughter, but it sounds charmed instead of judgmental. "Why don't you want to sell swimsuits?"

"I'm bad at math. There's lots of adding. I hate people."

"Thank you for calling, Rocco," Zane says in a lighthearted tone. "I needed this. Melanie, I adore you. I agree that managing the surf shop sounds like a big bunch of suck."

"Can we dance together again so I don't have to sell swimsuits?"

He snorts. "For you, I'll come back to the dance world. Would it help if we dance together some?"

"Yes. I'm scared. Swimsuits don't help."

"Zane, right?" Demitri chimes in.

"Who's asking?" Zane replies, suddenly caged.

"Demitri Cantrell."

"Fuck you, Demitri Cantrell," Zane barks, to the amusement of the surfers.

"Fuck *you*, Zane," Demitri snarks back.

"Whoa, whoa, whoa," Rich jumps in. "What happened to staying calm for Melanie?" Demitri cuts evil eyes at Rich, who admonishes, "Don't you glare at me, Demitri."

"I'm glaring too," Zane bellows through the phone.

Rocco, Luis, and Pepe all laugh.

"I heard *all* about you, Demitri," Zane snarls. "Why are you in Pierre's home?"

Demitri's cheeks are burning red. "Melanie had to come here.

She's rather attached to me in her current mental state. Let's just say that you don't want her driving right now, and her being away from my calming ability could get messy."

"Rocco," Zane calls out. "Get Demitri away from Melanie and kick his ass out of there."

"No can do, Beastie Boy," Rocco replies. "He's currently her emotional support barnacle."

"Then I'm leaving this movie set on a goddamn helicopter that'll land on Venice Beach," Zane says, his tone on edge.

In response to Zane's anger, my hands start shaking.

"I see you're handling this disaster as well as Melanie is. She's shaking. You need to slow your roll."

"Rocco," Zane screams before collecting himself. Much calmer, he tries again. "Rocco, I need to know if I should head over there. If Melanie needs help, I will seriously helicopter in."

"Why?" Demitri demands through clenched teeth.

I look up at him with huge eyes. He looks primally furious.

"Scary," I say, sliding my desperate, baby-doll gaze to Rich.

My stepdad appears baffled by the battle royale unfolding over the phone. "Get back on topic. Melanie wants to dance with you, Zane."

"Right," I say with a head rattle. "I want to dance with you and Demitri for my job. I don't want to sell—"

Zane cuts me off, "Swimsuits. Got it. Does the idea of the store scare you?"

I nod frantically.

"Terrified nodding," Rocco narrates.

"I can't live here. I'm sixteen." My eyes narrow as I look to the door. "There aren't any industrial locks here." Into the phone, I plead, "Help me."

"It's easy to see that this is a lot right now," Zane calmly replies.

"Okay, we'll dance instead of dealing with customers." Through the line, I can hear Zane smile as he sardonically says, "I would love to be your *only* dance partner."

"Nope," Demitri squawks. "Hang up."

"Quit screwing with each other!" Rich scolds.

"She likes dancing with me," Zane teases childishly.

"She's *my* partner," Demitri informs, leaving zero room for ambiguity.

"We'll see about that," Zane says. "Melanie, if you want to be a professional dancer, I'll pull some strings. Now, I need you to go back to what you were talking about with Jessica. Can you handle that?"

"Bank accounts are confusing." I whimper. "I'm really scared."

Zane sighs. "Jessica?"

"Yes?"

"Get copies of the account paperwork to me. I'll guide her through it when I get done with this damn shoot."

"Thank you, Zane," Jessica replies politely.

"You don't have to do this," Rich insists. "I can help her with bank accounts."

"And you are?" Zane's tone is caged.

"Her stepfather, Richard." Rich smiles. "I remember you. Whenever I went to the beach for a bonfire, I'd always bring twice as many s'more ingredients because of you. You're the mammoth guy with the striking face, right?"

Zane laughs. "That's me. Nice to speak to you again. Full disclosure, I'm the one who made the final decision to end life support. I helped Melanie through it."

"Thank you for doing that," Rich says, "but I promise it wasn't a long-term obligation you were committing to. Demitri and I have Melanie covered. Do your work."

"I'm not abandoning the terrified love of my best friend's life," Zane replies. "She and I are friends now, and apparently we're dancing together instead of selling swimsuits."

Everyone chuckles.

"I'll help where I can," Zane says.

"Are you coming to the paddle-out?" Rocco asks.

"I don't know if I can handle it." There is a quavering quality to Zane's voice.

"He's sad," I murmur.

"I'm okay, Melanie. Call me again if she needs help."

Rocco hangs up.

To Demitri, I pointedly say, "We don't run a surf store."

"Correct. We've never run a surf store."

"I don't want to sell things. I don't like people." I can't get unstuck from that concept.

My best friend chuckles. "A people-y person you're not, except with *your* people." He glares at the phone that Rocco's still holding.

"Annoying customers. Annoying store. Annoying commitment." I grimace and gesture at him flippantly. "You're also an annoying commitment, but you're prettier than a surf store."

Demitri's face scrunches. "Thank you . . . I think."

"Umm, Melanie, honey."

I look to Rich.

"I'm worried about you," he says gently. He looks to Demitri and quips, "I'm worried about you and Zane also."

I wave my hands about. "Clarity." I look to Rocco, Pepe, and Luis. "You like people."

Rocco shrugs. "We like customers because they have money."

"Eh." I shrug. "Tomato, potato."

"Right." Rocco glances around at everyone. "You all get it?"

Everyone nods, and Rocco looks at me quizzically, though he's clearly amused.

"If you can't tell," Rich says, "she gets a little weird when she's frazzled. Melanie, do you want to sell the surf shop?"

I grimace at him. "I'm not selling Pierre's dream." I gesture to Rocco and say to Rich, "He helps Pierre's dream."

"Do you know how to run the store, Rocco?" Rich asks.

Rocco nods. "I'm the manager. Luis and Pepe are the assistant managers."

"Adam says you sell weed," I inform Rocco.

He laughs a little. "A guy has to have a hobby."

Rich smiles at me. "There you go. You don't have to be people-y. You employ people-y people." He turns to Rocco. "And I'd like to buy some weed to help me get through this shitshow."

With a grin, Rocco pulls a dime bag from his pocket and hands it over. "On the house."

"Thank you much," Rich says with an appreciative chuckle.

I shake my head. "This isn't right." I become irritable, and on a wave of frustration, extreme clarity blazes through. "I don't steal from my friends," I bark at Rich.

Demitri grips my arms. "Calm down, Melanie." He sends a wave of calm through the touch, and I inhale deeply before exhaling in time with him. "Good," he encourages. "I need you to stay calm."

"What happens if she doesn't?" Jessica asks.

Demitri's jaw hardens. "I'm unsure, but what I'm feeling is alarming."

"You can feel things in her?"

"I've been able to for a while now," Demitri says. He clears his throat. "It's been incredibly pronounced since she returned from Hawaii. I know it's odd, but I need everyone to trust me on this." He looks down at me with deep eyes. "No one thinks you steal from your friends. This is just legal stuff. Tell us what you're thinking, but please stay calm."

I nod and curl up with my cheek against Demitri's chest as I study Rocco, Luis, and Pepe. "I shouldn't own this. You guys were his family. He built a business with your help. He lived his life with you, not me. The business goes to Rocco, complete with the business account."

Rocco's mouth drops open.

"Is this more looney Melanie?" Luis asks.

Demitri shakes his head. "No. This is the clearest I've heard and felt her since she had her psychotic break last night."

I glare up at him. "Judgy much?"

He gives me a look. "You fell off the old reality wagon for a hot second, Meley."

"Dance career," I say. "Us."

Demitri smiles. "I'll let you be as crazy as you want if you'll ditch dancing with Zane."

Playfully, I scrunch up my nose. "Nope. He's massive, and I feel like a tiny fairy when he dances with me."

"Ohhh eeew," Demitri blisters out. "Eeeewww! Are you serious?"

I giggle and nod. "He's gorgeous, and his cologne smells like warm caramel and naughty secrets."

Pepe, Luis, Rocco, and Jessica spurt laughter.

"That was descriptive," Rich says. "I'm going to need more weed."

Demitri's mouth drops open as he glares at me. "Oh, no you don't! Nope. You have to sell swimsuits now." His irritation snaps to Rocco. "Who exactly is this Zane tool anyway?"

"Zane *Drell*," Rocco informs, clearly loving this.

Demitri's eyes widen. "You have to be *kidding!*"

Rocco shakes his head. "Nope."

Pepe and Luis crack up.

"Your crazy sidekick adores him," Rocco explains. "He's her new partner. He was also Riptide's oldest friend. They've known each other forever."

I wince at the *sidekick* reminder and step away from Demitri.

"You aren't my sidekick, Melanie," Demitri says.

"I'm sorry," Rocco says. "I shouldn't have said that."

"You know how to run the store," I say to Rocco, intentionally steering the conversation from the reminder that Demitri doesn't respect me. "And you've busted your ass by his side. It's yours."

"Melanie, are you sure?" Rocco asks, clearly stunned.

I nod. "I don't take what's not mine. You've earned this through dedication and hard work." I look to Rich, who nods his approval with a soft smile.

Jessica gives me her card. "I'll be in touch. I have your stepfather's number."

After Rocco assures that he's got this situation under control, Rich says goodbye to me, promising to meet me at the paddle-out service. He leaves, walking Jessica to her car.

— —

I'm standing in a bedroom I've never been in. Everything's neat, and the room smells like Pierre. I study the pictures on the dresser but don't touch anything. I cross to a framed sketch of a seashell. It's beautiful, with soft shades of peach and light pink, and it reminds me of how Pierre would call me his seashell.

Through a door into a bathroom, I open a dirty clothes hamper and find a T-shirt on top. I pick it up and bury my face in it. It smells like Pierre. When I strip off my dress and pull the shirt on,

I completely fall apart, gasping and sobbing as I ugly cry. I sink to my knees and lose it on the dark-blue bathroom rug. It takes me forever to collect myself enough so that I can function. The tears don't stop, but I can at least stand.

I leave the bathroom and cross to the bed. I pull back the covers and slide in. The bed smells like Pierre's cologne, and I sob again, curled up hugging his pillow.

The door opens and light streams in briefly as Demitri comes into the room and closes the door behind him. "Hey. You're blasting the condo with more soul-crushing grief than I've ever felt."

"I'm sorry," I reply. "I didn't think to shield."

"Love, I need you to tone it down. Everyone in the vicinity, anyone with any *awareness*, is going to feel you." He studies me. "We can go back to Mabel's if you want. This is insane. You can't do this."

"I need to be here. I'm sorry that I need you, Demitri."

"I'm not, Melanie. I'll always be here to help you."

I sit up in bed. "It might be too much for me right now, but can we at least try to talk about us? I know you don't like the topic, but I need to clarify some things."

Demitri crosses to the bed and sits knee to knee with me like we have a thousand times before. He laces his hands with mine.

"I really need to level with you," I say as I squeeze his hands. "Darkest, deepest, best-friend time, D. Some of it might hurt."

"I need to talk to you also." He rushes to say, "I feel horrible that I made you so profoundly unhappy the morning you left with Adam. All of this could have been prevented if I'd handled that differently." He pauses before adding, "You know that I love you, right?"

I smile softly. "You don't have to do this. Just hear me out, Demitri. *I* was wrong, not you. I was clinging to you because the only time I was happy was when I was with you. But it's not your job to make me happy. Pierre made me happy, but it was effortless for him, and I made him happy in the same way. It's just not like that with you and me. I'm incredibly sorry."

He starts to argue.

I hold up a hand. "Easy laughter, holding hands, sleeping with my head on your chest, settling into comfortable moments. Those are relationship gifts, not Melanie and Demitri gifts. There's nothing appropriate about me spending the kind of time with you that I did. My emotional neediness strained the boundaries of our friendship."

Demitri's looking at me like he just watched me run over his puppy. "Melanie, I love that you need me."

I smile softly. "I'll never get what he gave me from any of the guys in my life. You've been more 'my guy' than either Trey or Adam has, but being someone's everything is asking a lot, and it was delusional of me to ask that. It's time for me to learn from Riptide, D. I don't know if anyone else will love me like he did, but even if they don't, I got what I needed in just a few days. Faking it with you sure as hell hasn't worked, and I'm so sorry."

"You weren't faking anything with me," Demitri argues, "and I took it for granted."

I squeeze his hand. "I'm not like that with anyone but you and Rip. But again, I shouldn't have been like that with you. You and I aren't on that level. You're kind, and gorgeous, and funny, and you love to dance as much as I do. That doesn't make us a thing, though. It makes me the quirky, mediocre best friend who turned into a stage-five clinger." A touch embarrassed, I scoff. "I turned into what I hate. There's nothing worse than the girl who decides to go for big air with the untouchable guy. I feel icky about it."

"I don't view you that way at all," Demitri says with desperation. "I love that you're fun, and silly, and buy me Fraggle pajamas that match yours."

I wince. "I did those things because I was comfortable. I viewed you as best-friend Demitri and forgot that you're *Demitri*. The second I stepped foot on that airplane to Hawaii, I got to be the Melanie I kept trying to be with you, except it was right with Rip. It was right with him because he wasn't Riptide with me. He was Pierre. You know what though?"

"What?"

I laugh a little. "He was *Riptide* with everyone else because he wanted to keep them at arm's length. You're *Demitri* when I get too close because you want to keep me at arm's length. I see that now and respect it."

Demitri closes his eyes and takes a breath. "A lot has changed for me, Melanie."

I shrug one shoulder. "For me too. What's changed for you isn't mine to know. That belongs to Victoria. I want you to really understand that I'm done driving you nuts. I'm a needy, immature, pathetic mess with you. I need to grow up, get my old-soul legs under me, and pull my shit together."

"Melanie, I'm your best friend," Demitri implores.

"And I love you so much for being that for me. With that said, I don't curl up with Presley when I need to sleep. I don't sit on Finley's bed and cry myself sick. I don't saunter into Tanner's house with a sack full of tacos and ask for a movie night. Riptide blazed in and brought extreme clarity into my life. I promise that I'm thoroughly and completely over you. I respect and appreciate you, but my feelings were totally inappropriate because they weren't shared. I'm deeply sorry, Demitri."

"Melanie, I need you to stop and listen to me," Demitri gasps out.

I shake my head. "You've been incredibly clear, without hesitation, from the start. I'm so sorry I fell apart last night." I grimace. "Vomit, and snuggling, and . . . ugh."

Demitri looks like I gut-punched him. "Being the one you chose to help you through this means a lot more to me than I let on."

"It was a revolting display," I say with a clear head.

"You just lost a man who asked you to *marry* him, Melanie! If you hadn't picked me to help you, I would have bulldozed my way in uninvited."

My mood shifts bashfully. Demitri squeezes my hands.

"The *me* now is different from the *me* before you left for Hawaii," Demitri insists. "Your apology was for the *me* from back then, not the *me me* that's me now."

I can't help but laugh a little. He's the only other person I know who riddles like I do. "All right, I'll hear out the you you who isn't you then."

Demitri takes a frantic breath. It surprises me. Because of his metaphysical calming gift, he rarely gets rattled. He glances around the room before saying, "Hang tight a second. I'm getting something."

He leaves, and I hear Ruckus ask, "Is she okay?"

"She's calm now," Demitri tells him, "but it's because she's attempting to best-friend-dump me."

"That's a thing?"

"Apparently," Demitri huffs.

He comes back into the bedroom a moment later and closes the door behind him. He slides a VHS tape into the VCR and sits next to me on the bed. I scoot back, propping up on the pillows.

"What's this?" I ask.

"Competition footage. I recorded all of it."

He hits *play* on the remote, and footage from the competitions comes on. He rewinds while I grimace.

"I don't know if I'm up for seeing footage of Pierre right now."

Demitri pauses the video. "Just hear me out, please."

He hits the *play* button, and the first piece from the opening show comes on. I can't help but smile as I watch the close-ups of Beastie Boy and me dancing. We're obviously having a blast.

Demitri pauses the video on a close-up of me. It's a full body shot, and I'm in a lift with a big smile.

He puts his finger on my sternum. "You're right that you aren't my girlfriend, and I don't get to be jealous. But," he says, pointing at the screen, "that girl right there is *my* girl! Mine!" He hits *play* again and pauses it quickly on a close-up of Zane. "I can't believe I didn't recognize him," he mutters. He points at the TV. "I hate that tool! Really, Melanie? Zane *Drell*!"

"He was great. Perfect partner. Not one slip. Never an issue. He took care of me."

"Ohhh eeew." Demitri gives me an offended look, and I laugh.

"What's the point of this, Demitri?"

He pushes *play* again, and we watch me wiggle, bounce, and make happy faces. In the video, I giggle at Zane and squeal when he turns me.

The piece ends, and Demitri pauses the tape again. "Melanie, you giggle, squeal, and make silly faces with me. It slaughtered me seeing you like that with him. That was when I realized something important."

"What's that?"

"It never bothered me when you were with Trey and Adam because I had zero doubt that you would leave either of them for me. It made me cocky. What I didn't anticipate was that freaking Riptide would come along and have a Beastie Boy dance partner sidekick." He looks sad. "Suddenly, you didn't need me to make you happy. You didn't need me to partner you in a show. You didn't need me to smolder at you. Then! *Theeen!* We all watched you in commercials and dance pieces and freaking look-see moments where you made girlfriend faces at the amazing Riptide. Adam, Trey, and I were completely screwed up. It was horrible. You were so happy, and gorgeous, and all sun-sparkly. Your life was exactly right, and none of us were in it. I sat on your parents' couch and had to fight not to cry."

He hits the *play* button, and "Wipe Out" starts. We watch my first tumbling pass, and then the shot switches to Pierre in the surfers' box. He's watching me with a big smile, and he and Ruckus side-eye each other while Pierre obviously says, "I love her," even though we can't hear it.

The announcer says, "Sorry, gals, but Riptide is officially off the market."

The shot changes to the full stage again.

I take a shuddery breath as my heart aches.

Demitri hits *pause.* "Yeah . . . that was a real treat. It took Bear, Darren, and my dad all damn night to get through counseling me, Adam, and Trey. Trey left first with Darren. He flat couldn't take it. Then Adam left with Bear. I was about to go when the promo came on. You two walked in slow motion out of the building. I swear, when you turned your head and panned past the camera, my heart stopped."

He turns off the TV, and I look up at him.

"What do you want me to say, Demitri? I'm sorry that you weren't interested? I'm sorry I fell madly in love with the most perfect person on the planet? I'm sorry that you had your head stuffed up Victoria's worthless ass? Or, how about, I'm sorry that my other dance partner was amazing, and I loved it?"

"Yes, Melanie. Please say all of that."

I laugh and shake my head. "It feels good to laugh, and I hate you for it."

Demitri breaks into a smile edged with fear. "Melanie, you're legitimately broken for a good reason. You lost someone who was perfect for you. If you have to be broken, which you do, then you need to do it with me by your side. *I* will help you through this. That's what we do."

"I didn't expect to fall so fast, and I sure as hell didn't think I'd lose him. I really thought I was staring down the barrel of a perfect life. Everything was magic." I quirk my mouth at him. "You know how I love your perfect abs, and the way you smell makes my head spin, and I think you're everything?"

He looks down contemplatively. "No, yes, and kind of."

I give a sad smile. "Well, it's all true. It was like that with him, but he'd get lost when he looked at me and forget what he was saying. People lose track of what they say around me out of terror or sick obsession, but never because they think I'm pretty. Certainly, no one like him does that anyway. He's everything that I want, and he's gone."

As tears fill my eyes again, Demitri pulls me over and puts my head on his chest.

After a long, tough moment, I whimper out, "I'm scared. Everything in me changed because of him. I don't know what I'm going to do."

"I know."

I pull it together, remembering my vow not to do this with Demitri anymore. "Now that I've heard you out, and I respect that you missed me and don't like Zane, I think it's best if you leave."

Demitri sighs. "Clearly, you missed my point."

"I didn't miss your point. You want to look hot with Victoria in public and hide in your room with me while I stimulate your need for humor and a brain, even though I'm not good enough for you."

Demitri winces. "Again, the me then is different than the me now. I'm not going, so where does this leave us?"

I smile softly at him. "I need to have my own movie nights alone, learn to cry alone, and somehow manage to sleep alone while being stalked by a murderer. I'm leaving you alone, Demitri. I'm not making you hold my hair while I hurl. I'm not going to follow you around and be amusing while you're gorgeous. You don't need a sidekick. You're so incredibly perfect without my dead weight."

"Someone has to hold your hair while you puke," Demitri insists. "Someone has to take off your stinky shoes." I glare at him, and he laughs. "Dancer feet," he teases, nodding knowingly. I scrunch my face up, and he squeezes me tight. "I'm here for your reality, Meley. Barf, feet, fear, weird riddles, and that craziness you blather when you spin *all* the way the fuck out."

"I do get weird, don't I?" I say bashfully.

"You get cuckoo for Cocoa Puffs, girl!" He gives me a look. "Tomato, potato?"

I rub my face hard while I laugh a little. "Tomato, tom-*ato*. You knew what I was saying!"

Demitri nods. "Exactly. I knew what you were saying. Frankly, we've hit the point where only I can decipher your shenanigans. I'm seeing that now."

I slip my gaze D's way with a face scrunch. "Hitting on me in this room belonging to my dead husband is tacky."

"First, I'm not hitting on you."

"Are too," I tease.

He laughs. "Are not. I plan to hit on you at some point, but now isn't the time. Second, it's so strange that you've never been here, but he asked you to marry him." He smiles softly at me. "Will you tell me about your trip?"

"Umm. You don't seem very fond of hearing my details."

Demitri holds an arm my way, and I hesitantly curl up against his side. "I want to hear all of it, Melanie."

I start the sordid tale full of romance, tragedy, laughter, and love. Demitri listens, open to all of it.

I held up okay through the story, until I got to the part about Pierre's leg being blown off. Demitri holds me tighter, and I fight to get through it.

"In the ambulance, he said goodbye to me when I dropped into meditation," I explain. "The doctors tried, but there was nothing they could do."

Demitri runs his hand down the back of my head. "I'm sorry, Melanie. I wish I had been there to help you."

"Zane helped me," I warble. "He held me while we waited forever. Time has never been that painfully slow before. We all kept saying that maybe it was taking so long because they found a way to fix him. The doctor got in the van and told us it was hopeless."

"How did you being Pierre's wife play into that?"

"It was weird. The paramedics and doctor took one look at my ring and respected what it meant. Zane explained my age, and lack of legal spousal paperwork. He has power of attorney, but he ran everything past me before he made the decisions. The doctor was supportive of my involvement."

"How did you feel about not having the final say in what happens?"

"Relieved. Zane's really good at this stuff. He made the right choices." I look up at Demitri. "I just want to be sixteen, you know?" I tear up, and he kisses my forehead before guiding my cheek back to his chest.

"I know, Meley." He huffs. "I suppose I should apologize for cussing out Zane."

"He cussed you out first," I remind him. "I guarantee he loved that little tiff you two had, if it helps."

The door opens and Rocco asks, "Can I come in? Ruckus is on the phone for Melanie."

I gesture him in, and he puts the cordless phone on the bed. "Melanie's listening," he says into the speaker.

"Melanie, it's Ruckus. We're all booked on a private flight that lands tomorrow. We're bringing Riptide home. I need to know the plan for his paddle-out memorial."

I look at Demitri with huge eyes. It's not the first time I've heard the term since Pierre's passing, but in the whirlwind of emotion, I didn't think to ask about it. "What's a paddle-out?"

"Shit. You haven't been planning it?" Ruckus asks, baffled.

I look to Rocco, who closes his eyes tight.

"Hang on." Pepe pulls his cell phone from his pocket and dials a number. "Listen in, please," he says quietly into his phone. "Ruckus is on with Melanie."

"A paddle-out service is like a funeral ceremony for a surfer, Melanie," Ruckus gently informs. "As his wife, you were supposed to be planning it."

Fear grips me suddenly as I realize I'm totally out of my element. "Okay," I whimper. "What do I do?"

"Oh, baby. Hang on." Ruckus hands the phone off to someone else.

Caroline's voice rings through. "Sweetheart, do you need me to fly out right now to help you?"

"There's already some lawyer talking to me about needing to handle Pierre's home and business," I blather through my panic.

"I have a stalker situation here. I have a ring on my finger from a guy whose condo I've never been to before today. I don't know what I'm supposed to be doing."

"Slow down," Caroline says. "Have you made any of the plans yet?"

From the background, I hear someone ask disgustedly, "Has she really not started to plan?"

My breathing gets shuddery. Tears fill my eyes.

Through Pepe's phone, Zane's familiar voice rings out. "Everyone stop! Caroline, can you hear me?"

"I'm here, Zane," Caroline replies. "Talk to me."

Rocco scoots the two phones closer together.

"Does everyone *seriously* expect Melanie to do this? She's *sixteen*!" Zane bellows. "What the *hell* is wrong with everyone? I get the whole surf marriage respect, but can everyone please take into account Melanie's reality?"

"I'm sorry, Zane. I figured you were helping her with all of this."

"Damn it. Melanie? What are you currently doing?"

"I'm in bed with Demitri, talking."

Zane makes a growling sound.

"*What*?" Caroline squawks. "The Demitri that Pierre didn't want you around because he's shallow and terrible for you?"

Demitri rubs his face with his hand.

"Get her out of there, Zane!" Ruckus hollers.

Apparently, everyone's now on speakerphone.

"Andreeew?" Zane calls out. We hear his mouth pull away from the phone a little. The conversation is a bit fainter as he says, "I need to go. I've got a mess back home. I can return in three days, but I have to plan this memorial paddle-out. This is all getting heaped on Riptide's girl. She can't handle it."

"Why can't she handle it?" comes a voice that must belong to Andrew.

"Because she's sixteen," Zane bellows, clearly fed up with everyone's assumption that a sixteen-year-old should understand the finer intricacies of funeral planning.

"You're best friends with a sixteen-year-old?" Mystery Andrew asks, sounding baffled.

"No. I was best friends with an eighteen-year-old who was dating a sixteen-year-old." Zane conveniently leaves out the whole not-at-all-legal marriage aspect, likely because it sounds wacka-doodle in normal society.

"They want a sixteen-year-old to plan a funeral?" Andrew asks, flummoxed.

"We've come full circle," Zane snarks. "I planned Riptide's dad's memorial. My parents planned the one for his mom when we were younger. I know what to do, and I need to help."

"Go. I'll get the schedule rearranged. We'll get everything done that we can while you're gone. We'll save your scenes for when you return."

"Get Brian, please. We're leaving." Zane is clearer now as he says into the phone, "I'm a fifteen-minute helicopter flight away. It's late enough that I can get away with landing on the beach, and then Brian will take off again."

"That's *beyond* illegal, my dude," Ruckus reminds.

"What are they gonna do?" Zane says. "Arrest me for being awesome?"

Ruckus cracks up. "Yeah, bro. That's exactly what they'll do."

"I'm Zane fucking Drell," Zane reminds. "I do what I want."

I giggle through tears, admitting, "I often say, 'I'm Melanie fucking Slate' when challenged."

Zane chuckles. "Well, I want you to be tiny young Melanie right now. Let me be the tough one. I'm on my way."

With that, he hangs up.

"What in the James Bond is happening?" Demitri asks, baffled. "Is this guy serious?"

"You have no idea." Caroline laughs through the phone. "For my wedding in Cabo San Lucas, his schedule was tight, and he had to helicopter in from set. Before he left, his pilot got pushback saying he couldn't get permission to land because the airport schedule wouldn't allow it. Instead of canceling his trip, he chartered a yacht with a helipad on the top, and let me tell you, he landed that son of a bitch right on that massive vessel, in full view of my oceanside wedding that was scheduled to start in ten minutes. Zane fucking Drell stepped off that helicopter in a tuxedo, hopped in a little transport boat, and entered in style just in time to be a groomsman. Zane does what he wants. He'll land on Venice Beach, and the helicopter will take off into the night. If he gets an FAA fine, he'll just pay it."

"What has happened to our lives?" I whimper to Demitri.

He shakes his head. "I don't know, Meley. Hollywood High being held hostage feels like it happened about a decade ago now."

"Damn, they really are young, and they deal with insane things," Rocco breathes out on a wave of disbelief. He, Luis, and Pepe stare down at us, worried. Rocco picks up the phone and promises, "We'll call you with details as soon as we get them hashed out with Zane."

Caroline says goodbye and hangs up.

Completely overwhelmed, I put my head on Demitri's chest.

"We'll give you two some time," Rocco says, and they leave the room.

Demitri holds me, keeping his metaphysical shields tightly in place while I blast wave after wave of anguish through the condo.

After thirtyish minutes, I feel the bed shift, and the guys all sit around me. My lungs seize, and I can't breathe. As I ball up tighter, Demitri gets me under the arms and pulls me up. When I curl my legs up by his sides, he adjusts the covers so my underwear-clad tush isn't mooning everyone. He gets a hand through my hair, and with his other hand on my back, he radiates calm as hard as he can. I take a gasping breath and finally calm some.

Rocco puts his hand on my back. "Whatever went on while you two were in Hawaii must have been something, because this is horrific. I know you two were new, but you're crying like you were married for fifty years. And I guarantee he's in no better shape right now."

I gasp and struggle to breathe like a toddler coming out of a tantrum. I look at Rocco with big eyes. "Can I ask you something totally inappropriate?"

"Heeells yeah, you can." Rocco breaks into a mischievous smile.

"Is it true that Pierre was new to . . ." I trail off as we hear the front door open, and everyone freezes. I sit up and scoot out of the bed. "You guys stay here."

"We're dealing with this," Rocco hisses.

All the guys get up, and I start to cross to the open bedroom door when a nightmare appears.

Jet's long black hair is disheveled, and his eyes are wild as he tips his head and stares at me. "I could feel you, Melanie," he breathes out on a filthy wave of obsessed energy.

Rage fills me, and I quake. My hands are shaking as my dark-water side blasts to the surface. The dark-water version of me, so full of grief and heartbreak that it's painful, says in my mind, *"End him."* I snarl and send out a blast.

Jet flies across the room and bounces off the living room wall.

"Holy shit," Rocco exclaims. "I didn't know she could do that."

"*She* didn't know she could do that," Demitri says.

I stalk out of the bedroom with the guys following and send out an energy line that wraps around Jet's ankle. When I whip the line, he goes flying across the room, hitting a wall and leaving a dent in the Sheetrock. He thuds to the floor, panting, his eyes huge.

Zane chooses that moment to stride through the open door.

I turn blazing dark-water eyes his way and growl, "Welcome to the Thunderdome. The spectators' area is—" Jet attempts to get up, and I toss a hand his way, whipping an invisible energy line around his ankle and hauling him upside down in midair. "Stay there," I bark at Jet before turning my attention back to Zane.

His mouth is hanging open, and his eyes are massive as he looks from Jet to me. "What the . . . ," he gasps.

"As I was saying, spectators' VIP section is over there." I gesture harshly with my head toward Demitri, Rocco, Pepe, and Luis.

Zane rushes to join the guys on the other side of the room.

"Don't go near her right now," Demitri instructs. "If she needs help, I'll step in."

"Do you know what to do?" Zane asks.

"I think so," Demitri murmurs.

Slowly, I turn a maniacal gaze back to Jet. "As you were," I snarl as I release the energy line.

He falls on his head and stares up at me with huge eyes. I send out an energy wave that pins him to the ground like an invisible net. Unable to move, he gapes at me in shock.

Something primally scary bubbles up in me, filling me with pragmatic clarity. My entire reality boils down to prey and predator. Jet's about to discover that I'm the predator. I sink to my knees, radiating menacing vibes as I slowly crawl toward him. When I get halfway to him, I snap out a hand and drag him with an unseen force as I sit back onto my knees. Harshly, I use my psychokinetic energy to tug him the last few feet to me while he hoarsely screams in protest. When I have him eye to eye, my lips pull back animalistically, and I breathe out a mentally audible purr. *"Fuck you, Jet."*

The incorporeal thought bounces and echoes from the walls.

I smile sadistically. My empathic gift rages around his terror. I nod. "You should fear me." I release an energy blast that thuds him against the wall. His eyes flutter about, and I can sense that he's not even close to mentally present. I slowly stand while he attempts to collect himself. Once there's clarity in his eyes, I raise an eyebrow and send out a blast aimed at his family jewels.

He screams and writhes as I grin sadistically.

"I'm going to kill you, Jet," I inform him, "and I'm going to enjoy it." The truth of my statement sends a panicked wave up my spine, but I ignore it, resigned to the reality that something dangerous lives in me.

I'm suddenly hit with an invisible force, and I fly back into the wall. I thud hard before thumping to the floor as all the guys exclaim. Demitri holds them back.

I maniacally laugh in my dark-water way as I get back to my feet. "Kinky."

"What the fuck?" Zane breathes.

I hold up a hand. "Hush."

"Wow. What happened to cute little Melanie?" Zane says, clearly not good at hushing.

I look his way, exasperated.

Jet seizes the opportunity of my distraction, and I get smacked in the chest with a sonic boom of energy. My ears ring, and the air is knocked out of me as I careen through the condo. It happens so fast that Demitri doesn't have time to do anything more than scream my name. I watch as the open sliding door whizzes past. Just as my calves meet with the balcony rail, and I know I'm about to plummet, Zane grabs me in a rush. I slam into his chest as he yanks me to him. He deeply inhales behind my ear. His eyes roll into the back of his head with an aggravated flutter.

"Weird, and hot," I think on an audible mental wave.

Zane turns with gritted teeth and then roars furiously at Jet, who races to the open door.

Jet stops short and looks at me with obsession that goose-bumps my whole body. "I'll be back." He smiles, slow and sinister, at Zane. "I'm going to kill you too. I'll save you for last though. You'll love it. The way the blood ruuuns." Jet slides his sick eyes my way. "You'll be the crowning trophy."

I draw a massive energy load from my last reserve, but just before I launch it at Jet, he says, "Huh-uh-uh." He hits Demitri square in the chest with an invisible attack, making Demitri scream and plunge to his knees.

In the confusion, Jet disappears.

Zane races out the door after him. Torn between helping Demitri and following Zane, I choose Zane because he's a Normal and doesn't stand a chance against a killer who apparently has energetic powers. I run for the door, arriving at the landing just as an energy attack nearly gets to Zane. I toss an invisible shield over him just in time. The energy hits, blasting the shield apart with visible sparks. My eyes widen as terror fills me. Jet is far more dangerous than I realized. I just used what was left of my reserves, and my legs are Jell-O. Luckily, Jet bolts out of view, and I sag against the railing.

"Get back here, Zane," I say, disgusted.

"We have to go after him!" Zane insists.

I roll my eyes and wrap him in another shield. I drag the shield toward me, knowing I'm going to pay for the energy use in a minute.

As Zane ascends, his shoes hit each step. In time with the smacks against each stair, he says fitfully, "No, no, no, no, no, no, NO!"

I release the shield around Zane as soon as he's on the landing. The others gather around the open door, clearly in shock. Demitri's hands are on his knees. His head hangs, but at least he's standing. The attack he was hit with could have easily killed him.

"I'm a *man*, Melanie," Zane barks, snapping my attention his way.

"Congratulations?" I reply, unsure what that has to do with anything.

Zane sputters. "You can't just *drag* me up the stairs!"

"Can too," I retort, gesturing with a flippant hand at the display I just made.

"Can *not*!" Zane bellows.

"Just *did*!" I volley back childishly.

Zane rattles his head, completely overwhelmed. "Damn, Mighty Mouse! Leave me with a little dignity."

I roll my eyes. "You're very impressive."

"Don't patronize me."

Rocco cracks up. "If it helps, my dude, she thinks you're a man. The adorably unstable teenage hardbody announced earlier today that she won't stop dancing with you because you make her feel like a fairy and your cologne smells like warm caramel and dirty thoughts."

Zane belts laughter at that revelation.

"That is *not* what I said." I huff. "Zane?"

He replies with a lilt, "Yes, Melanie?"

"I said you smell like warm caramel and naughty secrets, not dirty thoughts," I inform with a matter-of-fact head bob. "In two years, when I'm legal, I'll have dirty thoughts. For now, your virtue is safe."

This amuses Rocco, Luis, and Pepe.

As I saunter back inside the condo, Zane gives Demitri a snide look and follows me.

"Can we get back to what matters? We have to stop Jet," Demitri insists.

I give Demitri a nasty look. "You can barely stand. He just waxed my ass, D. I'm toast. We're damn lucky he ran, or he would have killed us all. My reserves are bottomed out. Did you not SEE that?" I slam the door shut, locking it. "Not only is that pervert obsessed, he's clearly deadly in more than one way."

"All the more reason that we go after him," Rocco rationalizes.

"We can't," Demitri says with a calculated look. He shifts his steely gaze to Zane. "You noticed it, didn't you?"

"Noticed what?" Zane asks, caged.

"You're eyes fluttered," Demitri accuses.

"What is happening?" Rocco demands.

Demitri growls out an aggravated exhale. "Apparently, Zane noticed something about Melanie."

"What?" I ask.

Demitri ignores me.

Zane clears his throat. "She's safe with me, Demitri. I know she's sixteen, and I'm very mindful. That pheromone is intoxicating, but I can think clearly through it."

"What is happening?" I ask Rocco, who shrugs.

"No, you can't," Demitri insists. "The fact that you helicoptered here is all I needed to know."

"What the hell is happening?" Rocco asks again, miffed.

"I want Pepe and Luis to steer clear," Zane informs. "Rocco, inhale behind her ear."

"This keeps getting weirder," Rocco mutters. He steps to me, and I look up at him with big eyes. "All right, prepare for a sniffin'," he quips, to my exhausted amusement. He inhales behind my ear, and his eyes flutter to the back of his head. His head lolls back and he gasps out, "Oh my God."

Pepe and Luis are staring at us like we're insane. Demitri shifts in front of me.

"Yeah, bud," Zane agrees.

My chin shakes. "What's happening?" I ask Demitri.

"She's unaware of it," Demitri cryptically informs.

"Oh shit," Zane murmurs. He clears his throat. "Demitri, she can never dance with anyone but you, or me. It throbs when she hypes up," Zane insists.

They're apparently allying now. *Yippee.* "Please explain this to me," I plead quietly.

Before Demitri can respond, Zane says, "Honey, you have an intoxicating pheromone. I've never experienced anything like it. It nearly took out my knees the first time you turned past me in rehearsal. Pierre couldn't resist it either. I've got my head on straight about it, though. It's why I pulled you away from Ruckus when we got to the van, and I held you myself while we waited for word about Riptide. You were upset, and it revved. I put my hand over that spot behind your ear to block it in that cramped van."

"Is that why you were harsh with Pierre about me?" I bashfully ask.

"Yes," Zane compassionately replies. "It took everything I've got to think through that pheromone and get my mind together. I was concerned that Pierre didn't have it together. Don't get me wrong, Pierre loved you soul deep. That pheromone got in his head, though. He said and did things that were so out of character for him. It scared me."

"Like what?" Rocco asks.

Zane sighs. "They were supposed to get the seashell tattoos."

"Whoa," Rocco breathes out. He side-eye's me. "Did he . . . ?"

"Oh yeah," Zane replies.

"Wow. Okay. I'll give her the seashell picture and explain what it meant to him." Rocco offers me a sad smile, but says for Zane's benefit, "Don't downplay where Riptide was at with Melanie. I'm sure that pheromone burned through his hesitation, but he wouldn't have waited all that time, and then tossed his morals aside flippantly."

"You think?" Zane asks.

"I know. I get your concern though. Now that the vanilla scent is in my head, I can faintly smell it every time I look at her."

"Vanilla?" I ask.

Demitri rubs his face hard. "I have no idea what it is, but it's why perverts are obsessed with her."

"Jet, guys," Pepe reminds.

I sigh. "He'll be back."

"How can you be sure?" Luis asks.

"Apparently, I waft woo-hoo. He'll return." I sneer toward the door. "He made that clear."

"There's so much evidence that Jet's killing people!" Demitri argues. "We can't just let him go!"

I hit Demitri with exhausted eyes as energy backlash gets the best of me. "I have nothing left, Demitri. My reserves are drained. If I go after him now, it'll kill me."

Demitri scans the group. "That energy blast *hurt*, so I'm useless for the night too. Anyone else capable of shooting fireworks out their ass at the pervert?"

"Out of my wheelhouse, my man," Rocco says.

Luis and Pepe nod their agreement that this is beyond them.

Zane snorts and pulls his phone from his back pocket. He dials a number and says, "Cody?"

He puts the call on speaker just as Cody replies, "Zaney Mania, what's up?"

"Code red. Batcave."

"Got it. Fill me in."

"Jet Trippley just attacked my girl. He threatened to hunt her down and kill her, and now he's headed down the alley from Rip's." Zane makes a hot-guy snarly face. "Can you deal with this, please?"

"Oh yeah, Trippley," the mysterious Cody says. "I know the detective in charge of that case. I'll call him and have patrols sent that way. Hell, I'll have one of my guys park in the alley and watch all night."

"Bill my accountant."

"I've got this," Cody says. "I'm so sorry about Rip."

"We all are," Zane replies quietly. "Thanks for helping me, Cody."

"She's not your girl, Zane," Demitri says the moment Zane ends the call.

Zane scrunches his face at Demitri. "You requested that I shoot fireworks out my ass, and I did. Cody Stirling owns the bodyguard company for half the A-listers in this godforsaken industry. He hires the best." Zane smiles. "Not only that, but he's calling the police for us. You're welcome."

"Thank you for helping us," I say. I tip my head curiously. "You actually have a helicopter?"

I receive baffled looks for my bizarre change of topic.

"Yes," Zane informs. "I hate traffic, my schedule is insane, and sometimes I helicopter in."

"But you're an *actor*," I squeak out. I wince, realizing that the way I said it was condescending.

"I am," Zane replies, looking amused.

"Doesn't that mean you're broke, in a studio apartment, eating ramen?" I ask bashfully.

Laughter peels from the surfers.

"Wait, wait, wait," Pepe says. "Does she really not know?"

"Nope, and I plan to keep it that way." Zane hits me with an amused expression. "Sure, Melanie. I like ramen." He looks to Demitri. "We must keep her safe. If Jet gets close enough to notice that pheromone—"

My gaze slides to Demitri as I cut off Zane, "At the TV station, Jet walked past us as we were getting our microphones put on. I was all sweaty and nervous. He leaned too close to me, and his eyes did that whole fluttery thing that guys sometimes do. Same thing Rocco did earlier."

Demitri's hand cups his mouth. "That's why he's obsessed with you! I need to call Adam." He pulls out his cell phone and dials frantically.

I swallow hard and quietly ask Rocco, "It's that bad?"

"It's not bad, Melanie. It's really *really* good. That's the problem."

Pepe says, "I need to know."

Rocco shakes his head. "Don't do it. I wish I hadn't. I can't get my thoughts in order."

Uninterested in further discussion about how I smell weird, I pull my cigarettes and lighter from my bag and head to the balcony overlooking the ocean. I light up and lean on the rail, watching the ocean ripple in the moonlight.

Pepe takes a cigarette from my pack and lights up. I can feel everyone's desire to ask about what the hell just happened.

Rocco chooses another tack. "Did Riptide know you smoke?"

I nearly laugh. "Nope."

"He'd hate it."

I turn deadly eyes Rocco's way, still thrumming with my dark-water side. "Well, shit in my scrambled eggs! He isn't here to judge now, is he?"

Zane chuckles as he grabs my pack and pulls out a smoke. "The stuff that pours out of her mouth . . ." He sighs and lights the cigarette with a shaking hand. "Let it go, Roc."

Rocco's eyes snap wide. "He might hate the smoking, but he'd love what you just did back there. You're a beast."

I look out at the ocean and don't respond. My thoughts are settling, clicking in my psyche with one resounding boom after another, and I experience the metamorphic shift in a distant, calculated sort of way.

"You okay, Zane?" Demitri quietly asks.

"No. What the hell just happened?"

"I take it you're not an energy worker?"

"Nope. Looks like I'm the odd man out of the Badass Balcony Club," Zane halfheartedly jokes.

"If it helps, what Melanie just did is new for her." Demitri studies me. "It's also incredibly rare. I've never seen it."

The other guys agree that my nifty display was new to them also. They all seem stunned, but they haven't run away screaming. *Points for them.*

As my fear and heartbreak settle into a part of me that can handle the monumental emotions, I finish my cigarette and put it out in an ashtray full of joint ends. I turn and lean on the railing, facing the guys.

"We got the pictures to the police like we promised before you left for Hawaii. We found out there's a lot of missing girls," Rocco says. "Most of them are from Hollywood. The police think Jet's responsible. I don't know where that freak's been hiding, but the police couldn't find him."

I nod.

"Melanie, you just invited a murderer to hunt you."

"He was already hunting me."

Rocco blinks rapidly at me. "So that makes it okay for you to egg him on?"

"You have no clue what my life is like," I snarl. "It's hell. Every guy who touches me loses his mind and either runs, or dies. I'm hunted, beaten, shot, tortured, not to mention attempted raped. When that isn't happening, I'm all pathetic and needy. The only man who really loved me for who I am is dead." I gesture to Demitri. "I torture my best friend by depending on him to pick up my pieces." I gesture to Zane. "Now I'm dragging Helicopter Hottie into my crazy." I roll my head around dramatically. "I need sweatpants, a freaking bra, and a hoodie."

Luis disappears inside.

I scrunch my face. "Flashing my ass while I crawl around on a pervert, with a gaping male audience, is a new low. Hooray for the hamster!"

The guys spurt laughter, the mood easing a bit.

"If it helps, it was hands down the hottest thing I've ever seen," Pepe informs while he puts out his smoke.

Zane and Demitri each glare at him, and then glare at each other.

Rocco belts laughter. "It was. You can't get mad at Pepe for announcing it. We were all thinking it."

I roll my hand the guys' way while I curtsy. "You're welcome."

Luis reappears with sweatpants and a hoodie. "Pierre's closet is fresh out of bras, but these were available."

I take the clothes with a quiet thank-you. I pull on the oversized sweatpants, rolling the waist twice so they stay up, and zip up the hoodie. To ground and center my rogue energy down and out, I take a deep breath. "I can't keep doing this. Can't live my life as a colossal disaster."

"I need to warn Big Joe, Trey, and Adam that you just encouraged serial killer Olympic games," Demitri says.

I look at him. "No. You don't. What you need to do is leave me to make my calculated decisions. I know precisely what I'm doing."

"How does Jet killing you help take him down?" Demitri snaps back.

Rocco quietly breaks in. "It doesn't. This isn't about Jet being brought to justice. It's about Melanie getting to Riptide."

Demitri looks at me in shock. "He was on his last lifetime. How do you know you'll even be with him if you die?"

Zane waggles his cigarette my way. "Not that I know shit about shit, but from what I just witnessed, she'd win that battle. If she dies, it's by choice."

I shake my head. "I felt what he unleashed. He was just toying with me." I look to Demitri. "He's gonna jackhammer my freaking soul if I don't figure out how to take him out." My head drops as exhaustion overwhelms me. "I need to sleep."

"Come on, love," Demitri says with an extended arm.

I shake my head. "I meant what I said, Demitri. I can't do this to you anymore." I flick a hand flippantly toward the inside of the house. "Apparently, I can blast people into walls now. I'm exhausted and on edge. I can't take a chance on accidentally getting startled and blowing you into the next room."

Rocco's face scrunches up comically. "*Any* blowing from Melanie might result in certain death."

I give Rocco a deadpan stare. "Down, boy. There will be no blowing."

"Wasn't requesting," Rocco blathers.

"Fantastic. Now I'm terrifying," I mutter while I cross the balcony for the door. "Thank you for your support while I proved to be a freak. Zane, I'd like to speak with you."

Zane pushes away from the railing, following me inside. I stop far enough away not to be heard by the guys outside. Zane steps up next to me while I stare at the wall.

"Hi."

"Hey, Melanie," he says softly. I watch from my peripheral vision as he blinks rapidly.

I need to fix this. I slowly turn to face him and look into his eyes. I radiate vulnerability, and it takes only a moment before he softly smiles.

"There she is. I recognize that girl."

My chin shakes a little. "I'm sorry you walked in when you did."

"Are you okay?"

I shake my head. "Not even a little bit. I've never done any of that before. I have no idea how to control it." I exhale hard. "Sorry. That's not your problem. Anyway, are you okay?"

"You should be a sobbing wreck, and instead, you're checking on me?"

"I've been a sobbing wreck. Now I'm . . ."

"You're what, Melanie?" he asks gently.

I close my eyes and whisper, "I'm so scared."

Zane's arms wrap around me, and quiet tears fall. He's so much bigger than me that I'm engulfed, but it feels safe. I hang on tight.

"I'm going to get you through this," he whispers. "You and me. I promise."

His declaration makes me sob harder. He patiently waits out my meltdown. My sobs finally calm enough that I can open my eyes. I look up at Zane, who's stoically crying.

"I'm so sorry you lost him," I whisper.

Zane's expression collapses. and he melts down.

A thought comes to me. "Will you please kneel for me?"

He doesn't question the strangeness of the request, instead just sinking to his knees. I put my arms around him and pull his cheek to my chest. I curl my shoulders around him, and he loses it.

Apparently, I was right. Sometimes we all need to be little and protected. He squeezes me tight around my hips, and I wait him out for a long stretch, just like he did for me. Judging from the severity of his racking sobs, I think this is the first time he's given in to grief.

When he calms some, I say, "Beastie?"

He looks up at me, and I wipe tears from his cheeks.

"Zane," I quietly correct myself.

He smiles a little.

"We need to work you through this before you go back to your movie set."

"I'm okay," he manages.

I shake my head. "Nope. Sorry, Zane, but this is as much about you as it is about me. You and me. We're going to get both of us through this."

His forehead drops to my chest, and I hug him tight again. After a long moment, he takes a solid breath. I loosen my hold on him, and he delicately takes my hands.

I smile softly and lace my fingers with his. "No holding back tears. You need to process this. Promise?"

He nods. "I promise." He stands and stares at nothing over my head. "Thank you, Melanie."

"You're welcome." I squeeze his hand. "Love you."

"Love you too," he murmurs.

I glance toward the balcony door. Demitri and Rocco are leaning against the railing, watching us. Demitri looks like his world is ending. My empathic gift flares as desperation pours from him. There's nothing I can do to help him tonight. Tonight, I have to face my fears.

I head to the bedroom, alone.

CHAPTER 38

When I sit up, everything is foggy. Fear shoots up my spine. It's replaced by awe as Pierre steps through the bathroom door. I gasp and start to jump up, but Pierre stops me with a raised hand.

"Stay there, Melanie." He crosses to me, whole and unharmed from the bomb blast. He's perfection as he slides under the covers. He hugs me tight, and I'm shaking in disbelief to be with him again. He lets me go and leans back against the pillows.

"You're here?" I gasp out.

He smiles softly at me. "I had to have one more night with you, and I was granted the request because I'm about to be unreachable for a time. We have things to discuss."

"Why is it foggy?" I ask as I glance around.

"You're dreaming, Melanie. It's the easiest way for me to reach you."

Pierre cups my cheek and kisses me delicately. My heart squeezes tight. I feel like I'm going to explode.

I sob as Pierre pulls away to look in my eyes. "I'm so scared," I say.

"I know you are. That's why I insisted on having tonight with you. I need you to keep a level head. I'm worried about how you challenged Jet."

"I don't care about whether I live or die," I express, exhausted and done.

He gives me a piercing gaze. "Put that idea out of your mind. I'm going to fill you in on some things. I'm not supposed to, but I need to do it because the pain you're experiencing could kill you—either from heartbreak or the rash decisions you seem to make sometimes."

Pierre pulls my head down to rest on his chest and wraps his arms around me. Tears fall as I work to wrap my mind around the notion that he's actually here.

"Melanie, you've got twelve lifetimes left. Very specific things are laid out for you in each of them. You've entered the tail end of your journey, where all unlearned lessons happen. Rule number one: you must suffer through life. If you die early, it just makes the process take longer."

"You died early, Pierre," I point out.

He says with extreme clarity, "No, Melanie, I didn't. I died because I accomplished my last lifetime goal. That goal was to find my forever soul. That soul is you."

My tears stop, and clarity starts to fill me. "I'm listening."

"I'm waiting, but you've got to finish this journey. Work through things with Trey. Shut off your connection with Adam. Back away from Demitri for now and let him figure out who he is. I'm going to help him. I'm taking over as his spirit guide."

This is a lot to process—more than I want to think about right now. "I don't know how to do this without you, Pierre!" I desperately plead, unable to focus on anything but my heartbreak over losing him.

"Yes, you do, Melanie. One day at a time. The sun comes up, and your feet hit the ground."

"I don't want to be with Trey."

He chuckles. "I'm aware, but he hurts you in ways that you need in order to grow. Trey's the pain that teaches you."

"Then what are Adam and Demitri?"

"Adam's already done his work with you over many lifetimes. He just likes to hang out because he's a pain in the ass." Pierre grins at me. "I triple dog dare you to tell him that. Adam's got some hard lessons to learn also."

"Done," I say with a laugh.

"Now," Pierre continues, "here's the big thing. If you can hang on tight and work through the last of your lifetimes, you'll spend spirit-guide eternity with me."

My eyes widen. "Eternity with you is a promise?"

"It's already set, Melanie. A little patience, and you're mine forever."

"Do you promise that this torment with Adam and Trey will end?"

Pierre chuckles. "You're almost to the finish line. In the grand scheme of things, you're steps away. Those steps will feel like a long road, though. Human time is different. It'll feel like the blink of an eye to me, but it will take a long time for you. Now, here's the deal . . ."

I gasp and roll over. Pierre exhales hard. Apparently, we can sweat in our dream state. We held nothing back, lost in the moment.

Now that reality is looming, panic fills me. "You can't leave me here!" I beg.

"I know, Seashell." Pierre's gaze is desperately sad. "Spending tonight together might have been a mistake, but I had to do it." He tears up. "I'm scared too. I'm not ready for what I face, but there's no choice. So you know, I'm headed into my spiritual debrief to tie up loose ends and work through the lessons I learned in this last lifetime. I want you to remember that you won't be able to reach me, but that doesn't mean I'm gone."

"I'm scared that we didn't get enough time together to really be ready for eternity with each other."

Pierre rolls on his side and puts a delicate finger on my jaw. "I know things that you don't. Trust me when I say that I made the right decision."

"I want a say in my own life," I insist. "I don't want all these monumental decisions made on my behalf, decisions that affect me without my approval."

Pierre considers this, worry marring his gorgeous face. "I'm sorry. I should have considered that."

"This was an *eternity*-altering choice."

"Would you have chosen me?" Pierre asks vulnerably.

"I don't know. I don't have the same view of this situation that you do. What I do know is that I apparently made very calculated decisions with Demitri that I stuck by for a very long time. There must be a reason, and I would have liked to explore it."

"I'm sorry. I promise to consult you in the future. There's no going back on that choice, but I made the correct decision. Melanie, he can't even give up *Victoria* for you. Remember what I told you, please." Pierre stares into my eyes. "I'm incredibly sad and scared that I've left you alone and broken. That's a big reason why I'm going to guide Demitri. Through him, I still have a connection to you."

Tears roll down my cheeks. "This is sounding like a goodbye."

"I'm not gone. I promise I'll be waiting for you when the

time is right. Don't trust just anyone, Melanie. You've got a lot of manipulation and evil coming your way." He looks toward the wall and appears to be listening to something I can't see or hear. He turns back to me and rushes to add, "I love you. I have no regrets. You're my everything. I need you to trust me." He kisses me hard, and then he's gone.

I frantically look around the foggy room. The realization that he's gone craters what's left of my sanity. I feel panic swell to bursting. I can't breathe around it. I inhale, tip back my head, and shriek his name.

I feel my body being rattled, and a voice says, "Melanie, wake up."

My eyes snap open, and I bolt upright in bed. My cheeks are soaked as I glance around the dark room.

"Close the door," the voice says. "Give us a second."

The door closes, and the nightstand lamp clicks on.

Zane runs his hands down my arms. "Hey. You okay?"

I shake my head. Tears roll again.

"Hang on, honey," Zane says as he gets up and grabs something. He sits on the bed again and puts Pierre's shirt around my neck. He guides my arms through and pulls the shirt down.

"I'm sorry," I manage to get out. "I shouldn't have sat up."

"It's okay," Zane softly assures.

Apparently, my nudity is excusable, given my night terror. My breathing is rough and choppy.

Zane pulls me in, hugging me. "I need you to slow down. Take an even breath in."

I do as he suggests.

"Good. What happened?"

"He came to me in a dream," I whisper. "He spent the night with me."

Zane waits until I'm a little more stable before asking, "How did the visit go?"

"We discussed everything. We did what we needed to." My face scrunches. "He left, though. I just lost him again."

"Oh, honey," Zane says, his voice thick with sorrow.

"He talked about you."

"What did he say?" Zane's barely holding it together.

"That he loves you. He misses you and says to thank you for being his best friend. You made his life so much better. He also said to thank you for taking care of me."

"He's not mad?"

I shake my head. "No. He . . ."

"He what?"

I quirk my mouth. "It's cryptic. Maybe you'll understand it. He said . . ." I look up with a scrunchy face. "I want to get this right, and it's weird. Okay. He said, 'Tell Zane that what he thought on the red couch is the route.'"

"Oh, shit," Zane whispers. His hand snaps over his mouth. He looks stunned.

"Where is the red couch?"

"It's in the break room on set."

I perk. "That means he visited you. That's really exciting!"

Zane's pained gaze causes me to wince.

"Does Pierre visiting scare you?" I ask.

"No. What I was thinking on that red couch does."

"Do you want to talk about it?"

"No. I'm okay. What else did he say?"

"Your instincts are right, but it won't be easy. Waiting is agony, and you need to figure out how to handle that. Also, that you aren't losing it, and there's a reason." I shrug a little. "I don't know what it means, and he flat refused to explain it."

Zane looks beside himself. He rubs his face hard, his eyes a bit glazed.

A knock at the door interrupts us.

"Come in," I call out.

Demitri opens the door and slides in, closing it behind him. He surveys Zane on the bed with me, and his brow furrows. "Hey. I was just checking on you. You okay?"

"No, Demitri. I'm not." I stare at him, suddenly blazingly uncomfortable. My heart clenches, and I can't breathe around my frozen lungs. "I need a minute," I barely manage to say. Unconsciously, I scoot back from Demitri and closer to Zane.

Zane side-eyes me before shifting and putting an arm around me.

Demitri stares absently at the bedspread, thinking. He finally says, "Please let me stay in here with you. I can't sleep in the living room."

"I can't. I need you to just trust me on that."

Demitri gestures to Zane. "Are you really picking Zane to help you over me?"

"I have to. I'll explain soon. Right now, I need to calm down. I'm sorry, Demitri." When he leaves, I let go of a heavy exhale. "That was harsh," I say quietly.

"No, it wasn't," Zane insists. "You were clear about what you need, and you communicated kindly."

I take an unsteady breath. "Can you stay in here until I fall asleep? I'm scared to be alone."

"Of course." Zane stretches out on top of the covers.

I curl up with my snotty, tear coated cheek on his chest. He lightly rubs the back of my head, and I start to calm.

CHAPTER 39

I take a deep breath, staring at the door. I took the world's longest shower, attempting to delay the inevitable, but now I realize that I must do this. I'm conflicted on a lot of levels. I genuinely love Pierre, but . . . I didn't expect to say yes to his marriage offer and then have that be the end of our time. At the moment, it seemed exciting, the future bright. Without that future, I'm left unsettled about my title of wife, along with all this responsibility. It's mine to contend with, though. Pierre understood my hesitation when we discussed it last night, but he insisted that we're right for each other. I know that, but *damn*.

I gather myself, ready to face today. In the end, I have no choice.

Last night with Pierre did bring *some* clarity. I'm still lost, but at least the finality of death is softened a little knowing that he is in a good place, even if I'm not.

In the living room, I find Rocco talking quietly with Pepe on the couch. I scan the room and spot Zane out on the balcony, leaning against the railing. To my surprise, Demitri is sitting on the other side of the balcony in one of the chairs. They aren't speaking, but they're coexisting. I'll take it.

"Made it through the night?" Rocco asks quietly.

I nod but don't have much to say.

"Demitri felt you wake up," Rocco informs.

My eyebrows rise. "That's new." Nerves bunch my stomach.

"Zane asked me to send you to him when you emerged. He's a hot-damn wreck, but we curbed the looming fistfight." Rocco is staring at me oddly.

"Fistfight?"

"Yeah, Melanie," he says, seeming a bit disgusted. "Zane and Demitri went at it when Zane came out of the room. I don't know what the fuck is going on, but I have questions."

"Ugh. I'll deal with it." Wanting to avoid a deep discussion with Rocco, I swiftly head out the balcony door. I need a few minutes to get my mind right and find out what happened.

As I step to the railing next to Zane, I decide to ignore Demitri for the moment and focus all my attention on my new friend. Zane pulls a cigarette from my pack and lights it. He hands it to me, and I take a drag. His eyes never leave the ocean as he casually grabs a blue coffee cup and hands it to me.

After an indulgent sip, I smile slightly. "You remembered."

"How could I forget that morning in the café?" Zane chuckles. "You like half your cup full of heavy cream, two heaping spoons of sugar, and a splash of coffee."

I laugh a little. "No judgy-wudgy, Beastie Boy."

"No judgment here. Good morning."

"Good morning," I reply, relaxing a little.

After I take a drag of the cigarette, he takes it from me and pulls a puff before handing it back.

"Did you manage to stay asleep after I left?" he asks.

I shift a cagey gaze his way, and his eyebrows furrow.

"Yes. Thank you for helping me."

He leans in closer. "Can I get some clarity on something?" When I nod, he murmurs, "There seems to be a great deal of confusion and opinions, so I'd prefer to get your answer. Are we going through this as acquaintances who are stuck in the same hell of losing Pierre, or are we friends?"

"We're friends, but I also want it clear that we're dance partners. That means I trust you unequivocally."

Zane side-eyes me curiously, and I smile a little as I look out at the ocean.

"I put my life in your hands every time you lift me over your head," I explain. "We're good friends, Zane, even though we have to get to know each other better." I finish my coffee, reaching around him to set my cup on the table. "Thank you for the coffee and a cigarette. You made this morning surprisingly tolerable."

"You're welcome. How long did you stand there staring at the door before you got up the nerve to come out?"

I look at him, stunned. "How did you know that?"

Zane scoffs. "Because it's what I'd do if I lost my spouse and had to face people the day I planned the memorial."

"You're a good guy, Zane."

He shrugs. "We're a lot alike. I'm figuring that out." He fires a hard look over his shoulder at Demitri.

I glance that way and huff. *Better get to a productive task.* "Well," I pat the railing. "Where do we start with all this?"

Zane holds a hand my way.

I laugh a little, surprised.

I take his hand, and he says, "We start with a morning walk on the beach, because I need a minute before I can do this for Pierre."

I exhale hard and squeeze his hand. "I do too."

Relief pours from me as Zane guides me around and starts to

lead me though the door. Demitri reaches up as I pass him. He grabs my hand and I stop.

"I'll wait for you," Zane assures. He heads in, leaving me with Demitri.

I meet Demitri's tortured gaze. He's far more upset than I would have expected. "What's wrong?" I ask him.

He hides nothing in his expression as he admits, "I don't think I've ever felt this lost, Melanie. Please."

"Please *what*?"

"Please don't be distant like this. I thought I was going to stay with you last night. I . . ." He falters.

"We'll talk, D."

It's not the answer he expects, and his eyes widen.

"I will completely understand if you decide to go home," I tell him.

"No, Melanie. I don't want to leave. I want to be here for you." He looks so unsure. "That's hard to do when I'm invisible to you."

This has taken long enough that Zane is leaning with his back against the open balcony doorjamb, subtly eavesdropping.

I debate with myself. I must discuss this with Demitri, but I have no idea how or when. "What happened last night between you and Zane?" I decide to ask.

Demitri purses his mouth in anger. "You screamed, and I headed that way. Zane beat me to the door and went in before me. I'd checked on you earlier and was aware that your clothes were on the floor. He had no business in that room with you."

"D, he was a perfect gentleman. He said and did nothing inappropriate. I get that you're used to being the one who rescues me, but I figured you'd be grateful to be off the hook."

"I'm not grateful to be shoved aside!" Demitri barks. "You just met Zane. He isn't one of us."

"Who's *us*?" I demand.

"*Us*. He isn't an energy worker. He isn't inner circle."

"You do realize I now have an inner circle that isn't *our* inner circle, right?"

Demitri gives me a disgusted look. "This new inner circle is full of guys that you don't know if you can trust!"

I snort. "Yeah, right. Because my *us* inner circle is full of such Prince Charmings? Trey and Adam haven't exactly been trustworthy. You treat me like a chore." I smirk as irritation bubbles up. "I think it chaps your ass that others don't view me that way." I tip my head. "I'm so full of drama, after all."

"Damn it!" Demitri gets to his feet in a rush, squaring off against me.

I watch from my peripheral vision as Rocco, Luis, and Pepe cautiously gather, ready to stop Demitri if this escalates. Zane turns, openly watching the exchange.

"I knew you overheard what I said to my dad!" Demitri accuses me.

"You have a right to feel that way," I insist angrily. "In turn, I have a right to back off."

Demitri scrunches his face, fighting his anger. A little calmer, he insists, "I already told you that who I was then, and who I am now, are different people. I'm *here*. I refuse to finally be the *me* you wanted, only to watch you be the *you* that was mine—with ZANE—while you ignore me!"

"You want to have this out with an audience? *Fine!*" I stab a finger into Demitri's chest. "How many times, D? *How many times* did you do everything you could, short of telling me that I'm pathetic, to get me to go away?"

"That is *not* true," he yells back.

I narrow my eyes. "Oh, but it is. You were with me in every way but one. You split your love life down the middle, giving Victoria half, and me half. The problem, *Demitri*, is that you had to keep me at arm's length so you could play your game."

Demitri runs a hand across his forehead. "I wasn't playing a game. I was scared!"

I roll my eyes. "Of?"

"Of turning into Adam and Trey. They aren't *right* anymore, Melanie. They're both so desperate to still be autonomous people that they run from you every chance they get. I don't want to be owned by you."

Maliciously, I crack up. "Owned by me? Are you *insane*? They do whatever they want, with gusto!"

"They have zero self-control left, Melanie."

"That's not my fault."

Demitri's eyes widen. "Maybe not, but you suck men in and destroy them." The second he gets that out, he breaks into a huge grimace. "I'm sorry, Mel—"

With a hand held up to stop him, I turn my back and saunter to the far side of the balcony. I wheel around and stare at him. "You want to play hardball? Fine." My dark-water anger is getting the best of me. "Stick with Victoria. You're right in your league there."

His mouth drops open. "Excuse the fuck out of you?"

My expression snaps to amusement. "I'm sorry, was that offensive? She's a gorgeous waste of space." I gesture to Demitri, making my point.

"You think I'm a gorgeous waste of space?" he sputters.

My anger flaring, I shake with the effort not to lose control. "*Why* is she worth it?" I growl and close my eyes, attempting to control my temper. I level Demitri with a look that hides nothing about the gravity of what we're up against. "You have *no idea* how badly you've screwed up."

The anger inside is suddenly riddled with fear bubbles. I shake my head, horrified at the realization of where things are headed. "What the hell is wrong with you?" I whisper. Before he can answer, I turn my back to him and lean into the railing. "Maybe the problem is whatever the hell is wrong with me." Panic boils. I collapse over my clenched stomach. *I can't discuss this now.* I take a deep breath, grounding out my rogue energy.

"What aren't you telling me?" Demitri asks, fear in his tone. His hands land on my shoulders.

"Please don't. I'm furious with you, Demitri." I turn to face him. "I have zero clue what we're going to do except survive."

He stares at me piercingly. "What did I do? This isn't about me saying I couldn't handle the drama in your life."

"We have a serious talk looming, but I'm not doing this with you right now. I think you should go spend time with Victoria. I need to talk to Zane."

"We need to discuss this now," Demitri demands. I shake my head, and he begs, "Please! I'm going to worry sick until I know what's happening."

"It's too late to fix it. No amount of worrying will help. You made your choice."

"What choice?" The color starts to drain from his face.

Losing him . . . A shaky inhale fails to steady me. *I can't handle the reality of losing Demitri right now.*

"How bad is this?" he asks.

It takes me two tries before I finally say, "You'll be okay, Demitri." My eyes widen. "*I* won't, but that's not new."

"*Out!*" Demitri bellows to our audience. He grabs my arms.

"Let her go," Zane orders.

Demitri lets my arms go and turns on Zane. "She isn't okay. I'm fixing this! Everyone, leave!"

Zane side-skirts him and holds a hand out to me "We have to talk."

"As much as I don't want to right now," I say, blinking rapidly and trying to wrap my mind around all that has happened, "I need to have this discussion with Demitri."

"You need a breather," Zane implores. When that tactic doesn't work, he smirks arrogantly. "It sounds like he's kept you sidelined for his own convenient ends. Maybe it's his turn to be sidelined."

"I can't do that, Zane."

My new friend smiles mischievously. "Pierre would be telling him to fuck off right now."

I take Zane's hand.

Zane smiles in his winning way, clearly relishing the *W* in his competition against Demitri. "Good choice, gorgeous. Now, let's chat."

Roiling with frustration, Demitri laces his hands behind his neck. Zane guides me through the living room and out the front door as Rocco, Pepe, and Luis watch. Just before Zane closes the door, he tips his head to the balcony. Rocco nods, and Zane guides me down the stairs.

My feet meet the sand at the edge of the walkway. "The beach is kind of a tough sell for me right now."

"Pierre loved it here," Zane says, putting his hands in his cargo shorts pockets as we amble toward the water. "The ocean is bigger than all of us. You can't forsake it because you lost Rip."

"I didn't know him very long."

"Sometimes it works that way. You meet your person, and they're just your person, you know?" Zane looks down at me, meeting my big-eyed gaze. He stops and inhales slowly. "Are you Demitri's person?"

I shake my head. "I was. I'm not now. That's what I needed to discuss with him."

"Is this about the talk you had with Rip?"

I nod.

"Do you want help getting your thoughts straight before you talk with Demitri?" he asks.

"Yes, but I can't. What Pierre revealed is incredibly complicated." I cross my arms over my chest and cower a little.

I look toward the condo. Rocco, Luis, Pepe, and Demitri are perched on the balcony, watching us across the distance.

"Can Demitri hear us somehow?" Zane asks.

"That's an excellent question. I don't know. He's never been able to before, but his ability to feel me wake up is new, and very unsettling given what was revealed to me." I look up at Zane.

He quirks his mouth. "I'm a Normal, so I don't quite understand all this. And I'm a stranger. Still, I'm not letting you deal with this alone. I'll keep everything between us."

"Thank you. The Demitri stuff I really don't want to discuss, but I'd like to know how you feel about Pierre's cryptic message for you."

Zane stares out at the ocean. "It's terrifying on a lot of levels."

"What did he mean?"

He starts to touch my arm and then stuffs his hands back in his pockets. "I'm not sure yet. It'll be okay. We need to deal with what you're going through."

"I don't want to." I stare at my feet in the sand. "I know that I got Pierre killed. I'll never forgive myself for that."

"I'm not mad at you for it," Zane assures. "I'm grateful that if I had to lose him, I got you in the process."

Unsure what to say, I stare up at Zane.

He saves me from having to speak. "I've danced with a lot of partners over the years," he says, "but never like it was with you."

This isn't the direction I expected this chat to go, but I like it.

"How so?"

He quirks his lips. "It's effortless. When I lift you, it's not work. You drape without hesitation. You become an extension of me. I've never had a partner who adjusted just as I thought of a slight shift that needed to happen. When I had you over my head, I thought, *She needs to settle into her hip.* You dropped into your hip immediately."

"There's a reason." I smile when he looks at me curiously. "I don't want to scare you with it, but I'm empathic. For the record, I don't use the ability to snoop through your feelings. With that said, I'm accustomed to partnering with Demitri. He opens up some, but it's different with you. He's an energy worker who can shield me off. It's second nature for us to shield. Because you're a Normal, you can't do that. It leaves your vibe open for me to pick up on." I shrug. "So I adjusted." I wobble my head. "Also, when you emoted your need for me to adjust, you squeezed my hip with your pinky finger. Clues, you know?"

Zane nods. "Somehow that makes sense, and I love it. I hated dance for a long time. I've had terrible experiences in the dance world. Torn muscles, severe pain, several surgeries." He rolls his eyes. "It's been a long time since I enjoyed it. Then, there you were." He laughs a little.

"I didn't know you've had injuries," I say, concerned.

He smiles softly. "They're all as healed as they're going to get. Choreographers took brutal advantage of my size one too many times. I couldn't handle the long-term abuse of lifting two dancers at once. I have an autoimmune disease that stretches tendons and ligaments."

My eyes widen. "Don't ever partner with me again without disclosing what's happening with you. I needed to know that. I get amped because of some metaphysical stuff that lives in me.

I launched hard into lifts and tricks because I knew you'd catch me. I could have been far more careful. That was selfish of me. I apologize."

Zane chuckles. "You're the littlest partner I've ever worked with. I never get partnered with the runt of the cast litter."

I giggle, not offended. "I'm usually the smallest one in a group."

"It was so easy. I didn't hurt. I didn't struggle." He gives me an open look. "I never let anyone know I struggled, because I'm supposed to be the big guy that can do it all. I prided myself in that, but ego landed me with a torn rotator cuff and a grade-three groin tear. That surgery was horrible. Anyhow, I always hurt after a rehearsal, and post-performances were miserable. I lived on painkillers." Zane takes a deep breath before adding, "You gave dance back to me, and I'll never forget that. It's like part of me died when I had to give it up."

"Promise that you'll always tell me if something hurts," I say.

With a nod, Zane takes his hands from his pockets. He wraps his arms around me as he watches the surf. "I was so excited when you agreed to dance in the circuit. After Rip passed and the circuit was canceled, I felt guilty about mourning the loss of dancing with you again. I needed to be focused on losing Riptide."

"Life goes on, Zane. It's okay to mourn Riptide but also realize your own reality."

"Before I met you, Pierre called and told me he'd found a partner that he was positive I could dance with. He had an uncanny intuition, and he was adamant that I come down to the competition. I doubted him until I met you." Zane squeezes me a little. "I need this with you, and I'm scared of losing it. I respect that Demitri's your partner, though."

"He's really not," I reply softly. "He's my partner, but he's uncomfortable with the vibe we have. We're put in a lot of sensual pieces together. He doesn't want to feel that about me, which I respect, but . . . you know?"

Zane nods. "Partnering is all touch. If you two are cast in pieces that are intentionally sensual, and he's not comfortable with it, then your partnership is doomed. He'll hesitate. You won't trust that he's got you. You'll both doubt and hold back. It's dangerous. That's how injuries happen."

"The pieces *we* got to do were fun," I say, unsure how to approach what I really want to say.

Zane nods, lost in thought. "I'd rather just be honest instead of wishing I'd said it. I don't have the reservations Demitri does. Yes, it's awkward that you're sixteen, but it's damn hard not to get lost in a partnership that I trust, especially when I've missed dance so much."

"I never considered my age from a dance partner perspective," I admit. "It literally didn't occur to me when I bounced up and introduced myself. I apologize that I wasn't more tactful."

"It didn't bother *me*," Zane assures. "I'm highly unlikely to dance professionally with anyone else, beyond the occasional movie scene. I'm really floored that the universe shifted you into my life. Thanks to you, I have dance back."

"You didn't know that you were sacrificing Pierre for it, though," I whisper.

"He was so sure you were his girl, Melanie. Knowing that I'll end up with a longer-term connection to you than he got is ironic and cruel." He meets my eyes and cups my cheek. "I refuse to make his death pointless. Something good came of it, and I'll do it justice."

I have a hard time breathing. Zane's gaze is intense. I finally manage to say, "I'm happy to give dance back to you, Zane. It's an honor to work with you."

He hugs me again. "Thank you. I'll get back on the dance roster at the Alice Agency and talk to her about you again once she's able to handle it. She's taking Rip's death hard." He lets me go. "We need to head back inside."

"Wait." I touch his arm. "This talk wasn't about you and Riptide like I intended."

Lost in thought, Zane stares out at nothing. "I think this talk was the one we were supposed to have." He seems to startle. "At least for me. Shit, Melanie. You didn't need to hear me whine about dance. You needed help processing losing your guy."

My huge eyes shift to meet his. "Knowing I had a part in you getting back your dance passion is exactly what I needed. Thank you for telling me. I spend more time than you know feeling like a dead-weight problem. It means a lot that you treat me like a valuable person . . ."

"You should never feel like you aren't valuable," Zane implores.

"People don't come to me with their deep stuff. They hide it from me . . . or I'm the source of their deep problems. I'm dreading the talk Demitri and I have coming . . ." I falter, and my voice cracks. "Demitri seems to adore me, and he hates it. He doesn't want to adore me. Who and what I am challenges him in ways that he despises. I told him I respect his need to be done with me, and I do, but damn it." I sigh hard. "I fell so thoroughly for him . . . He and his dad had a talk that was the single most humiliating moment of my life." I cover my face with my hands.

"I knew you were close with him, but I didn't know you had a thing for him. Pierre filled me in, but not to that extent. What did Demitri say to his dad?"

"The gist was that he wasn't going to give up the hottest girl in school for his quirky best friend whose life is a dramatic disaster."

I wince. "I left right after I overheard that. I met Pierre a few hours later."

"Ouch. Harsh."

"It was, but it was honest. I need honesty more than I need to be placated. It brought extreme clarity. Because of the realization that I'm a friend Demitri loves like an annoying little sister, I had room for Pierre. That led me to finding exactly what I want in a dance partner with you." I look up at Zane. "Dance is ego driven for Demitri. He's jaw-droppingly gorgeous and talented, but he knows it. I know that I'm just a means to an end when I dance with him. I don't want to be an accessory." I pause to collect my thoughts. "I like dancing with you because I feel like I'm good at my job. You make me feel like I matter, and like we're dancing *together*, instead of dancing for *you*."

Zane inhales deeply. "I have to admit I'm having a hard time understanding how you could ever feel like no one. I mean, I *saw* what you did to Jet."

"Yeah, that's a whole big thing," I admit. "It's just that everyone who makes me feel like someone always winds up leaving. Or dying. Or distancing themselves. Guess I'm a tough sell."

"Pierre was sold. So am I," Zane assures me. "I'm on Team Melanie."

I raise a mischievous eyebrow and look up at him. "You sure you're not on Team Vanilla Pheromone?"

Zane scrunches his nose playfully. "I refuse to answer that question on the grounds of your age."

I crack up. "I'll curb the giggly flirt in me on the grounds that I have no control over the vanilla woo-hoo."

"The vanilla woo-hoo really is WILD." Zane chuckles.

"Just so I don't have to ask Demitri, will you explain what it does?"

Zane winces. "I have zero business discussing this, but I'm pissed that none of your guys ever told you. They should have—for safety reasons alone. Safety reasons are the only reason I'm willing to discuss it."

"Understood and respected." I nod eagerly.

"All right, then here goes. The vanilla woo-hoo, as you call it, smells just like really expensive vanilla extract. It could be confused for girly lotion or perfume. The problem is what it does when it gets into the bloodstream." Zane looks down at me with self-deprecating amusement. "I'm in no way a scientist, so my theory may be bullshit."

"Got it. I'm not real science-y either. Continue."

"All right, you turned past me, and I thought, 'Even her perfume is adorable,' and then it got in my head. I couldn't think. Then it got in my bloodstream, and I had some serious work to do to curb every reaction. It wasn't a normal response to an attractive female. It was obsession. I had to have you."

I shrug bashfully. "Guys are guys?" I say timidly, trying to understand.

"Nope," he says pointedly. "This wasn't a sexual thing. Well, it was, but it went far beyond that. My reaction was primally protective. It was soul deep. It had an almost *ritual* drumbeat pound in my blood. I wanted to take on everything you are and be a part of it. It was fucking terrifying. I didn't know you and had never felt anything like that about someone. It hit hard and fast, and it was monumentally overpowering."

My mouth drops open, and I stare rudely at Zane.

He nods as he glances my way. "Your reaction is right. I'm a good guy at my core. I mean that honestly. I'm very protective of the women in my life. I don't view women as objects, and I'm very stable. I believe that's why I reacted in a protective way and

was able to curb my immense sexual reactions to what you exude."
Zane clears his throat awkwardly. "I know that was blunt."

"It was, but I prefer blunt," I assure him, even as my mind rattles.

There's something like fear in Zane's eyes as he shakes his head. "It scares the shit out of me that Jet smelled that pheromone. I mean, the first time you got in my head, every primal, hidden secret started boiling inside me."

"Secrets?"

"We all have our kinks and dark side," he says with a shrug. Then he gets serious again. "If you could boil my dark side to the surface like that—to the point where it almost rolls over my ethics—imagine the malignance it's pulling out of someone like Jet. He won't stop, Melanie."

I hold up a hand. "Hang on and back up. I'm going to ask something difficult of you, Mr. Ethics."

"All right," Zane says as he stares out at the ocean. "I'll attempt to answer."

"You're right that we all have our kinky darkness. Full disclosure. I rarely hide mine. I'm called Wildcat among your crew for a reason. I'm not a saint, and one of my metaphysical abilities runs the extreme seduction route. So, knowing that you don't have to tiptoe around the topic to save my delicate sensibilities, what do you mean about rolling your ethics?"

"I'm twenty-one. I have a very public persona because of my career. I also have a best friend who's eighteen . . . *Had* a best friend who was eighteen," he corrects. "Anyhow, my best friend, who I also view as a little brother, was madly in love for the first time. Had I had a little less self-control and a weaker ethical foundation, I would have said 'fuck it' to everything in my life, happily destroyed my future in a gleeful blaze of glory, and landed in jail with a smile on my face." He looks down at me. "That's what's wrong with Trey and Adam. They gave in and lost control. I guarantee they act out as a coping mechanism because they want control over their decisions, even if they're making the wrong ones."

I nod. "Thank you for telling me that. This conversation will never go beyond us, for the record."

"Thank you. I'm incredibly uncomfortable about any of the feelings I had after I first met you. I've been consumed with curbing those instincts."

"I'm about to make it worse," I admit, "but you deserve to know something. It'll come up if we continue dancing together."

"What is it?"

"You need to understand what lives in me." I look up at him with steely eyes.

He takes a deep breath. "I think Pierre may have already filled me in."

"It'll affect you. I lose control of what I call my dark-water side when I dance. It's connected to passion, and unless we always do adorable bouncy pieces together, you *will* be hit with it." I smile a little, keeping it quirky and apologetic. "I'm sixteen, but I'm also *really* not sixteen, Zane. So you understand, I think I need to unleash it while my creepy pheromone isn't on overdrive. If it hits you without warning, the combination of the two may buckle you."

Zane's eyes widen. "What exactly are you saying?"

"That I respect your age, and that we're just friends, but also that I'm a primal beast at my core."

He squints. "Phenomenal. Do the thing."

I take a grounding breath and put a delicate hand on Zane's tank-top-clad chest. I drop my shields and send a controlled wave of my dark-water energy into him. There's no rage in it. I'm careful to allow the seduction at the core of the energy to gently pulse. My efforts at only sending the calmest version are fruitless. Zane's knees give out. He thuds to the sand, his head hanging.

Startled, I toss up my shields, putting them tightly in place. My hand snaps to my mouth as I realize that even the lightest version of my energy managed to take out the knees of a Normal. Energy workers handle it better.

I kneel in the sand, careful not to touch him. "Zane," I say softly.

His eyes are squeezed closed, and he doesn't reply.

"Love," I say, "I can't touch you right now because the energy in you will reconnect with me, but I'm here. It'll fade. I sent the lightest version. I'm sorry. I've never done that with a Normal, and I didn't realize how it would affect you."

Finally, Zane manages to open his eyes. He stares at me with such vulnerability. "That was insane."

I nod. "I'm a lot."

"That energy . . . What *is* it?"

I sit in the sand facing him. "It can be a weapon, as you saw last night. It can also be a source of extreme sensual connection. I'm still getting a handle on it, but it flares whenever I dance. It didn't flare at the competition because the pieces we did had zero sensuality. It's why Demitri runs from me. It's also why he can't give up dancing with me. That energy is addictive, and I think he hates it. It's created great conflict in him because he doesn't want me romantically. You need to understand that it lives in me, and it'll eat you up slowly."

Zane draws a breath as if to speak but then hesitates.

"I know you wanted to dance with me," I say, "but that energy, in combination with my pheromone issue, may not be worth it."

He flops back to lie in the sand. "That energy isn't making me run, which honestly, is incredibly scary. It makes me want to stay." He gives me a quirky look. "You know when you see a dangerous critter that looks friend-shaped, you're aware it's deadly, but you want to pet it anyway?"

I giggle. "Sure. Like a bear?"

He nods. "You're that."

"Well, that's better than you running away because I'm a freak." I flop down in the sand next to him.

"You *really* are," Zane quips.

I crack up, giving into the insanity of it all. "Pierre didn't run. He embraced all of it. It was nifty."

"My God, he was so obsessed with you. He couldn't get you out of his head after he met you. He tried. I attempted to help him. So did Rocco. It was so bizarre, and totally unlike him. I didn't get it until now. If he couldn't curb it, no one stands a chance." He rolls onto his side to look me in the eyes. "He was genuine, for the record. He truly loved you, but he couldn't control his common sense. He chose to give in to it because he viewed being with you akin to harnessing lightning. He said, 'When given the option to hold that kind of power in your hands, you have to take a chance.'" Zane shrugs. "I get it now."

"Where do you stand with me?" I ask fearfully.

Zane props up on an elbow, lounging in the sand. "More determined to protect you than I was before. I'm glad you showed me the reality. I'm also glad that you didn't let me get blindsided. You're my brother's girl, and I'm going to make sure no one hurts you."

I sit up and wobble my head. "Big brother that thinks I'm woo-hoo. Freaking awkward." I chuckle.

"Meh. We can work with that. At least I know it was metaphysical trickery, and I'm not just a giant pervert."

We both dissolve into comfortable laughter. "If it helps, my dark-water side makes *everyone* uncomfortable." I look at Zane and quietly inform him, "I harm people simply because of what I am. The fact that they stick with me is a miracle. I need you to understand that I recognize the importance of personal boundaries. You, for instance, aren't a teen chaser, and yet you had to grapple with your instincts and ethics. That's not fair to you."

"True, but you've been honest about it. So, I propose that we work together with the understanding that if I ask for a minute to get myself together, you grant me space."

"Done. I can do that."

He smiles. "Then we're good." He stands and offers me a hand up. "Let's go tackle planning the kind of memorial that our Pierre deserves." He puts an arm around my waist, and we make our way back to the condo to face the impossible.

CHAPTER 40

"**P**olicy of Truth" by Depeche Mode is playing. I can feel Demitri's hyper-focused gaze on my back. I'm tired, soul deep, and I feel lost.

"Yes, sir. I'll have the obituary to you in the next few hours, but I don't want it to run until after the paddle-out. The memorial is by invitation only." Zane listens for a moment before ending the call.

Zane hands me a pad and a pen. "Ready to write the obituary?"

I shake my head with huge eyes.

"Do you want me to do it?" he asks quietly.

"Yes, please. I don't even know Pierre's middle name." The awkwardness of being included in all this planning is making me more and more uncomfortable. I really don't know Pierre, and the past few hours were bizarre.

"His middle name was Love," Rocco informs.

"You have to be kidding!" Demitri barks. "Was *everything* about him perfect?"

"Pretty much," Luis interjects.

"I need a minute," I whisper to Zane. I hand him back the pad and pen and turn to go who knows where. This condo isn't big enough for all of us, and I'm feeling suffocated.

My gaze catches Demitri's. We stare at each other, and he says, "That's the look you give Trey."

"That tracks."

Demitri shakes his head. "I don't want the look you give Trey. My goal in life is to fix that look every time you get it from someone else."

I sigh and shake my head. "I'm just really tired."

"Can I please help you sleep?"

"No, thank you," I reply, aware that Zane, Rocco, Pepe, and Luis are listening.

"Your metaphysical abilities go haywire when you're exhausted. Given the new one, you need to sleep." Demitri flourishes his hands. "That's what I'm for. Please, Melanie."

I grumble on my way out to the vacant balcony. I sit in one of the chairs and stare at the ocean.

Demitri follows, closing the sliding door behind him before he sits in the chair next to me. "Talk to me, Melanie."

"Pierre came to me in a dream last night."

Demitiri leans forward in his chair and rubs his face hard before steepling his fingers under his chin. "Tell me."

"This is going to be a difficult discussion." I draw my knees up and rest my chin on them. "You've been with me from the start of my existence."

Demitri's eyebrows rise.

"You aren't my soulmate for a reason, Demitri. When we met, there was a meteoric connection. Apparently, in the spirit realm, after our first lifetime together, it was so perfect that we chose to be more than soulmates."

"There's more than soulmates?" Demitri asks with dread in his voice.

I nod, and tears brim painfully. My chest tightens. "Thank God for that." I give in to the tears. "I can't handle soulmates being the end all, be all, because soulmates leave." The realization that my forever bond with Demitri isn't enough for him to even take a chance on me crashes in. I scoot from my chair, leaning on the railing to watch the ocean waves.

Hands land on my back. "If we're discussing this, I'm holding you," he gravels out as he wraps me up tight.

My eyes close. I hate that I always want to be held by Demitri. Now that I know why, it makes this even more painful to discuss.

"I need an honest answer out of you before I reveal more," I implore. "What is your instinct with me?"

"I always want you around," Demitri quietly admits. "I gravitate to you. I feel obsessed with you, and it's a bad look, Melanie."

"There's a reason. This is hard to explain, but I'm going to try. Once a soul completes the lessons of their lifetimes, they become spirit guides. Pierre was on his last lifetime, and he's a spirit guide now."

"Okay," Demitri prompts as I falter.

"You and Pierre are a very rare kind of soul, Demitri. You were created with the utmost values. Think of it as you being a spirit guide in a living body. It's a difficult position you were in because you were responsible to maintain your values and keep your focus. Anyhow, we became soulmates our first lifetime, but chose to forego that to run the eternity gauntlet for two hundred and fifteen lifetimes because we wanted forever. The idea is that I experience the pain, and you provide the healing and guidance while we journey together through our paths. Apparently, I wanted eternity with you so much that I agreed to experience a series of mortifying horrors over the course of my lifetimes as payment for the possibility of us becoming eternally bonded as a spirit-guide pairing. You see, I didn't have a soul-path plan with the depth of yours. I was never meant to be on your level. To become your eternal equal, I had to earn the necessary knowledge through experiences built of pain. In turn, you've had to work through the agony of watching me destroyed over and over."

"Hang on a second. I need clarification." Demitri inhales through heavy emotion. "Are you saying that we both *chose* lifetimes full of impossible torture?"

I nod. "Apparently, although Pierre doesn't seem to have all the details about why Adam was my soulmate, and then there you were."

Demitri squeezes me painfully tight. "That explains why you experience horrific things so often." He's radiating despair and confusion. "It's my fault, and I ran from you because I thought it was drama?" he adds in disbelief.

"You need to understand how things have shifted," I say, gutting up to drop this bomb. When he doesn't reply, I hit him with the first round of tragic news. "You caused the shift this lifetime. A soulmate bond is fusing between you and Victoria. It's why you can't let her go."

"*What?*" Demitri's tone is steely.

I nod. "She's your girl, D. Welcome to hell." I stare at the ocean while Demitri's heart hammers against my spine.

He tries three times before he manages to get out, "I can't be soulmates with Victoria."

"Why?"

"Because I like her for shallow reasons," he admits.

"There must be something deeper there. You're a perfect soul, and you love her. You see something in her subconsciously that was worth more than the connection we built over so many lifetimes. Find the depth."

There's concern in Demitri's eyes. "I don't think there is any depth."

"You better hope like hell that there is, because soulmate bonds are cataclysmic even when life is good," I say with no emotion.

Demitri shakes his head. "Being brutally honest, I don't like her at all. I'm with her because of her body."

The confirmation that he gave me up for a hot body is not entirely surprising, but it's still heartbreaking.

Apparently, Demitri realizes that also, because he asks fearfully, "Are you saying that I traded your soul for hers?"

I nod. "We have twelve lifetimes left. We made it through two hundred and three lifetimes, only to be derailed by Victoria's rack and stack. We stuck together for a long time, but it's over, Demitri."

"Hang on. Pump the brakes. I just found this out!" Demitri insists. "It's not over, because I can fix this."

I shake my head mournfully. "Now for the next atomic bomb. Pierre's become your spirit guide. That's excellent news for you because he deeply understands you. There's bad news, though. Pierre asked me to explain that he's replaced you as my eternally bonded." As I speak the words, I feel dead inside.

Demitri sputters. "He *what*?"

"He didn't ask me. He gave me no time or consideration. In his defense, people don't get a lot of say in this stuff, but I wish he had waited. We argued about that. He did it because you, Mr. Perfect, have slid down the ranks after losing sight of your larger purpose. I've worked up the ladder because, apparently, two hundred and three lifetimes of torture and commitment taught me a lot. For the record, had I been given a choice, I would have stuck with you and just accepted that you're an idiot, because you're my person when it boils down. Pierre says it's already done, though. No backsies."

Demitri's hands quake as they cover his face. "No, no, no, no. Wait, wait, wait. Everything needs to slow down." He bends at the waist, gasping out, "I should have listened to my dad." Panic is alive in his eyes as he looks at me. He attempts a deep breath that rattles, before he calmly says, "Wait. Let's go through this slower."

He plops down on the balcony floor. I sit knee to knee with him.

He takes my hands and asks, "Do you want eternity with Pierre?"

I shrug and tear up. "I didn't get enough time with him to discuss eternity. He and I were together part of one lifetime before. Then there were the few weeks I knew him this lifetime."

"Okay," Demitri says, "so, you *have* spent a lifetime married to him?"

"No. I was married to Trey then. I had an affair with Pierre, apparently."

Demitri's eyes widen.

I nod, forlorn. "You've been the one constant I could count on in my lifetimes, but not as soulmates."

"Explain that again."

"Here's how Pierre says it works. To be spirit-guide paired, you must only have pure love for the other soul. It's like the super version of a soulmate bond. Soulmate bonds are a love contract only during the duration of a soul's lifetimes. Their purpose is to teach hard, and profound, lessons. Once you reach spirit-guide status, soulmate bonds dissolve, and a soul moves on to be with their spirit-guide-bonded soul, or they ride solo. We were positive we could make it through without things getting tainted." I smile a little, but it's a pained kind of smile. "We almost made it, but we fizzled this lifetime."

"Fizzled?" Demitri barks. "We *fizzled?*"

"You lost focus, fizzling our bond. Victoria wins."

"*Nooo.* Nope. No, ma'am. I don't want Victoria! Forever? *Forever*, Melanie? With her?" Demitri's completely spun out. "If the world were to end, I'd rush to you, because when it all boils down, you're my person!" He gasps. "How did I not see that before?"

"Because knowledge brings clarity. It's okay," I assure him. "You can move on, Demitri. I'm apparently covered."

"What kind of an arrogant *jackass* makes an *eternal* decision about FOREVER without asking you?" Demitri bellows.

"Shhh," I hiss at him. "Secret chat about insane hush-hush stuff."

It does nothing to quell Demitri's panic.

I grasp his cheeks. "Love, you didn't think I was yours, and you didn't want me to be yours. Now, I'm not yours. Nothing has changed except that you *really* got your wish."

Demitri takes a frantic breath. "*Everything* has changed!"

I shake my head softly. "You didn't want us," I remind him compassionately. "Unfortunately, the powers that be took your sentiment into account. I *did* want us, and the thought of you made my heart hurt. I didn't understand why I felt like that until Pierre explained all of this. I thought I was immature and obsessed with a gorgeous guy. I now know that wasn't the case. I feel better knowing that I'm not just some unhinged stalker freak. I want you to be happy. I'm okay with this."

"I'm not okay," Demitri begs.

I smile softly. "We can still be friends, but your obligation is done. I'm Pierre's problem now, and I have to trust that he knows something I don't, and that's why he made these monumental decisions."

"Two hundred and three lifetimes?" Demitri gasps out.

"Two hundred and three lifetimes of you fighting every second to hold it together while my pathetic ass tried to survive pain and torture so I could learn enough to be with you for eternity. I give you credit, D. You held on for a long time. I tried. I can promise you that. I don't know what went on in our past lives, but I know that, for you, I'd do anything." Humiliation burns red up my neck. "I know I destroy men. You're right about that. I'm relieved that you avoided a relationship with me. You're perfect, and I could never destroy you."

Demitri inhales frantically. "Melanie, wait. I'll face all of it. I was being a shallow asshole. I get it now."

I shake my head. "You shouldn't be with someone you feel that kind of hesitation over." A small smile crosses my lips. "Apparently, we've had a lot of time together. I'm so grateful for that."

Demitri's complexion runs gray. "I think I'm going to be sick," he mutters.

"Then I'll wrap this up," I say, steeling my resolve. "Now you know why you felt so irrationally attached to me. I thought you'd be relieved to find out that your servitude to my dead weight is truly over. You're free." I smile softly. "You were adamant about no 'us.' I truly believe in you. This must be the right thing."

I start to stand, and Demitri gets a death grip on my wrists, pulling me back to my knees. "I did *not* know I was making this decision!"

"Victoria will be far easier to deal with." I gently extricate my wrists from his shaking hands. I kiss him on the forehead. "Enjoy simplicity. You've earned happiness. I'm releasing you from our commitment. I love you."

I stand and leave the balcony, headed back inside. Now that Demitri knows everything, I feel oddly content in the realization that he is free. Life with me is hellacious.

Maybe I should become a nun. I snort before cracking up at the thought.

Zane and Rocco are sitting at the dining table going over what they've written. They look my way curiously.

"You okay?" Zane asks.

I grin and give him a sarcastic thumbs-up. "I'm planning to become a nun, Helicopter Hottie."

Zane belts surprised laughter while Rocco looks at me like I'm insane.

"She's so fucking bizarre," Rocco squawks.

"I love it," Zane says through his laughter.

"Oh Lord, don't you start," Rocco grumbles at Zane.

"Please go back to accomplishing my obituary duties," I say with a hand flourish.

Uninterested in further disturbing them, I cross to a big cabinet by the stereo. I pull open the cabinet doors and find row after row of records. I've never seen so many in one place. Marveling, I thumb through them and smile. Pierre had incredible taste in music.

Just as I start to pull a record, Demitri frantically rushes by, headed into Pierre's bedroom. I follow and get to Pierre's bathroom just in time to witness a truly impressive waterfall hurl that only halfway makes it into the toilet. When another bout hits, I cross to Demitri and put a hand on his back. Rocco and Zane lean on the doorjamb, watching with huge eyes.

When Demitri finally finishes, Rocco says, "Goddamn, man. I think you just barfed up what you ate in the fourth grade!"

Demitri sags to the floor, pale and coated in sweat. He wraps his arms around my waist and gasps out, "You can't do this."

"I didn't do it, Demitri," I softly remind.

"This isn't happening," Demitri desperately moans out with conviction.

"It's already happened. We can't change it," I reply with no emotion. I clear my throat. "I need to get through the loss of Pierre before I can even begin to unpack losing you. I also haven't dealt with Trey leaving me, although I don't think I even care at this point."

Without warning, Adam barrels in. He skids to a halt in the middle of the bathroom and surveys Demitri clinging to me. Demitri flops to the toilet again and hurls a fresh round of impressive goo.

I wince. "Why are you here, Adam?"

Adam grimaces comedically as he watches Demitri. "What the hell is wrong with him?"

"He's sad," I huff. "Why are you here?"

"Demitri told me you had a battle with Jet, who likes how you smell."

I roll my eyes. "And?"

"And I'm here!" Adam waves his hands about, like that's the answer to everything.

"Who is this?" Zane asks with a scrunched expression.

"This is Adam." I Fraggle my face, and Zane chuckles.

Adam looks at Zane for the first time. "Zane *Drell*?"

"Is it weird being recognized everywhere you go?" I cut in.

Zane nods. "Pitfall of fame. It blows."

Adam flaps his hands about frantically while Demitri yaks up another round. "What's the haps?" Adam demands.

I roll my eyes. "Oh no. *This* version of Adam arrived." I look to Zane and Rocco. "There are two versions of Adam," I inform them. "Cool, collected Harley guy, and this train wreck." I flourish toward Adam. "Buckle up. It's time for *The Melanie and Adam Show*."

Zane and Rocco spurt laughter.

"Wait, wait, wait," Adam blathers. "Why is Zane Drell here?"

I smile sarcastically. "Oh, well, you see, he got a whiff of my vanilla pheromone and decided I was a giddyap good time."

Adam gives Zane a challenging look. Zane just chuckles in response.

I snap my fingers repeatedly at Adam. "Yo, asshat, over here." Adam looks at me and I nod brightly. "Wanna explain why you didn't fill me in that I apparently smell like a pornographic cupcake factory?"

Adam runs his neck out at me. "Was that a mystery?"

"Umm, yeah . . ."

"You have a nose!" Adam gestures at my face.

"I can't smell it!"

His face bunches. "You can't smell that? You're all pissy in this little room, and it smells like the damn cookie store at the mall." He grins. "Thanks for that, because Demitri's barf is repugnant." He reaches without looking and flushes the toilet on Demitri's behalf.

"After everything we dealt with regarding Joel and his unhinged father," I seethe, "you should have told me that I have an irresistible pervert-lure."

Adam scratches his head. "I guess I didn't make the connection."

"You're a pervert, Adam," I reply sarcastically. "I lured *you*."

"You lured me because I'm your soulmate," Adam replies, exasperated. "Also, you're a pervert, too, so don't get all uppity. That's why we get along."

"Oh, eeew. I get that you're all hopped up on your newfound heaven with Valerie, but I thought you at least had my back enough to warn me. You knew about Jet, and you *still* didn't tell me. I don't appreciate that, Adam."

He glares at me. "Heaven? Are you shitting me? Do you have any *idea* how trapped I am?"

"Wah? Are you?" I give him a disgusted look. "Pregnancy with your fiancé isn't a trap, you jackass."

Demitri manages to stand. "I should have told Melanie about her allure," he says unsteadily. "I didn't want to discuss it. I wanted to pretend it doesn't exist so I could fool myself into thinking it was nothing. Now, she's being attacked by yet another psycho."

"If you didn't tell her, then who did?" Adam asks.

"I did," Zane says.

Adam looks his way, and Zane waves a little.

"Why do *you* know about it?" Adam demands.

"Oh, well, I dance with her. And apparently, I've got a little pervert in me because I helicoptered in to make sure she's okay." Zane grins.

"You *what*?" Adam looks at me judgmentally. "Adding to your collection, I see."

"Oh, fuck off, Adam. Clearly my collection is doing stellar. Demitri wants nothing to do with me. Pierre is now murdered because of me. You're, well, you're *you*. Trey left me. Zane's just my dance partner."

"Hey, now!" Zane barks. "I'm also your friend."

"Thank God *someone* is," I huff. I cross my arms over my chest. "I can't deal with you right now, Adam. There's a line at the Melanie's Life Sucks Department. Take a number and wait your turn."

"I'm here to protect you," Adam insists.

I give him the look he deserves. "Why are you *really* here?"

"Ugh." Adam's hands flop. "I needed an excuse to catch a breather. Valerie is driving me *insane*. I just *can't* with her. 'Baby this' and 'baby that.' We just moved into a *house* that I bought."

"Congrats," Zane offers.

Adam gives him a look, then points at me as he says to Zane, "She's my soulmate. My soulmate I *gave up* for a Normal who's pregnant and wants me to paint a nursery mint green!"

"Oh my God, what did I do?" Demitri moans before spastically bending over and letting loose a fresh round of vomit quite loudly.

"What's wrong with him?" Adam asks.

"Oh, well, we got some fun news," I inform.

"That looks a lot like pregnant," Adam says emphatically. "Is he pregnant?"

I laugh. "Nope, and I'm mad enough to fire off a few shots your way, so I'm gonna tell you." I gesture to Demitri. "Guess who was supposed to be my forever?"

Adam studies Demitri. "Really? *Him*? I thought I'm your forever!"

"Nope!" I shake my head with a smirk. "You're my original soulmate, one who's run his course but still sticks around to be a pain in the ass." I gesture sarcastically in his direction. "Case in point. You're being a pain in the ass right now."

Adam gives me a look. "How do you know all of this?"

"Well, that's a big honking secret," I crow.

"So, then what's Pierre?"

"Pierre's the new Demitri."

Adam nods. "Oh. Then what's Demitri?"

"Demitri's Victoria's arm candy." I smile as Demitri dramatically moans, clutching his stomach.

"What's Trey?"

I nod vibrantly. "Trey's the pain that teaches me."

Adam cracks up before jutting a thumb Zane's way. "What is he?"

Before I can reply, Zane cuts in. "I'm trying to keep myself in check, because Cupcake Cathy passes out obsession and erections like they're gifts with purchase. And I'd rather not get arrested on statutory."

Adam leans my way while he surveys Zane. "You sleeping with the famous guy?"

"Nope. Helicopter Hottie and I have decided to be respectful friends with boundaries."

"Fantastic," Adam crows. "Sounds like you're single. I'm beyond stressed and need a head-clearing explosion. Will you sleep with *me*?"

"Ugh," I hack. "Adam, I'm in my kind-of-married dead husband's bathroom. Don't be you, please."

Demitri stands again.

I gesture to the bedroom. "Go lie down, Demitri."

"Will you lie down with me?" he asks pitifully.

"No," I snap.

Rocco and Zane crack up.

Adam laughs. "I see that your grief over your dead fake-husband has effected your libido."

"Shut up, Adam. Go home and paint the nursery! Lord!" I push through the door and head back to the living room.

Rocco, Zane, Adam, and a clammy Demitri all follow. Just as I reach for the record again, Trey strides through the front door.

I sigh. "What are *you* doing here?" I whimper.

Pepe and Luis are watching from the open balcony door.

"Who are you?" Trey asks, glaring at Zane.

"You don't know?" Adam caws. "*Everyone* knows!"

"Never mind," Trey says dismissively. "I don't care." He struts to me and tips my chin to the side, surveying my bruised face. He gives me a hard look. "You do understand that you're supposed to call me when you get attacked by a serial murdering psycho, right?"

I gesture about the room. "I believe I'm covered. Besides, I can blow people through walls now, so *eh*."

"Melanie . . ." Trey glares around, then demands of everyone, "Can we have a minute?"

"No. Get the chat over with." I cross my arms over my chest.

"I made a mistake," Trey says.

I roll my eyes. "Not you too. Stick with your decision, Trey. I'm over this." I turn my back to him and reach for the record.

Trey grabs my arm, turning me around. "I'm sorry."

I stomp a foot. "Damn it! I want to listen to Chaka Kahn."

Zane leans to Rocco. Before he can ask anything, Rocco says, "That's Trey, the super dismissive shit-stick who dumped her."

I shoo at Trey. "Go stand over there. That's your area."

Trey goes where I indicate, and I look to Demitri. "You're over there." I point Demitri toward the opposite corner of the room from Trey, and he dutifully goes to his spot. I raise an eyebrow at Adam and just point by the balcony door.

He chuckles and heads that way, though he disappears into the kitchen instead of going to his spot.

Whatever. I just want him out of my way.

"Nice! Riptide has beer," Adam calls out from the kitchen. He leans around the doorjamb. "Yo, Mrs. Strader, can I please have one of your inherited beers?"

I blink, stunned.

"What?" Adam asks.

"I can't believe you called me that."

Zane winces. "Damn."

"Take what you want, Adam," I say flippantly.

Adam goes back in the kitchen.

"He's impossible when he gets like this," I mutter. I give Trey a pleading glance. "Will you please get him out of here?"

Trey looks bored. "No. I'm not here to babysit Adam. I'm here to get my girl back."

"Crap on a cracker," I belt.

"My stomach is bubbling again," Demitri whines. "Can I please leave my corner?"

"No," I snark. "You're fine. You're happy this way, remember?"

Adam returns to his corner with a beer in hand. "Reporting for duty." He salutes.

Zane and Rocco crack up.

I rub my face. "I hate my life." To Zane, I say, "You're over there." I point to the one remaining empty corner.

Zane smiles at Rocco. "I get a corner." He happily strides to his spot.

"Where do I go?" Rocco asks.

I smile at him and blink sweetly. "You get to be in charge of those three!" I point to Demitri, followed by Adam, and then Trey.

"No one's in charge of me," Trey informs.

Rocco gives Zane a thumbs-up. "I get a special job. This is fun."

Zane chuckles.

"All right, let's hash this out," I announce. "Trey, we're staying broken up. I'm done. Demitri, we are what we are. I'm done. Adam, you get one beer, and then *you're* done. Zane, I gave you a corner just to piss off the Three Stooges. We're not done." I scrunch my face. "That came out wrong. We aren't a *we*, and we aren't done."

My mother and Rich choose this moment to stride through the door and survey the collection of guys stuck in corners, with Rocco in the center of the room with me.

"What's going on?" Rich asks.

"An excellent question," Pepe crows from the balcony.

"I'm covered up in all of this." I gesture about the room. "I needed to organize my mess."

Rich and Mom turn in a slow circle, surveying the guys.

"What roles do each of you play today?" Mom asks, amused.

"I'm becoming a nun," I announce gleefully.

Mom and Rich grimace.

"There goes Christianity," Rich snarks, to the amusement of Rocco and Zane.

I point toward Adam. "This upstanding gentleman has decided that he'd like naughty-time with me to assuage his sadness about how his baby mama ain't stellar."

Mom grimaces. "Ugh."

"Agreed!" I point to Demitri. "He's a sad panda because his desire to not be with me has left him without me, but now I'm suddenly just so *nifty*."

Mom shakes her head and chides Demitri, "So sad. She thought you were magic."

"Meh. Over it," I say, to Demitri's dismay. I point to Trey. "He made a mistake, apparently."

Mom just rolls her eyes dramatically. Her gaze lights on Zane mid eye roll. "Heeello," she purrs.

Zane gives a charming smile. "Hello. Zane Drell. Nice to meet you." He looks to Rich. "Any chance you brought s'more stuff? We need snacks for this farce."

Rich chuckles. "Yes, but don't tell anyone. It's a surprise."

Zane laughs a little. "Secret's safe with me."

"I'll be thrilled when you reveal the secret," I tell Rich.

"Can we *please* get back to what's important?" Mom cocks a hip and surveys Zane. "What exactly are you doing here?"

Zane grins while I inform, "Helicopter Hottie is here to rescue me from planning a memorial."

"Well, aren't you thoughtful!" Mom flirts.

"I certainly try to be," Zane replies agreeably.

Mom looks to me and hisses, "Yes, girl."

I give her a disbelieving stare. "I'm not after Helicopter Hottie. He's twenty-one."

"Well," Mom says matter-of-factly, "you can't become a nun because you've been married." She gestures to Zane. "And when you got it, you got it."

My face squashes up comically. "Twenty-one," I remind. I turn in a dramatic circle, indicating the guys. "Plus, I have these."

Mom gives Trey, Demitri, then Adam disgusted looks. "They're broken. You need a fresh model." She puts her hands on her hips and tilts her head adorably. "Rich is fifteen years older than me. Granted, we got married eleven years ago, but let's be realistic. When I was sixteen, he was *thirty-one*."

My mouth drops open.

"Damn, Rich," Rocco says. "Nice work!"

Rich is glaring at my mother. "Hush, Carol."

Mom gives him an aggrieved look. "I think Zane is the clear winner in this bingo game."

I toss my hands. "I'm not trying to *pick* one of them! I'm trying to make them stop!"

"I approve." Mom smirks mischievously in Zane's direction.

Zane grins. "There's so much you don't know. Don't green-light the red couch."

Everyone appears confused, but I look at Zane with huge eyes. "Interesting twist."

He rolls his eyes. "We'll get there. For now, just keep squabbling with the Three Stooges. It amuses me, and it distracts you from your Pierre heartbreak."

Flustered, I turn on my mom. "I'm supposed to be mourning Pierre's death! Instead, all I've done is deal with all of this. It's revolting. I'd like to be sad now."

I'm interrupted as Ruckus, Caroline, and the circuit crew come through the door. Ruckus is carrying an urn, which causes everyone to freeze. He crosses to me and hands it over. I blink rapidly and stand statue still, staring at the blue metal container that I'm now holding.

"Ask and you shall receive!" Adam crows.

"May I please be released from my corner?" Zane asks frantically.

"Yes, please," I whisper.

Zane rushes to me, taking the urn. He hands it to Rocco before hugging me tight. "Let's go talk for a second."

"I'm okay," I manage to get out. I let go of Zane. "Hello to all who just arrived." My stunned gaze shifts to the urn Rocco is holding. "Welcome to my own little slice of heaven." I clear my throat, deciding on a route. "All right, where are we at with all this planning?"

"Obituary is done and ready for your approval," Zane says.

"We've got the paddle-out scheduled for tomorrow at four," Rocco says. "We need to get word out, but only to the invited list. I've got it ready."

Rich clears his throat. "I have your account statements, Melanie, and the paperwork you need to sign."

"Okay," I say, worn out. "I'd like to get this stuff handled, and I want Chinese food."

"I'll get food," Pepe offers.

"Orange chicken, beef and broccoli, egg rolls, egg drop soup," I instruct. "And whatever everyone else wants."

Pepe raises his eyebrows. "Where do you plan to put all that?"

"I'm stressed. Grab cash from the nightstand." Apparently, Pierre kept large amounts of cash on hand. There's plenty to afford eggrolls.

"I'm on it, boss," Pepe says, grabbing the phone and going to the kitchen to place the order.

"Rich, please approve the obituary. If you approve, then I'm happy."

My stepfather smiles. "I'd be honored."

"Please give the legal paperwork and bank statements to Zane."

Rich's eyebrows rise. "You sure?"

I nod, uninterested in arguing or explaining myself.

He retrieves the paperwork from a duffel bag, then hands them to Zane. "I brought clothes for you, Melanie," he says to me over his shoulder. He sets the duffel bag by the stereo cabinet.

Rocco hands him the notepad bearing the obituary. Rich steps out to the balcony to read it.

"Ruckus, Caroline, Luis, Rocco, Adam, and Trey, please start calling people regarding the paddle-out memorial," I request. "Rocco will instruct you."

They all nod and head to the couch to make a plan. Caroline squeezes my arm and smiles at me as she passes, looking proud about how I'm handling things.

"Mom," I say quietly. "Would you please talk with Demitri? I trust you with the topic, but it stays between us."

"Of course," she says before heading to Demitri.

He looks like a lost puppy as he follows my mother into the bedroom.

With everyone occupied, I look up at Zane. "I need to fall apart, please," I say.

Zane follows me to the bedroom. As we pass through, I announce, "Pardon, so sorry. Headed to the bathroom, because everywhere else is occupied."

When we get into the bathroom, Zane closes the door behind us. I take a moment to survey the mess Demitri made. I sigh and open a cabinet, finding cleaning spray and paper towels. I get to work on the floor and toilet, scrubbing harder than I need to.

After a long stretch of scrubbing, Zane grabs my hand, stopping me. "I think it's clean."

"Are we doing this right?" I ask while I throw away the paper towels and wash my hands.

"Yup," Zane replies. "I'm pissed that they handed you Pierre's urn. I'm going to talk to Ruckus."

I lean against the counter and stare at Zane.

"If you need to talk about this insanity with Demitri, Trey, and Adam, I'll help you," he offers.

"Thank you. I need help."

"I know you do."

"I can't with those guys. I have to, though." I sigh. "They're my monkeys, and this is my circus."

"You don't want Adam, Melanie. I've heard enough about him. He treats women like toys. The Trey guy seems annoyingly intense. There's no fun there, so he's out. You said there's no help where the Demitri situation is concerned. He's out. Problem solved. You're a widow with no attachments."

I bark a laugh. "Is there a reason you have to be twenty-one?" I mutter before wincing. "Sorry. No filter."

Zane snorts. "I was thinking it, too, if it helps."

"Hooray. Helicopter Hottie was thinking it." I grumble about, fussy. "This is all really weird, right?"

"Which part?"

I wave my hands about. "Pierre is dead, but I'm hosting guests at his house and cleaning his shitter that Demitri is throwing up in. My two soulmates are making phone calls for Pierre's funeral. You're writing his obituary because I don't know him well enough to do it myself, but I'm apparently 'Mrs. Strader of the inherited beer.' My mother thinks you're a real treat. You're twenty-one, but I have to fight not to hold your hand." I spin around and lean on the counter with my head hanging. "I'm so tired of being a codependent sleaze who lives in a constant state of panic."

"Melanie, all of this is going to take time. You're doing really well, all things considered."

I push away from the counter and stomp my feet irrationally. "Goddamnit! I've got a math take-home test that Demitri's supposed to help me with. Now I can't ask him." I make a sound that reminds me of a frustrated toddler.

Laughter peels behind me, and I turn in slow motion to glare at Zane. He plunks down on the floor and laughs louder. A giggle bubbles up, and I join in the merriment.

"Where's your homework?" Zane asks.

I flourish toward the door. "In my backpack next to the bed Demitri is currently sobbing on."

"Go get it. Everyone else is handling the memorial stuff. We've earned some normalcy. I'll help you."

I raise my eyebrows. "You helping me with math in Pierre's bathroom is normalcy?"

"Today it is."

With a grateful smile, I slip into the bedroom and grab my backpack.

"What are you doing?" Demitri asks.

"Getting my take-home test. Zane's going to help me."

Demitri looks at my mom with huge eyes. "Now I don't even get to help her with *math*?" he blathers.

"For the love of . . ." I huff back into the bathroom, closing the door. "It would appear that helping me with math is important to my former forever," I inform Zane.

The movie star in my dead sort-of-husband's bathroom scrunches his forehead. "Demitri really fucked up, didn't he?"

I nod. "And Pierre greatly overstepped by replacing him."

Zane pats the spot next to him, and I plop down and start digging through my backpack for the test.

"Is there any fixing it with the Pierre and Demitri switcheroo?"

I shake my head.

"Pierre has always been bad about that," Zane says. "Success came very easily to him. His arrogance was one of his only bad qualities. I'm not surprised that he decided what he wanted and took it without permission."

"I need someone who's honest and upfront in my life." I look to Zane pleadingly. "Will you be that?"

"Yes. That I can do," Zane replies. Hesitantly, he adds, "Please don't disappear when this tragedy is all over. People tend to disappear from my life. My fame and schedule eventually start to overwhelm them. I get really lonely."

"*You* get lonely?"

"You have no idea. Pierre called me every night." His head drops. "I did that for a year after his dad died. Then, when he was doing better, I started having issues with depression, and he started doing it for me. I'm really going to miss it."

"No girlfriend?"

Zane shakes his head. "I have the same problem Pierre did. Women use me for money and prestige. I hate it."

I scrunch my face. "Who does that? How do people even know you have money?"

He slides baffled eyes my way and grins ironically. "I helicoptered in, Melanie."

I shrug. "I have no idea what that costs. I mean, I know it's not a taxi fee, but who the hell knows about helicopter fundage?"

"You really don't care about that stuff, do you?"

"Honda Civic. Helicopter. Bicycle. Eh. Transportation, right?"

Zane chuckles. "Bicycle?"

"I don't care if you Fred Flinstoned or George Jetsoned your ass here. I care that you walked through that door. Didn't matter if I was screaming in a night terror, energetically attacking a pervert, demanding egg rolls, or fighting with my exes, you were here for it." My expression melts into vulnerability. "You showed up for me."

Zane really studies me. "Adam, Demitri, and Trey also showed up for you."

I shake my head. "They showed up for themselves. Adam needed an excuse to avoid his reality. Trey's doing his usual flip-flopping. Demitri felt obligated. Why did *you* show up?"

"Pierre would have done it for me."

I smile softly. "Thank you for being an actual man."

His eyebrows rise.

"I was raised by Rich," I explain. "He always shows up. He loves my mother so thoroughly. He's not selfish, forgetful, or arrogant. He works his ass off every day, and still has time for us. He's what I thought *every* man was . . . until Trey abandoned me, Adam used me, and Demitri dismissed me. Now I realize that men like Rich are very rare. You, Zane Drell, are the kind of man Rich is and Pierre was." I smile.

Zane gets a little misty-eyed. "Nobody has ever said anything like that to me before."

"Then we're even, because nobody's ever helicoptered in to take my dead husband's urn from me while I tried not to crap my pants."

We dissolve into a laughing fit.

I sprawl out on my stomach on the floor. "Wow. Heated floors. Weird."

"Pierre also had money, you see."

"Apparently, given the bank statements—the thought of which give me bubble guts." I curl up on the radiant floor.

Zane digs through my backpack, pulling out a pencil.

"What are you doing?"

"Your test. I'm a math whiz, and you've earned a break."

"Isn't that cheating, Mr. Ethics?" I ask with a grin.

He lounges on the floor and kicks his feet a bit, bent at the knees, while he starts writing answers on the paper. It's adorable, and it reminds me that it hasn't been that long since he was in high school.

"Everyone treats you like you're the sage old guy of the group, but you're not," I point out as he breezes through the test.

"Yeah, I know. I'm not a real person to people. I'm *Zane Drell.*" He says his name sarcastically, causing me to giggle. "I'm really Zaney who likes playing pinball and eats peanut butter from the jar. I like math and read Archie comic books."

"You fancy movie star, you," I tease. "Now for the real test to see if we can be friends." He looks my way, and I narrow my eyes from my prone position. "What brand of peanut butter?"

Zane gives me a very serious look. "Crunchy Jif, duh."

"Oooh, eeew!" I dramatically flop to my back and grab my heart. "The agony."

"What brand then?" Zane asks with a suspicious lilt.

I sit up challengingly. "Goober grape. Peanut butter and jelly in one jar. *And,* there's a cartoon grape and peanut on the label! Jif has a boring label."

Zane narrows his eyes. "Curveball, but it's quirky, so I'm on board." He gives me a no-nonsense look. "You must admit that Goober is crappy, though. It's all grainy."

My mouth drops open. "Well la-di-da! Helicopter Hottie is a peanut butter snob!"

He chuckles and pushes the completed test my way. "Done." He sits up, grabbing the papers that I left on the counter. "Let's get to this bank statement business."

— —

"I don't want any of it," I announce as I stride into the living room.

"Melanie, you can't run from money," Zane insists.

"I'm not. I'm realistic. That money needs to go to a different cause." I clear my throat. "Rocco, as you know, I'm signing the business account over to you, along with the shop. I'd like for you to use the personal account to create a charity surf school. Zane seems to understand all this investment stuff. Please figure out how to fund the surf school long term."

Zane shakes his head. "You're making a mistake. I can guide your investments, and you'll be set. There's two million in that personal account."

"I'm not making a mistake." I look up at Rocco. "Can you run a charity division of your surf school?"

Everyone's staring at us with their mouths hanging open.

"I can, but Melanie, you need to listen to Zane," Rocco implores.

I sigh. "Rich, are we set?"

He nods. "If you want to do this, then you should."

"Done. I'll feel better about this. None of this money is mine."

Rich smiles. "Well, you aren't out of hot water yet, Melanie. You're receiving the insurance settlement for Riptide's death. I got the call from Jessica this morning. There's a trust being set up."

I look at Zane. "What does that mean?"

Zane smiles softly at me. "It means I'm not going to fight you about the surf school funding." He looks to Rich. "How much is it?"

"A million."

"Can it be invested through the firm I use?"

"We'll talk," Rich promises.

Zane's eyebrows rise. He stares at the bank account sheets in his hand. "I've never seen a girl give up two accounts totaling four million before, but there's no stopping her."

I exhale, relieved. "The last thing I can handle is living a life that Pierre funded, only after knowing me for a few weeks."

"All right, that's settled," Rich says. "Everyone, get into suits. It's time for the first round of the memorial send-off. Pepe and Luis, can you get a bonfire going?"

They high-five and scurry out the door.

I grab my duffel bag and head into Pierre's bathroom to change.

Settled between Rich and Zane, I lean back on my elbows as Rich sings Don McLean's "American Pie." Rocco and Luis are strumming guitars while Pepe accompanies on a set of bongos. The fire crackles while the ocean waves lap and crash. We've been at this for an hour, and I'm loving it. A lot of the Beach Bar patrons have joined us. Zane checked, and his hired security are scattered all around Pierre's whole neighborhood. We should be safe.

Zane bumps my shoulder lightly with his as I sit up. "This was Pierre's favorite thing to do."

"Yeah?"

"I can't tell you how many bonfire sing-alongs we've had over the years."

The song ends, and my mother holds a hand my way as the next song starts. I take her hand, and she hauls me up. She guides me to a quiet spot and asks, "How are you holding up?"

I shrug. "I'm overwhelmed. I'm scared and feel lost."

Mom nods. "I'm proud of you. You did the right thing with Pierre's accounts."

"I'll be able to sleep better at night. I'm glad you approve."

"Melanie," Mom says, "tonight, I want you to be you. I know you hold back around us. Don't. You need this." She looks down and exhales hard. "Demitri was really honest with me. He's broken, but you don't need to worry about that right now. These guys must learn that you aren't a toy at their disposal. They'll figure it out, but I hope you leave them in the dust."

"If you'll give me tonight, it'll make this easier. I've got a lot on my plate right now."

Mom nods. "Tonight, you're you."

"Thank you." I hug her.

"You're welcome. Now come on." Mom leads me back to the group just as the song ends. "It's Melanie's turn," she announces.

I look at her like she's insane. "I can't sing!"

"Oh, yes you can," Mom says sternly. She gestures for the tequila bottle in Adam's hand.

He gives it to her, amused. She takes a wicked swig from it before handing it to me.

I take a healthy pull from the bottle while Mom says, "'I'm the Only One.' Melissa Etheridge. Let's go, Melanie. I've heard you belt it, and it gave me chills."

I hand my mom the bottle and rub my face. "Fine," I reply, not at all pleased to embarrass myself. I snag Adam's cigarette, and he chuckles while he lights another one.

Rich starts the guitar strum, and the other instruments join, building the rhythm. Mom nods encouragingly as I start the song.

Unexpectedly, a hand presses on my stomach. "From here, Melanie," is murmured in my ear.

I open my eyes, and Zane's staring at me penetratingly. I breathe from my diagram and belt the next section of the song. Indeed, he's right. The song suddenly has life.

I close my eyes and give in to the song. All I hear and feel is the musical rhythm and sensation of singing with everything I have in me. I throw my head back and inhale hard during the musical break. I open my eyes, and everyone's mouths are hanging open. Everyone's but Zane's, that is. He's smiling at me with a gleam in his eyes. The next section comes up, and I confidently belt it, not giving a damn what anyone thinks. The bonfire flares high as I perfectly hit a long crescendo note. People gasp and marvel. It drops as the note ends. I finish the song and exhale hard, letting my head drop. I nod to myself, silently affirming that I need to give in more to experiences that are as freeing as this.

When I open my eyes, Rich says, "That's my girl. Yes."

Applause rings out. I smile a little and return to my seat.

Rocco starts a spirited version of "Spirit in the Sky" by Norman Greenbaum. I glance at Zane. "Thank you for helping me."

"You told me you can't sing," he reminds me softly.

"I can't."

"I beg to differ. I'm about to grab that guitar in a minute. I want you to do one more song. You'll see." When the song ends, Zane says, "Luis, can I snag your guitar?"

Luis hands it over, and Zane gets it situated.

"Melanie thinks she can't sing," he announces. "But she doesn't understand her voice. I'm about to fix that." He looks to my mom. "Carol, can you sing?"

Mom nods with a smirk. "Whatcha got?"

"Hop up, Melanie. It's time. 'Piece of My Heart.' Janis Joplin." He starts playing before I can argue.

I stand and meet my mom by the bonfire. She takes my hand and belts the first part of the song. Her voice sends its usual chills up my arms. We get to the softer next section, and I join her. It comes time to belt, and I let go of my insecurity again. Eyes closed,

I pour everything I've bottled up into the overwhelming song. I get consumed in the experience, and don't realize it until the last line of the song. I open my eyes to discover that my mom bowed out and took a seat at some point. Adam and Demitri have tears in their eyes, and Trey's hand is over his mouth. Everyone appears stunned, and most are softly crying.

"You dropped your shields over your empathy," Rich informs.

Chelsea appears truly overtaken.

She looks to Zane, who says, "I told you. She can dance and sing. I suspect her acting abilities are just as good. You're staring at a triple threat."

"We'll talk," Chelsea says to Zane as she marvels at me.

"Hi," I quietly say, having not noticed when she slipped into the group. People have been arriving as they can.

I take my seat as Zane hands back Luis's guitar. "Thank you for pulling for me," I quietly say as Caroline starts a haunting rendition of "Summertime."

"You're a Janis, Melanie," Zane informs me. "You aren't a Whitney Houston. If you sing from your gut and let loose, you're mesmerizing. I'll work with you on it."

"I don't want to take up your time," I murmur. "I know how busy you are."

Zane rests back on his elbow in the sand. "I need to work with you on this, because you're going to be my partner at the agency. I won't let up until it happens. Ms. Alice will give in."

I quirk my mouth and lean to Zane. "I have no idea who you are professionally, but you seem to impress people. You sure about an unknown, unseasoned partner?"

"It's one of the draws." He smirks at me mischievously. "Do you know how many people I've partnered with that this will piss off? Most of those girls have attempted to use me." He shakes his head. "I've declined every partner Ms. Alice offered me."

I sigh. "The good news is that I won't use you. I want it clear that I'm not willing to hold you back."

Zane chuckles a little. "I'm beyond that point, Melanie. You can't hold me back."

"Well then, I'd love to partner with you." The flutter of excitement about this passes, and I grimace. "I never sing in front of people. I feel weird about it."

"You shouldn't. Everyone was gutted. The emotion that rolled off you was incredible."

I bite my lip. "What happens tomorrow at this paddle-out?"

Zane starts describing what I can expect, and worry boils just under the surface.

CHAPTER 41

I stare at myself in the mirror. I'm in the black bikini Pierre gifted me. My hair is wet from the shower, and I've opted to leave it that way and skip the makeup. I'm going to the memorial how Pierre liked me.

In one sense, I feel oddly empty. In another, I'm alive in the knowledge of where I'm headed, and also destroyed by the fantasy of what almost was.

I leave the bathroom and walk into the living room. The surfers are all in their board shorts, along with Demitri. The door opens, and Mr. Cantrell and Rich slide through.

"Everything is loaded in Demitri's Jeep and my van," Rich says.

I chose the items I wanted, and we got them packed in a few boxes in record time.

After a deep breath, I'm ready to tackle another layer of the to-do's. "Now," I say, as I gesture to a mountain of surfboards leaning against the far wall of the living room, "I'd like Rich to pick out a board first."

Rich smiles and crosses the room to survey the boards before pulling a long yellow surfboard that I'm guessing was once a vibrant shade before it faded with age and wear. "I'm taking the long board." He juts a thumb at the guys. "None of these yahoos know how to ride it properly."

The guys laugh, and Luis says, "We wouldn't be caught dead on that thing, old man."

Rich grins. "It was Riptide's dad's, so it's an honor to have it."

I nod to the guys. "Go pick your boards, please."

Rocco holds up his hand. "Hang tight, vultures." He pulls a black Rusty board from the choices and hands it to Rich. "A lot of people think the board Riptide rode in competitions was his favorite. But it's not true. Those were just the ones he had to ride as part of his sponsorships. *This one* was his favorite, and I think it's only right that Melanie should have it."

"Nope," I reply. "It goes to Zane."

He looks my way, surprised.

I laugh a little and point at the board. "Can you imagine me on that."

Zane chuckles. "It's more about sentimental value than practicality."

I shake my head. "For you, it's both. It's yours."

Looking a bit taken aback, Zane takes the board. "Thank you, Melanie," he says softly.

After I nod my appreciation his way, I find myself fighting back tears again. I watch as the guys each pull a board from the pile.

Zane grins and takes the final board left after all the guys made their selections. He hands the red board with a black center stripe to Demitri, and all the guys laugh. "This one's yours," Zane explains. "Riptide hated it. It pulls right for some reason. He called it, 'Goddamnit.'"

We all crack up, and Demitri wobbles his head, amused. "Thank you, I think."

"Riptide had a sense of humor," Pepe says with a chuckle. "I guarantee he's watching us right now and laughing."

Rocco clears his throat. "Demitri, all kidding aside, you need to know that Riptide didn't hate you. He planned to talk you through some stuff, but he wanted to sink his claws into Melanie first. He saw zero threat in Adam and Trey, but you were a different story."

Demitri nods but doesn't say anything. We both know that Pierre is now Demitri's spirit guide, but we have no business announcing it.

Rocco leaves briefly, returning with the framed sketch of a seashell. He tears up for a moment. After a deep breath, he pulls it together. "One night, we were having a party at Surfrider. We were covered up with girls. All of us were all over them, except for Riptide. He was fifteen at the time. He had a sketch pad, and he sat on his favorite beach blanket by the bonfire. The guys gave him never-ending shit because he wasn't into the Bettys. I sat next to him and asked what he was drawing. He explained that he believed in the code. He was an otter waiting for the right seashell, and he had no interest in the girls. He was drawing a picture of a seashell that he planned to get tattooed on him and his girl whenever he found her."

Rocco hands me the sketch. "It belongs with you."

"Thank you." I hug Rocco. I take one last look around the condo, really absorbing the feel of Pierre's personal space before I give it up for good. Sorted, and as ready as I can be, I hand Pierre's house keys to Rocco. "The condo is yours."

He hugs me. "Thank you, Melanie. As I come across items I think you might like, I'll box them up for you."

Demitri holds a hand to me. "I'll drive you."

"Nope," Zane says, clipped. "She's coming with Riptide's crew. You guys can drive there."

Zane guides me out the door as Demitri argues, "I need to talk to you, Melanie."

"We've talked, Demitri," I reply as we round the bottom of the staircase.

The surfers and Zane guide me to the sand. Ahead, in the ocean, await the Beach Bar crew, drifting on a collection of jet skis. There are four unmanned jet skis waiting on the shore.

We leave Rich and Demitri by the driveway and head to the water. Zane and Rocco strap our boards on the cargo dollies attached to a few of the jet skis.

Zane takes my hand and loads onto a blue jet ski. "Come on, Seashell. I'm taking you to the paddle-out."

I swing my leg over the back and wrap my arms around my hulking escort. He hits the gas, and we take the lead, with all the surfers following in succession. I rest my cheek on Zane's bare back and stare out at the calm ocean. He takes my hand that's gripping his waist and squeezes it. My heart hurts. I'm not ready for this paddle-out, but I need to move on. The last few days have been bizarre at best.

Zane releases the throttle, slowing down to beach the jet ski. The beach is covered up in the circuit crew, along with Rich, my mom, and a bunch of randoms I don't know.

Rocco smiles down at me. "I give you credit. Everyone who meets you loves you. I can't believe Demitri's dad is even here," he says as we watch Mr. Cantrell parking in the distant lot.

"Not everyone," I mutter as I spot Trey walking our way with Adam. They're both carrying their surfboards.

"We don't need drama, Trey," Rocco calls out.

Trey holds up his free hand, looking miffed. "I'm here to paddle out and pay my respects."

"Why would you want to pay your respects?" Luis asks. "You didn't even know Rip."

Trey curbs his irritation that I can feel through our soulmate line. "Riptide's girl is being hunted by a freak. Consider me her security detail today. To answer your question, though, Riptide made Melanie happy. Melanie's devastated by his loss, and I give a shit about that. I'm here in support of her."

Zane mutters to me, "My security team was booked today. Trey serves a purpose."

I sigh dejectedly but let it ride.

Mama Mabel walks up holding a surfboard under her arm. I hug her, and she flirtatiously says, "Hello, boys. Aren't you all tanned and stunning today."

They're all clearly charmed.

"You surf, Mabel?" I ask.

She smiles. "I was a teenager once. I used to surf often. At least until my business took over my life." She puts an arm around me. "Let's get through this together."

"Thank you for being here, Mabel."

"Grab your boards," Rocco yells loudly enough for the crowd to hear. "Time to paddle out."

We wade into the ocean and lie on our boards, paddling out together.

Rocco waves me to him. "I'd also like Richard to join me."

Rich and I paddle his way and get situated on our boards next to Rocco. Zane takes my other side with Mr. Cantrell, Demitri, Adam, and Trey. Everyone creates a circle, sitting on their boards.

"We're keeping this simple," Rocco says. "Only the basics. Riptide wasn't formal, and he didn't like all the extras." He clears his throat. "Riptide was a simple man. He liked easy laughter and saw the beauty in nature. He kept only his true friends close."

He smiles softly at me. "For those of you who don't know, this is Melanie Strader. Riptide's wife."

Some look surprised. Zane takes my hand and holds it up, revealing my double pearl ring. Eyebrows rise, and everyone smiles softly.

One of the girls I don't know yells out, "Welcome to the family, Melanie," across the expansive circle.

"Thank you," I whisper.

"Now that you've met Riptide's girl, I'd like to say that he was loved deeply by all of us. He was a good friend, a good business-man, and a hell of a surfer."

A cheer goes up, and everyone smiles.

Rocco tears up. "This is the last thing I expected. I always thought we'd die off one at a time, doing stupid shit, and Riptide would be sitting on his surfboard doing this ceremony for the last of our dumb asses to go before him. I was convinced that he was just hitting his stride. He fell in love with Melanie."

Someone yells out, "Finally!"

Everyone laughs, and I smile sheepishly.

"He fell in love with Melanie, and that was supposed to be the start of a perfect chapter for him. While his death is tragically unexpected, it's our job to see him through and close this lifetime for him." Rocco hands the bag of Riptide's ashes to Rich, and tears roll down my cheeks. "Melanie," Rocco says, "you're new to this. Can you handle the spouse's job?"

"What is it?"

"As Riptide's godfather, Rich is going to dump the ashes. It's your job to dive in and swim through them, dissolving them and making him one with the ocean. It's your final act as his wife before you're free again."

I get my knees under me and lean down, putting my forehead on my board while tears roll down my face. Zane puts his hand on my back.

"Rocco, don't make her do this," Caroline implores him.

"You said yes to him, Melanie," Rich says. "This is part of the deal. I need you to gut up. He'd do it for you, I guarantee."

"I can do this. Just give me a second." I cover my face with my hands and fight to get through my meltdown. My tears don't slow, but I finally give up and say, "I'm ready."

Rich looks at me, and I nod. He holds up the bag. "Melanie Strader and I are returning Pierre Riptide Love Strader back to the ocean. He always caught the best waves and made the crappy ones look damn good. To you, Riptide."

A cheer goes up as Rich dumps the ashes in the water in front of Rocco's board. Rocco steadies my board, and I slip into the water and swim down deep through my husband's ashes. Submerged in the underwater world, I feel a bubble of energy drift through my chest. It bursts, and the purest love I've ever felt slowly drifts through every part of me. As it gets to my hands and feet, a tingle sparkles and then synergizes.

I send, *"I love you, Pierre. Wait for me."* I get no response, but I don't need one. Knowing Pierre is still with me bolsters my resolve.

I resurface and watch as everyone splashes water toward the center of the circle.

The boom box that Rocco left on the shore for a dance party after the paddle-out ceremony suddenly clicks on, and "Impossible Love" by UB40 wafts across the ocean to us. Tears roll again. Rich paddles to me and helps me onto his board.

Everyone listens to the lyrics, and I quietly say, "I love you too, Pierre."

Tears fall all around the circle. The song ends, and everyone paddles into a straight line.

"Your Seashell is going first, Riptide," Rocco calls out. "Give her a hell of a wave."

I gesture to the calm ocean and look at Rocco like he's nuts. "It's nothing but glass, Roc."

The boom box switches to Aerosmith's "Sweet Emotion," and Rocco grins. "Nice choice, Riptide." He says to me, "Oh, don't worry. Rip will send us waves. He was magic in life. Something tells me he's even more incredible in the afterlife. Paddle out, Seashell."

I swim to my board that Zane has next to him and hop on. I paddle out and wait at what I'm hoping will be the break line. To my shock, a massive wave starts to form in the distance. I put up devil horns and yell, "Yes, love!" I turn and paddle before popping up. I catch the wave just right and hit a hell of a set.

When I'm done, Rocco yells, "Hang ten, Seashell! You could've won a competition with that set!"

I raise up devil horns and yell, "I love you, Pierre!"

In the calm of the shallows, I sit on my board and watch everyone take turns on the waves that keep coming. Rich goes last, and he catches a perfect wave on the long board.

"You handled your shit, old man," Rocco compliments when he's done.

Rich grins as he floats on his board next to me. We all stare out at the ocean.

"We love you, Riptide!" Rocco calls out.

We all yell our love just as one last monster wave comes. We watch the wave, and when it crashes, Rich says, "Riptide just caught his last ride."

Everyone heads back to shore, leaving me alone on my board.

Mama Mabel paddles over and sits on her board next to me while I stare out at the ocean. "What do you need, Melanie?" she asks quietly.

"I need Pierre."

"I know you do. How do we get you through this?"

"What I really need to do is go back to my life. Surfing, the beach, all of this is the life I was supposed to have with Pierre, but without him, it brings nothing but pain."

Mama Mabel nods. "We're going to find some normalcy with your people who don't remind you of Pierre. I can get you back to your life."

"Yes, please. I'd like that a lot." We paddle back to shore, and as I carry my board up the beach, I stop short. "Trey," I quietly call out.

He looks my way.

"We have a problem."

Trey follows the line of my gaze to the "Trippley Media" vans parked in the lot. Cameras are aimed our way.

"No one look that way," Trey orders quietly. "Everyone, act normal. Jet Trippley, Melanie's stalker, has arrived with media vans." He stands facing me.

"How did he know where we are?" Adam asks. He's facing Demitri, pretending to talk to only him. "The paddle-out was kept quiet."

"There has to be an insider," I murmur.

"You all keep acting normal," Adam says. "I'm doing recon. Gonna grab a pack of smokes from my Harley side bag."

"Melanie, I'm getting you out of here!" Zane insists.

"No," I reply with my back to Zane. "You need to get my parents out of here. Keep them safe."

"Then what the hell do we do with you?" Zane demands, his back still turned to me and Trey as he pretends to talk to Rocco.

"I'll get Melanie out of here," Trey says.

"We need to call the police," Zane insists.

"We've tried that already," I reply while smiling and nodding at Trey, keeping up my part of the charade. "Even when Jet attempted to kidnap me, they did nothing. We did it again when the murder bag and photos were found. The police are useless."

"Melanie, you're coming with me and your parents," Zane snarls.

I move subtly backward until my back presses against his. I grapple with my hand that the media can't see. I grab Zane's hand, and he laces his fingers with mine.

I squeeze. "Zane, you said it yourself. Jet isn't going to stop. He's obsessed, and he's after me. He's proved to be Teflon where the law is concerned. I have to deal with him myself."

"Baby, you can't do this," Zane whispers with desperation.

"I'm going to be okay," I assure him.

"Jet's here, Melanie," Adam informs as he rejoins Demitri. "His black BMW is in the parking lot across the highway."

"Okay, Trey and I are leaving."

"Please don't," Demitri begs.

"No choice. I need the surfers to get my parents out of here. The rest of you, get back to Mabel's." I give another squeeze before running my thumb over the top of Zane's hand. "I love you all. Thank you for being here for the paddle-out."

I let go of Zane's hand and reach for Trey.

He wraps his arm around me. "You ready?" he asks.

"How good are your driving skills, Trey?" Zane asks from behind us.

Trey laughs while staring into my eyes. "That and a mean right hook are all I've got." He smiles softly at me. "You and me, babe?"

"You're going to have to get over that, Trey," Demitri says. "She's mine."

"Wrong," Adam argues. "She's mine."

"You're getting married, douche-canoe!" Trey snaps at Adam, who's pretending to talk to Demitri.

"I'll leave Valerie," Adam says.

"You can't leave your pregnant fiancé, you fuck-stick," I snark. "Ew. I don't want *that* guy!"

"Ugh," Adam groans.

"I don't like that look in your eyes, Zane," Rocco mutters.

"That look is going to get worse soon. In case there's confusion, you guys need to enjoy your time, because it's running short with Melanie. I plan to step in, and I assure you, when I do, you'll be out."

I'm whipped around, and Zane cups my cheek.

"We're supposed to be casually talking, Zane," I remind.

"Listen to me," Zane says intensely. "You're Melanie fucking Slate. You're a badass, energy-attacking beast. You take down that asshole. Do you hear me?"

I smile and nod. "And you're Zane fucking Drell, who's going to keep my parents safe."

Zane grins. "Let's do this." He speaks a little louder so the group can hear him. "Keep doing the grilling and partying thing. Several of us are headed back to Pierre's." He takes his phone from his bag and dials a number. A moment later, he says, "Brian, pick up. Pierre's." He ends the call.

"Where's Jet parked?" Trey asks Adam.

"Across the highway at the Beach Bar."

"Here we go, Mel." Trey drapes an arm around my waist, and we casually head to the parking lot. Cameras stay focused on the party, and the two cameramen seem to ignore us. We get to Trey's Z28 and scurry in quickly. He fires it up and moves swiftly for the exit.

I hear Adam through our soulmate connection as he informs, *"They're in the car."* I watch through his eyes as the jet skis splash at warp speed through the water.

"Shit," Trey barks as he looks in the rearview mirror. "Here we go!"

He hits the gas as I turn to look behind me. There's Jet's BMW pulling out of the Beach Bar parking lot.

"Drive, Trey," I bark while I hit the button for the sunroof.

"What are you doing?" Trey screams.

Through our soulmate connection, Adam yells the same thing at the same time. He's watching everything through my eyes.

Over the sounds of the jet skis, I hear Zane holler through Adam's ears, *"What's happening?"*

"I'm seeing if he's armed," I reply as I unbuckle and get to my knees.

"Are you insane?" Trey screams.

"Yuuup," I reply as I slowly stand. Media vans are following Jet, managing to keep up. I raise my arms to my sides.

"Get down here," Trey orders as he tugs on my swimsuit.

"She's essentially telling Jet, 'Come at me, Bro!'" Adam bellows through our connection. Sounds like he's keeping the jet ski crowd in the loop.

"What?" Demitri screams through Adam's ears.

From his car behind us, Jet does nothing more than glare at me with pathetic menace while he revs his engine. I plop down in my seat.

"No gun," I snark. "Hit the gas."

"Put on your damn seat belt!" Trey bellows.

I hit the *play* button on his dash CD player, and Rage Against the Machine's "Bombtrack" blares. "Perfect!" I crow. "A little driving music." I buckle up and smile at Trey. "Hey, babe! It's been a long time since we took a joyride."

He looks at me like I'm nuts.

"Now they're flirting!" Adam yells.

All my guys, and my mother, groan out an *"Uuuggghhh."*

Trey can hear it through Adam's open connection, and he grins. He laces his fingers with mine and puts my hand on the gearshift like we used to. He shifts gears, speeding up. He takes a hard left at the last minute, and Jet flies past. Now Trey hits the gas, shifting rapidly. "I think we lost him," he announces.

I glance through the back window as Jet skids dangerously around the corner we just traversed.

"Nope," I inform as Rage Against the Machine screams their protest.

"He's still on their tail," Adam informs as the jet skis are ditched on the sand. Rocco, Pepe, and Luis start racking them as Zane, my mother, and Rich make a mad dash for the helicopter on the beach. Lifeguards are holding back spectators. I watch through Adam's eyes as they jump in and the helicopter takes off.

My phone rings. I put it on speaker. "Hey, Helicopter Hottie. Whatcha doing?" I joke.

"My diligent duty," Zane replies. "Your parents are airborne."

"I know. I watched through Adam's eyes. Get them somewhere far away."

Trey chooses that moment to say, "Umm, guys?" I look his way, and he grimaces. "We're going to need to make a pit stop."

"Snacks would be awesome," I joke.

"Agreed. You can get us snacks while I gas up the beast and fistfight with Jet in a parking lot."

"You have to be kidding me?"

Adam fills in the beach group about our empty gas tank situation, and Zane groans and tells my parents.

"How close to empty?" I ask just as the gas light clicks on. "Well, shit. Looks like I'm killing Jet in this canyon. Trey's got maybe ten miles before this hunk of steel becomes a useless paperweight."

"Keep driving, Trey," Zane barks. "Keep following them," he says to someone else on his side of the line.

I stand enough to look out the open sunroof. The helicopter is tailing us, quickly approaching.

"This is *not* getting my parents out of danger," I scold Zane.

"Adam told us Jet isn't armed. What's he gonna do to us?" Zane chuckles. "We're gonna 'Air Patrol' my girl out of there."

"*Shit!*" the mystery voice says. "Are you serious?"

"What's your plan, Zane?" Trey hesitantly asks.

"Ever seen the movie *Air Patrol*?"

"Yeah," Trey replies.

"I trained for four months on that shitshow. I do my own stunts." I can hear Zane grinning as he asks, "Ready to come aboard, gorgeous?"

My mouth drops open as I watch the door slide open on the side of the helicopter, and a chain-and-steel ladder unroll.

"Oh. My. Goddd," I breathe out. "You aren't serious, are you?"

"Yup!" Zane says. "Clock him, Brian."

"Holy shit, you *are* insane," the voice apparently belonging to Brian replies as the helicopter pulls up above us. "Have Trey tell me his speed."

"Eighty, but we're about to hit curves," Trey bellows. "Do it fast!"

I watch as Zane swings his legs over and takes the rungs down so quickly that my mouth drops open. I stand on the seat when he motions for me, leaving my phone on the center console.

"Lower, Brian," Trey bellows in the direction of the phone as he looks up at me through the sunroof.

Zane grabs me around my back and hoists me up. The helicopter rises as Zane grips me hard. "Hang on, gorgeous. I need two hands." He hefts me to his front, and I wrap my legs around him. I grab on around his neck, and he starts to climb the ladder.

"You're fucking wild," I cry out as I stare into his eyes. "Hate to tell you, but holy shit, you're a serious thing."

I survey the scene bellow as Trey whips his Z28 around. I'm guessing the closest gas station is the one back down the hill where we took our wild turn. Jet whips around to follow, and Mama Mabel's limousine screeches up, drifting sideways to a halt to block his way. Demitri is right behind her. He pulls up, followed by Adam on his Harley. They all stare up at me hanging from Zane on the ladder. I throw up my right arm, flashing devil horns, and hear them all yell, *"YESSS!"* through Adam's ears.

"Two hands, baby," Zane says. "Hang on."

He grapples to ascend the ladder. I glance over his shoulder to discover that the Trippley Media vans have pulled over and parked. There are video cameras pointed our way.

I grin at Zane. "Fucking hot."

He smolders at me. "You didn't think I was gonna make you cool your heels at a gas station, did you?"

I giggle before kissing his neck. I let just a touch of my dark-water seduction loose, and he gasps.

"If you do that again," Zane warns, "worst case, we're going to fall off this ladder. Best case, I'm going to heft you into this helicopter with a raging erection in these board shorts. In front of your parents."

The helicopter jolts harshly, and his foot slips. I scream and hold on tighter while he hangs with one arm. "Damn it, Brian," Zane yells. He gets his footing again before saying to me, "Erection's gone."

I laugh through the tension as we reach the top of the ladder. Rich gets me under the armpits and pulls me in just before Zane hefts himself up. Zane sits with his legs hanging out of the helicopter and flips Jet a double set of birds. Everyone drives down the hill, disappearing around the corner as we disappear in the other direction. Jet speeds as fast as he can but can't keep up with us. We lose him.

I sag on the floor of the helicopter, terrified now that the threat is over. I sit up as Zane closes the helicopter door after hefting the ladder in. He flops on his back next to me and puts his hands over his face. "I hate helicopter stunts. The way that ladder swings. My hands get clammy, and . . ."

I lie down again and curl up against him. We're both panting in fear. He puts an arm around me and squeezes me tight.

My cheek lands on his bare chest, and I hang on with shaking hands. "I need a second. Holy crap, that was terrifying."

"Thank God you decided to be scared once you were in here," Zane replies. "You did good, gorgeous."

I sit up and look at him. "You've done that before?"

He nods. "The actress was Kate Bondue, and she weighs one forty. I knew that with your bitty ass, I could swing it without a safety harness." He sits up.

Trey says distantly through the speaker, "Package delivered to Movie Star. Jet's following the helicopter. Give me a second, and I'll be gassed up."

I look around, surprised by Trey's voice.

"I have a system in here," Zane explains. "You left your phone with Trey. I called you through the helicopter line." He points toward the cockpit. "The microphone picks us up. We hear Trey through the speakers." Zane turns his attention to the pilot. "Hang up, Brian. I need to talk to Melanie."

The speaker crackle ends, and Zane's head drops. He presses his cheek against mine. "We did it. We're okay."

"I need a cigarette."

"Me too, gorgeous." He cracks a window and starts handing out smokes from his backpack. Brian reaches behind him, and Zane gives him a cigarette with an anxious chuckle. "Nice flying, bro."

"Sorry about that jolt," Brian says. There's a calm, confident, certainty about him that my empathy picks up on. He has a calculated feel, which relieves me. We don't need another wild card at this phase of our day.

My mother takes a drag, her hand shaking. "Thank you for getting Melanie," she says to Zane. "And don't you two *ever* do that again."

Rich is grinning from ear to ear. He slides the cigarette back into the pack and sparks a joint that he pulls from his own backpack. "That was awesome," he crows.

Zane tips his head back with his eyes closed. His cigarette hangs from his lips as he says, "I'm glad I was awesome, because I'm gonna hang with your girl." He hefts me up with one arm and plunks me in a seat. "Meet my wingman, the seat belt," he snarks. "We need safety precautions. I'm tapped out for the next twenty minutes."

I giggle while he thuds down in the seat next to me and taps his cigarette, the ashes scattering instantly on the roaring wind.

The speaker comes to life with a harsh, "Identify yourself."

Brian answers, "*Drell Two.*"

There's a chuckle, followed by, "Zaney Mania. What's up, bro?"

Zane exhales hard. "Joseeeph. Just doing my thing, brother."

"Your *thing*?" Joseph snorts. "We're getting so many 911 calls, it's like Godzilla's stomping through the canyon."

"He is," Zane announces. "I had to rescue my girl. Put us in blackout status for the next hour. I've got another illegal landing coming up."

"Done and done. Just an unknown movie stunt. I'm on it. Hang ten, brother."

The speakers go silent.

"Thank goodness for Malibu Joseph, or I'd be getting arrested when we land." Zane turns to Brian. "Call Seashell's phone."

Brian must have hit redial because the phone starts ringing through the speakers.

Trey answers.

"We're landing on the Marmont helipad," Zane says. "They'll cover me. The law isn't taking kindly to this hero bullshit."

"The Hotel Marmont has a helipad?" Trey asks.

"Yup, and the best bar in Hollywood," Zane crows.

"On it," Trey says. "I'll call Mabel so she knows the plan."

Brian hangs up, and we listen to a call to the Hotel Marmont.

I scrunch my face. "This is weird, right?" I ask my parents.

Rich shrugs. "Welcome to show business."

My baffled gaze slides to Zane.

He looks back at me like I'm the one who's weird. "What? They have a helipad." He gestures about. "We have a helicopter. Tomato, potato."

I crack up and take another drag of my cigarette.

CHAPTER 42

The helicopter blades whip relentlessly as my parents and I hop out, crouched even though the blades can't hit us.

"Call me!" Zane yells over the racket. "I need to know she's safe."

"You're a lifesaver," Rich replies. "We'll let you know when she's locked up at Mabel's."

"Love you, Mighty Mouse," Zane says with worried eyes.

"Love you, too, Helicopter Hottie." I look to my parents and yell, "Trey just pulled up. He's ready for us."

We make a dash down a path and out a side gate, finding Trey's Z28 ready for us. We hop in, and I exhale hard.

An engine revs behind us. I whip around and spot Jet's BMW.

"Fantastic," I snarl. "Fuck-stick found us."

"How the *hell* did he find us?" Rich bellows as he stares in disbelief out the back window.

"He has to be tracking me," I reply, disgruntled. "He's a powerhouse energy worker. I don't know why I'm surprised."

"He's got us blocked in," Rich warns. "How do we get out of here?"

"This car's made of steel," Trey says through gritted teeth. "His is made of aluminum. Mine wins."

Trey puts his car in reverse, and I glance over my shoulder. Trey mashes the gas, slamming into Jet's car as it skids out of the way. Just when we've cleared the car, Trey yanks the steering wheel hard, and we skid to the right. There's a red light ahead. He shifts out of reverse, and suddenly, my window explodes and I feel something whizz by my head.

Trey grabs my neck and shoves my head between my knees as he hits the gas. "Get down!" he yells.

I have to trust that my mother and Rich are down in the back seat.

"Looks like he found a gun!" I squawk.

I wiggle free of his iron grip as Trey hits the gas on Sunset. We're flying down the road as I look over my shoulder to see that Jet's BMW is keeping pace.

Teeth gritted, Trey says, "Put on your seat belt, Melanie. I'm going to outrun him."

"Can his car outperform yours?" I gasp out.

He gives me a baffled look that would be hilarious if we weren't running for our lives. "We're in a muscle car, and he's driving a shitty sedan." He watches the road again, accelerating.

"It's a BMW," I remind him.

"Oh please!" Trey scoffs.

I open my connection line with Adam and feel his head snap up. He shushes everyone in the room, and I can see them through his eyes. Our line has never been this clear before.

"We're in a high-speed chase on Sunset," I send. *"Jet shot out my window. Get ready! We're coming in hot!"*

Adam sends alarm through the connection, and I feel him split his attention. After a moment, he says in my mind, *"We're heading that direction."*

Trey is apparently getting the messages because he responds through the connection, *"Stay where you are. We're coming to you."*

"We've got a problem over here!" Adam says. *"Dead body in the parking lot."*

"What?" Trey barks.

"Yup. She's wearing a shirt with Melanie painted across the front."

"Damn it!" Trey snarls. *"That means Jet knows where Melanie was staying before she headed to Riptide's."*

"There's nowhere else to go," Adam insists. *"Get over here. The police are here. Lure him in, and this ends."*

"Get the cops out of there," Trey yells aloud.

"Not this time," Adam assures. *"A guy named Officer Striker is heading this up. He's an old-school Hollywood kid, born and raised. Apparently, Mabel coached his sister's cheerleading team twenty years ago. She trusts him, and he seems pretty up-and-up."*

Trey makes a reckless U-turn and hits the gas. He flips Jet off as he passes, and Jet looks furious. Jet makes a sharp U-turn and almost careens into a bank.

Trey smirks as he watches this in his rearview mirror.

"Shouldn't his car have a better turn radius than yours?" I ask.

"The car isn't the problem. The *driver* is."

"Think you can out-drive him?" My eyes are huge.

Trey growls, "We're about to find out." He hits the gas.

My cell phone rings.

"Did you make it?" Zane asks as soon as I answer.

"High-speed car chase!" I inform.

"I feel alive again," Rich yells out. "Hot damn, Trey. You can drive, son!"

"Get me out of here, Zane!" Mom pleads over my shoulder.

Trey takes another sharp turn, and Mom and I scream.

"Damn it!" Zane bellows. "Talk to me, Trey."

"I've got them, Movie Star. It's my turn. Get out of town. Hurry. Jet knows that you're connected to Melanie now. If anything happens to you, she won't make it. The rest of us are locking down behind Mabel's security system. You, Rocco, and the boys need to hide."

"Are you positive you're safe there?" Zane asks.

"There's a dead body in Mabel's parking lot, so who knows?" Trey says through gritted teeth.

We careen through yet another red light, leaving screeching cars and blaring horns behind us. I'm watching as Jet's car dodges through the intersection, right on our tail. Trey takes the turn by Mabel's at breakneck speed and whips into the alley.

My heart races when I realize that all Jet needs to do is make this last turn and we have him. Then I see it: there's maybe a dozen police cruisers parked in Mabel's lot, their lights flashing. Jet clearly sees it too, because he speeds by and avoids the alley, heading off into the night.

"The police in this town are special," Trey seethes.

He brakes hard in the parking lot and storms out of his car. Big Joe and Stubbs are standing in the center of the lot, looking like they're in an argument with several officers.

I come up beside Trey just as Officer Striker introduces himself.

"Real stealthy!" Trey hollers. "Jet saw your lights and took off." Officer Striker winces.

Big Joe bellows to the officers, "I *told* you!" He and Stubbs fire up their Harleys and take off after Jet.

Just as my mom and Rich join us, Adam rushes over. He hits Officer Striker with a disgusted look.

"I apologize," Striker says. "This was a rookie call on my part. I know better."

Several officers get in their cars and head in the direction that Trey indicates, with a car description fresh in their minds.

Trey turns and sees Adam holding my hand. He glares at Adam, what's left of his patience having been abandoned back on Sunset. He freezes, and I follow his line of sight. There, propped up against the wall, is the body, my name scrawled across her shirt. My head drops as emotional exhaustion fills me.

"Everybody inside," Trey belts.

Still reeling from what I just saw, I step into Mabel's to find all my school friends, along with several of the Hellhounds, waiting. Presley and Finley rush over and hug me hard.

"You okay?" Presley asks me.

"No."

Her expression softens as everyone gathers around. "Married, huh? That's intense."

That's what she wants to talk about right now? I think with a soft laugh. "It was very simple. No ceremony. Just a discussion. I got none of the marriage perks and skipped right to taking him off life support a few hours later."

"Shitty. Did you at least get some good naughty time out of the deal?" Presley raises an eyebrow.

I smirk knowingly. "Hell yes. Oh, and also a helicopter ride, a dolphin swim, and some time on a yacht."

Presley makes a sarcastic expression as she nods. "Kick ass. That makes up for all this heartbreak for sure." She shakes her head slowly and says with conviction, "Girl, he was so fucking hot."

I laugh. "That he was." *Leave it to Presley to somehow make me feel a little better at a time like this.* "Today, we helicoptered in, landed on the Marmont, got shot at, and discovered that Trey's a race car driver." I throw my head back and yell, "I'm so sick of *thiiisss.*"

Big Joe looks around at all the occupants of the parlor. "It's time to lock down and have a breather."

"A *breather?*" I stare at him like he's nuts.

Mabel nods. "A breather. Once those gates drop, we're safe. It's time to celebrate Riptide and let off some steam." She turns a hopeful glance Mack's way. "Are you up for dropping those gates and staying here for a few days?"

Mack nods. "Done. Everyone, settle in and relax. You're safe." He disappears down the hall, and we hear the gates slam down a moment later.

I exhale hard.

"You got that seashell sketch with you?" Big Joe asks.

My first instinct is to tell him that they're still in the boxes in Demitri's Jeep, but then I see that someone has apparently delivered them into the room.

"I've got you, Meley," Demitri says as he crosses over to the boxes. He's clearly trying to keep me from melting down. He takes out the framed sketch and brings it back to me.

Big Joe looks the picture over. "Riptide's accountant wired payment to me for a pair of seashell tattoos. You and Rip were supposed to come in together the day after you returned from Hawaii. He was thinking you'd get it on your hip, but I'll put it anywhere you want."

I smile. "Put it where he wanted it."

"This is my assistant, Needle," Big Joe says, introducing me to the man standing beside him.

When I survey the man, I decide that I'll just have to trust Big Joe on this one. Needle's covered from head to toe with tattoos, complete with a pot leaf on his cheek.

"He's going to outline your firebird tattoo on your shoulder while I freehand your seashell," Big Joe informs.

"Two at once, huh?"

Big Joe laughs. "You've been through a lot of changes. Sometimes life moves fast, and we have to rush to catch up."

I snort. "You're telling me." I put my hands to the sides. "I'm currently covered in Riptide's ashes and dried saltwater. Before we do any ink, I need a shower."

Big Joe looks at Needle. "That's a new one. We've had people covered in weird stuff, but husband's ashes is a curveball." He says to me, "Don't sweat it. We have to disinfect the areas anyway. Come lie down." He looks to everyone. "Crank up the music. Let's party in honor of Riptide while I ink his girl."

The music blasts as everyone starts passing out drinks. A party rages around me while I lie on a padded tattoo table. Now that I'm safe, I'm filled with post-traumatic shock. Big Joe and Needle rub my shoulder and hip down with something cold. Adam pulls up a chair and sits next to my face.

"What am I in for, Adam?"

He grins. "It'll sting, burn, tickle, and sometimes feel like someone's scratching on you. Whatever you do, don't move. Two at once is a lot. Here we go." He takes my hand as two tattoo guns hit me at once.

My fear quickly dissolves. There's something incredibly balancing about the two spots being worked on at the same time. Adam rubs his thumb over the space between my eyes. I sigh happily and slip away.

"Melanie, wake up."

I open my eyes to find Big Joe grinning down at me.

"You fell asleep. We're done."

I sit up and stretch while Adam, Arch, and Bear all stare at me.

Awed, Arch says, "I cried when I got my first tattoo."

Bear laughs. "I screamed. Not Melanie, though. She takes a freaking nap!"

I laugh. "If it helps, I'm exhausted, and that's likely why."

Big Joe takes me into the bathroom to show me the work he and Needle have done. Pierre's seashell sketch is perfectly replicated on my hip. It's exact, down to the tiniest detail. I tear up as I look at Big Joe.

He hugs me. "It's a really pretty sketch, Melanie. Thank you for letting me ink it for you. I know how important it is to you."

I nod. "Thank you for doing it."

Big Joe turns me around and hands me a mirror. I look at my reflection in the mirror behind me, and my gunshot wound is perfectly covered by a firebird. It's beautiful with its shades of red and burgundy.

I grin and bounce. "I love it! Thank you."

Big Joe smiles at me. "I'm so glad. You're welcome."

We head back to the living room, where Trey looks over the tattoos. He nods after a moment's contemplation. "Hot."

I laugh.

Demitri steps up next.

"More imperfections," I warn him. "I know how you just love those."

He laughs. "Shut up and turn around. I love your imperfections."

I turn to let him look over the firebird and seashell. His sudden smile has weight to it. He kneels next to my hip and explains quietly, "Riptide wants to see it. He's in my head."

Demitri's expression morphs sad as he studies the seashell. He looks up at me, but his eyes don't feel like him anymore. He takes my hand and pulls me to the hallway. Mama Mabel rushes to unlock my guest room door and then closes it after us.

I look up at Demitri.

He quietly says, "I'm going to let Riptide take over for a second."

The energy behind his eyes shifts.

"I love you, Seashell."

"I love you too, Pierre."

He cups my cheeks and leans down. He kisses me like only Pierre did. Somehow, it's not awkward coming from Demitri.

After a lingering moment, he pulls back and assures, *"You're going to be okay. I'll be in Demitri's head some."*

Demitri's eyes shift back. He's staring down at me with a world of pain and confusion in his expression.

"Thank you," I whisper.

"You're welcome, Meley."

He gathers me up in his arms and holds me. I'm uncomfortable with how perfect it always is when Demitri hugs me. It still feels that way even though our spirit-guide bond has dissolved.

There's a knock at the door, and Demitri opens it.

"Surprise time," Tanner says. "Come on, you two."

"Give us a second. We'll be right there." Demitri closes the door and pulls me in again, holding me against him. He puts his cheek on the top of my head, and it makes me uncomfortable, knowing he can't be my safe place anymore.

"I already miss you," I whisper.

"Let me talk to Riptide," Demitri says. "I can't lose spirit-guide eternity with you."

I shake my head. "I guarantee he isn't giving that up with me, Demitri. I know that man." I shrug. "I'm really happy for you."

Demitri looks at me quizzically.

"You get to try out some new freedoms. The old future-spirit-guide ball and chain is gone. Have fun, Demitri. Screw randoms, cut loose, maybe marry Victoria."

He scrunches up his face like he just smelled something terrible. "Oh, eeew. No, no, and no. I have zero interest in any of that.

Being honest, I'm not going to touch anyone again until I get a handle on all this. Casual sex no longer interests me."

I make a shocked face. "Who are you, and what have you done with my best friend?"

Demitri chuckles. He crosses to the suitcase I took with me to Hawaii, taking out a pair of sweatpants and my favorite T-shirt. "Change out of that swimsuit, Meley." He hands my clothes over, and I head into the bathroom.

A couple minutes later, I return in my fresh clothes and take a deep inhale.

"Better?"

I nod. "Better." I look up at him. "You okay after you kissed me?"

"Nope. Confused. It wasn't me, but it *was*."

I laugh softly. "We're screwed *up*."

"That we are." He really studies me. "I can't believe you climbed out of Trey's car and were carried like a koala bear into that helicopter."

"My life is so insane."

"That it is, Meley."

Demitri escorts me out the door, and we make our way back to the group in the parlor.

"Everyone, hush," Arch barks as he turns up the television.

There on the screen is Newscaster Kitty. "Police have released the name and photograph of a serial murderer at large," she's saying. Her eyes steel up just before Jet's picture is flashed on the screen. Considering that Jet's her brother, I'm sure Kitty isn't happy. She comes back on the screen long enough to inform, "Viewer discretion is advised."

A perfectly edited video of the car chase starts. We watch from the media van's vantage point behind Jet as I stand in Trey's sunroof and turn to survey Jet. I disappear into the car again, and Trey takes his sharp turn. The image cuts to the helicopter hovering over Trey's car, and Zane getting down and then up the ladder. I'm clinging to Zane far tighter than I remember. There's terror in my expression as my hair whips in the wind.

The image cuts to the newscasters sitting side by side, and Randy takes over.

"Jet Trippley has been identified as the killer known to local police as the Boulevard Butcher. During an afternoon raid of his home, investigators uncovered the remains of as many as nine victims, these in addition to other cases currently being connected to Trippley. Police are asking for diligence by the community. If you see Jet Trippley, do not approach him. He is considered armed and dangerous. Immediately call police."

The newscast changes to another story, and Arch clicks off the TV. He turns a skeptical gaze my way. "Was that *Zane Drell* climbing out of a helicopter and pulling you out of a car in your underwear?"

I sigh. "It was a swimsuit, for the record, but yes. Zane Drell is helicopter-stunt-trained."

Mabel holds up her hands. "Everyone, take a deep breath."

Everyone in the room inhales and exhales.

She nods. "Good. We're here, we're safe, and the whole city is now searching for Jet. Let's let everyone else do the hard work. We don't have to leave until he's caught."

Tanner raises his hand and is called on. "Wrong. We've got *The Crucible* opening tomorrow."

I grimace. "Damn it. I've missed *weeks* of rehearsal."

Tanner shrugs. "Ms. Ferry seems positive you'll be fine."

I rub my exhausted face before leveling my parents with a look. "While I understand that I'm sixteen, and school is important, I don't know how much longer I can keep splitting my life like this. I'm busy signing legal paperwork, taking helicopter stunt flights, and getting shot. I can't handle chemistry class every day on top of all that."

"This will all blow over and you'll be back to your normal schedule," Rich assures me.

"Normal?" I bellow. "*Normal*? I don't have a *normal* that's normal. I have this life, Rich. We hadn't even finished a media interview at Trippley Broadcasting," I say, gesturing wildly toward the TV, "before I had a fresh stalker. A *stalker* who's apparently called the Boulevard *Butcher*!" I point Rich's way. "DO YOU NOT GET IT?"

Before he can answer, my cell phone rings. I toss it to my mother. She answers, listening, before she starts speaking quietly with Mack.

Mack disappears down the hall, and a moment later, we hear the sound of the gates sliding up. My mother heads to the foyer.

"I understand what you're saying," Rich says, returning to my point, "but this kind of thing *can't* continue forever. This is likely to be the last of the drama."

My stepfather doesn't know what I do—about how my life-path is built out of pain and torture.

Giving in to fear, I shake my head at him. "You don't get it. It's never going to end until someone ends *me*! In the past year, we've dealt with Joel, Coach Stamp, the hostage takeover, Jet . . . , and I'm standing here covered in Pierre's ashes . . . after hanging from a helicopter and getting shot at *again*! ALL IN ONE YEAR, RICH!"

There's no reply. What can he say?

I stride into the kitchen, coming back out with a jar of pickles. As I struggle to open the jar, I ignore everyone completely. I'm hyper-focused on the task, but it quickly becomes clear that no amount of effort is going to pop the seal on this stupid lid. Tears fill my eyes and spill in a torrent. "GOD DAMN IT!" I scream before cocking back my arm to launch the jar.

Zane strides into my view and takes the jar out of my hand before I can throw it.

"WHAT ARE YOU DOING HERE?" I scream. "You're supposed to be running from the Boulevard Butcher!"

Effortlessly, Zane pops the jar lid loose.

"Show-off," I snark.

He looks amused.

"Thank you," I mutter.

"I can't fly away knowing you're in danger." Zane looks to Mabel. "Got room for two more?" He gestures to Rocco.

Everyone who wasn't a part of the past few days at Riptide's is now staring at Zane with their mouths hanging open.

"Zane Drell?" Tanner asks in awe.

Presley asks, "Melanie, what is Zane Drell doing here?"

"I'm here to open pickle jars and dry tears," Zane replies on my behalf as he sets the jar on a table. He gently runs his thumbs under my eyes, wiping away tears.

"You're okay, Melanie," Mabel says quietly.

"She's not okay," Zane says, "and everyone needs to stop forcing her to be okay. Enough with that." He smiles sadly. "Time to fall apart, Seashell."

I give in so thoroughly to tears that I can't even make a sound. I collapse over my straining lungs. Zane picks me up, hugging me while everyone watches, and lets me cry it out. Once I calm a bit, he hands me a pickle from the jar on the table. I chomp on it like a toddler.

Zane gets another spear out and takes a bite. "Pickles and a good cry." He smiles at me. "Easy-peasy."

I take another crunchy bite and whimper, "Thank you."

Big Joe clears his throat. "Melanie, I have a surprise for all you kids."

I shake my head dismissively. Without a word, I open and close my hand rapidly like a needy toddler. Zane snags another pickle spear from the jar and hands it to me.

"No surprise," I whimper. "So tired."

Zane nods. "Me too, Seashell. Bedtime. Where are we headed?"

Demitri steps forward. "I've got her."

Trey shakes his head. "No, *I'm* going to stay with her."

I point to Zane before taking another bite of the pickle. Zane snags the jar and then carries me down the hall. I turn the doorknob, and Zane pushes the door open. Demitri and Trey are barking their protests as we head in and Zane closes and locks the door. He thumps the pickle jar down on the dresser and sets me on the bed.

"Scared," I whimper.

Zane kneels by my knees and puts a hand on my cheek. "Nothing is going to get through that door. If it does, I'll kill anyone who tries to hurt you. We're showering and sleeping. You go get a shower first."

"Swear to me that you won't leave while I'm in that shower!"

He shakes his head. "I was in my helicopter, headed to Delmar, and turned around because I couldn't just leave you. I'm not going anywhere. I need to sleep, too, and I can't do that unless I know you're okay."

I rush into the bathroom and take the quickest shower of my life. I put my sweatpants and T-shirt back on and return to the bedroom. Zane has half of the covers pulled back. The other half of the bed has a fuzzy gray blanket draped over it.

"Get in bed, Melanie," he says.

I slide under the covers that he pulls up to my chin.

"I'll be out in a few moments." He disappears into the bathroom. From the quickness of his shower, it seems like he didn't want to be in the shower any longer than I was. He emerges moments later in a pair of black gym shorts. He clicks on the nightstand, turning off the overhead light. He slides under the fuzzy blanket, careful not to get under the covers I'm using. He silently holds out an arm, and I snuggle up. I shudderingly exhale.

"You're safe," he whispers. "Go to sleep."

My eyes drift closed.

CHAPTER 43

Now that it's morning, I've slept, and Zane made us coffee, I feel human. Unlike last night, I feel ready for whatever Big Joe didn't get a chance to show us.

Big Joe breaks into a grin as everyone spreads out around the parlor. "The Hellhounds have a surprise."

Tanner carries two huge duffel bags to the spot of honor next to Big Joe.

"I'd like to present each of you kids with a gift." Big Joe gestures to Tanner. "Your friend over here has quite the skills with a sewing machine." He sweeps his arm to a handful of the Hellhounds all sitting to our right. "The guys pitched in the paper to get this project accomplished."

The Hellhounds raise their beer cans, saluting us. Apparently, we're at the morning beer phase of mayhem.

Stubbs says, "You're too young to join the Hounds, but we all think you deserve to be one of us, so . . ." He gestures back to Big Joe.

Tanner unzips the first duffel bag and pulls out a little black leather vest, which he hands to Big Joe.

Big Joe holds it up to show it to us. *Hollywood Hellcats* is embroidered in bright red across the back. Below, it reads *HHP*. "That stands for 'Hellhound's Protected,'" he explains. "Anyone who should know will understand what it means." He turns the vest around to reveal the name *Firebird* embroidered on one side. He grins at me. "Come get your vest, Firebird."

My mouth drops open as I step up and take the vest from Big Joe. I hug him gratefully.

He smiles down at me. "You've been through hell, but here you stand. Keep rising from the ashes, Firebird."

"Thank you," I say quietly.

Big Joe turns back to the crowd of teens. "You don't get to pick your nickname. You earn it. We've taken the liberty of nicknaming each of you." He smiles mischievously as Tanner hands him the next vest. "We had to whip this monster together last night." He raises an eyebrow Zane's way. "Helicopter Hottie, come get your cut."

Zane cracks up as he crosses to accept the gift. "Nice to meet you," he says to Big Joe.

"You as well. Rocco filled us in on the past few days. Thank you for helping Firebird." Big Joe hands over the vest, and Zane puts it on before returning to me. "Arch, come on up. You're Anarchy."

Arch pumps a fist in the air. "YES!" He hops up and bounds over to Big Joe, taking the vest and giving the big guy an exuberant hug.

Big Joe laughs and takes the next vest from Tanner as Arch sits back down. "Marcus, you earned the nickname 'Chomp' because you never stop eating." We all laugh as Marcus crosses to Big Joe to accept his vest. Big Joe grins at him. "We had to name you something tougher than 'Snacks.'"

Marcus beams. "I love it. Thank you!"

Tanner hands him the next two.

"Victoria and Demitri, you're up next."

The two join Big Joe at the front. Demitri is clearly trying to keep some distance from her, and it's awkward.

"Victoria, you're Besos. It means 'kisses' in Spanish. The way you distracted everyone at the television studio was brilliant." He looks Demitri over. "And you, my dude, are Travolta, due to your incredible dance ability."

Demitri throws his head back and laughs. They thank Big Joe and make their way back to their seats, where they put on their vests.

Big Joe takes the next two vests. "Adam, you are officially Diesel."

Adam grins and hisses, "YES!"

"And you are Little Mama," Big Joe says to Valerie with a soft gaze.

Valerie tears up and hugs Big Joe tight. "Thank you," she whispers.

"That baby is going to have a whole lot of godfather Hellhounds."

She smiles at Big Joe, and Adam guides her back to their seats. "Presley and Hiram."

They traverse the living room to Big Joe.

"Hiram, you are hereby known as MacGyver because you can fix anything."

Hiram bows his head at the compliment, taking his vest and putting it on with a grin.

"And Presley, you are Va-Va-Voom, because . . . well . . ." He stammers, clearly not wanting to say something inappropriate.

We all laugh. *Looks like Presley's showstopping figure strikes again.*

Presley grins sarcastically as she hits a curvy supermodel pose. We all chuckle and clap. She takes her vest and hugs Big Joe.

"Tanner and Finley, you're up." Big Joe accepts the next two vests. "Finley, you're Sugar. I've literally never met a sweeter little lady than you."

She blushes and smiles at him, gingerly taking the vest with a shy, "Thank you."

Big Joe turns to Tanner. "And *you* are Strut."

Tanner takes his vest and puts it on before performing a quick supermodel pass. This earns him applause from the Hellhounds.

Big Joe continues passing out the vests to everyone. Susan earns the nickname Patent because of her patent leather Doc Martens. Dante is Diablo. Javier is Gazelle because of his grace. Bear is Yoda. Darren is Samurai. Drake is Ojos Locos because of his stunning eyes. Deb is Throttle because she always revs up her Harley. Jayla is Split because of her dance training.

The ceremony continues until everyone but Trey has a vest.

Big Joe takes the last vest from Tanner and turns to Trey. "Last but not least, I present to you, Shivers."

Everyone cracks up as Trey crosses the room and gives Big Joe a hug. He takes his vest and looks at Kendra. "Well, Spark, I guess something good came of it."

Kendra winks at me, and I crack up.

CHAPTER 44

We made it through the afternoon show and act one of the evening performances with no issues. Trey was adamant that we had no business leaving our place of safety for something like this, but most of the cast was locked in at Mabel's house, and we couldn't just blow off the show completely. Zane argued at length with Trey, who finally relented on the grounds that the "show must go on."

I peek out the gap between the main curtain and watch as Trey, Rich, and my mom take their seats in the front row right, positioning themselves next to Kelsey and the dancers who aren't in the show. Dante and his band are in the front row on the other side. Zane and Rocco are in the back row. The Hellhounds are spread out all along the back of the audience. Administration at the school is probably wondering why every biker in Hollywood is here to see *The Crucible*, twice. It's not their thing, I'm sure, but they're here to watch over us while we're in our vulnerable positions onstage. Most of them are genuinely excited to help tear down the set after the show ends. With Jet still on the loose, the stakes are higher than ever, so the bikers will be serving as our personal bodyguards through everything we do until my stalker is caught.

Presley comes to me and peeks through, spotting Mama Mabel and her girls in the first row of the balcony. "I can't believe the Hellhounds and all of Mabel's girls have wasted their entire Saturday to take in both shows."

"I was just thinking the same thing," I say. "We owe them big."

"It's remarkable that they've taken us on like they have," Presley says. "Imagine the impact this is having on all their lives. One day, they're a bunch of happy-go-lucky bikers and prostitutes, and the next thing they know, they're saddled with a bunch of teens on the run from a murderer."

We look at each other and laugh.

"Our lives are insane!"

Presley nods. "*What* are our lives lately?" She hisses, "He has a helicopter?"

I shrug, nodding.

Presley gives me a blazingly serious look. "So hot," she whispers.

"Twenty-one," I remind her.

"Who gives a damn? Do it."

With a grin, I steer the conversation away from the topic of Zane. "It's a good thing I was put in jail, or we wouldn't have ever met Big Joe, Mabel, and their posse."

Before Presley can reply, Susan calls, "Places," from her podium on stage right.

Presley squeezes my hand. I head to the wings on the side of the stage. The lights dim, and we hear the audience quiet down. I take a breath as the curtain opens, revealing the interior house set designed by Hiram.

Tanner steps out on the stage and delivers the first line of act two.

Presley is seated at the table center stage. When I notice her eyes widening, a chill washes through me.

"Something's not right," I whisper to Susan.

A scream pierces the air from the balcony. Susan speaks over the headset to Hiram in the booth. Suddenly, the house lights come up. I peek around the wings. A fire is burning in the balcony. I gasp as the downstairs lobby doors are thrown open. The roaring orange flames flicker in the lobby as well.

Chaos ensues as people start leaping over each other, pushing and screaming. The doors at the back of the auditorium are shoved open, and the audience jostles and pushes for the exits. I turn around to find smoke billowing from backstage left.

The performers start panicking and trying to get off the stage. I turn back to the audience just in time to spot a familiar face. Jet leaps from out of the chaos, lands on the stage, and runs for me. Trey and Rich lunge for the stage, jumping up and getting between Jet and me.

I look down and scream to my mom and Kelsey, "RUN!"

Panic in her eyes, Mom grabs Kelsey and starts pushing her through the crowd toward the exit.

Zane and Rocco try to force their way through the crush, to no avail.

"Ruuun!" I scream again.

When Dante and his band join us onstage, the homicidal maniac seems to take new stock of the numbers stacked up against him. He takes off running, disappearing down the boys' dressing room hall with Dante and his bandmates giving chase.

Demitri tries to push his way through the crowd but can't get to me. "Melanie!" he calls out, panicking.

I look up at the balcony to see Mama Mabel, one of her scarves over her mouth and nose to block the smoke, guiding her girls out another emergency exit. The Hellhounds seem to be pinned back by the crowd as well. We're on our own.

Trey and Rich grab my arms and pull me through the side door. "Scene shop," I yell over the raging noise.

We turn the corner to discover that it's too late. The exit is blocked by flickering flames and billowing smoke. I rush down the hall to costume storage, where the costumes, perfect fuel for this inferno, are already engulfed.

We run down the hall into the dressing room, where Adam grabs a lamp and smashes a window. Outside is a fire escape—along with four thugs waiting for us, crowding the tiny space. One grabs Adam and jerks him through the open window.

Adam is taken by surprise, and has to go limp to avoid getting cut by the shards of glass as he's pulled through. "Keep Valerie safe!" he screams as the struggle begins on the fire escape.

Valerie's frozen in a state of panic.

I grab Susan's arm. "No matter what happens to the rest of us, you get Valerie out of here! Go! These guys are after me. You can't stay with us."

Susan nods and pulls Valerie through the door.

I turn back in time to see Rich crawling out through the window to help Adam. Trey breaks the other two windows that are painted shut, and now we have a view of the mayhem. Thugs are crushed along the fire escape and down the ladder. There's no chance of sneaking past them. Apparently, trust-fund-boy Jet has hired every evildoer in the state to do his bidding. Adam ducks a flying fist just as Rich gets one of the thugs by his jacket and throws him over the edge of the fire escape. Every time they get one thug off them, another crawls over the edge. They're like swarming locusts.

When I start to panic, Trey grabs me and pulls me back. Big Joe makes it to the fire escape landing just then.

"Big Joe will get Adam and Rich out of this," Trey insists to me. "We have to get out of here!"

Trey and I turn back to the door that Susan and Valerie just exited, but it's too late. Flames are eating at the edges of the doorway. I turn and run to a ladder that goes up to a trap door in the ceiling. There's another story to this building that hasn't been used since the 1950s.

I have to get out of this heavy costume! I pull the bonnet, long skirt, and blouse off quickly, dropping them in a heap on the floor. I'm wearing a sports bra and black leggings. It'll have to do.

Trey starts up the ladder just as I remember that all our backpacks are in this room. Not wanting to lose everything to the fire, I turn and grab the bags, then rush back to the windows. Through the scrum of fighters, I spot Stubbs down below. When I scream his name, he looks up. I start tossing bags down to the pavement below, careful not to hit Rich and Adam as they battle the thugs. Stubbs catches them.

"Melanie, quit dicking around!" Trey yells.

I look up at him. "All our keys and my pearl ring are in the backpacks!"

He rolls his eyes. "We're going to die in this building if we don't move!"

I scoff. "I'm not leaving my ring behind."

He snorts and pushes the hatch open. We climb up into a maintenance room. We try the door, but it's locked. Trey braces and kicks the door open. On the other side is an old-fashioned classroom with old-fashioned desks. The chalkboard on the wall, the teacher's desk, everything in this room feels as if time stood still. Trey runs across the room, sending plumes of dust up wherever his feet land.

He wrenches open the door, and we look into a long hallway. Smoke is billowing through the cracks in the hardwood floor to the right. "Left," he orders.

We take off left down the hall, and he kicks open the next door. "No windows!"

"I remember Ms. G saying something about how they abandoned these rooms in the fifties because they aren't up to fire code."

He kicks open another door and smoke billows out. "She wasn't kidding!"

My heart is racing as smoke rises from the cracks in the wood floor under our feet. "What do we do?"

He grabs me. "Don't panic. I'm going to get us out of here."

"What if you can't?"

"Then we die together!"

I nod. "Okay."

"NOT OKAY." He rushes to the next door, kicking it in, but we find the same smoke-filled nightmare. "DAMN IT!"

Out of the smoke, Jet steps through a doorway at the end of the hall. Lit in this way, murder in his eyes, he looks like a demon straight out of Hell. I scream.

Adam chooses this moment to send a pulse to me, asking if I'm okay. I pulse back the image in front of me: Jet and the fiery inferno. The panic he sends back almost drops me to my knees. I quickly block off the connection. I can't be distracted.

Trey turns and spots Jet. He breaks into a full-blown man-trum. "GOD DAMN IT! I'M SO DONE! FUCK YOU, JET!"

My ex-boyfriend charges at my stalker. Jet runs toward Trey through the smoke. Trey grabs him by the shirt and tosses him through the door he just kicked in. Jet hits the floor, which dissolves under him. He falls through as flames lick at the broken wood floor. We watch as the paint starts to blister on the walls.

"Hey," I squawk. "*I* wanted to kill him!"

Trey gives me a look before grabbing my hand. "RUN!"

We run down the hall in the direction Jet first came from.

"He had to get up here somehow!" I yell over the sound of the raging inferno.

We turn the corner.

"This way!" Trey yells.

There's a hall that leads to another collection of classrooms. He kicks open another door, and finally, we see a window. He grabs a chair and uses it to smash the window. Fresh air rushes in from outside. Through the opening, we discover that there's no fire escape.

"I swear the universe hates us!" Trey growls.

"There's not even a damn drainpipe to shimmy down. Do we jump?"

"We're how many stories up, Melanie?"

His irritation strikes me as irrationally hilarious. I double over laughing.

Trey looks at me like I'm insane as I gasp out through my chuckles, "This is hilarious, and you know it."

"You might be ready to die," he barks, "but I'm not."

The building starts to creak and crack as its support beams burn up.

Trey turns and yanks down the curtains. The old material tears easily. He rips it into shreds. Working quickly, we tie the strips end to end, creating a long rope.

"This material's older than my grandmother," I say. "What if it doesn't hold?"

"It has to," Trey says. "This is our only chance."

I turn and stare into the flames. *I've died by fire before*, I recall from a past life. *It's quick. Maybe this is a good thing.*

Trey grabs my face with both hands. "No, you don't. Melanie Slate, I love you. I know you've been through a lot, but I'm not letting you die in this hellhole. You're my girl, like it or not, and I'm not giving up on you." He knots the material on the radiator below the window. "Now, come on. You go first. When you get to the bottom, I'll come down." He tosses the makeshift rope out the window.

I grab hold, put my legs out the window, and brace myself. I take a few hesitant steps down the side of the building before looking up at Trey. "Here I am dangling from another deathtrap."

Despite himself, he smiles. "Move, fast. The fire's at the door."

I pick up the pace and run down the side of the building, making it all the way to the ground. I look up as Trey swings his legs from the window. Smoke billows out behind him. He's almost all the way down when a fireball bursts from the broken window, burning the makeshift rope. Just as the rope breaks, he turns and pushes off the wall, landing like a cat on the dumpster lid below.

I let out a breath I've been holding too long.

He hops off the dumpster and rushes to me, wrapping his arms around me tight.

"I'm okay!" I assure him as he looks me over.

"We have to get out from behind the building. The whole thing's about to collapse." He grabs my hand and we run.

My intuition blazes to life. "FASTER!"

I feel the building give way before we hear it. The energy of impending doom roars in my head just as the building starts collapsing behind us. We run just ahead of the destruction and rush out past the alley just as the last of the structure comes down in a billowing black cloud of debris and smoke.

Trey screams and grabs me, launching us to the side as hard as he can. We land and roll to the edge of the paved track by the field. We lie there panting for a time, trying to catch our breath in the air thick with smoke, ash, and dust.

"Thank God all the fences are gone," Trey gasps out, "or we would've died."

We lie there trying to relearn how to breathe as sirens scream and screech down the road. I look at Trey lying on top of me, and he smiles down at me with a face covered in soot.

"You saved me again," I say.

"Seems like it's the only thing I do right."

I laugh.

"I know you love Riptide," he says softly, "but he's gone, Melanie."

"He *did* tell me to reconnect with you."

Trey's eyebrows rise. "Interesting. You've heard from him?"

I nod, but decide not to fill him in on the details.

"I like that perfect fucker. I'm gonna trust him on this." Trey leans down and kisses me passionately. As we kiss, he rolls us twice, clearing us from the smoke.

He ends the kiss, and it takes me a moment to wrap my mind around the familiar brand of ice and earth that blasts through me. That feeling is distinctly Trey.

I exhale hard as he helps me up.

"You ready to walk out of hell together, yet again, soulmate?" he asks.

"That's what we do best." I raise an eyebrow. "You seem not at all worried about the Zane factor."

Trey smirks. "Zane made Rocco and his boys promise to force him to cut off communication with you after Jet's gone. Well, Jet's dead, and I'm getting my girl back."

I'm too damn worn out to worry about any of that right now.

Trey wraps his arm around me, and we walk down the field, turning into the quad. Water shoots in wide swathes over the debris as the half dozen firetrucks at the front of the school try to put out the smoldering mess. Trey turns left through the teachers' parking lot, and we exit through the far driveway.

All our family and friends are standing with their backs to us, watching the debris smolder. Mom and Rich are surrounded by our friends. Everyone's crying, and Adam's holding my mother while she sobs. Demitri's on his knees crying, with Bear's hands on his back. Zane's gripping the iron railing with tears rolling down his face.

"Hey, losers!" Trey hollers. "Whatcha crying about?"

Everyone whips around and stares at us with their mouths hanging open.

Mama Mabel throws up her hands and yells, "Hallelujah! They made it!"

Mom screams and rushes our way. She pulls us both in for a hug.

"Did everyone make it?" I ask.

"You two were the last. Everyone else is here." Rich hugs Trey. "Thank you for pulling my girl out of the fire—*literally* this time."

Adam rushes to me and nearly smothers me to death, he hugs me so tight. He's followed by Demitri, who wipes his tear-streaked face before gently pulling me in. His arms shake.

Zane comes up to me last. He picks me up and whispers in my ear, "Damn it! I thought we lost you."

"We need to get out of here!" Adam insists. "We have no idea where Jet is."

Trey points toward the burning wreckage. "Jet bulldozed his way toward us, and I tossed him into the inferno. He's ash." He smirks my way. "Melanie's salty about it. She wanted to be the one to kill him."

I laugh and shake my head. "Thank you for taking out the trash for me."

"I always will," Trey replies, putting an arm around my shoulders.

"Looks like the dance show is canceled," Arch says as we watch the fire billow. "But on the bright side, at least we don't have to tear down the set."

We all crack up, overcome by the usual post-trauma hysterics.

Demitri takes my hand and steers me away from the group. He's clearly distraught. "Pierre," he says aloud, "you knew Melanie was alive. Why didn't you tell me?"

When Pierre's voice rings out in my head, Demitri's eyes snap wide, indicating that he hears him also.

"*Because you needed to learn what it feels like to lose her.*"

"Asshole," Demitri mutters. He shakes his head and hugs me.

Zane and Rocco stride up. Zane's eyes are pinched at the corners.

"I promised Zane that I'd drag him out of here when you were safe," Rocco informs. "We're hoofing it back to his place a few blocks up the road."

"Thank you both for everything you did to help me."

Rocco smiles. "You're welcome, Seashell." He hugs me before stepping out of the way.

Zane wraps his arms around me with a heavy sigh. "You're insane, Wildcat," he says quietly.

I smirk up at him. "Don't you ever forget it." I tip my head. "I won't be sixteen forever."

Zane grins. "And I won't be gone forever."

"One day, you need to helicopter your ass in, scurry down that ladder, and rescue me forever," I quietly request.

"Done," Zane replies before kissing me on the forehead.

He and Rocco head down the sidewalk, and I rejoin the group.

"How many days do you think we'll get off this time?" Tanner asks.

We survey the school, and laughter starts to spurt.

I shake my head. "I swear, we never learn anything here."

Trey chuckles. "I don't know. Our running, ducking, careening, and shooting skills have improved."

"I've got a mean right hook now," Jayla says.

"Yeah, you do," Deb caws proudly.

We all crack up.

CHAPTER 45

Officer Striker grins at Mama Mabel. "I had to deliver the news to my favorite gal," he says coyly.

We all exhale, not liking the police invasion just as we started a spirited party.

"Not all police are evil," Mabel insists to us. "For those of you who haven't met him, this is Officer Striker."

We go through the proper introductions, and then Striker's gaze falls on me. "So, this is who all the fuss was about, huh?"

I huff. "If it helps, I'm sick to death of being the creator of fuss." I shake my head as I survey my friends. "We're now fuss-free, and I plan to keep it that way."

Officer Striker chuckles. "The case has been officially closed."

"Was Jet's body found?" Trey asks.

Officer Striker sighs. "That inferno blazed so hot, there's nothing but ash and cinder left. He couldn't have survived it. We're in the clear."

Mack, Big Joe, Stealth, and Stubbs stride through the door and clap hands with Officer Striker. Apparently, they all know each other.

"What's up, Firebird?" Big Joe grins at me. "We're ready for the next catastrophe. Whatcha got?"

"There will be no more catastrophes. You're gonna have to settle for an old-fashioned beer fest instead." I smile endearingly. "Please thank the Hellhounds for me."

Officer Striker glances around the group. "Does everyone have nicknames?"

Big Joe gestures proudly to our group of teens. "Meet the Hellcats, Hollywood's newest underground group. We named all of them."

Officer Striker shakes his head. "Makes me wish I hadn't gone into the force. I miss the underground."

My intuition twinges. I freeze. Trey and Adam feel the shift and glance at me. My gaze falls on the bikers across the room. Suspiciously, I ask, "Stubbs, Stealth, and Mack, what brought you here tonight?"

"Just checking on you," Stealth answers.

"I've got a work shift," Mack quietly informs.

"Interesting." My intuition flares stronger as I look them over. I send to Trey and Adam, *"Bingo. One of them is the informant."*

Trey's and Adam's eyes narrow as they survey the trio.

I ponder a moment before breathing out, "I wonder . . ." Just at the edge of my mind, I can sense a new ability emerging—an energy that feels like *seeking*. I send out a touch of that energy, finding that I can use it to probe the guys. I've never tried this before, but at this point, I don't question new abilities.

Invisible to the eye, the energy swoops around Stealth. I send to Adam and Trey, *"Nothing from Stealth."*

I send the energy around Stubbs.

"Nothing from Stubbs."

The moment I send the energy around Mack, I'm met with a slight flare of malevolent challenge. Almost imperceptibly, Mack shakes his head, warning me not to mess with him. The energy in the room electrifies, and everyone collectively shivers.

"That's the one." Trey and Adam start to move, until I send, *"Not yet. I'm going to deal with him myself."*

They both look my way, radiating concern.

"Bear and Darren," I say quietly, "come here, please."

The two boys who first introduced me to energy work step up next to me.

"What's happening?" Bear asks.

Everyone in the room is statue still, watching suspiciously.

"I'm drained. Boost me."

Bear and Darren each put a hand on my shoulders. I feel them do the opposite of our usual grounding and centering. Instead, they open twin channels from the earth and start pulling energy up and through them, channeling it into me. I immediately get a splitting headache.

I send to Adam and Trey, *"I need you to store this energy for me."*

Though they're both hesitant, they drop their shields. I grab their hands and channel the energy from Bear and Darren into them. When they're full, I fill up too, vibrating from head to toe.

Bear and Darren are quaking with the effort to hold it together. Just when I feel them on the edge of panic, I gather the energy and hurl it at Mack, unsure what it's going to take to crack him. His shields hold firm.

I growl. *He's better than I thought.*

I pull harder, channeling all the stored energy from Adam and Trey through me all at once. My spine burns as the energy passes through. My head feels like it's going to burst. Finally, just when I can't take it anymore, I send a blast Mack's way.

Mack's eyes widen as he gasps. I feel his shields start to buckle. He hits his knees. His shields blast apart, sending an energetic wave of evil through the room. When it's over, Mack looks up at me, panting.

I stalk away from my guys, and the energy flow cuts. The effect is disorienting, but I ignore it. I get to Mack and snarl, "You're the plant."

Big Joe's mouth drops open. "There's no way. I've known him since I was a kid."

"That's him, all right." Adam says.

He and Trey stalk across the room, where Adam gets behind Mack and hauls the giant man up. I step back, glaring.

"What the hell is a little sprite like you gonna do?" Mack snarls.

My friends all laugh. "Rule number one," Presley says, "don't ever challenge Firebird."

Demitri puts his hands on my shoulders, and the headache immediately stops. I meet Adam's gaze as I drop all my shields, and Adam and Trey see what's coming.

"ROUND TWO," Tanner caws out, delighted.

Trey crosses to me and takes my hand. "Level him."

Adam snarls, "Do it. Then this whole disaster is behind us."

My dark-water side boils up in my mind and shines, hugely sadistic, from my eyes.

Trey feels the energy writhing in me and laughs. "You'll be lucky to ever unscramble your mind after this," he says to Mack.

Mack panics, but Adam has an iron grip.

I pull a massive wave of energy from Demitri. I channel the energy into a finely honed point and blast it at Mack. When it hits its target, Mack's eyes roll into the back of his head. He gasps and wheezes, the sound bubbling and frothy. Adam lets him go, and Mack face-plants on the floor.

Mama Mabel's eyes widen. She looks at me like she doesn't recognize me. "I thought you only played for the light side?"

I roll my neck as the energy seethes. I lean my back against Demitri's chest and meet her judgmental gaze unflinchingly. "Just like the Hellhounds have their good and bad factions . . . so do we. Adam, Trey, and I don't fuck around."

Officer Striker's jaw drops. "You a witch or something?"

I smirk. "I'm Melanie. No further explanation needed."

CHAPTER 46

I sigh in the dark and slide out of bed. I can't sleep, but Trey's finally sunk into a much-needed deep sleep. He had no intention of falling asleep with me, but he's worn out. The book he was reading aloud is lying open where it slipped from his hand when his eyes closed. Instead of disturbing him by turning on the reading lamp on my nightstand, I grab my book and slip out the door, quietly closing it behind me.

Mama Mabel's is silent. As I've realized is her custom, the lamps in the parlor are on for anyone who wants some quiet time at night. I settle into my favorite love seat and crack open my book. The story takes me away. I'm completely consumed with Alice's journey down the rabbit hole when my intuition blazes to life.

Ignoring the pain in my chest, I hop up from the couch and mentally reach out to Trey and Adam. Trey's so dead to the world that I can't wake him, but Adam's eyes snap open.

I get as far as sending Adam, *"My intuition's screaming,"* when an alarm sounds through the building and a recorded voice starts saying, "Lockdown, lockdown," over and over. I hear bolts on the doors locking into place all through the building.

I rush to the hall, headed to my room, but stop short. There at the other end of the hallway, wearing a gas mask, stands Jet. My pulse pounds and I can't breathe. I send the image to Adam, who's panicking down our connection as he struggles to open his door.

Adam suddenly stops and sends, *"Wait, wait, wait. Jet's dead. Maybe we're asleep and dreaming this."*

"Are you SHITTING me?!" I mentally bellow back. *"We aren't asleep! Give Jet credit. He's like the damn post office! Come rain, sleet, police, or fire, this motherfucker somehow shows up!"*

"HOW did he survive that inferno?"

"I have no idea how he's standing here, but he is, clear as day."

I rattle my head. *Focus, damn it! You can ponder impossibility later!*

"What's up with the creepy gas mask?" Adam sends while Jet and I have an off-putting gas mask stare down.

I shudder. *"Who knows. Probably some weird kink of his."*

A hissing sound streams through the air just as the recorded voice says, "Exterior lock countdown. Ten . . . nine . . ."

It occurs to me all at once that this must be the panic room system Trey mentioned, and Mack must have told Jet how to trigger it. *I have to get out of here!*

I turn in a rush and spot a set of car keys on an end table. I grab the keys and race for the building exit that leads to the parking lot. I hit the *alarm* button on the key fob, and a beater car chirps lethargically.

Fantastic. This might not work.

I run for the car and slide in just as I hear, ". . . seven . . . six . . ." from Mabel's building.

I start the car and wince at the loud blast of music I really don't need pounding in my ears right now. I ignore it, reaching for the gearshift. My eyes snap wide at the realization that I have no idea how to drive this thing. I try to reach Adam, but he's somehow out cold. I fumble through my sweatpants pocket for my phone. With shaking fingers, I hit redial before pushing the *speaker* button.

"Hello?" Zane answers, half-asleep.

"Help me!" I scream.

Fully alert now, Zane barks, "What's wrong?"

"Jet! Car! Strange gearshift!"

"What do you mean, Jet?" Zane bellows over the music.

I hear Rocco in the background. "What's wrong?"

"Jet's there, and something about a gearshift."

Rocco's voice comes in clearer. "Talk to us."

"I have to get this car to move!" I scream, panicking as I watch Jet stride confidently out of the building. He surveys my car with a smirk before strutting across the parking lot.

"Look at the floorboard," Zane orders. "Are there three pedals?"

"Yes!"

"Shit. It's a manual," Zane breathes out. "All right, push in the left pedal with your left foot. All the way down."

"Done." I wrench my head around, expecting to see Jet standing behind the car, but he's nowhere to be seen. My heart is pounding in my chest.

"Now, press the brake with your right foot and put the car in neutral," Zane coaches.

I do and he says, "Put it in first gear and give the car a little gas while slowly letting up on the clutch."

The car starts moving jerkily. "It worked," I gasp as I roll forward.

"Good girl. Now, shift gears as you speed up."

The car makes a terrible sound, and Zane coaches, "Shift."

I do and pull out of the parking lot. In my rearview mirror, I see Jet slide into his luxury car and roar it to life. He's quickly on my tail.

"He's following me!"

"Turn off that damn music so I can hear you better!" Zane orders.

None of the dials and buttons seem to control the stereo. "It won't turn off. This piece of shit!"

"I'm getting you a new car," Zane yells back.

"It's not mine! Hence why I didn't know how to drive it."

"Where'd you get it then?" Rocco asks.

"Stole it," I inform.

"Of course you did," Zane seethes.

"Now isn't the time for a morality check, boys," I bark.

"See if you can find a quieter song, at least," Zane requests.

"It's Thrill Kill Kult, Zane—there are no quieter songs," I retort as "Final Blindness" starts blasting.

The voice in the song talks about teenagers prowling Hollywood Boulevard searching for sex.

"Classy," I seethe.

I try to send a mental message to Adam but find him completely still. I can see through his eyes, and something is very wrong. His mind is working now, but he's on the floor, frozen in place.

He sends back red-hot rage. *"Drive, Mel. Some kind of gas came through the vents. I can't move. I have to wait for it to wear off."*

"Jet's following me," I send back. *"All the doors inside and outside of Mama Mabel's are locked. You should all be safe in there."*

"But you aren't safe!"

"You guys are. That's what matters."

"Melanie," Zane bellows, and from his tone, I suspect I missed several "Melanies" before that.

"Sorry. Mental chatter with Adam." I fill in Zane and Rocco about everyone having been gassed.

"She's on her own," Zane says. "Grab my keys!"

"Check for Trey," Adam sends. *"See if he can move."*

I check down the line. *"Trey was asleep when everyone was gassed. He's out cold."*

"Drive faster, Melanie. I don't know how long it's going to take for this to wear off and I can get to you."

Zane's voice bounces in a way that says he's running. "Tell me where you are."

"Headed up Hollywood Boulevard."

I check my rearview mirror and leave open the connection that allows Adam to see through my eyes. Jet's right behind me. I take a sharp turn from Hollywood onto Vermont Avenue and hit the gas. This piece of shit car is hopelessly outgunned. A moment later, Jet pulls up next to me. He grins sadistically and swerves right, slamming into me.

I fight to keep my borrowed car on the road. "On Vermont now," I scream.

"What was that sound?"

"Jet's ramming the car."

Through the phone line, I hear a car starting. "We're on the way."

"Zane's coming to help me," I send to Adam.

"Ugh," Adams grunts disgustedly in my head.

"Adam, would you rather I die instead?"

"Slow down, Zane," Rocco yells through the phone.

"Not a shot," Zane says. "Just hold that phone and hang on."

"We're being lit up," Rocco warns.

"Good. We need the police. I'm not stopping. They can follow us!"

"Keep driving, Melanie," Adam sends as he watches through my eyes. *"Shift gears."*

I skid onto Los Feliz and pull ahead of Jet. I realize that he's just toying with me. He can run me off the road at any time. "Turned onto Los Feliz," I yell over the music to Zane. "I'm headed up the hill."

The car struggles on the hill.

Adam panics in my mind. *"You're going to be trapped up there! It's a dead end when you get to the observatory. TURN AROUND!"*

A nearly brutal wash of clarity settles over me as I realize he's right. Strangely, the thought brings an unexpected sort of contentment. I radiate the sentiment through our connection.

Adam gasps in my mind, choking on fear as he sends back, *"Don't you dare, Melanie. Get out of there!"*

I send him waves of calm. He fights them, sending heartbreak and panic.

Jet revs his engine behind me and slams into the back of the car. I grit my teeth and try to accelerate, but the gas pedal is floored. *Of all the cars, it had to be this one.*

"It belongs to a client who wasn't good to drive last night," Adam informs. *"Mama Mabel made him leave his keys, and her chauffer took him home."*

"It's not looking good, Adam. I don't think the client is getting his car back in one piece."

"Find a way, Melanie." His mental voice is racked with anguish.

"This is the way I'm supposed to head." I send a wave of my intuitive clarity.

Jet slams into the back of my borrowed car again, and the impact rattles my teeth. I unintentionally send a fresh wave of terror down my connection to Adam.

I feel Adam emotionally buckle.

After a pause to collect myself, I say aloud, "Adam, tell our friends and my parents that I love them. Tell Bear and Darren thank you for always guiding me. Tell Presley and Demitri thank you for being my best friends." My voice cracks.

"Stop saying goodbye, Melanie," Zane screams.

I look in the rearview mirror as new lights come into view down the hill. "I see you, Zane." His car is being followed by more red and blue lights than I've ever seen in one place.

"Cavalry is there. You might be okay," Adam sends as the Griffith Park Observatory road looms up on the left.

Jet slams into me again as I clear the top of the hill and pull into the expansive observatory parking lot.

"Brake, Melanie," Zane yells through the phone.

I hit the brake pedal, and nothing happens. "Brakes are out," I scream.

"Downshift!" Zane screams.

Absolute calm fills me. "Adam, tell Trey and Demitri I love them. Make sure they understand how much."

Adam screams in my mind, *"CIRCLE THE PARKING LOT AND GET OUT,"* but I know it's impossible. I've only got one route.

I send the image, and say, "I love you, Adam. Take care of everyone."

Zane screams, "DOWNSHIFT!"

It's no use. The gearshift is stuck. "No can do, Helicopter Hottie. Shifter won't move. I love you."

I hit the gas as hard as I can, and the car accelerates now that I'm not on the hill. The stone banister looms up quickly as Jet slams into the back of the car again.

Adam screams in my head as Zane screams through the phone, "MELANNNIEEEEE!"

I careen off the west observation deck, the same place where Trey kissed me the first time, and glance in my rearview mirror.

"I'm taking Jet with me. He just made the jump. You're all safe."

Adam's anguish ripples through our connection as he watches through my eyes.

"NOOOOO!" is the last I hear through the phone as the car free-falls and suddenly smashes into the tree branches below.

My world goes black.

CHAPTER 47

I wake to the distinct sound of flames. I struggle to clear my vision, blinking several times. My head feels heavy, and it takes me a moment to realize that I'm hanging upside down and all the blood has rushed to my head. I glance to the side. The car is collapsed in on the right, mangled, with the passenger seat twisted against my shoulder. I look to the left and see flames and Jet's car engine on fire twenty yards away.

"Melanie!" comes the familiar voice.

That's when I notice Zane, Rocco, and all the police officers straining against an unseen force. Jet's hyper-focused on them from his car. I probe to figure out what's happening and quickly discover that he's holding his pursuers back with an energy net.

Let's put an end to that, I think.

With all the strength I can muster, I release an energy blast, directing it into the fire in Jet's car. The flames expand into an inferno, and the fire blazes in the cab. I can feel the pain and terror rise up from him, and for the briefest moment, I hesitate about the idea of killing someone, even the stalker serial killer who has been terrorizing me for so long. *I have the ability to put the fire out,* I remind myself.

And then I remember what he did to Pierre.

With clenched teeth and a pounding heart, I watch his body burn. He screams, trapped, and then he goes still.

I know he's dead when the police, Rocco, and Zane come unstuck from his energy net and start running my way.

I tap into my connection with Adam, and it roars to life on a wave of his nearly inconsolable panic. He's driving his Harley.

Realizing that this means Trey might also be awake, I tap into my connection with Trey, struggling to hold both connections together through my shock. Trey roars into the connection, and he's close to hysterical.

"I can't be the one to hold the line open," I murmur to them.

Both guys send massive waves of relief that I'm alive.

I feel Trey almost double over and hear through his ears as Bear asks, *"What is it, Trey?"*

"Melanie's alive. She just tapped into the connection."

Adam bolsters the line between the three of us. I mentally exhale, relieved. I let them see what I see. The upside-down car is disorienting for them, and it takes them a second to realize what's happening.

"Look for fire. That's where I am."

My eyes fade to a spotty black again just as Zane grabs my hand.

I feel both Adam and Trey rushing to me before the sound of the sirens invades my shocked, disoriented mind.

An authoritative voice says, "Wait here. You can't touch her. We have to extract her properly or she might end up paralyzed."

"Where is that life flight?" someone yells.

"Unavailable!"

"We have to get her to the Riverside Trauma Center," someone else yells. "Cedar Sinai is full."

Zane scrambles back, grabbing his phone from Rocco.

Mama Mabel's voice floats in next. "You don't understand these kids, Officer Striker. Let them do what they need to before you remove Melanie."

After a hesitant moment, Officer Striker says, "Everyone hold. Let the boys in."

Bear's voice booms, "Go! Go!"

I hear footsteps racing up the incline, and Adam and Trey drop to the ground by the crushed driver's side next to me.

Bear says, "You two, get physical contact. Darren and I are going in through you. I'm going to tap in and hold everyone steady. Get in there, Demitri."

Adam, Demitri, and Trey reach through the missing window, and I moan but can't get my vision to clear. The moment they touch me, the fog in my brain instantly lifts. Trey moans and Adam gasps when they open the connection between us. I feel pain radiating from each of them, and it takes me a moment to realize that it's my pain, but I'm in shock and can't feel it from my own body. I send that down our connection, and both guys slam walls up on their sides of the connection to prevent me from feeling what they feel.

"Open up, guys," Bear orders. "We need in."

Adam murmurs to Bear, "She's in shock and can only feel the pain she's in through our connection."

"The pain is information," Bear insists. "We need it. Drop your walls."

The walls crash down, and I'm hit with waves of excruciating pain. It burns through the rest of my fog. Even gasping hurts, but it helps me take mental stock of where the pain is located.

"Airlift inbound," Zane yells. "I can get her to Riverside General."

Demitri and Darren slide into the connection. Bear's presence hovers under everyone. I faintly experience all five guys in my psyche. Demitri feels like he's rummaging around in my body, while Darren starts doing energy work at a rapid-fire pace, trying to fix what he can of my mental shock. My head lolls, and I let them do what they need to without resistance.

Demitri calls out, "Several broken ribs, one broken wrist . . ." He pauses, taking further stock of the damage. "Broken neck! Unsure about lower body. Her legs are trapped. I won't know until we release that pressure." He pauses again, and I feel him try to survey my spine. He says to the guys, "Light up her spine."

The guys send a pulse of energy through me, and it travels up my spine.

Satisfied, Demitri announces, "Her spine is intact. Her legs are a wild card."

Bear, Darren, Trey, and Adam extract themselves from my mind and back away from the car. Demitri lies down flat on the ground and grabs my hand, sending a steady wave of calm.

I exhale, the pain raging up. I hurt so bad, I can't even cry. I can't control the flow of pain down my connection with Adam and Trey, and I feel them quaking.

Bear turns to them and orders, "You two, pull it together. Support her while they pull her from the wreck. It's going to get worse when they move her."

Officer Striker asks, "How did you do that?"

"We'll explain later," Bear says. "Demitri's keeping her calm. He needs to stay there, if possible. Get her out of there."

I watch as Trey and Adam sit on the dirt outside the car. They close their eyes. Bear puts a hand on Adam's shoulder, and Darren puts a hand on Trey's shoulder. Through our connection, I feel twin lines of energy. They come through just in time because a buzz-saw sound roars to life.

Officer Striker loudly informs, "Jaws of life. We're cutting you out, Melanie. You have the engine block pressed sideways on your legs. Don't move."

I hold still. The sound is overwhelming as sparks fly. The police and firefighters work around Demitri. I internally panic, and Demitri sends a stronger wave of calm, his hand shaking with the effort. Trey comes through our connection, radiating calm, with Darren backing him.

The sound cuts out suddenly, and an incredible weight is lifted off my legs as I hear a lot of people grunting.

The sound of a helicopter whomp-whomp-whomps nearby.

"Airlift is here!" Zane yells over the noise.

I open my eyes.

Officer Striker says, "Here we go, Melanie. We're cutting through the seat belt. It's all that's holding you. Be ready for us to grab you. It's going to hurt."

Demitri lets go of my hand, backing away. Adam blazes brighter through the connection and sends the equivalent of an energetic adrenaline rush through me, backed by Bear. A neck brace is put on me, and I scream. The borrowed adrenaline gives me a boost. I can suddenly handle it better. Officer Striker gets hold of me and pulls me through the sawed-out hole in the mangled car. The pain is almost blinding as it seers through every part of me. With the help of two paramedics, he sets me on a stretcher. I finally have a view of the car. *It's barely even recognizable as a car anymore.* Shock and terror reverberate through me as I stare at the twisted wreckage.

Trey, Demitri, and Adam jump to their feet and rush to my side. Demitri puts a hand on my shoulder and washes my fear away while Trey grabs my hand and starts pulling pain from me.

My eyes widen. "I didn't know you can do that."

His voice shakes with effort. "I didn't either. You need it, so I can do it."

I ask the guys, "Jet?"

Adam sends an image of a body bag being carried down the dirt hill to an ambulance below. I exhale and close my eyes, relieved.

We start to move up the rugged terrain to the waiting helicopter in the parking lot above. The jostling of the paramedics carrying me up the hill sends a fresh wave of pain through me.

Zane grabs my hand as I'm hefted into the helicopter. He climbs in while Officer Striker argues with him.

"It's my chopper!" Zane yells over the whipping blades. "I'm going with."

A paramedic hops in behind him, and the door is closed.

I pass out cold as the helicopter ascends.

CHAPTER 48

I slowly rise in the dark water in my mind. It goes from a blackish gray to a light blue, but it feels like an eternity before my head breaks the surface with a gasp.

"She's coming to," a voice says. "Someone turn out the light."

"The light?"

"We've been through this before," Rich's voice says.

I open my eyes, blinking heavily. I survey the room, moving only my eyes because I quickly discover that my head won't move. "Not this again," I groan.

Quiet laughter wafts through. "Welcome back, Mel."

I glare at Adam. "Ugh. How bad is it?"

Rich steps to my side, taking my hand. "You've been in a medically induced coma for several weeks now. You had neck surgery, and they think it worked, but we won't know until you move. Your wrist is in a cast. You have three broken ribs that are improving with each x-ray."

I slowly pan the room with only my eyes. Adam, Rich, and Zane are there. Adam's in the corner on the phone.

I survey Zane. "Looking a little worn out, there, Helicopter Hottie."

Zane chuckles.

"He's been here almost every night," Rich informs.

"The movie wrapped," Zane says with a shrug. "I had the time."

I smile a little. "Your dedication to my pathetic ass is impressive. Thank you."

Zane smiles and nods. "You're welcome. People have been coming and going, giving me breaks."

"He rarely takes them," Adam snarks.

It hurts when I laugh.

A doctor comes in and surveys me. His gaze is serious and intense as he steps to the end of the bed. "I'm Doctor Shaffer. Are you up for some tests?"

"We'll see. Hit me with it."

"Move your fingers on your right hand," he requests. I do, and he smiles the slightest bit. "Left hand." I move the fingers on my left, and he nods. "Can you lift your arm a few inches?" Quickly, I lift both arms, and he scolds, "Take this slow."

I give him an amused look. "Slow isn't my forte, Doc."

He chuckles. "I need you to go slow on this." He uncovers my feet from the bottom of the bed. "All right, Melanie. Here we go."

Rich's jaw is set tight with worry.

"Wiggle your right toes," the doctor requests. I do, and he chuckles. "Those were your left toes, but I'll take it."

"Typical dancer. Sorry." I wiggle my other foot.

"Good. Now lift your right leg."

I pull my knee to my chest and extend. My ankle touches the top of the bed railing near my head. Luckily, the sheet still covers me.

The doctor's eyes widen. "Oh no." He rushes to me and grabs my ankle carefully. He lowers my leg and gives me a look.

"You said to lift my leg."

The doctor looks to my guests, baffled. They laugh.

"She has dancer brain," Rich says, "not normal brain."

The doctor rattles his head. "I've never seen someone do that." He gives me a gruff look. "Lift the other leg a few inches please." I do as requested, and he nods. "No paralysis. She's in the clear, pending a whole lot more bedrest."

"Woo-hoo!" I crow. "Paralysis would make running from the grim reaper a real task."

Zane's smiling from ear to ear. "Thank you, Doctor Shaffer."

They shake hands as Doctor Shaffer says, "It's been really good to see you again. How's the shoulder?"

"Better, and I'm dancing again now that Melanie's my partner. She's light enough that I can handle it."

Doctor Shaffer surveys me. "I bet you two are adorable," he says to Zane. "She's tiny." He smiles at me. "I thought you were twelve when I first saw you. We've got you in a pediatric neck brace." He looks to Zane. "Her ribs on the x-ray are surprisingly slight. It looks like she has incredibly delicate bones. You need to be really careful when you lift her in dance shows."

Zane nods. "Done."

The doctor takes his leave.

"Am I going to have to repeat this school year?" I ask Rich. "I've been at school all of a few days this semester."

Rich shakes his head. "You're out on medical leave. Graduation is in a month, and we're hoping to have you on your feet for it. Adam and Valerie are getting married that weekend."

"I am NOT lying in this hospital for a month," I argue. "You've lost your mind."

"Correct," Zane retorts. "Tomorrow, they're airlifting you to Cedar now that there's room. Then you'll lay in that hospital." He pulls a stack of Archie comics from his backpack. He plops down in what I suspect has been his chair for the past few weeks. He scoots so I can see the comic book and announces, "It's Archie time."

"Comic books?" I ask, a little baffled.

"Got a better suggestion?"

"Nope. Let's see what Betty and Veronica are up to."

Zane scrunches his face. "Who cares? It's all about Jughead and Archie."

I roll my eyes. "Typical boy."

Rich and Adam each snag a comic book and have a seat.

CHAPTER 49

"**I**'m not riding in that thing."

Trey rolls his eyes and gives me an exasperated look. I shake my head again at Trey, and I feel Adam's amusement radiating to us from the distance.

"Just pick her up and carry her. There are so many steps at the Hollywood Bowl that the wheelchair is useless anyway."

I grin at Trey and send through the joint connection, *"See! Adam would carry me."*

Trey sends back, *"Yeah, yeah. Adam's the best."*

Adam sends amusement. *"I agree."*

Trey scoops me up gently and carries me through the parking lot. We get to our seats with our friends and wait for the graduation ceremony to start.

I turn, surveying Trey's profile, and can't help but chuckle quietly. When he hits me with an irritated look, I grin and whisper, "At some point, you're going to have to get over that you were passed out and Adam was the last one I said goodbye to."

He frowns and puts on his sunglasses.

The school band hits the first notes of "Pomp and Circumstance" as the graduates take the Hollywood Bowl stage one row at a time. Adam and Valerie are together, both in their red graduation caps and gowns.

I smile and take Trey's hand. He switches hands with me and puts his arm around my shoulder. I lean in and happily think to Trey, *"The graduation gown covers Valerie's baby bump. It's a good thing the wedding is coming up, or she wouldn't be able to fit in her dress. Tanner's had to take out the waist twice."*

Trey meets my gaze as he squeezes my shoulder.

"I talked with Bear and Darren," I send to him. *"They've worked out a way to shut down the connection with Adam. Pierre advised this."*

Resistance crosses through our connection as Trey inhales sharply. *"If it weren't for that connection, you might not be alive right now."*

"I know, but we have to let him go. He needs to take care of his family and run his new business." I snicker a bit. *"Just think, we only have to get me through three more years of high school."*

Trey sends amusement tinged yellow. *"Right. The first year was a cakewalk. How hard could the next three be?"*

Both of our mouths twitch as we try not to laugh during the ceremony.

CHAPTER 50

I survey my image in the mirror. Other than the wrist cast, I look fairly normal. My neck is still sore, but I have full range of motion again. I nervously ponder the possibility that my hospital problems will rev back up while I'm wearing this gorgeous dress, but I harshly shove the thought aside.

You're better. Don't even think about that.

My face burns fuchsia as I recall what Zane and I went through after I woke up from the hospital.

I swear he'll never speak to me again. That was vile. I ignore the thought, hoping to never ponder it again.

Back to the task at hand, I study my reflection. My strapless red bridesmaid dress is gorgeous. It has a heart-shaped neck with a delicately draping long skirt. I turn and look at my shoulder. My new firebird tattoo is stunning. Big Joe outdid himself with the artistry.

Presley and Finley cross to me wearing dresses that match mine. Both hug me.

"You think you can handle this?" Presley asks.

I nod. There was a great deal of speculation about whether I'd make it out of the hospital on time. Zane worked double time to get my muscles to function again after they started failing. We made the finish line, to everyone's relief.

Valerie smiles at me from across the room. She's breathtaking in her wedding dress. I carefully clamp down on my connection with Adam because accidently sending the image would ruin the wedding anticipation.

"I'll be right back." I exit the bridal suite and traverse the hall to the groom's room. I tap lightly on the door and send a pulse to Trey and Adam.

"It's Melanie," I hear Adam say. "Let her in."

The door opens, and all the guys are jaw-dropping in their black tuxedos with red ties. I smile and make the rounds, hugging each of them.

When I get to Trey, he shakes his head. He smiles and pulses through our connection, *"Every time I see you, I think you'll never get more beautiful. Yet here you stand."*

I smile at him. *"You're a charming devil."* Considering how he didn't visit me at the hospital, I'm relieved that things seem fine.

He grins.

I cross the room to Adam, who gazes down at me. I take his hand and silently pull him into the private waiting room next to his suite. He closes the door and clamps down on his connection with Trey, looking unsure why we're here.

"You ready for the wedding?" I quietly ask.

He takes my hand, sending a pulse of nerves but no internal conflict. I nod, and he pulls me in, hugging me.

"You're beautiful," he whispers.

"Your tux is perfect. Val's gonna lose it when she sees you."

He lets me go and smiles softly.

I gather myself. "It's time."

Adam looks confused. "For?"

I open the line between the three of us and send to Trey, *"You guys can come in."*

Adam puts an arm around me and turns to face the door. It opens, and Trey, Bear, and Darren enter. Tanner scoots through behind them with his makeup case and closes the door.

Bear and Darren cross to Adam.

"We're shutting down the connection," Bear informs. "It's Melanie's wedding present to you and Valerie."

Adam's face falls. He shakes his head. "Absolutely not. I can't do this now."

I know why Adam's so distraught because I feel the same way. We've had a soulmate connection for what feels like forever. It's become a sanity line for both of us. The thought of not having that with Adam scares me. At the same time, I have no interest in feeling Adam's wedding glee over Valerie.

Adam juts his chin Tanner's way. "Tanner's here because?"

Tanner clears his throat. "I'm going to need to fix Melanie's makeup after."

Just the mention of fixing my makeup brings tears to my eyes. I look up at Adam, and the first line of hot tears spills down both my cheeks. I've experienced so much loss recently, and losing Adam may be more than I can stand. I have to do this, though.

Tanner hands Adam a T-shirt and helps him shrug out of his tuxedo coat. Adam pulls the T-shirt on over his dress shirt so I don't get makeup on it. He reaches for me and pulls me in.

I hold it together for all of half a second before my knees buckle and I'm overcome with racking sobs.

Adam picks me up and crosses the room, facing us into a corner. He holds me and waits while I relearn how to breathe. "Can you handle this right now?" he asks.

I shake my head frantically. "I won't ever be able to handle it. We just need to get it over with. It's now or never. This gives you a clean slate with Valerie."

Adam's head falls back, and he sharply inhales. *"I love you, Melanie. You know that, right?"*

I nod and pulse back, *"I love you too. I'm scared to death of never feeling it again, though."*

"I am too."

He sets me down and wipes tears from my face. I look up in his ocean-blue eyes and take a deep breath. I squeeze his hands and whisper through our connection, *"Goodbye Adam."* Of course, I'll see him again, but it's different. Our soulmate connection deserves a goodbye.

Adam holds his breath for a long moment and finally exhales sharply. He quietly sends back, *"Goodbye, Melanie."*

We turn, and I fight not to lose it again. *We have to do this.*

Bear and Darren step forward, and Trey and Adam take my hands. Bear and Darren put a hand on each guy's shoulder. We all close our eyes, and the familiar sensation of the four guys looms in my psyche. They start by walling off the connection between Adam and Trey because it will make things easier. I feel Trey exhale through our connection when his is sealed off with Adam.

Bear and Darren turn to me in my mind and get on either side of the connection between Adam and me. They close it off with a rush of what cuts like cold steel. I suddenly feel like half of me is missing.

Bear and Darren back out of my mind, and I'm left reeling.

I open my eyes and stare up at Adam. He looks lost as he stares back at me. After a long moment, he wordlessly turns on his heel and heads into the bathroom with Bear.

Darren leaves through the hall door.

"Are you okay?" Trey asks softly as he steps up to me.

"I need a minute," I whisper.

Trey nods and departs into the groom's dressing room.

The door opens from the hall, and Darren returns with Valerie in tow. Darren says to Tanner, "Make sure Adam doesn't come out of the bathroom and accidentally see Valerie."

Tanner nods and slips into the bathroom. We hear him talking to Adam as he pulls the door partially closed.

Valerie looks at me, and her expression constricts as my face falls and tears stream down my cheeks. I kneel, barely able to breathe. Valerie crosses to me in a rush. She sits on the carpet in her wedding dress. Darren hands her a towel to drape across the front of her dress. She pulls me against the towel, holding me.

After the tears calm, she asks, "What do you need to hear?"

"I need to know that you're going to take care of him."

Valerie puts a hand on my cheek and tips my face up to meet her gaze. "I swear to you with everything in me that I've got this. No matter what, hell or high water, he's going to be okay."

I nod. "I had to let Bear and Darren shut it down. He needs to be yours."

Valerie smiles the tiniest bit. She quietly says, "Thank you."

The tears subside as I nod. I take a shaky breath and collect myself. Valerie gingerly helps me stand. I'm still struggling from my neck surgery, but I'm determined to make it through this. She squeezes my hands and leaves through the hall door.

I cross the room to the slightly ajar bathroom door, where the guys have been listening. Adam looks at me through the open door. I don't need the connection to know that he's a mess of conflicting emotions on the inside. I try to test the connection, and the barrier holds.

"Nothing."

He shakes his head. "I can't get through on my side either."

Uncharacteristically shuttered, I nod once, hard and fast. "It's done."

Adam looks uncomfortable but grateful for the clipped finality. He smiles ruefully at me before heading into the groom's room.

When the door closes, I sink into a chair, folding at the waist. My head hits my knees. I sob. Tanner grabs a towel to drape over my knees to avoid spotting the satin. He sits with me until I cry myself out. Then, when I'm done, he works his magic on my makeup.

So . . . How did it go? Well . . .

The entire crowd gasped when Valerie came down the aisle. She was radiant. Adam cried. The ceremony was perfection.

The after-party celebration was a blast. We partied like we're known for, and with half of the Magnet kids in attendance, it felt a lot like our school dances. Red-rose bouquets and vanilla-scented candles graced the center of each table. The fragrance wafted heavily through the banquet hall.

They served chicken, and Adam and I exchanged an amused look across the banquet hall at an old private joke. I even got in a dance with Mr. Isley, which turned out to be my favorite part of the evening.

Toward the end of the event, my wrist was throbbing and my neck was stiff and sore, so I headed out to the balcony for a break and to take in the cool night air. The venue's balcony had a gorgeous view of the city lights.

Soon after, Adam came out to join me. He leaned on the railing next to me and quietly asked, "You okay, Firebird?"

Drained from the day, I smiled wearily and nodded. There wasn't much to say.

He squeezed my shoulder. "Love you."

"Love you too, Diesel."

The rest of our group came out and joined us. Most were oblivious to what Adam and I had dealt with earlier, which was for the best. With a grin, Tanner carried out a duffel bag full of the black leather vests he collected from each of us a few days before the wedding. He handed them out to us each in turn. The photographer came out on the balcony and snapped a picture of all the Hellcats, vest clad, with the Hellhounds. The picture now hangs on the wall in my room next to the picture of me shooting double birds outside of Snow White's Café. They're my favorite pictures of our group. Only Zane was missing, and he had been missing ever since I was released from the hospital. Zane had insisted to Rocco that he enforce a little separation between us. Otherwise, Zane might grow too attached. Despite arguments from both Zane and me since, Rocco has done his job well. I haven't heard from Zane. I know it's for the best, but I'm lost without him. The battle we waged in the hospital bonded us. I don't want to depend on him, though. A six-week hospital nightmare was the last thing he needed. My humiliation keeps me at a distance. I can't call him, and I won't.

Valerie announced at the end of the reception that it was time to toss the bouquet. In my Hellcats vest and red bridesmaid dress, I jostled into the fray of unmarried girls, ready for the silly ritual tossing. Everyone bumped and scrambled, jockeying for position. Valerie launched the bouquet, and it headed straight for me, just like I knew it would.

Everyone cheered as I caught it easily. I made eye contact with Drake and grinned because we'd made a plan about this after my intuition sparked a week prior. Crossing the dance floor, I handed the bouquet to Deb as Drake dropped to one knee. He proposed, and she practically screamed "Yes!" Everyone in the room roared and cheered as Deb and Drake kissed. Our group all put up devil horns as Extreme's "More Than Words" hummed through the speakers.

"I take it you knew you were going to catch the bouquet?" Trey said.

I smiled. "Sometimes this intuition comes in handy for something other than life-and-death nightmares."

He took my hand and turned me twice before pulling me in to dance. "This song?" he said.

"Somehow the right song always plays."

"Are you going to be okay without Adam, Zane, and Pierre?"

I closed my eyes and laced my fingers with Trey's. The perfection of *us* hummed through our connection, synchronized. Without Adam's looming presence in the other half of me, the energy that's purely Trey had filled in the empty places. I closed my eyes, studying it. After a long moment I said, "You and me, babe. We've got a shot."

Trey leaned in and kissed me. It seemed I had followed Pierre's advice about reconnecting with Trey after all. The entire world disappeared as the candlelight flickered.

Two weeks after the wedding, I finally decided to call Trey. I'd spent the past few weeks alone, unsure about why so much distance had grown between my friends and me.

"Is it true that everyone got together last night?" I asked him bashfully.

Trey sighed. "Yes. We went bowling."

"How come no one called me?"

Trey cleared his throat. "I think we all just need a breather."

"From me?" My heart sank.

"It's been a lot, Melanie," Trey said hesitantly.

"So, I've lost my friends too? Losing Pierre wasn't enough?" Tears filled my eyes.

"I'm sorry, Melanie, but I can't take anymore. I want to enjoy my summer." With that, the line went dead.

The radio silence from Zane had continued since the wedding as well, and my parents were on a Big Bear trip. On my bed rested a package labeled with Caroline's return address, and I told myself that I wasn't about to open it alone.

I picked up my bedroom phone, deciding to take a chance, and called Demitri.

"There's a package I need to open," I said to him hesitantly, "but I'm a little out of sorts. Are you a part of the 'No Melanie' club?"

I could practically hear him smile. "I didn't know there was a 'No Melanie' club. Me and Dad are hanging at the house. Want to come over with it?"

"You good with that?"

"Hell yes. I miss you."

I smiled. "I'll be right over."

At Demitri's house, Mr. Cantrell presented me with a Cactus Cooler before I even got out of my car. He hugged me and then swept me through the door. Excited, Demitri ran across the living room and hugged me gingerly. His dad took the soda from me, and despite my recent injuries, I wrapped my arms and legs around Demitri and hugged him like my life depended on it.

My best friend finally put me down and handed me a shirt and sweatpants, with tags still on them. I unfolded the shirt to discover that it had Red the Fraggle's happy face on it. I laughed.

Demitri tipped his head to his bedroom. "Go change and wash off that damn makeup."

I rolled my eyes. "I'm fine like this, D."

"No, you aren't. Get." He pointed and I relented, heading to his room.

Freshly changed and makeup-free, I made my way back to the living room.

Demitri rolled his finger around, and I turned my back to him. He took my scrunchie from my wrist and piled my hair up in a messy bun. He turned me around and nodded. "Perfect."

I shook my head. "You didn't have to do this, D."

"Did too. I want you happy while you're here. I'm hoping you'll come over more often."

I swallowed hard. "I've spent a lot of time by myself."

Demitri brushed a stray hair from my face. "Let's sit down and talk about it."

We made our way to the couch, where Demitri sat next to me while Mr. Cantrell took his usual place in his recliner.

"You haven't been at any of our group outings," Demitri said.

"There's been more than just bowling?"

He nodded. "We've been to a movie, to Snow White's, to a party at Mabel's, and to the laser show at the observatory."

"No one invited me," I informed sheepishly. "I called Trey today. He said everyone needs a breather before he hung up on me." I quirk my mouth. "Zane's also MIA."

Demitri and Mr. Cantrell exchanged a glance.

"I wasn't there for any conversations about needing a breather," Demitri said.

Mr. Cantrell snorted. "That's probably because they all knew you'd push back."

Demitri's brow furrowed. "I'm sorry, Melanie. I'll talk to them."

I shook my head. "I don't want to be where I'm not wanted."

"Well, we want you here." Mr. Cantrell gestured to the package I'd brought with me.

Demitri reached to collect it from the coffee table and handed it to me. I opened the box and pulled out several seashells. The accompanying card read:

> We found these on the kitchen counter in your villa
> and thought you might want them.
> Enjoy everything in this box,
> and know how much Riptide loved you.
> Love you to pieces, Seashell!
> —Caroline

I handed the note to Demitri, and he read it while I set the seashells aside. Mr. Cantrell gestured curiously to them.

"Pierre picked them up for me as we wandered the beach on our trip," I explained.

Next, I pulled a beautiful, light-peach photo album from the box. Demitri curled up with his arm over my shoulders as I opened it. The whole album was full of pictures Caroline had taken, still shots from the media footage, and pictures of the villa covered in flowers that she must have taken after I left. We got to the last picture, one of Pierre and me as the sun set with the ocean in the background.

I closed the album and took a deep breath. Demitri took the album from me and set it on the coffee table. I steeled up, knowing what I needed to do.

Demitri closed his eyes a moment before looking at me. "Pierre's telling me that it's time and you need to do this. Hang tight, Meley." He got up and went into his room. A minute later, he came back with the little black leather jewelry box in his hand. "We need somewhere to put it."

My hand shook as I started to take the ring off.

Demitri handed the box to his dad and took my hand. "Deep breath, Meley." I inhaled as he slid the pearl wedding ring off my finger. He carefully put it into the cushioned slot in the box, and Mr. Cantrell closed the lid. Demitri gently set his hands on my cheeks. "Are you okay?"

I shook my head no and then nodded yes.

He chuckled. "Do you want to sob this out, or should we order pizza and watch a special prize I got you?"

I smiled curiously. "I'm so tired of crying. Think Pierre would be offended if we do pizza and fun instead?"

Demitri kissed me on the forehead. "Nope. He spends a lot of time in my head. We already discussed you taking off the ring, so I know he doesn't want you to fall apart about it."

"There's only so much crying you can do, Melanie," Mr. Cantrell assured. "It's time to enjoy your life again." He gave me a pointed look. "Please spend some time with Demitri. He's a lonely mess without you."

Demitri started drumming softly on my legs. "Pizzaaaaaaa. Pizza, pizza, *pizzaaaaaaa!*"

I laughed. "Done. Order it."

Mr. Cantrell grinned and called for delivery while Demitri hopped up and went to his room. He came back dangling a Tower Records bag in his hand. I took the sack and raised a curious eyebrow as he sat down next to me.

"You seem to have done a lot of Melanie-shopping lately that you had no business doing," I said.

Demitri smirked. "I wanted to be ready if you ever came over again."

"That's really sweet. Thank you, Demitri." I pulled out a VHS box set, and my mouth dropped open. I squealed at him, "Yeeesss! *She-Ra: Princess of Power*, season one." I launched myself at Demitri, and he hugged me. "Best present ever!"

"You're welcome," he said with a laugh. "Now, we're going to watch She-Ra kick ass in her sleazy little outfit while I pick pineapple off that damn Hawaiian pizza you always insist on."

He put the first tape in the VCR before settling against the armrest of the couch and stretching out. He held an arm my way, and I lounged with my back against his chest. He wrapped an arm around my stomach, and Mr. Cantrell got a throw blanket situated over us.

As the *She-Ra* theme song started, I squealed. "This is the best, Demitri."

He kissed the side of my head. "It certainly is."

I inhaled deeply. Demitri inhaled with me, and we exhaled together.

Special thanks to the incredible team of models that keep pulling through for me over and over. Thank you to Deidre Michelle for her endless ability to find the right people to depict these characters. Thank you to Anna Hall, Kyle Fager, and Stephen Knezovich for making this series magic. Thank you to Jordan, Bear, and Carol for their endless conceptual support.

MELISSA VELASCO is a true explorer of the arts. With a well-rounded background as a choreographer, professor, dance teacher, stage manager, author, and Crystal Grid teacher, she thrives in creation. At her core, she believes that the arts save lives and provide a route for passion and connection. The artistic ride makes life a whole lot brighter.

With a quick wit, often edgy mouth, and loud laugh, Melissa exuberantly embraces life. To find balance from the mental cacophony in her head, she enjoys expansive views in her mountain home. Her ideal day involves a mug of hot tea, music playing, and a whole day to write. Her greatest loves are her three children and husband. The four pillars of her ultimate happiness include her family, friends, dance, and laughter.